The Mysterious Life Of The Heart

The Mysterious Life Of The Heart

WRITING FROM *THE SUN*
ABOUT PASSION, LONGING,
AND LOVE

EDITED BY SY SAFRANSKY
WITH TIM McKEE & ANDREW SNEE

The contents of this book first appeared in *The Sun*. The following pieces were subsequently published in books. We gratefully acknowledge the authors and publishers for their permission to reprint the work:

> Christopher Bursk, "How Far Did You Get?" *Ovid at Fifteen* (New Issues Poetry & Prose, 2003).
> Tess Gallagher, "Sixteenth Anniversary," *Dear Ghosts* (Graywolf Press, 2006).
> John Hodgen, "This Day," *Bread without Sorrow* (Eastern Washington University Press, 2007).
> Brenda Miller, "The Date," *Season of the Body* (Sarabande Books, 2002).
> Kirk Nesset, "Still Life with Candles and Spanish Guitar," *Paradise Road* (University of Pittsburgh Press, 2007).

Published by:
The Sun Publishing Company
107 North Roberson Street
Chapel Hill, North Carolina 27516
(919) 942-5282
www.thesunmagazine.org

Cover photograph: Nicole Blaisdell
Cover and book design: Robert Graham

Ordering information:
To order additional copies directly from the publisher, please visit www.thesunmagazine.org.

Library of Congress Catalog Card Number:
2008911349

ISBN 978-0-917320-04-0

Manufactured in the United States of America.

10 9 8 7 6 5 4 3 2 1

Contents

■ Introduction

When I was in my twenties, I came across a new essay by Henry Miller, then nearly eighty, about his obsession with a beautiful, mysterious, and, as I recall, not entirely available young woman. One of the twentieth century's most influential writers, a fearless cultural provocateur and irrepressible ladies' man, Miller was shamelessly in love. Hopelessly and pathetically in love. He thought of the woman constantly. When he couldn't be with her, he wrote to her every day. At the end of his rope — unable to work, unable to sleep — he was, he admitted, as confused and insecure as a love-struck teenager.

Not that many years removed from adolescence myself, I didn't know whether to be discouraged or relieved. On the one hand, I'd always assumed that, as I got older, I'd get better at handling this elusive and tempestuous force called love. Surely by the time I was thirty, say, or forty, I'd have developed a modicum of self-possession and would have stopped running around with my emotional shirt-tails flapping in the breeze. Perhaps I'd even be able to look at an attractive woman without assuming she was put on earth to fulfill my longing for completion. Yes, in a decade or two, I'd have it all worked out. But Miller's misery suggested that Cupid didn't care if you were a young fool like me or an old fool like Miller: those cute little arrows were going to pierce you, and, before you could even find out the perfect stranger's name, you'd have stained the carpet with cute little drops of blood.

Yet Miller's honesty also had a liberating effect on me. If — despite his genius, his worldliness, his many marriages, his innumerable affairs — he'd been brought to his knees by this latest infatuation, maybe I didn't have to judge myself so harshly for regularly tripping over my own two feet. Were the cultural icons I worshiped smarter than me? Yes. Were they more accomplished? Of course. But why assume they were any better at loving another person or at dealing with the pain love inevitably brings? It seemed as if we were all in this together, the geniuses and me.

On some level, I already knew this. But it's one thing to realize something intellectually; it's another to experience it viscerally because a writer is unafraid to be naked on the page. By laying bare his emotions without embellishment or embarrassment, Miller had given me something of great value. He'd shown me the power of being vulnerable, and he'd helped me feel less alone.

Decades later, as editor and publisher of *The Sun*, that's the kind of writing that moves me the most, and it's what you'll find in *The Mysterious Life of the Heart*.

All the works in these pages originally appeared in *The Sun*, a magazine that has been published monthly out of Chapel Hill, North Carolina, since 1974, when I sold the first copies on the street. *The Sun* itself has been something of a romantic endeavor: born of youthful idealism, built by the hard work of many people, and kept alive by passion — for the written word, for an honest story well told, for fragile humanity in all its guises.

Love is a house with many rooms, and *The Mysterious Life of the Heart* explores only one of them: not a child's love for a parent or a parent's love for a child or love between siblings or love between friends. It's about the room upstairs at the end of the hall, shared by two lovers who've decided to stay — for a weekend or forever, no one can say. Sometimes they kiss, sometimes they bite. They dream they're in heaven. They swear they're in hell. *That* room.

The sheer volume of writing on this subject that's appeared in *The Sun* made it difficult to decide what to include. Choosing fifty essays, short stories, and poems out of the hundreds we considered might have been easier if we hadn't already fallen in love with and published them all. So we set to work reading and rereading, Venus sitting on one shoulder and Mars perched on the other, and when we finally finished making our choices, what did we end up with? Exactly twenty-five works by men and twenty-five by women. Well, how about that!

We'd hit the bull's-eye without even trying.

This isn't a book in which you'll find the seven steps to connubial bliss, with exercises at the end of each chapter to simultaneously tighten your buttocks and open your third eye. But that doesn't mean the stories, essays, and poems are randomly arranged. Instead, we follow a winding, sometimes treacherous path from the innocence and impetuousness of young love through marriage and devotion, temptation and betrayal, divorce and heartbreak, and finally forgiveness and mercy. When read from front to back, *The Mysterious Life of the Heart* is a journey worth taking. (Naturally, you're free to ignore our counsel, begin reading anywhere, and jump from piece to piece, just as you're free to throw caution to the wind and jump into bed with the next attractive person you meet. Don't say we didn't warn you.)

This book is the fruit of many people's labor. That we managed to publish it while also putting out a monthly magazine is a testament to the intelligence and hard work of my colleagues at *The Sun*. Specifically, I'd like to thank art director Robert Graham for his elegant design and fine eye for detail, and photographer Nicole Blaisdell for her evocative cover photograph; manuscript editor Colleen Donfield for helping to determine the final selections; senior editor Andrew Snee for his sensitive editing of every piece; and managing editor Tim McKee, who shepherded the book from idea to finished product. My deepest gratitude goes to the writers themselves, whose willingness to share their glorious and painful experiences is itself an expression of love.

As the editor of a book about love, I'd be guilty of hubris, and all but inviting the gods and goddesses to smack me silly, if I didn't acknowledge that, despite being marginally wiser than I was in my twenties, and despite having been married most of my adult life (to three different women, though not at the same time), I'm hardly an authority on the subject. For if you took everything I've learned about love from the women I've lived with and the nights I've spent alone; from the sacrifices I've made and the sacrifices I've foolishly demanded of others; from the unforgettable moments I've already forgotten and from the ecstasy of spirit I'll never forget, that ineffable state beyond the veil of separateness where the "I" that says "I love you" is no different from the "you" that hears it — yes, if you took everything I've learned about love and dropped it in the ocean, there would be a little splash, and there would still be room for an ocean.

Sy Safransky
Editor and publisher

P.S. The best place to read *The Mysterious Life of the Heart* is in a quiet corner away from the usual distractions. (Avoid public places where laughing or crying is frowned upon.) The publisher grants permission for portions of the book to be read aloud to a loved one, by candlelight, between the hours of 10 P.M. and 2 A.M. But using this book to try to seduce someone or to justify the unbelievably selfish way you acted last week is expressly prohibited.

The Mysterious Life Of The Heart

Ecstasy

a short story by **STEVE ALMOND**

I'd fallen in with a group of beautiful blondes. I have no clear idea how this happened. Something about a friend of a friend. Something about a party. They'd caught me on a good night, I think, and the impression had never quite worn off. They called me "Lush," not because I drank but because, in their eyes, I embodied some verdant aspect of hope. This was a terrifically inaccurate notion, but flattering, and certainly worth preserving.

I lived that year, my second at college, in a flurry of winks and kisses, minty breath, the cream of necks and décolletage. We must have gone to classes, though I remember now only the classrooms: yellow, wooden desked, and faintly diseased, suggesting privation, the loss to be swallowed on the path to wisdom. Wisdom was something we desperately wanted, from books and lectures and so forth. It sounded sexy and protective. We had, in other words, an authentic thirst for wisdom, but it had occurred to none of us that the acquisition of wisdom might entail loss.

The real business of those years was experience: dawn confessionals and inside jokes, bouts of incompetent hedonism chased by flamboyant displays of empathy for the have-nots (whoever they were). What were we hoping for? An end to the lacerations of self, I guess. An alleviation of guilt. A single moment of emotional extravagance that would allow us to believe, wholeheartedly, in our youth. Grace.

It really happened only once, on the day we took Ecstasy, which was a new drug then, though old to the therapists. The blondes appeared at my door. "Take this," Kath said.

"What is it?"

"Medicine."

"Take it," Maddie said. "We already took ours."

"It'll make you feel better," Dana said.

"I'm OK how I am, really," I said. "I've got to finish this paper."

They were smiling, all three of them in loose dresses, the tops of their breasts purring with sun. The other guys on the hall hung from their doorways, cursing me softly. Then a fourth woman appeared, and the blondes began singing. "Solange," they sang. "Solange, Solange." I wanted to sing it myself: *Solange*.

Someone said, "This is our friend Lush."

She was pushed forward, a figure as dark as me and nearly as tall, elegantly slanted, and smiling, but quizzically, as if she had walked into the wrong wedding reception. "Hey," she said.

I looked at Solange, trying to look away at the same time. I was desperate in that moment not to fall in love with her; with the way she looked, her cheeks and heavy lips, her sloping hips, her feet — my God, her feet! — in sandals whose leather strips circled the stems of her calves. With some awareness of how much I loved her, of how happy I would be to wake up beside her every morning for the rest of my life, both of us naked and smelling of sleep — with all this, I set out not to love her.

"Hey," I said.

The blondes laughed musically.

I took the pill from Kath's palm.

The day was aimless beauty, the hill green and moist from the first rains, wisps of cloud above and softball players threading the fields below. In the distance, the library's ivy rippled like a coat of mail. We lay on the grass, touching at the edges.

Just past Kath, I could see Solange's leg, bent at the knee, traversed by a delicate scar.

"I don't feel so hot," I said.

"That's 'takeoff,' " Maddie said.

Kath reached over and rubbed my belly.

Dana ran her hands through my hair, which curled down my back in those days. Then the three of them smothered me in kisses. This was something they did from time to time. My role was to behave like a knickered lad beset by bosomy aunts. The blondes' real beaus were older guys who lived off campus and played varsity sports. They enjoyed the blondes' company at night. During the day, the blondes were mine.

I'd had girlfriends, of course, but always dull girls. On this day, the day we took Ecstasy, I was fresh off a breakup with a girl named Temple: pale, blue-eyed Temple, pretty in a fragile way and scared to death of herself. Our last night together, she had shed her turtleneck and — in an approximation of passion much closer to rage — yanked up her bra, cinching the flesh around her ribs, a wire-rimmed cup cantilevered under her chin like a spittoon. "They're not very big," she'd said glumly.

The blondes had squealed when I'd told them this story. "That girl," Maddie said.

"What were you thinking?" Kath said.

"I thought there might be something there," I said. Truth was, I was nothing much to look at. My nose was pretty solid, and I had the hair going for me. But my teeth were oversized and, no matter how much I brushed, slightly yellowed. Tiny blackheads pebbled the skin around my nostrils. According to the dermatologist, my pores were too large.

None of this was about to matter, though. The blondes were still kissing me, laying their pretty heads on my chest and chattering. The queasiness faded, and, as when the sun emerges from behind the clouds, everything gathered a bright intensity: the bodies of the women touching mine, the soapy smell of them, the grass beneath me, the library's red bricks, and the softball players below, running and shouting. Without my quite noticing the change, I no longer felt I had to put one over on anyone to be liked.

Maddie turned her face to mine and stroked my shoulder. "You're beautiful," I said. "I guess you know that. But I don't want our friendship to obscure that, you know? That appreciation. The way you move, you know? That grace you have, the way you scissor along. Your 'carriage,' I guess they call it."

Kath said, "He's right. The way you move — God, how delicious. Your ass does this thing."

"A little hop-skip."

"That's it. A hop-skip."

"When you wear that one skirt."

"The purple one."

"Right."

"Like a shelf," I said. "Like you could set something on it."

"It makes me want to take a bite of your ass," Kath said. "Turn over, Mad. Come on, let's see that thing."

Maddie giggled and flopped, and Kath squirmed down her body and cupped a cheek in one hand, and I cupped the other, and we took the flesh into our mouths and pretended to bite her tush while Maddie, far away up her spine, shrieked happily.

Kath glanced at me, across Maddie's splendid cleft. "You're there, aren't you, Lush?" Her face flashed under her bangs. She looked like Claudette Colbert, impish and knowing.

"I guess. Yeah."

She kissed my forehead. Her lips smelled of grass. "Lush has arrived," she called out, and, from somewhere closer than I expected, Dana laughed. Then there was another laugh, a contralto, and Solange pushed her head around my shoulder until we were cheek to cheek, her smoothness making me wish I had shaved, though also making me feel rough-hewn and slightly dangerous.

"So this is the famous Lush," she said. Her voice was lower than you'd expect, full of husky mischief. She turned to me, and her lips hung there an inch from mine, plump and arrowed. She had chocolate on her breath.

I t would be impossible — and sad, finally — to revive the entirety of that afternoon. We sat around the way people on Ecstasy do, in a kind of tantric spell, melting onto our tongues squares of Lindt chocolate, gulping ice water from a pitcher and talking about the *experience* of the chocolate and the water, scratching backs and massaging shoulders and praising each other ardently, without hesitation or guilt, a satisfaction of the harrowing needs toward which our bodies lunged.

And Solange. *Solange.* I lingered over the word, let the syllables hum in my chest. She looked like her name: French and elegant, a long nose, snaggled teeth, green eyes flecked with hazel. And when she spoke, one sensed the sweet insecurity caused by her teeth, which made her smile feel like something bestowed. She had a passion for silent films and for what she called the "rescuing tone" of Chopin. Her father had died when she was six, and her mother, though kind, had clearly been overmatched by the duties of love. Everything Solange said sounded a little lonely, a little hopeful.

All afternoon, the blondes had been calling out to passing friends for refills of water, vamping like Blanche DuBois and Mae West. But now the afternoon was dimming, the light penumbral, and everyone was gone to dinner.

"I'll get some water from Clark," I said.

"Me, too," Solange said.

Those words actually came from her mouth; they were not something I imagined, though they had the ring of fantasy, as did the vision of her falling down the hill toward me, a young woman torn from the pages of Victor Hugo, hair carried up by the breeze, her brown neck tilted, her hips wrapped in a red skirt. And her hand reaching for mine, shyly but without hesitation.

Clark dorm was an old brick monstrosity where the frosh were packed onto damp hallways. We wandered in through the basement, where the laundry machines were, and dropped onto a sofa. Light poured through the window in front of us, turning everything golden; the shadows danced in sinuous rows, like Bedouins. We gasped, in unison, at the dusk.

"This is my favorite time of day," Solange said. "The time for remembering, you know?"

"A nostalgic light," I said.

"That's right. But not in the Hollywood sense, all that manipulating the past for sentimental effect. More like remembering things as they were, another time."

"What do you remember?" I asked.

We were sitting side by side, our legs laced, the ticklish flesh of our feet brushing down below. I breathed in the smell of pink detergent.

The dryers softly droned. I watched Solange in profile, the way the tip of her nose dipped when she spoke:

"Westport, I guess. This lake we used to go to with my dad. Being a little kid running around naked. Making a fire on the beach, roasting hot dogs on sticks, curling up in my dad's lap. He wore one of those Greek fisherman's hats — you know the kind, with the cord across the front? And I used to sneak into his study and sniff the lining, just to smell him." She giggled. "Does that sound weird?"

"No."

She frowned, as if I might be giving her too much credit. "My mom says I made the whole thing up about the lake. 'There's no lake in Westport,' she says. She says my father hated the beach: all that sand and salt. She says I must be thinking about going to the Long Island Sound with my stepdad."

"What do you think?"

"I don't know. I guess it doesn't matter." Her voice was drowsy. I had the feeling she was going to lower her head onto my shoulder; the wish that she would. "It's not the thing that matters, right? It's the memory. Like what they say about dreams: it's not what happened; it's how you feel about it, what it means to you. My mom gets mad when I bring it up. Probably that's why I bring it up."

I put my hand on the nape of her neck, and my fingers made circles on her skin, which was dusted with salt. She hummed a pleased hum and let her head droop, hair falling across her shoulders. Outside, the copper sun was dipping behind the hill. I could smell both of us, ripe from our day in the heat.

"What was I saying?" she asked.

"About your mom."

"She's just so controlled. So brisk. I love her. I do. She doesn't make it easy, is all."

"Maybe she's scared."

I can hear myself speaking back then, and I know how I sounded: like some charm-school *sensitivo* who can't wait to get his hands on the goods. But that's not what it was. The drug had simply wiped away the inhibitions, the fears that normally curb our tremendous natural affections. We were just who we were: two young people yearning after possibility.

"You still miss your dad?" I said.

"I don't know," Solange said. "My memory misses him, if that makes any sense. I can't remember him, really. It's more these snapshots: Him in a suit in the morning, all shaved and handsome. Or me in his lap at the lake. I'm sure I loved him. But it's kind of sketchy, honestly. My older sister remembers him better, and I'm never sure how much I'm picking up from her. . . . That feels good."

I could feel the cords of her neck under my fingers. The room was darkening, the laundry smell rippling against our own sweet reek. Her right leg rested atop my left, her skirt rolled up and her kneecaps shining like plums. She'd taken on the aspect of a Goya, slightly elongated and backlit.

She tapped my thigh. "You OK?"

"Yeah."

"Your leg's not asleep?"

I shook my head. No, nothing asleep.

She lifted her head and looked at me. My hand fell down her back, landing on the swell of her bottom. We leaned forward, and our chests pressed against each other, just our chests — her breasts, my boyish muscles, each of us licking our lips, looking at the other, the miracle of mouths and eyes.

"What about your family?" Her voice was hoarse. "They're in California, right?"

"Maybe we can kiss," I said.

"We can kiss," she said, and laughed. "Tell me about them."

"They're good people. Dad's a lawyer. Mom teaches special ed. My older sister is in divinity school. She's an expert on Saint Thomas Aquinas. Good people. Good suburban people."

"You don't miss them?"

"Not really," I said. "A little, I guess. We're not the closest family. Everybody kind of does their own thing."

"What's that mean?" Solange leaned back, out of the sun, and I missed her breath.

I thought for a minute. "Like, I can remember sleeping over at this friend's house, the first time I'd really slept over. I must have been eight or nine. My parents were at some conference that weekend. And all I kept thinking was how much I missed being at my house, with my family, you know? I had this mental picture of all of us sitting in the living room, real cozy, reading or playing a game, whatever. But the crazy thing was, we never did that kind of thing. The whole parlor scene. My folks were tired all the time. My sister was always off with her friends. It was just some idea I had of the way things could have been."

"That's sort of sad," Solange said.

And it was. It was. But I couldn't feel it just then, with her next to me, her electricity. "Not once you're used to it," I said. "That's just how some families are. They feel a lot, but they don't say much. You can't force things. Maybe I just needed too much."

She frowned again. "How could you have needed too much? You were a little kid."

"I just mean that sometimes I can come on a little too strong."

Solange lifted her leg off my thigh and swung herself around. For a second, I thought she was going to get up, that I'd upset her somehow. Then she brought her hand to my cheek and moved her face in front of mine. I leaned forward too quickly, and we bumped foreheads, a dull little pop that made us both giggle.

She ran her fingers through her bangs and took a deep breath. "OK," she said. "We need to relax a little bit."

"We do?"

"Yeah."

"Really?"

She laughed softly and patted her lap. "Put your head here. We can talk some more."

I lay down, my head cradled beneath her belly. I could feel the swell of her mons pubis against my cheek, and I caught a musky smell: amaretto, her body lotion, her body.

She told me she wanted to raise her kids in the country, that her dream house was all mapped out: a renovated old barn with exposed beams and a mud room and a potbellied stove and the master bedroom in the grain loft.

"And a pond out back for swimming," I said.

"Sure. A swimming hole."

"A couple of dogs from the pound."

"An herb garden."

We agreed on everything, even the small hardships of the place: snowdrifts and muddy roads. I wanted this woman so fiercely that I could feel the blood drum in my ears, which I know sounds absurd, given that I'd met her only a few hours earlier, and we were both under the influence of this drug. But my longing was not just for her; it was for the story she told and my place in that story. Solange was not a simple woman. She was deep and troubled, and she needed me. And I needed her. That was my idea of love: two people who fix one another. It hadn't occurred to me then — this would take some years — that the best we can hope for in love is the graceful management of one another's disappointments.

The light had nearly fallen away. I began playing with her knees, testing her reflexes with the side of my hand. She kicked her foot out. The pitcher tumbled.

"The water," Solange said. "Fuck."

"Shit," I said. "That's right."

Up we leapt, taking the stairs two at a time, holding hands like characters in a bad musical. "We'll have to fill it up in the bathroom," I said.

"I'll do it," she said. "I've got to pee anyway."

We dropped each other's hands, and she took a step toward the door.

"Maybe we could kiss goodbye," I said.

We collapsed against one another and kissed deeply, our mouths open. I ran my tongue along the silk of her gums. Her neck was warm and salty. A clamoring group of frosh appeared at the end of the hall, back from dinner. "OK," Solange said. "You'll be here when I come out, right?" And I watched her face as she said this: the soft apprehension in her eyes, the slight protrusion of her mouth, the question that hung there between us. I was ready to wait ten years, twenty.

"Right here," I said. "This spot."

We were worried that the blondes might have gone to eat. But they were right where we'd left them, gorgeous and leering in the cool dusk. Someone had brought them a blanket, and someone else a bowl of fruit.

"Where have you two been?" Maddie asked.

"Sightseeing?" Kath said.

Dana tossed me a pear.

Dining-hall smells hovered overhead: calico skillet, roast chicken, mashed potatoes with brown gravy. I looked at the pear. "Aren't you guys cold?"

"We've been planning dinner," Kath said. "Cheeseburgers and Greek salad from the Hungry Pirate. You'll love this place, Sol."

"Perfect," I said.

"What's the matter?" Maddie asked.

She was talking to Solange, who looked suddenly stricken. "My bus," she said.

"What do you mean, your bus?" Kath said.

"Shit," Maddie said.

"You're not serious?" I said.

Solange nodded.

Then Kath and Maddie climbed to their feet and tackled her. They had it down to an art. Solange tumbled, her skirt rising so that I saw the shiny swell of the backs of her thighs and a flash of purple underwear. She squealed and kicked her brown legs as if she were juggling a beach ball with her feet. The blondes forced her down and cawed like pirates: "Aye, matey! We'll have none of that rot! Yer staying put, where ye belong!" That sort of thing.

The sky was turning dark, and a breeze came up. It suddenly felt like autumn again. But the drug made sorrow difficult and beside the point, and Solange herself seemed more heartbroken than any of us. "I know, it sucks," she kept saying. "Shit, shit, shit."

And even when Kath muttered something about letting "Andy stew in his own juices" — even when a certain part of me grasped that Solange was returning not just to somewhere, but to some*one* — even then, the drug kept me from envy and woe. Because the important thing was to make the most of this chance, to acquit myself well, to authenticate what we'd shared and trust her to return, eventually, to those feelings.

We walked her to the bus station, through the blue gloom of a New England October evening edging into night, all of us arm in arm and oblivious to downtown's tinseled menace. There was no intense departure scene, no anguished violin notes or faces pressed against glass. Solange and I hugged, and then she disappeared onto her bus, and the blondes and I shambled back to campus to eat dinner and let our high taper off.

I woke the next morning fuzzy headed, vitally bled, and certain that my vertebrae were grinding against one another. The blondes and I met for brunch, hoping to revisit the previous day's spirit, but our talk was hollow, forced. The blondes were still young and beautiful and gay. They sang out phrases like "Somebody's got a crush" and "Solange plus Lush," but I felt sullen. They were trying to buoy my spirits, I suppose, or expressing the hope of matchmakers — offering her in place of themselves. I never figured it out. I knew only enough to recognize that I was a kept man, and this knowledge was all it took to break the easy rhythm of our days and set me adrift.

I suppose it might make sense at this point in my life — with a wife and a son and long afternoons of contentment drawn around me — to disavow my passion for Solange. Or, at the very least, to relinquish her memory. But you don't relinquish anything when you've fallen in love, no matter how briefly. The heart writes in indelible ink.

And no matter how long you live and whom you love next, you are also there, all those years ago, with your head in her lap, your cheeks pressed against her thighs, her eyes and your eyes, and the future hung like a pear between you. And sometimes the memory is so beautiful you lose an entire life all over again; and even when you return to the present — to your place by the window, your wife warming soup in the kitchen, your son calling to you from outside — even then, it's so beautiful you can't tell the difference. ■

How Far Did You Get?

by **CHRISTOPHER BURSK**

Often the first
question other boys would hit
a boy with, as if the kid
hadn't gone out on a date
but tried to
swim the English Channel,
and they knew he couldn't
cross such a distance
without their help,
and this was their way
of helping him. *Go on,*
tell us exactly how far,
not knowing yet how to
understand what a boy did
with a girl,
except by measurements:
how long,
how often,
the precise calculations
of sex. What was a kid to say
to his buddies? *It was like*
grabbing hold of a boat
and being pulled aboard
after treading water
for days. I lay there

like someone who'd been rescued,
        looking up at the stars
as if they'd been part
        of the search party, too,
the breeze on my neck,
        the whole dark
sky. Imagine a boy
        telling that to his friends.
It is more
        than they wish to know.

Foreclosure

by **DOUG CRANDELL**

At thirteen, I wanted to be a father.

Our failing family farm had two trailer homes sitting vacant. To make ends meet, my parents rented one to Valerie, a pregnant, unwed twenty-three-year-old with tomato red hair who worked at the Kroger deli, where my mother was the manager. The day Valerie moved in, I watched from my bedroom window as she toted a suitcase up the three steps to the trailer. That's all she had: a faded pink suitcase, the vinyl peeling. I thought her hair looked pretty. A small herd of Holsteins, my 4-H project, bawled at her from behind a fence. It was springtime but still cold out, and from my window I could see Valerie's breath escaping her body. My mother, who'd opened the door for her, patted Valerie's swollen stomach. I stopped spying from behind the curtain and went to the stereo to put on Air Supply's "Lost in Love." Then I lay in bed and thought of how I would propose to Valerie: I'd tell her the baby needed a father. I would get down on one knee, my hair feathered just right for the occasion, and present her a ring. Maybe my sister Dina would let me borrow one of hers.

My father and mother had been renters all their lives. Then, in 1980, both of them forty years old, my parents had signed a mortgage agreement with Dennis Rice, a farmer nearing retirement who wanted to sell his place to a "hardworking family." My father was tired of renting run-down homesteads, doing all the work, and splitting the meager profits from the corn and soybeans seventy-thirty with the landlord, who got the lion's share. The problem was he couldn't qualify for a regular bank loan with what he earned from his union job at the ceiling-tile factory. So Mr. Rice, playing the role of benevolent father figure, had agreed to be the mortgage lender himself. He'd arranged for a lawyer to draw up a contract, and my father had signed it. The interest rate was nearly 18 percent. If we missed more than three payments, Mr. Rice would be able to evict us and repossess the farm.

The day we moved in, Mr. Rice stood in the bare kitchen and went over the terms of the loan with my father. "Of course, Dan," he said, "I know we won't ever need to think about this last part" — the part about evicting us. "My lawyer made me put it in." Before he left, Mr. Rice invited us to come to his church in town. He was almost seventy but strong and lean, and he hugged us all, reminding us kids to pray to the Lord Jesus Christ. My older brother Darren, who was fifteen and wore a black Van Halen T-shirt over his long-sleeved thermal underwear, just rolled his eyes.

E ach evening, as darkness settled over the farm, I'd watch Valerie's mobile home from my bedroom window. My mother had sewn Valerie some drapes from leftover U.S. Bicentennial material: the words "Don't Tread on Me!" with an eagle soaring above them and flags of all sizes raining down. I had drapes of the same pattern in my room, and I fingered the cloth. I'd not met Valerie yet, and I was afraid that when I did I might lose the ability to speak.

A knock rattled my bedroom door, and my father said, "Let's go. We've got chores to do." The paddock where we exercised the livestock was a mess. Old Man Rice had not kept up with repairs or manure removal. We'd been breaking our backs patching, painting, hauling, and making the place respectable. My hands were blistered and torn, and I don't think my parents, who held down full-time jobs, slept more than a couple of hours a night.

I t was in the middle of a long Saturday of chores, after I'd greased the two planters and prepared the tractors for the fields, that I ran into Valerie. It was the first warm day of spring, birds twittering in the trees, and I was jogging toward the house as she walked across the verdant yard.

"Hi," she said, her flaming hair lifted by the breeze. The sky was bright blue, the trees tipped with red buds, the green daffodil shoots that my mother was ecstatic about forcing their way up along the garage. Valerie smelled of cigarettes and perfume. She shook my hand and crinkled her button nose. "Your mom showed me your picture at work, but you're even cuter in person." I thought I'd pass out. She had on her Kroger uniform, the dark blue polyester like armor. The top was cut to fit to her growing belly, and her soft-soled shoes — for standing on her feet all day — broke my heart. She looked at her watch. "Oh, fiddle," she said. "I've got to go. My shift starts in ten minutes. I don't want the *boss* getting mad at me." She winked. We both knew my mother was her supervisor. Valerie dashed across the gravel to her car, a 1970 Ford Maverick, rusted and tilted to one side, that I viewed as exotic. She climbed in, fired up the engine, and rolled down the window. "Since it's Saturday night, why don't we play some cards when I get off work," she said, a cigarette dangling from her mouth, blood red lipstick on the filter. The car tires spit gravel as she tore out of the drive. I was so excited, I forgot about the chore I'd been doing until Darren approached me: "Did you get the ether?"

"Huh?"

"The ether, dimwit. I can't get the MF started." We called the Massey Ferguson tractor the "MF."

"I guess I forgot." My face was flushed.

"You look weird," said Darren, smirking. "I saw you talking to her." He punched me in the arm.

The fields seemed as limitless as the canopy of blue sky above them. While our dad planted corn with the John Deere, Darren and I disked and harrowed another field, getting it ready for the eight-row planter. Darren drove the MF with the disk behind, and I followed with the harrow on the old Allis-Chalmers, a tractor so slow you could walk alongside it. Both tractors had AM radios, and we listened in tandem to WOWO. Every so often, Darren would rev the MF's engine to get my attention, or hang halfway out of the cab, whistling and acting the nut — anything to make the time go faster. We went up and down a field with no apparent end under a beautiful spring firmament, the air so crisp it hurt our lungs.

At lunchtime a familiar truck rolled across the flat land: red and spotless, stark black tires glistening with Armor All. Mr. Rice had started showing up at all times, even during supper or in the morning, making my siblings and me late for school. He made many suggestions, sometimes turning sour and bossy. It was clear he still saw the place as his own and my family as just borrowing it, but my father was polite to him and expected the rest of us to be as well. Now Mr. Rice waved me down, and I pulled over, the harrow fishtailing behind, thinning the rich loam like chocolate cream. The earth smelled ripe with the scent of decay from last year's clover.

I left the tractor idling and climbed down from the cab. Mr. Rice walked up and pointed a finger at my chest. "You're not going fast enough out there to break up all the clods. Quit daydreaming and give it some horsepower." His eyes were watery and cast a notch too far up, as if he were reading the words he spoke from a sign above my head.

"That's as fast as it goes," I said. "It's a slow tractor."

"Don't lie to me, young man. Get moving." He spun around and walked back to his truck, whose radio blared the voice of a preacher getting all worked up. As Mr. Rice sped to the next field, a flock of Brewer's blackbirds exploded from the tangles of fescue he drove over, their nests likely crushed by the old man's tires. I thought of Val, her little baby growing inside her belly. My brother and I finished up the field just past sunset with the tractors' lights on. It was tilled in perfect concentric circles, like designs left by aliens.

I rushed through dinner and showered until my skin was red, steam rising from the tub as if a fire had been doused. Then I put on Mitchum deodorant and sat by my window to wait for Valerie to get home from work. It was past 10:30. Luckily Darren, who shared my room, was playing euchre at a friend's house. A swath of yellow-blue light cut across the yard, headlight beams tracking the east side of the garage. I could tell by the thump of the motor it was Valerie's Maverick. My mother wouldn't be far behind, maybe thirty minutes, the time it would take her to do some light shopping. We mostly ate from our freezer and pantry, making do with the preserves she'd put up the year before, eating canned vegetables with pork shank.

I raced downstairs and bolted toward the back door, then slowed to a stroll, nonchalant, as if I were leaving the house to check on the paddock as part of my Saturday-night routine, having forgotten about playing cards with Valerie. I shoved my hands in my pockets and kept my head down. The night was cold and quiet except for the pings of Valerie's motor settling.

"Hey," she said, "are you ready to play cards?" She tossed her baggy denim purse over her shoulder and snapped her gum. "I need to shower first, though," she said. "I hate the way that deli makes me smell." A faint aroma of basting barbecue surrounded her.

"OK," I said, "I'm just making sure the tractors are locked." I kicked the ground, my armpits heavy with Mitchum.

"Great. Come over in fifteen minutes," she said.

Sixteen minutes later I knocked on the door of Valerie's trailer. I'd opted for some Big Red gum, the cinnamon burning my chapped lips. She opened the door, and I stepped inside to the sound of "Crazy Little Thing Called Love," by Queen. The interior of the trailer was dimly lit, lamps casting pinkish light onto the sagging couch and tattered La-Z-Boy. Valerie wore a robe that didn't quite cover her knees, and she gave off the scent of balsam and Ivory soap. Through the bathrobe, it was difficult to tell she was pregnant.

"You look nice," said Valerie, struggling to pull a comb through her wet hair, which appeared brown instead of red. "I've got a rat. Will you help me?" She turned around and backed up, handing the yellow comb to me over her shoulder. I was confused, but I took the comb and began trying to fix her hair. The teeth caught in the tangles, and she yelped, then giggled. The long, wet strands were still warm from the shower. Finally, after I'd made her cry out several more times, the comb slid through easily.

We sat down in the kitchen alcove. A candle flickered on the table as Valerie dealt the cards. "Do you know how to play two-man euchre?" Her agile fingers shuffled the deck, first overhand, then in a riffle, the cards flipping faster than I could see. We played several hands, and I lost. Valerie laughed and winked a lot. When she crossed her legs, the robe slipped up, exposing a freckled thigh that scared me. All of a sudden she tossed the cards on the table and said, "Let's pig out!" She got up and yanked open the freezer door. "Frozen pizza! Pepperoni!" she cried, trying to sound Italian.

We sat on the sofa and ate Hershey's Kisses while we waited on the pizza. I'd never been out on a date, but I assumed this was what a first date felt like. Valerie turned the music down so that it crackled softly from the speakers. She put her feet in my lap and leaned back. "God, my back hurts," she said. Her bare toes wiggled. In the watery light she looked like a girl I knew in study hall.

"When is your baby due?" I asked.

"Not until October," she said. "What do you think about 'Rolin' if it's a boy and 'Taylor' if it's a girl?"

"I like them both," I said, feeling grown-up.

"Do you know I'm ten years older than you?" Val said, puckering her mouth. "God, that sounds so weird." The timer on the stove dinged, and she pulled her feet from my lap and shot into the kitchen. I breathed into my cupped hand and smelled melted chocolate.

While we ate, she told me all about the guy who'd gotten her pregnant and then run off: a Hormel-chili truck driver named Randall. They'd met at Kroger and dated for almost a year. When she told him she was pregnant, he said, "I'm not wanting a family." The next week at work, another truck driver delivered the chili — and the news that Randall had quit. Valerie tried for a while to find him, then gave up.

"I can raise this baby myself," she said, a scared smile on her cherry red face.

It was getting late. The wind rattled the mobile home. "That Mr. Rice is a creepy guy," Valerie said, munching on pizza crust.

"I know," I said, pleased that the conversation had turned to a familiar subject. "He's always showing up, telling us how to do stuff. Darren says he's a complete dick-face."

Valerie threw her head back and laughed. "Your mom can't stand him either. She told me he invites himself to meals all the time. He stares at me when I get out of my car."

We went on gossiping about Mr. Rice until it was almost 1:30. Finally Valerie walked me to the door. "Good night," she said, and she kissed me on the cheek. "Come over tomorrow night at the same time. I'll rent us a movie."

As I walked toward the house, across the small patch of yard, I looked up into the clear, dark sky filled with pinpoints of light. I wanted to be Rolin's or Taylor's daddy. *I could do it,* I thought as I opened the door to my house and crept quietly in, like a father coming home late from work.

For the next two weeks I went to school, worked planting the fields in the afternoons, and spent my evenings at Valerie's. We watched movies on her Betamax video player and ate junk food and told each other secrets we'd never uttered to anyone else. I rubbed her back, which hurt because of the baby. Valerie cut my hair and pierced my ear, numbing it first with ice cubes and holding a potato behind it as she pushed a corsage pin through the lobe. She gave me a gold stud to put in it, and she wore the other one.

Mr. Rice continued to pop up like an apparition, shaking his head and pointing out things he didn't think we'd done right. Darren flipped him off behind his back. Our dad was exhausted, working twelve-hour shifts at the factory and coming home to plant corn and soybeans in the dark. Once, he fell asleep at the wheel of the tractor and nearly drove into the river. After her job at Kroger, Mom didn't have any extra time or energy to give to us kids. People from the fuel company had been calling for their payment, and the seed bill hadn't been paid. The farm looked great, tidied up and repaired, but financially we were losing ground. Then, on a Saturday afternoon in early April, a thunderstorm ripped through, and sheets of rain sent most of what we'd planted two days earlier rushing into the culverts. All we could do was inspect the damage. My dad smoked a cigarette and used a stick to pick through the loam, Darren and I trailing behind him. Then Old Man Rice showed up, his truck splattered with mud.

"Well, what are you going to do now?" he demanded as he jumped out.

My dad wheeled around on him but didn't answer. His cigarette hung loosely from his lips, smoke coiling in the humid air around us.

"I told you not to plant this week," Mr. Rice continued. "That's what the *Farmer's Almanac* said. I told you God came to me at church and said you and your family needed to repent, or he'd deliver punishment."

Darren made a face behind Mr. Rice's back.

"Go home, Mr. Rice," said my dad, tossing the stick aside. "This isn't your concern."

"Not my concern? Not my concern?" Old Man Rice's eyes widened, and his wispy gray hair swam in the breeze. His veined hand trembled as he pointed at our dad. "You're two months behind on payments. If this isn't my concern, I don't know what is."

Our dad kept his back turned and didn't speak to Mr. Rice. "Boys," he said, "fill the planter up. We can replant this tomorrow."

Old Man Rice seemed to vibrate like a reed as our dad walked right past him to the barns.

That night, as we were eating dinner, Mr. Rice showed up again. For the first time, he actually knocked instead of barging in. Dad answered the door, his hand on the knob blistered and nicked across the knuckles. He had to be at the factory in two hours for another shift. I was trying to rush through my meal so I could go buy Valerie a present.

Mr. Rice was dressed in a suit and tie and smelled of aftershave. Dad offered him a seat at the table. "No thank you," he said, more reserved than I'd ever seen him. "I just wanted to come and carry you all to the worship service tonight." He looked at his silver watch. "You have an hour to get ready. I'll wait in the car for you." His wife was already waiting there.

Our mother shot our father a look as she stood up from the table, starting to clear it. Old Man Rice added, "And it would do that woman with child to come along too."

I felt a flame surge inside me.

"Thank you, Mr. Rice," said our dad, "but I have to work, and Doris and the kids have chores to get done. But thank you."

"You're going to have to get some help from God, or you'll never make it," Old Man Rice said, anger bristling underneath his soft tone.

"Maybe next time," my father said, and he showed Mr. Rice to the door. When Dad came back to the table, he looked worn and beaten down. Maybe he'd realized that signing a mortgage agreement with Mr. Rice was no different from having a landlord.

The next day we replanted the storm-ravaged field and moved on to the other sixty-acre plots, all outlined by rusty fence rows, their wooden posts leaning. With the crop in, we were able to take a little break for the first time in two months. Dad called in sick at the factory over Memorial Day weekend so he could stay home and sleep. Our mother cooked all his favorites: yeast rolls with chipped ham, rhubarb pie, savory dill potatoes, Salisbury steak. We even invited Valerie over for meals; she asked me to carry the behemoth Betamax machine, and we watched movie after movie. Nervous my family might see how in love I was, I pretended to be only slightly interested in her conversation. She wore glistening lip gloss and a long black cotton dress over her round, compact stomach, and I snuck glimpses of her all night.

During the last movie, a James Bond film that my mother called "risqué," Valerie sat next to me on the couch. I remained upright and stiff, ignoring Darren's attempts to get my attention. My mother turned the light off, and before long Dad was snoring. He slept fourteen hours a day that weekend, and we were all happy for him. There was no sign of Mr. Rice. It felt good to be together, all the work done — for three days, at least. I suppose that was the last night of our dream of owning a farm.

After the movie had ended, I walked Valerie to her trailer. She invited me in, and I pulled the present from my pocket.

"What's this?" she asked, her face glowing. She pushed a red nail under the Scotch tape and pulled away the wrapping paper. It was just a baby rattle, but she acted as if I'd set up a college fund for her unborn child. She hugged me tight, her swollen stomach pushing against mine. I wanted to bury my face in her hair. Then she took a deep breath and started crying, still clutching me. I patted her back as I'd seen my father do to my mother's when she sobbed after a hard day.

"Are you OK?" I asked.

"Yes," she said, as if irritated by her own emotions. "It's just I'm scared sometimes." She backed up, and a few of her red hairs clung to my shoulder like tethers. "Besides, you shouldn't be worrying about me." We sat down on the couch, and Valerie leaned back, put her feet in my lap, and closed her eyes, exhausted.

"You know, you've never told me if you have a girlfriend," she said, sleepiness slurring her words.

I stiffened. "Not really. I mean, no."

"Oh, I can't believe that. If you were five years older, I'd snatch you right up."

I rubbed her feet as she drifted off. I wanted to be her baby's father; to marry her, work the farm, and feed her child. But I only vaguely knew what was required of a husband, and the thought made me feel both excited and overwhelmed. I pulled a blanket over Valerie and slipped out the door.

The night sky was clear, and the weather had warmed up. Crickets trilled near the cistern. The cattle moved along the fence; I couldn't see them, but I heard their hooves padding the soft earth.

In less than three months, Old Man Rice had his lawyer foreclose on us. By then, we'd gotten everything fixed up as good as new, including the house. (Dad would later say we'd rented the idea of owning our own place.) When Mr. Rice and his son came and took it back, they could barely hide their excitement at the coup they'd pulled off. They'd brought the sheriff to make sure we didn't protest. Mr. Rice also had an orange Gideon Bible for each of us. He handed them out before we climbed into our vehicles. Valerie clutched the same faded pink suitcase she'd moved in with, and Darren hauled her massive video player out to her car. Dad told Mr. Rice he could keep the Bibles; he may not go to church, he said, but he remembered something about the Golden Rule. Mr. Rice tried to tuck the Bible inside Dad's shirt pocket, but Dad pushed his arm away and said, "Don't touch me."

I saw Valerie only once more, in the hospital after she'd delivered. I rode along with my mother to see the baby. The Hormel-chili driver had come back. He was shorter than I was and wore a bushy beard. Valerie looked worn-out but happy, little Taylor swaddled and lying on her chest. We didn't stay long, and my throat ached the whole time. On the drive home, to a rented house inside the city limits, my mother said, "For a while there I thought Val's baby would be fatherless."

I didn't know how to say that I would never have let that happen. ■

Beach Boy

by HEATHER KING

New Hampshire, 1970

I am a moody, bookish teenager living in a small town on the coast. Ten miles offshore, the Isles of Shoals seem to hover, whispering of mystery, a promise unfulfilled, a gift forever withheld. In fact, the islands are easily reached by boat in an hour, and the one time I went there it was bleak and cold, and a sea gull swooped down with its sharp yellow beak and stole my sandwich. I prefer to regard them from the shore, imagining a paradise just beyond my reach.

My penchant for fantasy stems from the fearful conviction that even the smallest action in the real world is fraught with danger. It is like living on a tiny atoll amid shark-infested waters — a state of anxious isolation that I am desperate to escape. Already, I crave the oblivion of alcohol and drugs, which, paradoxically, will isolate me even further. I do not yet have a name for this craving, nor do I know that my loneliness, my terror of other people, and my desire to escape all flow from alcoholism, which has run like slow poison through both sides of my family for generations.

In my last two years of high school, I get drunk every weekend, smoke pot incessantly, and drop acid every chance I get. I have slept with boys, but I have never had a real boyfriend. Graduation night, a friend introduces me to Mitch, a boy from Massachusetts. Mitch is a carpenter, but his true calling is surfing. The ends of his hair are sun bleached, his nose is always peeling, and he carries an ever-present board under his arm like a mutant flipper — all of which I find achingly attractive. Within weeks, we are inseparable. We drive around in his brother's green MG, listening to Rod Stewart, Neil Young, Cream. At his rented beach cottage, with its flimsy towels and sandy linoleum floors, we cook Rice-a-Roni and Pillsbury biscuits. In the back pocket of my jeans, I carry a bottle of Silk of Intimate, a perfume that looks like melted pearls, with which I drench my wrists and neck.

Mitch seems to understand my notion of some plane other than the one we live in, a parallel universe of peace and harmony. We talk haltingly about this, though we have neither a name for it nor words with which to describe it. We sense that there is something between us — something sacred, huge — that is part of a transcendent whole. One afternoon, after we have been dating a couple of months, we are walking along the beach, and Mitch puts a name to it: love. We're in *love*! The word spoken aloud is blinding, explosive. We tremble in its presence, walk around in circles, shaking our heads and laughing. We are shellshocked, dazed at our good fortune.

In a friend's workshop, Mitch builds us a bed frame of rough pine planks. Lying in that bed, I memorize him, trace his contours like a map, study his face as if it were some ancient text that held the secrets of the universe. If they lined up a million sets of hands, I tell him, I'd know which ones were yours. I lick his eyelids, his neck, the hollow above his collarbone. He tastes, always, of salt.

This perfection is marred by one small stain: for me, our love — and my other passion, literature, which I feel only enhances, ennobles, confirms our love — is everything, but for Mitch there is surfing, too. He and his friends speak a language I do not understand: swells, breaks, some mysterious place they call "outside." When the waves are up, they drop everything, grab their boards, and head to the beach like lemmings. I try my best to fit into the surfing culture. I watch as Mitch shows me the best way to wax a board, secretly wishing I were reading. I wear a choker of puka shells, feeling like Eleanor Roosevelt gotten up as a hula girl. I slather myself with Hawaiian Tropic, then lie rigid in the sun feeling guilty for lounging around smelling like a coconut while other, more-deserving people are working. The stomachs of the other surfers' girlfriends are tan, taut, and undulating. Mine, warily exposed between the top and bottom halves of a pink-and-blue two-piece, is whiter than my arms and legs and has the shadow of a beer belly.

I drink, but so does Mitch. Everyone we know drinks. I cannot yet see that, for Mitch and most of our friends, drinking is an adjunct to life, not life itself; an expendable pleasure, not a necessity they are willing to pay for with the DUIs, hangovers, and morning-after horror stories that have become a fact of my life. For me, drinking is not social; it is pharmacological, the relief I crave for my low-level paranoia and overwrought nerves. When Mitch gathers up his gear and bolts for the beach, my shoulders slump, my face sags, and I feel as if I will die from being so cruelly abandoned. But then it gets dark or the waves turn mushy, and he comes back, and it's time to start drinking again. Everything is miraculously transformed. With Mitch in my arms, *Gasoline Alley* on the stereo, and a river of Almaden Mountain White Chablis coursing through my bloodstream, the familiar feeling of peace descends, filling the void that was my miserable, lonely life up until now. Eighteen years old and my life is mapped out, a path of joy stretching all the way to the horizon.

Rincón, Puerto Rico, 1973

I have dropped out of college for a semester and quit my waitressing job so that I can participate more fully in Mitch's surfing, a part of his life from which I am usually absent. From our rented white stucco house, a dusty trail leads down to a sweep of turquoise ocean. Cocks crow at dawn, the air is thick with the smell of frying peppers, and the heat presses down like a hand. We pick lemons from the tree in the yard and squeeze them over tins of sardines. At dusk, we walk to the store and buy hard, dry white rolls, a hunk of orange cheese, and shots of 151 rum, which we drink outside on the patio.

Alcohol is no longer the reliable elixir it was at first: instead of assuaging my innate terror, it is beginning to make it worse. The rum burns like gasoline, and the sun sets in a fiery blaze, flickering ominously near the edges. A restaurant farther down the beach specializes in conch fritters, but every time we go, they are closed or sold out or nobody has caught any conch that day.

Rincón is a mecca for wave worshipers, its beaches crawling with surfers — with their golden tans, their zinc-covered noses, their girl-friends who sit around stringing African beads or cleaning stemmy wads of pot. Mitch is in heaven, but I am focused on the cockroaches in the shower, the overfriendly local men, the endless hours of un-structured time. Every morning he goes surfing with his cronies, and I set off by myself for another portion of the beach with a towel and a book. The sun bludgeons me, and the waves foam in, hissing on the sand like snakes. There is something sinister in the air: no sky should be this clear, no water this warm. Although I am beginning to see that my paranoia may be connected to the fact that I drink until I black out every night and spend every day in the grip of a vicious hangover, it does not occur to me to cut back or stop.

When the sun gets so bright it hurts my eyes to read, I wade around in chest-high pools of seawater and pluck shells — coral pink, orange, banana yellow — from the sand. I am mesmerized by the variety of striations, ridges, and whorls, astounded that they are free for the taking. I arrange them in rows by color on my towel and try to decide whether they are more beautiful vividly wet or dried by the sun, when their colors become subtler: the pinks fading to rose; the oranges and yellows growing paler, sadder, more delicate. I cup one in my hand, an ivory scallop with lavender stripes, and will a miniature Venus to rise from it, a tiny friend with streaming golden hair, flowers fluted around her head, one elegant hand shielding her breasts.

When I am not drinking or lying on the beach, I am reading on the terrace. Due to the steady stream of Mitch's surfing buddies in and out, my presence there frequently gives rise to one of those awkward, depressing exchanges every die-hard book lover dreads: What are you reading? *Something by this guy Flaubert.* Who's Flaubert? Or, Who's Jane Austen?

"Who's Dostoyevsky?" asks Greg, a bronzed, green-eyed hunk from South Carolina who is so ridiculously good-looking it is like sitting on the terrace across from a 3-D *GQ* photo.

"This Russian guy who had epilepsy and almost got killed by a firing squad but was sent to Siberia instead."

"What's it about?"

"Um, this guy who kills an old lady because he doesn't want to have to take money from his mother and sister, sort of like he was so bad he was good."

Long, dead pause.

"Yeah," Greg says, "books are great," and he gives a twenty-minute synopsis of *Carrie*.

My days of solitude leave me stiff and uncommunicative. By the end of the month, I am collapsing under the weight of my own alienation and loneliness. Mitch and I eat fish and rice at mom and pop stands, watch cockfights, and take walks on the beach, but it feels increasingly empty, and I drink even more than usual to fill up the emptiness. Mitch has decided to stay on a couple of extra weeks, but I am going home as scheduled. For the first time in more than three years, I am relieved to think of our being apart.

The night before I leave, I toss back a few shots of rum at home, softening my perpetual sense of impending doom with the alcohol's rancid warmth. Later, we walk down the hill to a thatched-roof outdoor bar on the beach. While the Beach Boys croon "God Only Knows" from a tape deck, I swill Cuba Libres, and we talk about how much we will miss each other. I wonder if Mitch is as ambivalent and confused as I am, but I don't ask; I no longer share with him my every thought.

After a while, Greg, ridiculously good-looking Greg, materializes and settles in at our table. We take turns buying rounds, and the drinks make us dreamy and voluble. Mitch talks about building a house overlooking the ocean. Greg muses about opening a surf shop. Studying the blond stubble on Greg's jaw line, the swell of his biceps, I feel the stirrings of a newfound affection for Rincón. The moon hangs low over the water, and a scented breeze rolls in with the waves — things I have never much noticed before. "It's so gorgeous here!" I say, slurring my words, and I impulsively divulge to Greg the dream I keep locked away in the deepest recesses of my heart, the dream only Mitch knows, the dream I think about constantly but never act on: I want to be a writer.

I'm ready to stay up all night, but Mitch isn't feeling well. "I'll walk her home," Greg offers, and Mitch heads back, and there is more rum, more sweet, deep, swirling talk. The hours pass in a blur; everyone has left but us. Finally, the music stops, they turn out the little Christmas lights that twinkle along the driftwood bar, and we leave the silvery black ocean behind and lurch up the hill, singing. When Greg stops in the middle of the road and kisses me, I feel the twitchy, doomed thrill of a convict being strapped into the electric chair. We go to his cottage, where I stay till dawn. Even the rum cannot drown out the knowledge of the barrier I am crossing. I have never disappeared like this, never cheated, never not come home at night.

When I stumble in the next morning, Mitch is frantic. "Where have you been?" he yells. "I almost called the police."

"I'm sorry," I say, hugging him tight. "I was so wasted I ended up sleeping on the beach."

It is a measure of how much I drink that this is received as a valid excuse. Mitch takes a cab with me to the airport, but my betrayal squirms between us, and I am on the verge of throwing up.

On the flight back to Boston, I wear a peasant blouse with pink flowers embroidered on the shoulders. On my lap, I cradle a wrinkled paper bag full of shells.

New Hampshire, 1974

I am on shaky ground, and Mitch is not exactly the soul of emotional health either. He cuts short a trip to Baja after he has a quasi–nervous breakdown because he misses me so much. When his brother and I pick him up at the airport, he is palsied and pale, like a traumatized war veteran. We go mountain climbing with my father and brothers, and, when we reach the summit, Mitch takes my father aside and confides that he feels the urge to jump. One afternoon, I come home from my waitressing job to find him kneeling in front of the stove, his head inside the lit oven.

"What's wrong?" I ask, cradling him in my arms. He doesn't know, can't articulate it, thinks it might have something to do with his father. I review what I know of his father but can think of nothing out of the ordinary: He drinks like a fish, of course, downing highball glasses of straight VO in one gulp, but who doesn't? He is constantly hung over and losing jobs and depressed, but who isn't?

Then one afternoon we are driving along the beach road when Mitch confesses he has slept with someone else: a girl I knew from high school; a strapping, blond beauty; a surfer. She is everything I am not. In the space of ten seconds, all the light leaches out of the world. It is like being kicked in the stomach; I feel as if I will never catch my breath again.

He drops me off at my parents' house. They are on vacation, and I am supposed to be baby-sitting my eight-year-old sister, Meredith. I lead her to the cupboard underneath the kitchen counter. The shelf is lined with newspaper, and the vodka is way in the back, behind the grapefruit squeezer and the pressure cooker. I show her how to put in a few cubes of ice, fill the glass three-quarters of the way with vodka, and top it off with tomato juice. "But mostly vodka," I repeat, and then I go upstairs and crawl into my parents' bed. When I come to, Meredith's brown eyes are watching me anxiously. Her head is not much higher than the bed. She holds out a fresh Bloody Mary. "I could put a little salt and pepper on top," she says. "Would you like that?"

I stay drunk for three months. I stop working, stop going to school, stop eating, and lose fifteen pounds. That last, fateful night in Rincón gnaws at me constantly, and the fact that I can't quite get the memory of Greg — those gorgeous arms; those long, hot hours in bed — out of my mind makes me feel even more guilty. It doesn't matter that Mitch doesn't know; deep in my heart, I'm sure his betrayal is the price for my treachery.

Mitch and I patch things up and limp along for another year or so, but it is never any good again. "You are really lucky in one way, because you always seem to be able to ignore everything else but me," he writes in a letter from Hawaii — where he's gone, of course, to surf. "You are hurt when you don't have that one thing" (meaning *him*), "but I can't be happy without doing things on my own, too."

This is the death knell. There is something wrong with me, some perverse flaw that turns every good thing sour. A few months after we break up, I hear through the grapevine that he has married someone else.

I do not know it then, of course, but I will be alone for the next fifteen years — fifteen years saturated with the smell of ground-in cigarette smoke and ammonia-drenched bathroom floors and soiled pillows on strangers' beds.

When I finally stop drinking, I will undertake a long, faltering search for meaning and convert to Catholicism. I will have no trouble grasping the concept of the Fall — the desperate, slavering compulsion to return to an Eden from which, paradoxically, incomprehensibly, one is continually expelling oneself. I will fall in love for the second time and get married. I used to think I would never again love anyone the way I loved Mitch, and I was right. You undergo that particular rite of purification only once. Afterward, you have learned the hard lesson that no mere human being can fix what is wrong with you.

Every so often, I will hear bits and pieces of news about Mitch: he's moved to California; he's had a daughter; he's gotten rich. Sometimes, thinking about his suicidal leanings, his father's drinking, the way alcoholics and people from alcoholic homes are unconsciously drawn to each other like magnets, I will wonder whether things might have turned out differently if we'd understood the connections, seen how badly we needed help. For a long time I will fantasize about running into him somewhere and having an if-only-I'd-known-then-what-I-know-now chat. Finally, I will resign myself to the fact that we will never see each other again and that it is probably just as well.

There will be years when I'll hardly think of him, but then, I won't have to think of him because he will have incorporated himself into my bones and blood. I will still remember him every year on his birthday, will still feel a pang every time I drive by that spot on the beach where he first said he loved me, will still cry two decades later when I hear "Mandolin Wind" in a Hollywood coffeehouse. Eventually, the wound will heal, all the pain and all the wild, self-annihilating joy distilled to the shadow of an image whose details become more blurred with every passing year. But I do not know any of this yet. I know only that, for a long time, I feel as if I were drowning.

New Hampshire, 1995

O ne of my oldest friends, whom I have known since I was thirteen, is dying of cirrhosis. I leave my husband in LA and fly to Boston, where I drive directly to the hospital. My friend's skin looks green, his legs and belly bloated. "Remember the time we were hitchhiking back from Montreal and my feet were frozen and we finally got a ride in that old, unheated van?" I ask him. "Remember how you made me take my boots off and held my feet against your bare chest to thaw them out?" He tries to answer — his eyes and scrabbling lips frantic — but I can't understand a word. Finally, he gives up. I sit by his bed, and we hold hands and doze while the heavy snow falls like flakes of cement outside the window. When I come again the following day, he has just died. They cover his face with a sheet and wheel him to the elevator. As the doors close, the last thing I see is his tangled hair on the white pillow.

The night of the funeral, I am lying on the couch at my parents' house watching television with Meredith and a couple of my brothers. There is a knock at the door; my father answers it, and a voice that I haven't heard in twenty years says, "Hi, Mr. King."

"Is that *Mitch*?" I yell, racing into the kitchen.

"I heard about Michael," he says, standing in front of the stove. "I thought you might be here."

I throw my arms around him as if he has risen from the dead, and we all crowd into the kitchen, leaning against the counters, to gawk. He is trim, almost too trim. He has the same crinkles in the corners of his blue-green eyes, the same head-thrown-back laugh. I can hardly believe, after all this time, that he is here in the flesh, intact, alive — the person who, for five years, knew me better than anyone else on earth.

While my mother passes around cheese and crackers, I ply him with questions. He says the last two years have been difficult: he got divorced, lost everything, moved back to the Maine coast. He is framing houses. He still surfs. His daughter is seventeen. "Pulling the same stuff Heather and I did," he says to my mother. "Shacking up with her boyfriend." His mother died a year ago, and Mitch delivered the eulogy. He has become a Christian and remarried. He and his new wife belong to a church with an elaborate name I do not quite catch, something with the words *abundant* and *house* and *light* in it. I am so excited to see him that it is half an hour before I realize that he hasn't asked me a single question, and another fifteen minutes before I notice that he keeps mentioning Satan.

"I stopped drinking," I offer, trying to change the subject.

Mitch fixes me with a penetrating stare and replies, "Ah, but the problem was never drinking. The problem was *evil*."

"It's funny," I try again with a hollow chuckle. "You've become a Protestant, and I've become a Catholic."

"Catholic? Sheer idolatry!"

My father comes to the rescue, pointing out that the apple trees Mitch planted back when we were dating are still growing at the edge of the backyard. "Picked five bushels last year," Dad reports proudly. "We made some nice pies."

"Do you spray?" Mitch asks. And while they discuss the pros and cons of DDT, and Meredith reminds him of the clambake we had once in the backyard, and my brothers reminisce about the '66 Falcon he used to drive, I think of all the things that are going to remain unsaid. I'd always imagined, if I ever saw Mitch again, hurling myself at his feet and keening, *Wasn't it wonderful? Wasn't it terrible? Didn't it fuck you up beyond all belief?* Instead, we have become strangers standing on opposite shores of a gulf I have no idea how to bridge.

"I guess I should get moving," he says finally. "My dog is outside in the truck." I think of Bernie, the slobbering Saint Bernard, Mitch's family dog: Is he still . . . ?

"No," Mitch says, "we put him down years ago."

We exchange addresses, and I see him to the door. There is so much I want to tell him. I want to thank him, to bless him, to tell him that I have carried him with me — the ocean, the music — wherever I have been. But I don't say anything except "Take really good care. It was great to see you." I kiss him on the neck, and he stiffens a little, perhaps catching a whiff of Satan on the cool night air.

I send him and his wife a Christmas card, but he never answers.

Los Angeles, 1998

My life is full of blessings now. I have been sober for ten years; married to a wonderful, extremely funny man for eight; and writing for five. Everything has changed — and nothing has. I am still plagued by the same nervous anxiety I had as a teenager, still tend to view my life as a nuisance I have to get through so that I can curl up in a corner and read: Tolstoy, Dickinson, Saint John of the Cross; books about inner journeys, books about the desert, books about prayer. I am still, in many ways, lonely.

For months after I saw Mitch, I was numb with shock, thinking him a fundamentalist fanatic. But eventually I saw that, though I didn't use the same language he did or think in quite the same way, I, too, had come to believe in evil, and that sex is holy and love a terrible power that burns like a flame. Whether it was the dark current of alcoholism or a thirst for God or sheer animal lust that had drawn us together, it was no coincidence that we'd been attracted to each other, and no accident that, in middle age, we had both ended up in church. Perhaps the amazing thing was not how much we had changed, but how much we had stayed the same, the outlines of our younger selves filling in like photographic images beneath the watery shimmer of developing fluid: Mitch, a wild-eyed Old Testament prophet, Isaiah in a wet suit; I, the perpetual observer, clothed in black, scanning the horizon for the Second Coming.

The details of his picture, though, are starting to fade. I can no longer conjure up his face, can barely remember what his voice sounded like, have forgotten the shape of his hands. Even the relics I tried so hard to preserve are disappearing like a receding tide: the bed Mitch made converted by my husband to kindling; the hundred-pound slab of oak Mitch found in an old lumber mill, which I'd used as a table for years, left behind when my husband and I moved from Boston to LA.

All that remains are the shells from Rincón, in their glass bowl on a shelf in the hallway. I have carried them around with me all these years without thinking about it, and I cannot remember the last time I really looked at them. They are faded now, the colors muted, like a head of hair gone gray. I thought I had buried every last feeling, but when I pick one up — an ivory scallop with lavender stripes — and touch it to my tongue, an electric thrill jolts through me, as if I have licked a live wire. It still tastes, ever so faintly, of salt. ■

Still Life With Candles And Spanish Guitar

a short story by **KIRK NESSET**

The story goes roughly like this: Girl meets boy in chat room, agrees
to meet downtown for coffee. And does, and after three minutes
of coffee can see it's not good. The story goes like such stories do. Girl's
got to ditch boy but can't simply snub him outright; he's not for her,
but he's human, and not stupid, either. What's more, he isn't ugly, has
what you'd call middling good looks, with a kind of weird dark charisma, despite the clothes: he spent eighteen months in the army, was
discharged for ambiguous reasons, and still wears mainly khaki. So
girl not only suffers the droning self-centered barrage but says, well,
OK, yes, she'll join him for dinner, and, get this, hops in his *minivan* in
the freezing parking garage (boy has no children, no trade, not even a
job), leaving her own car there on level three, trusting the universe to
protect her, as it must, asking herself why in God's name does she do
these things that she does.

Lucky for her and for us, the story doesn't end in this vein. Boy does
not pull off into a dimly lit lane to rape her and cut her with his knife
and burn her and maybe cannibalize a bit for good measure. Girl does
not become a statistic, another in a long list of sorry bodies that turn
up piecemeal in dumpsters. This is a happier story, unhappy as both
girl and boy seem to be. First he sideswipes a wall, descending the
parking garage. Turns out the van is his mother's, he borrowed it and
in fact rarely drives (this in part was the rub with the army), though
he's just turned thirty-three. With forced nonchalance he pilots the
damaged van to the valet lot at Atherton's, the city's most illustri-
ous eatery, and in they go. Into the tableau of Italian suits, diamonds,

candles, magnificent dresses — to the dismay of said girl, clad humbly in Levi's and tennies and white poly-knit top. The boy has brought his guitar in its uncomely case. They like me to play here, he told her outside. Anytime. Really.

The bar upstairs is a degree or two less formal, if not quite your jeans-or-khaki locale. And it's brimming with murmuring holiday tipplers. Boy squeezes through with his instrument, followed by girl; they claim the single unoccupied table, a tiny walnut thing trimmed in brushed chrome, like the bar. He unsheathes the guitar, tunes briefly. The girl motions as the waitperson passes, but he's looking in every direction but theirs. The boy kicks off his set with a burst of flamenco. The murmur halts in the bar for a moment as this new element registers. This Spanish brashness so forwardly flung, unprompted, so at odds with the holiday music. With "God Rest Ye" issuing still through the invisible speakers.

The boy retunes between songs. He hadn't gotten the guitar tuned in the first place. He doesn't get it right now. He's tone-deaf, or nervous, or both; he's only been playing eight months. The waiter glides over at last, addressing them — boy, girl, guitar — as if from some immeasurable distance. Beer for the boy, Scotch on the rocks for the girl. And an order of fries and steamed clams, since the boy said there'd be dinner. Boy blasts off again. Another fervent song by Montoya. It's all flamenco, actually. Flamenco's what the boy knows; it's his passion, his love. That and playing in public. Which he does with much flair: head jerks, grimaces, dramatic down-strums.

Two songs later the girl slips away to the bathroom. She opens her purse on the spotless, mica-flecked marble counter, extracts her cellphone, and dials her housemate. Sharon, she'll say when said housemate picks up, I blew it, come rescue me, *now* — no, better yet, invent an emergency, something terrible, just call my cell in ten minutes. But Sharon's not home. Girl leaves message on voice mail, conveying just a fraction of the desperation she feels, then enters a stall, latching the elegant latch on the veined marble door, and, unzipping, sits. She doesn't have to pee, but, well, here she is.

She's gone out of her way lately to find these least-feasible men. Tonight seems to epitomize them all, the whole sad, vivid tally. There was the bewildered professor, a guitar player also, who didn't and would never know what he wanted, who couldn't say what he meant, for all his fondness for words, and who was, by the way, married. There was the brother of her ex-roommate Stella, psychotic, volcanic, a bona fide stalker after the fact. There was the computer astronomer, whose very face made one want to yawn, and Ken, who was addicted to pot; there was the lovable drug-and-alcohol counselor with his less lovable herpes. And yes, the man who comanaged the greeting-card factory, too old for her, really, who couldn't be pleased unless she played boy to his girl, unless she forcefully "took" him; and she *likes* being a girl, and feels strange, not sexy, with plastic accouterments strapped to her hips.

For sure, one can be forgiven for doing what one does again and again and again. Girl meets boy after boy after worst-possible boy. But what hurts is knowing you do it, and knowing you know, and knowing you haven't learned. What hurts is playing the role willingly, knowing in your bones how dire the ending will be. Even in the oldest, most basic stories the wolf hides its teeth badly. And the girl knows what a wolf is, and knows about teeth, and still dares the thing to bare its teeth fully.

She sits biding her minutes, jeans at her ankles. Then gets up and zips up and checks herself in the mirror and then exits. She passes the Christmas ficus with its tiny white bulbs, the row of gleaming bar stools, the cheerful holiday couples; she settles again at the table, where the boy is playing full tilt. Bargoers glance over occasionally. A few look embarrassed. Above all they don't know how to respond. *Why are these people here?* they seem to wonder, this smiling pretty girl with the mole and all her white teeth and this manic young man in black boots and khaki. They don't see a bowl or a tip jar. Will the girl walk around in a while with a hat, a sombrero? And the boy might choose, if he would, to play a bit softer.

One more clam, she decides, one last sip of Scotch, and she'll say she's got to go. She's feeling sick, she will say; it's her stomach, the seafood perhaps; she hasn't had a clam since she was seven. She looks at the antique leaded windows, which are just slightly steamy, then at the bar, squinching her face up, trying to will her guts to rebel. That's when she sees the woman. A short, erect lady, midseventies maybe, clad in cobalt chenille. The lady's not drinking, nor is she with anyone. She's just standing there gazing — at the girl, at the boy — three paces off, serenely smiling.

The boy ends his song with a flourish. The woman applauds emphatically, edging up, inciting the first general applause of the evening.

Wonderful, she says, beaming.

Her face is exuberant, radiant, rosy. The house music intones yet from on high, cautiously operatic. *And heaven and nature sing, and heaven and nature sing!*

Thanks, says the boy.

The woman beams at the girl, the boy, the guitar. Do you know "The Hunt," by Albéniz? she asks.

Still working on that one, the boy answers.

Marvelous.

Thanks, says the boy.

Are you here every Saturday? We're downstairs. I never come up here.

I just come around when I can.

I see, the woman says.

She's swaying minutely, touching the girl's chair to keep herself steady.

Would you play for us? she asks the boy. At my table? Downstairs?

The boy looks at the girl.

Just two songs, the woman says. We'll pay you.

The girl's got her hand on her gut, face squinched, but doesn't speak up in time.

OK, says the boy, and stands up. And the girl says, I'll wait here, and the lady says, Oh, honey, no, he's playing for *you!*

Downstairs it's a soft-spoken party of six. White linen, candles, maroon linen napkins. At the table's head a pair of diners slide over, making space for the girl and the boy and the acoustic guitar. The lady's husband, who resembles Marcus Welby, MD, orders a beer for the boy and a Scotch for the girl, looking like the last thing in the world he wants to ask his dear wife is What have you gone and done now? The boy tunes, then rolls into the Montoya piece he opened with earlier.

This time he gets every note right, the song is flawless, minus a few rhythmic stumbles. He concludes, panting almost. The whole table applauds. As do others: other tables, other diners, who seem at least vaguely interested in what is transpiring at this end of the room. The piped-in Christmas carols have been summarily silenced. The waiter hands the desserts around, coffee. The boy rolls into song two.

The woman seems entranced by the girl. She's beaming and beaming, confiding, utterly wrong but somehow also right in her way, her fine silver hair swept in a bun, gazing over the bouquet of hibiscus and holly, the candles, the neck of the Spanish guitar. The boy moves into song three, and then four. There's no stopping him now, he might play forever, and that's fine with her, with the woman, even if her party's begun again to converse, and the old man on her left, liver spots, baggy red velvet vest, half blind and half deaf and maybe touched by Tourette's, is nodding off slowly.

This is how it feels to be young and in love, her face seems to say. This is how we're made love to; this is how love comes at us, deliciously headlong. This is how we flower and live in it, because it's all that matters, ever. I know this well, her face seems to say. And I refuse to forget it, or lose it. And I know you'll remember it, too.

And now the girl's phone is going off; it's clipped to her hip, not ringing but vibrating in its imperative way. And in this happier unhappy story of girl and boy, this story that could and does go on without end, the girl lets it buzz. She melts into her chair and her Scotch and stays where she is. ∎

Alone With Love Songs

by **EDWIN ROMOND**

It was an old motel
overlooking
Lake Michigan,
the rooms converted
to tiny furnished
apartments
for people like me —
single, straight
out of Catholic seminary —
for $85 a month:
just enough space
to live for the first time
by myself.
Some days
I'd stand for hours
gazing out at the waves,
sipping coffee and
smoking the cigarettes
I needed like air —
not the last time
in my life
I would crave
what was killing me.
And I'd listen to records.
In solitude
I fell in love

with love songs.
Years before mortgages
and picking out patio furniture,
I shared my time
with Sinatra and Mathis,
Linda Ronstadt
and Carole King, just music
and me, my eyes set
on restless Lake Michigan,
vast as the future when
you're twenty and in love
with the promise of love
from James Taylor
or Joni Mitchell.
When Wisconsin snow
would erase the lake
from my window,
I'd feel a blizzard of flames
inside me as I listened
hour after hour
to haunting ballads blurring the
distance between the romantic
and the real, and I,
love's lonely apprentice,
taking it all in,
getting it all wrong.

I Will Soon Be Married

a short story by **JOHN TAIT**

I will soon be married, though it's nothing I would have believed, nothing for which I'm prepared. The bride is asleep across town, and she and I have made no real plans. We've scarcely discussed it. Yet I feel a pang of anticipation each morning. I feel that same ache now while I sit with my guitar across my lap, drunk and trying to stay conscious at four in the morning. I've spent too many nights like this, drinking beer, holding but not playing my Telecaster, writing songs in my head. Mr. Galvez, my downstairs neighbor, pounds his ceiling (my floor), though I don't know why. I've annoyed him many times with parties and loud music, but I haven't made a sound tonight, haven't had it in me to play a note while I compose "I Will Soon Be Married," a song for my bride-to-be in her distant bedroom, her black hair arranged in sleep in ways I can't imagine. Mr. Galvez bangs again, and I wish he would go to bed, that he would even be happy for me, that he would leave me in peace and let me finish writing my song.

Elzbieta, my fiancée, is the singer in my band. I met her a year ago, in the summer, after I lost my job at Record King. I was living in a rehearsal space and sleeping on a stinking mattress where something else lived that bit my legs at night and left scarlet marks that didn't itch but still troubled me. I knew the bites came from that mattress because I would circle each one with blue ballpoint pen before I slept, and the next morning I'd find four or five new ones. I felt a simmering, sick anger all that summer, and I wasn't sure if I'd been poisoned by what had bitten me or if it was just the indignity of wearing those marks.

I had just formed a band called Farrago. I've been in bands for the past twenty-four years, since I was fourteen. The other members were old friends: Aaron, the drummer; and Carl, the bass player. We came together because we had few complaints with each other as human beings, unlike the members of my previous band, which had dissolved when I punched the drummer in the eye. Farrago jammed for hours in the space where I slept, captured ideas on a four-track when we weren't too stoned to hit RECORD. Over time we developed a repertoire of slow boleros, sleepy waltzes, and lugubrious country ballads that I sang passably.

One night we played the Love Hospital, a small club here in Toronto. In the sparse audience, a black-haired girl sat alone, her backpack balanced in her lap. A skinny punk at the next table was trying to make this black-haired girl, leaning his chair back and rattling his bracelets. A college boy two tables away was trying to make her too; I watched while he stroked his damp upper lip and gathered advice from his friends. Even the barmaid was trying to make this black-haired girl, trailing a hand along her freckled shoulder, pulling a braid aside to whisper in her ear. The girl smiled serenely at each of them but kept her eyes on the stage throughout our set, her braids bracketing her pale, serious face, her eyes the color of varnished teak. I decided if I was going to approach her it should be right after the show, while I was still stoked from playing. After the encore, I headed to the bar to plan my next move, but she was already at my side, so suddenly it startled me. I introduced myself and prepared to discuss what girls usually want to discuss after shows.

"I'm Elzbieta," the black-haired girl said. "I would fit with you."

She was younger than she'd looked from afar, twenty-four at most. I couldn't place her accent, with its nasal lilt and swallowed syllables.

I smiled. "Fit with me?" I was about to ask what she had in mind when her eyes dropped. I thought maybe she was shy, until I followed her gaze to where my wool sock had fallen and saw she was staring at the ring of scarlet bites around my right ankle, some circled in faded blue. They looked like plague sores. I forgot the words I'd been about to speak, drew my foot back, and felt the same heavy anger I'd carried all summer.

"I'm sorry. I mean I would fit with your band." She looked up with timid insistence. "I sing."

"OK," I said, and gave her the address of my rehearsal space before she hurried off. The next day she left two items there: a battered cassette wrapped in newspaper and a jar of fragrant cream with a Polish label that made the marks on my legs fade.

Each night for a week I lay on my infested mattress, headphones covering my ears, and listened to her singing over a Casio organ, her voice breathy and close against a cheap microphone. She sang mostly pop songs from the seventies — the Carpenters, Linda Ronstadt, Bread — along with a version of "Raindrops Keep Falling on My Head," which she sang in the singular: "Raindrop keep falling . . ." Toward the end she sang along to Polish songs on the radio, very softly, sometimes too softly to reach the high notes, her voice dropping to a broken whisper.

It never occurred to me then whether her voice was good or bad, skilled or unskilled. It was just a voice in a distant room that had become a voice in mine, a voice singing late at night, trying to empty some restless sorrow while not waking the parents in the next bedroom. I listened to the tape every night, rewound and replayed it until the battery light on my Walkman dimmed to a tired amber eye.

I invited her to a rehearsal. Aaron and Carl sat and watched while she laid out her yogurt and bottled water, placed a small stuffed ape by her microphone stand, took off her shoes and socks, and stretched as if she were about to run a sprint.

"We would never subject *you* to this," Carl muttered as I passed.

We began the first song on the practice tape I'd given her, her voice timid at first, then rising and gaining strength in the small room. I saw the others exchange glances during the second song, which was followed by a silence that Elzi broke with nervous laughter. We ran through our set once, then a second time. Afterward Elzi sat on Aaron's stool and asked him to teach her simple drum patterns, then cooed at wallet pictures of Carl's daughter. There was no consultation or vote. She came to our next rehearsal and sang at our next show.

Elzi and I dated for a few weeks, went to matinee movies where I gave whispered explanations when the actors spoke too quickly, window-shopped in front of Bay Street boutiques where we could afford nothing. She came to my place a few times, though she would never stay the night, because her aunt would worry. She always dressed and left after the evening news. One night, after a downtown gig before our largest crowd to date, she told me she didn't think we should continue.

"I'm too old for you," I muttered.

"It's not that. I like you, Tommy. I just think our music is more important. It's more important to me right now than anything. The band is just about to get big, right? If you and me stayed together, and things went badly between us . . ."

"Sure, I understand."

"You are OK, Tommy?"

"I'm fine," I told her, though afterward I walked the streets all night until the cold forced me into a busy cafeteria, where I stood in line with weary construction workers and cops for ten minutes before I realized I wasn't hungry.

Elzi's predictions about Farrago were right. Things have gone well in the year since then, better than any of us imagined, with growing crowds and a successful EP on a local label. Or, rather, things were going well until one night a week ago when I walked Elzi home after rehearsal. She'd been quiet all evening, not joking or teasing as usual. At her door she invited me in for coffee. Elzi lived with her aunt in an apartment squeezed into the right half of a two-story house. I'd been only as far as the small kitchen, which was just past the front corridor, with its hung jackets and vacuum cleaner. I'd never seen her aunt, only heard her muttering in Polish at the top of the stairs, seen her slippers on the bottom step, and drunk the coffee she'd brewed, though her doctor wouldn't let her drink it.

I was sitting at the kitchen table, sipping strong coffee with whiskey and describing a scuffle with a bouncer the previous night, waiting for Elzi to sigh and scold me, when she asked solemnly if I would "get married" to her.

I laughed, too drunk to catch on.

"I'm serious, Tommy. My visa expires soon." She smiled mirthlessly.

"I have to go back. Or they deport me."

"I thought you were getting your permanent residency." I blinked at her. "Why didn't you tell me this before? Jesus. What about the band?"

"Don't be mad, Tommy. I'm embarrassed. I read it wrong, the information. I thought my aunt would be enough for them. But I got a letter." She stared down at her folded hands. "You think I'm stupid, don't you?"

"I don't." I stared at my own hands, scraped and nicked from the previous night's fight, and laughed. "Why me, Elzi?"

"I don't know anyone else I can ask."

She cried then, muffling her sobs in the crook of her elbow. When I told her — when I *promised* — that I would do whatever she needed, she cried louder and kissed me on the temple, dark braids wagging, then said good night and climbed the stairs to her bedroom. I finished my coffee, let myself out, and walked home like a sleepwalker in a spray of rain that failed to rouse me from my dream.

That was a week ago, and tonight our band is playing an "important" show — important because industry and media people might be present. Jonny Woodbine will probably make an appearance, as he has at a few recent shows. None of this means much to me. Over the years, in different bands, I've been wooed and courted and have even signed contracts. I've heard whispered promises that made me walk the streets all night, too stoked to sleep, predictions that made me quit jobs and lose friends and spend money I never saw. My expectations now are modest. Farrago is specialized and offbeat. We've built a respectable following, enough to fill most smaller clubs, but we've plateaued. Without a major financial push or solid distribution deal, we're better off staying small and local.

Tonight I play guitar and watch Elzi, who stands between me and the faces ringing the stage in her thrift-store cocktail dress, barefoot as usual. I watch how her shoulder blades fan with each breath, how she leans forward on the balls of her feet when she comes to a note she's struggled with, toes curling as if gripping the stage.

Elzbieta is our main attraction. No one but her would deny this. Many of our fans are young men who stand rapt as she sings in her closed-eyed, swaying style, cupping the mike in her hands as if it were a small bird. I suspect many of these young men imagine hearing this voice across an unlit bedroom. She appeals to women, too, though in them her voice awakens a pleasurable brooding. After our shows, the men look stirred, sharp-eyed with longing, ready for adventure. The women look pensive and morose, ready to go home early, to think and reevaluate. A small throng waits for Elzi after each show. She talks and shakes hands, accepts the adulation gracefully.

As I watch her sing tonight, it occurs to me, as it has in every still moment this week, that she and I will soon be married, and I'm embarrassed to say the idea sends an electrical current through my insides — until I remind myself that it shouldn't. Though Elzi and I have hardly discussed our plan (at her request), it hasn't much left my mind. Tonight, after our important show, Elzi makes the announcement to our bandmates over a bottle of wine backstage. Carl claps and whistles. Aaron says nothing, only looks from one of us to the other.

"Talk about taking one for the team." Carl punches my shoulder.

"Oh, yes, so awful to marry me." Elzi pretends to sulk until he kisses her forehead.

"I'd do it myself, sweetie, but they'd have me in jail for bigamy." Carl frowns. "Though I'm still an accessory to immigration fraud now, right? Great."

After the others leave, Elzi wants to finish the bottle with me and make wedding plans. I pretend to be annoyed, though it's something I have thought about, late at night or in the morning before I'm fully awake.

"You must wear a suit and good shoes, Thomas," Elzi announces, putting on the stuffy manner she uses to tease me now and then, "or I will be very embarrassed."

"I'll see what turns up."

"And it must be in a church."

"For fuck's sake. Are you serious?"

"Of course." I see a mischievous gleam in her eyes, but perhaps some sincerity too. "It must be."

I scowl and sip wine. "OK, how about that little chapel in the Annex, the Polish one near the IGA dumpster that smells like cat piss?"

She gasps and wrinkles her nose. "Saint Stanislaus? No. So dirty."

"Why are you the one calling all the shots? I'm doing you the favor. Saint Stan's or nothing."

She throws up her hands and sits back grumpily.

I lay out my other conditions: that we must be serenaded by a sweaty fat man playing mazurkas on an accordion; that I must have all the homemade pierogies I can eat, preferably greasy ones; that the service must be conducted in Polish by an old drunken priest with bad teeth and gin blossoms.

"What are gin blossoms?" Elzi asks. I tap the bridge of my nose, the broken blood vessels there. She leans close and squints but claims she can't see anything. "Well, I want a little girl to carry flowers," she says defiantly.

"Yes, an angry, ugly little Polish girl from the neighborhood who makes faces all through the ceremony, with a limp or a stutter or a lazy eye or —"

Elzi sniffs. "I should have listened to my friends. They warned me about you. I should have found a nice boy who will be good to me instead of . . ." She sighs and stands, unsteady from the wine, her expression one of convincing martyrdom. Then she kisses my cheek playfully and heads home to her worrying aunt.

After most of the crowd has left and we're breaking down the gear, Aaron stops me and, with the same tone he might use to criticize a guitar solo in rehearsal, asks what the hell I think I'm doing.

"If I don't do it, she'll be deported. We'd never replace her."

"That isn't why you're doing it." He doesn't look up from the patch cords he's untangling. "You know she could find some nice guy to help her out. You don't have to be that guy."

I say nothing, feeling shamed and cross, like a schoolboy caught passing love notes in class. I'm not sure how he knows, what exactly he's witnessed from his perch behind the drum kit. Though I know he's right, I also know that I will do whatever Elzi needs.

Jonny Woodbine has appeared, sniffing around the stage with his Chairman Mao hat, engineer boots, spiral notebook, and tattoos. He greets Aaron but not me. Jonny is a local boy made good. Over the years I've watched his cranky reviews move from a student paper to a 'zine to an entertainment weekly to a column in a Toronto news-paper. In the photo by his byline he twists around to get his Celtic shoulder tattoo into the shot. I've seen him in panel discussions on rock culture, where he lectures like some combination of Iggy Pop and Robespierre. Jonny has his own midnight alternative-music show on the local cable channel, which he ends every week by shouting, "Live it, people!" and giving the camera a supercilious salute. He's on every guest list in town, and his drinks are always paid for.

Jonny Woodbine never lets on that he knows me, though we've drunk together a few times, and though he's written a dozen reviews of my bands over the years and even mentioned me by name, seeming most intrigued by the fact that I don't move much onstage. In reviews he's described me alternately as "the band's brooding, still center . . . emanating a Brian Jones–like menace and charisma," and as "a do-nothing weak link . . . a drunken, inert lump." I think I'm caught at some awkward intersection in his imagination.

Jonny is looking for Elzi. For a week or so he's been pursuing her, like so many others, though he might have a better chance than most. I've been present a few times when he's impressed her with his name-dropping and impassioned rants or made her giggle with his gossip about other musicians. Tonight Jonny makes small talk with us before asking, with practiced indifference, "So, where's *la jolie chanteuse*?"

"Gone home," Aaron says.

Jonny glumly helps Aaron tumble the kick drum into its case. I sus-pect he is considering how to ask for Elzi's number without making his intentions too plain. A respected music journalist shouldn't have to stalk an artist like some groupie.

"I like how your sound is developing," Jonny tells Aaron. "You're moving into this polyrhythmic, early-Beefheart territory that I really dig. And, of course, the vocals are tremendous."

"Of course," Aaron says.

Jonny regards him uncertainly. "Anyhow, I'm going fishing with Doug Gordon from Archer Records this weekend. If you gave me a tape, I could play it for him."

Aaron and I exchange looks. Archer is a successful Chicago indie label that would be a good match for us. Aaron digs through his backpack and flips me a cassette. While Jonny Woodbine pauses to write some pressing thought in his notebook, I hesitate. In my own pack I have Elzi's worn cassette, the one she gave me a year ago. On impulse I put away the band's cassette and hand Jonny Elzi's in its place.

"Need it back when you're done," I tell him, though I suspect I won't see it again.

Jonny looks puzzled, then pockets the tape and salutes us before he leaves, just like on television.

"Live it, asshole," Aaron mutters behind his back.

Later that night, I lie on my mattress like a capsized tortoise, unable to get to my feet or even pick up the beer I set on the milk crate just a moment before. I wonder why I gave Jonny Woodbine Elzi's tape. Maybe it was a joke. Or an experiment. Or maybe I wanted Jonny to hurt like I did when I first listened to it — not just the pain of knowing you will never hear that voice singing only to you, but the ache that you were not present at the moment the sounds were made in some dark Krakow bedroom.

My amplifier is switched on, sizzling, and I have the cord in my hand. I touch the bare lead to my tongue, and the amp faintly pops, but I feel nothing — no energy, no charge, no release. Mr. Galvez downstairs bangs on his ceiling, but I'm not making any noise. There's just the hum of the amp and the ringing of tinnitus in my ears. I wonder what he hears that I don't. Perhaps he's banging in his sleep, an angry reflex. Or maybe the music in my head, my "Soon to Be Married" song, is keeping him awake. He's a bachelor too, and if he's hearing the same song I am, then he won't sleep a wink tonight.

"Get married onstage," the owner of the Love Hospital insists at a table in the club's back room. "We have nothing booked Wednesday the twelfth. You got it if you want it. Play a set, then get hitched."

"No way," I say immediately, though the others at the table are grinning.

"We could make it a benefit show for Canada Immigration," Carl says, and everyone laughs but me. "Sponsored by the Polish-Canadian Friendship Society."

"I'm not taking part in some freak show," I grumble, though I seem to be alone. "I'm not Tiny fucking Tim."

"It could be fun, Tommy. Don't you think?" Elzi asks.

I study her earnest, amused eyes, then tell them they can do whatever they like, and laugh along with the rest. Later, when the others leave to check out a show across town, I beg off, and Aaron follows me.

"If you don't want to do it, tell them," he mutters. "Tell her. I will if you can't."

I break away from him and duck into the bar down the street.

Late that night I get into a fight outside the Jerk Pit. My opponent is a big kid with blond dreads who thinks I'm someone else, though this is probably only a pretext to fight, and I'm too drunk to point out his mistake anyway. I have my chance to run, but I stay and go down quickly. The beating is nothing special. As I feel his fists and boots, I know it isn't the last pummeling I'll receive. That thought and the alcohol give me the patience to wait it out. My attacker's bored friends eventually pull him off, and I sit up and catch my blood in my palm, cupping it as if I could pour it back into me. A waitress I know, Kristine, stops to help. She's a nice girl who sells leather goods on the street on weekends. I've sat by her stand once or twice, talked and flirted. Her hands gently touch my face.

"I live just down the street," she whispers. "C'mon."

I feel in her touch a desire to comfort and care for me. I almost go with her. I might have only a week ago.

"Sorry," I lisp through swollen lips. "I'm getting married soon."

She helps me to my feet and watches me stagger off.

Back home I look in the mirror. The bridge of my nose and my lower lip are so swollen I look almost simian. The beating has chipped a top front tooth, and I feel the shocking absence with my tongue. I look less like a bridegroom than I do the bum in the alley beside the church who watches the bridal party leave with an uncomprehending stare.

Before our next rehearsal, Elzbieta sees my face.

"What happened this time, Tommy?" She's angry, almost.

I say I don't remember, which is mostly true, and continue unloading the van.

She grabs my sleeve. "Tommy, will you talk with me?"

"About what?"

"Aaron says I should talk to you." She studies me carefully. "We don't have to have the wedding at the club if you don't want to. We don't have to do it at all."

"It's fine." I lift the hi-hat and snare through the van's side door. "I just don't like that fucking stage they have over there. It smells like beer and sweat, and the boards are rotting, and the lights are too hot."

"Maybe I don't like it there either. Maybe we cancel."

"No, the show's booked. The flyers are up. I don't care."

Her brow is knit. "It's strange to think we are married soon." She chuckles. "Married people, how do they live? What do they do? How are they different? I have no married friends, so I don't know. How do you *be* married?" She's not entirely joking.

"From what I've seen, you mostly ignore each other and collect grievances to use at some later date."

Elzi's face shows alarm, then incredulity. "That's what you think?"

I shrug, but I'm glad that she disagrees.

"But did you ever think you would get married like this, to some stupid foreign girl at a rock show?" She gives me a shy smile.

"I never thought I'd get married at all."

"Me, I have thought about getting married from when I was small, but I never thought it would be like this." She looks up quickly. "I don't mean you. I feel so happy you would do this for me. But I mean on a stage, in a bar. It isn't what I imagined when I was a girl. Do you understand?" Her eyes fall. "Maybe we could go to a church. Maybe even that one you like."

I resent how she can seem so earnest, how she can make me hope for things I shouldn't.

"Elzi, it doesn't matter where or how we do it, because it's pretend." I can't keep the exasperation from my voice. "We wear pretend rings. We pretend to live at the same address. We go on a few pretend trips and take pretend pictures to show at the interview. I'm doing this as a favor. So please don't lay some trip on me about spoiling your girlhood dreams."

Her eyes are moist as she walks off.

Aaron comes out soon after. "Just so you know, I told her to talk to you. I told her I thought she was taking advantage. That I didn't think it was right. That she should find somebody else."

"Uh-huh."

Aaron rubs his eyes in exasperation. "Tommy, I don't get it. Why?"

"Maybe it's a selfless act."

"I don't believe that. What do you hope is going to come of all this? Until you tell me something that makes sense, any way I look at it, she's using you."

"It's OK." I lift the kick drum with a grunt. "I wasn't using me much anyways."

The big day has arrived. Some of our friends have draped a banner — CONGRATULATIONS ELZI AND TOMMY!! — across the stage. They've drawn a caricature on it of us holding hands. I'm shaggy and troll-like, with my chipped tooth. Someone has added a beer bottle and a burning spliff to my picture with black marker. For some reason the artist has given Elzbieta pointed ears, like a pretty elf.

For the occasion I'm wearing a tuxedo and a bowler hat that Carl dug up. The tux is too small and doesn't reach my wrists and ankles. I look like a cross between Charlie Chaplin and Charlie Manson. "I feel like an idiot," I whisper to Aaron, who doesn't reassure me.

Elzbieta arrives late. Her hair is tied back in a way I've never seen it, coiled above her nape. Her skin is so pale that I can detect the fine blue veins at her temples, perhaps even their quick pulse. The gown she wears is real, I see with surprise, white floor-length lace with a bodice. Only when she turns do I see where the hem has fallen in ragged strips and a safety pin holds a shoulder strap together. Elzi's hand shakes as she sips a beer at the bar. She's avoiding me — I don't know how much out of wedding-day superstition and how much because of our argument a few days back. When I approach, her eyes look naked and frightened.

"It'll be fine, sweetheart," I whisper. She smiles, though her hand holding the bottle still trembles.

I'm right, as it turns out. We play that night with pleasing synergy, that one-mindedness that happens every few shows. I sweat through the old tux by the third song and feel a clammy chill the rest of the set, but it doesn't matter. At midnight, after our three-song encore, the Unitarian youth minister from down the street mounts the stage, gangly, red haired, and thin wristed. He squints uncertainly at us before he begins. The ceremony is brief and ironic. The audience prompts Elzi when she stumbles, blushing, on her vows. Aaron plays rimshots on his drums after mine. When we chastely kiss, Elzbieta stands on her toes and leans against me, her small fingers splayed on my chest. The audience cheers, and cameras flash. Our wedding will be a back-page novelty story in the entertainment weeklies.

Afterward my drinks are on the house, and my back is slapped sore. The DJ plays polka music with wheezing accordions. There's dancing. The bar is filled with our friends and fans and, later, people who've wandered in from the Blue Jays game looking for a party, out of place but happy. I sit for a long time on the lip of the stage with a beer. Elzi is dancing in a whispering huddle of girls, their faces close and conspiratorial. Watching them, my heart is full, and I couldn't move or speak if I wanted to.

Then I see Jonny Woodbine moving through the crowd, heading toward Elzi. He whispers in her ear, and she exclaims and clutches his shoulders. He stays near her through the next song, and I'm mildly gratified to see that Jonny Woodbine can't dance, only sway self-consciously, as if balancing on a plank. I drink more, and to my surprise I'm soon dancing, too, in a huddle of Jays fans who encircle me with their arms and keep me on my feet. I feel light, my legs rising and kicking until the song ends and they lean me against the wall by the side exit.

Aaron comes to check on me twice and bring me a fresh beer. Then Jonny Woodbine is before me, his face flushed with drink. He moves like a man who suspects he's being observed from a number of positions at once.

"Congrats, dude," he shouts into my ear, the one that is not pressed against the cool brick. "I was just talking with your lovely *wife*." Is that an ironic emphasis he places on the last word?

"Thanks," I say, uneasy with his new interest in me and with his broad grin.

"I think you gave me the wrong cassette the other night," he says, looking slightly troubled. I'm pleased that Elzi's tape has wounded him in exactly the way I intended. He clears his throat. "It's OK. I gave Doug my own copy of your EP. He's excited and wants to meet all of you. He thinks Elzi's amazing."

"She is."

"I've got better news."

"Archer Records?"

"Better. Doug Gordon's just been offered a job at Matsuhiro Music. The big leagues. If he takes it, you guys will be the first band he signs." He waits for this to sink in. "Doug and I have a few ideas for you. We want to develop a sound that will showcase Elzi's voice to a broader audience. Doug knows some great musicians in Chicago. We're thinking about experimenting and adding a few players. If that's OK."

I've had a lot to drink, but the "we" hasn't escaped me, nor has his proprietary tone. I've been through this dance before. The fire-exit door opens, and a draft chills me through the damp tux. "I suppose you'll be subtracting players too."

"We haven't thought that far ahead." He prods my shoulder with his knuckle. "Hey, I was digging your playing tonight. That solo in the new song — Django Reinhardt on acid, I'd call it. Too much."

"Can I ask you a question, Jonny?"

He nods.

"You remember me, don't you?"

His expression shows no disagreement for the first few seconds. Then he frowns and shakes his head. "Should I? Maybe I've seen you around."

"We've talked before. We've had drinks together. I've read reviews where you used my name. It's no big deal. I know I'm not somebody worth remembering. None of my bands were any good. Until this one."

Jonny squints, as if taking me in for the first time. "Sorry, dude. I've lost a lot of brain cells over the years. Yeah, maybe I remember. You were in Ubik, right? And the Headtakers? Good stuff." He gives a slow smile, though it's too late now to be gracious, to reminisce.

"This band is the best I've been in. And it's because of Elzi. I want good things for her. Which is why I'm not sure I like your ideas."

He leans in closer. "I want the same thing you want, Tommy. And to be totally honest, I can help her a lot more than you can. If you want to keep playing shitty little clubs and passing out a box of CDs to your friends every few years, go ahead. But that's not for her. I can take her a lot further."

"I'm not arguing that," I say. "I know you're going places. And if you're really going to help her, that's great, and I thank you. But if you're not, if you mess up and drop her off somewhere along the way. . . well, I'd have to cut your throat."

Jonny smiles uncertainly when he sees me smile. "It's up to Elzi to decide what she wants to do next, not you or me, right? Go sleep it off, bro. We'll talk later. Again, congrats."

"Live it, Jonny." I salute while he heads back out to the dance floor. Moments later, someone flips off his Chairman Mao hat, and it falls under dancing feet and is trampled into a flat blue wad. Jonny stoops to retrieve it before remembering his dignity. Then he straightens, chuckles, and runs his fingers through his hair. I'm about to laugh until I see him beside Elzi again, whispering in her ear for a full minute before the two of them leave by the back door.

I stumble down the sidewalk outside the club at two in the morning. I know I'm heading due west, but little else. Too many nights I've navigated like this, the CN Tower a compass needle on my horizon. I feel a spray in the air, something between mist and rain. Then I hear the sound of pursuit behind me, the rapid footfalls, and a weary part of me wonders what beating I'll receive now.

But it's only Elzi, her gown lifted to reveal sandals and painted toenails. She stands beside me expectantly, and we burst out laughing like a con man and a shill rendezvousing after a swindle. I almost topple.

Elzi takes my arm, and we walk, not speaking. I don't know where she's leading me. We pass a Portuguese club surrounded by patio torches, with garlands and vines hung from wooden frames. Old men speak in urgent voices around a table, leaning forward, smoking cigars and drinking port wine. They turn and watch Elzi and me in our wedding gear, and we stare back until one of them lifts his small glass and toasts us solemnly. We wave to them and walk on.

"Did Jonny talk to you?" Her eyes are so bright I could see them without the streetlights.

"Yes."

"He said he will do everything he can. Use all his connections with promoters, with TV, with radio. I still can't believe this is happening."

"It's great, Elzi."

She's leading us through a suburban neighborhood, away from the city streets, a block with Portuguese and Italian and Serbian flags on lawns, with meticulously baroque gardens, soccer balls and nets. She hums a tune.

"I like that house." She points to a stately Victorian with a rock garden. "A nice married couple could live there. Don't you think?"

"How about that one?" I say. "Great for kids. Roomy. A nice yard. I could fix it up, put a swing set and a barbecue pit in back. What do you say?" What began as a joke has come out sounding oddly mirthless. I'm grateful when she doesn't laugh.

Elzi stops walking. To my surprise we've arrived at her apartment by an unfamiliar route. She gestures me up the narrow stairs in front. We sit in the kitchen and drink her aunt's coffee. When she takes my hand and opens her mouth to speak, I'm afraid she's going to thank me. I'm relieved when instead she begins to sing — quiet and embarrassed, two short verses in Polish. I sit and listen. It's the voice from the tape, aching, hushed so as not to wake her aunt upstairs.

"A wedding song," she explains, blushing. "I can't remember the rest."

It occurs to me, through the haze of drink, that these few minutes may be the only chance I'll have to sit like this with the woman I love, who is now my wife. And though it doesn't feel anything like I'd imagined, it's sufficient.

I'm about to speak when Elzi leans across the table to kiss me. I'm surprised again because the kiss is gentle and tentative and sad. And it may contain a question and maybe a careful, generous invitation, though I understand that any offer made tonight will be good only for tonight.

Elzbieta heads to the stairs, her dress's torn hem trailing, and though I know I'm free to follow, I remain at the table. Whether I follow or not seems irrelevant. Whether in the next hour I am in Elzi's bed or walking the streets back to my apartment in the spray of rain, it couldn't compete with this present moment. Whatever I've denied in the past, whatever regrets I'll suffer in the future, I can live with them. I've lived with worse. No, I'm digging my heels in for just a minute or two, and I won't be budged. I know I should move or act, that anyone watching would hasten me beyond this instant to the next. But I've just been married, and I wonder why I can't stay here awhile and have my moment's peace. ■

THE MYSTERIOUS LIFE OF THE HEART

The Leap

by **LARRY COLKER**

We stood in groups of twos and threes
on the sidewalk outside the bar,
talking, smoking, watching traffic and each other,
one quiet old guy by himself looking at the moon,

when a quick motion caught our eyes
as the girl pounced on her boyfriend,
shimmied up his tall torso,
squeezed her legs around his waist,
clasped her arms around his neck,
pressed her face into his hair.

If I were a prophet, I'd say
a burst of light surrounded them
like a glory. Like revelation, like satori,
we were all converted on the spot:
for the rest of our lives we'd wait
for such a rapture,
our bodies suddenly made heavy
with bone and flesh not our own.

I caught the old man looking, dumbstruck,
until he collected himself
and went back to staring at stars.

At first the boyfriend took it like a puppy's exuberance,
continued the conversation as though that leap,
still rebounding in our chests,
were nothing special. But his girl did not unlatch.
She tightened her arms and legs around him
until who knows what was let loose inside,
and he hugged her back, with a shy smile at us,
as if embarrassed by his riches.

The Woman With Hair

a short story by **ROBERT MCGEE**

The first time we met, she didn't say much but instead let her hair do the talking. Her hair had a lot on its mind. It went nearly down to her knees. This was in July, at a Hollywood Hills party thrown by the friend of a friend. There was only one person in the house we both knew. At midnight we sat on a couch with a cat between us. Pretty soon she and I started petting the cat at the same time. When our fingers touched, the cat's hair stood on end, and I think mine may have too.

When she came to my house the next day, I tried to be a gentleman and not kiss her too soon, but after eating the mango she'd brought, I couldn't refrain. For three hours we lay on my floor kissing — just kissing, which was more than enough. Never had I known lips so soft.

And her hair!

Her hair was unlike anything I'd ever seen. It straddled time zones; it lived and breathed, making deep exhalations down to her toes. Sometimes her hair seemed nearer the ground than her feet did. It blossomed like the fig tree growing outside my door, floated like the hummingbird that fluttered above.

Sometimes I kissed her hair instead of her lips.

Five nights in a row, after she'd visited, I curled up in bed with strands of her hair. I was like a boy who takes a football to bed, so deeply in love is he with the game.

"OK," my friend Frankie said. "Seeing that you're a man who's never known love, how do you know that it's love?"

"Your very question is the answer," I said.

"Explain, but without any Zen nonsense."

I stated several facts that Frankie already knew: I'm shy. I like quiet. I like living alone. I like to know everything that's in my fridge. I like my clothes folded a certain way. I don't watch TV or wear shoes in my house. I don't talk in the mornings. I don't like sharing a bathroom or breathing aerosol sprays. But this woman didn't get on my nerves. We'd spent the whole day together, and I couldn't wait to see her again.

"Well," Frankie said, "if she can put up with all that, you two deserve each other."

Soon it was August, but how could it be August if I wasn't miserably hot? Each night for a week the woman with hair lay in my arms. To lie beside her was like resting on a pile of leaves. Mostly she slept without a sound, but one night her breathing was troubled; she talked in her sleep and said she wanted to stay. I had made a vow never to speak before 10 A.M., but at 7:30 I asked her to move in with me. I promised we'd be happy until we were gray. I told her all this without thinking and still didn't regret a word. The woman with hair smiled as if it all might come to pass. Her fingertips consulted her hair. She never said yes, but she didn't say no, and so I kept hoping, even after she and her hair had driven away.

"Hair! Hair! Hair!" Frankie screamed. "If I hear one more word about hair . . ."

That September she and I stayed in the Venice Beach bungalow of a friend who was in Italy shooting a film. Mornings I went to work while the woman with hair wrote poetry and walked in the surf. I didn't like my job very much. In the afternoons I'd sneak down a stairwell and escape. I'd come back to the bungalow to find her reading Rumi in the shade of a tree, wearing a sarong. I looked forward to leaving for work each day, because only by leaving could I return. For the first time ever I entertained the idea of having a wife. In my daydreams I became "the man who married the woman with hair."

That week at the beach we made love three and four times a day. It got to the point where I went to work mainly to rest. After lunch I'd do my Houdini act, vanish by the stairwell, and go home to that small cottage, where we would talk, laugh, read poetry, hold each other in silence, kiss like teenagers, walk around naked, and make love again and again like lost souls who'd finally ended their search. We wore each other out, barely stopping to eat. I'd never spent more than a week with a woman under the same roof, but for eight nights running we slept with our bodies intertwined, and it wasn't enough.

Some nights we took walks hand in hand. I'm no hand holder, but now I felt lost if I didn't have her palm against mine. I began to pity other couples when we went to restaurants and shops. These couples would see us and realize how little they had. They didn't know what it was like to fall madly in love — to be thirsty for so long, and then to have that thirst quenched. I felt sorry for these other couples, who would envy our romance and go home completely depressed.

I loved her so much I wanted to climb inside her head and swim around awhile. Mornings I would fall into her eyes. Sometimes they were brown, but other times they turned green. When I told her this, she tried to cover her face.

"They're not supposed to do that," she said.

"Why not?"

"They only turn green when I'm sad or in love."

"Are you sad?"

"Not at the moment," she said.

O ur last morning in Venice she leaned against my car, tilting her face toward the sun. Her eyes became one with the light, and I knew I'd found all I'd ever wanted in life. I'd been with some wonderful women, women I'd cared about, but none of them had been the one. I'd hurt more than my share of women by not committing, and each time I'd been sorry, but I hadn't wanted to settle or make a mistake. Now I felt lucky to have waited, because I was ready when the woman with hair came into my life.

She said she loved me and wished she could stay. We hadn't talked much about what her life was like where she lived. I had been to her town once, long before we'd met — or, rather, I'd been through it, on a moonlit night, which had left a lot to the imagination. I hadn't asked about it for fear I might scare her away, but now, I thought, might be the time.

"So, where you going?" I asked as casually as I could.

"Crazy," she said.

I wanted to know more, but I just left it at that. Crazy might be a fine place to go. It didn't matter where crazy was, or who would be waiting for her there. I watched as she backed up, pulled away from the curb, and vanished.

I called in sick, then drove from Venice to my apartment near the HOLLYWOOD sign. In a way it was true: I was sick. I just didn't know the name of my illness or what would cure it. My apartment felt too big, too empty, too lonely; from every corner it called me a fool. I thought maybe I should paint the walls. Instead I sat down to write to her.

My plan was to send an e-mail before she got home, so that when she arrived she wouldn't feel the same loneliness I'd felt when I'd walked into my apartment. But I never had the chance to click SEND. As if conjured by my thoughts, she walked in as I wrote the last line.

"Forget something?" I asked, trying not to seem so thrilled.

"Not exactly," she said.

She'd driven sixty miles into the desert, she said, but she'd been unable to go any farther. She wasn't ready to go back, not yet.

I put out my hand but didn't touch her for fear that she might fade away. "Is this real?" I asked.

"I don't think I like reality much anymore."

M orning light caressed her face, and shadows of leaves danced on the walls. Through the open windows the scent of honeysuckle floated into our room. As she slept, I gazed at her naked body, which was graceful and willowy, as if an extension of her hair. Then I noticed that my own body had changed since the woman with hair had entered my life. Normally stocky and tense, my body now seemed to reach the end of the bed, and my hands and feet were more relaxed. It was as if I were growing, stretching outside of myself.

"I adore you," she said when she opened her eyes.

"Marry me," I said suddenly, surprising us both. I'd never proposed to anyone before, and when she closed her eyes, I was sure I'd done it all wrong.

When her eyes opened again, I saw that she had something to say.

For six years she'd been living with a man, she told me. At first they'd been a couple, but over the last two years he'd become more like a brother. They shared a large house and had separate bedrooms. They did things together; they did things apart. They loved one another, but she wasn't in love. The man understood and accepted this. Their life together was so comfortable that neither felt the need to move out. She'd resigned herself to having a companion who would always be there, but who would never want or need more.

From the moment we'd met, she'd begun to feel her life was madness; it was all turned around. She hadn't expected ever to feel this way again: like a woman, a lover. Now she wasn't sure she could go back.

"So you're leaving him," I said.

"It's not that simple," she said.

She told me she was afraid *not* to go back. When she slept, she had visions. Things that happened in her dreams later happened for real: Bombs exploded. Buildings collapsed. Cars and planes crashed. Ever since she was thirteen, disasters had appeared first in her mind, and then on the news. Until recently, the victims in her dreams had always been strangers, but for the past year she'd had dreams about him. The man she lived with was a fireman, and night after night she dreamed of him dying alone on a mountainside, calling for help, and she would run or drive faster to get to him, but she was always too late. She was going back, she said, because she feared he would die if she stayed with me. I pulled her close, thinking I might be the one to die if she left.

After that we didn't talk so much as hold one another and breathe. I knew time was running out when the scent of honeysuckle started to fade. When it was gone, we walked to her car.

"I love you madly," she said.

But you're leaving, I thought.

I started to tell her I'd wait for her, then realized that was the same as saying I would wait (and maybe hope) for another man's death.

"Marry me anyway," I said. "Keep living with him, and come to me when you can."

"And you don't think that would be strange?"

"It is what it is. We could elope tonight if you want."

"You have no idea how wonderful that sounds."

"Think about it."

She nodded, then told me she had to leave and might have to stay away for a while.

I said OK, but didn't ask how long it might be.

Our kiss was a shared breath. We held it for a full minute, and she smiled as our lips slipped apart. It wasn't until she drove off and I glimpsed her hair through the rear window that I realized her smile had been an odd one. A smile that seemed to conceal dark thoughts. A smile, I decided, that may not have been a smile after all.

I didn't see her for months. That fall was a season of weeping trees and creeping hours. I went to work, but I wasn't there. I felt invisible, yet also exposed. I watched clocks, counted minutes. Day after day I sneaked away from my desk only to realize that I had nowhere to go. I escaped from one door only to return through another, like some absent-minded professor who keeps forgetting his hat. By Thanksgiving the receptionist had grown weary of my constant comings and goings and had stopped saying hello.

I didn't see the woman with hair, and yet she was everywhere. I would find strands of her hair in strange places: my refrigerator, my coffee, my soup. At times I even found her hair in mine. It was as if the strands magically appeared. Once, I pulled off the road to remove a strand from my mirror, and an out-of-control truck barreled into my lane, narrowly missing me. Had it not been for her hair, I would have been killed. I got off the freeway and took a walk to calm down. When I came back, a parking ticket beneath my wiper blade flapped in the breeze. I considered fighting it by throwing myself on the mercy of the court: *Your Honor, I would have been killed had it not been for her hair.*

She finally returned on Christmas Day. She'd called the night before to set a time, and in the morning I rose early to clean — not because my apartment was dirty, but rather to make time disappear.

At noon she arrived carrying two pale blue mugs she had made herself. I couldn't help but be encouraged by the fact that there were two. I remember how hopeful I felt as we drank from those mugs. I pictured us living on an organic farm where she could fire her own clay pots and I could raise sheep. All I wanted was for her to stay so we could be one of those couples with matching sweaters and mugs.

As it turned out, she could stay just an hour and had other things on her mind. We kissed only once, and there was no talk of the future. We didn't talk much at all really. Mostly we drank tea and held one another on the couch as we tried not to cry. Then, just before leaving, her green eyes started to tear.

We had shared seventeen nights. Now she was gone.

Four years later I found myself alone again on Christmas, having just ended things the night before with an Argentine woman who'd come to me on the rebound from a bad marriage. She'd fled after opening — and being disappointed by — my gift. She'd been expecting an engagement ring. After she'd torn away every last shred of wrapping paper in a mad search for diamonds and gold, she threw my present (a mohair sweater) into the fire and stormed out swearing she'd never speak to me again — but only after telling me, in both Spanish and English, exactly where I could go.

I didn't go to hell, as my Argentine ex suggested. Instead I moved to the southern tip of Africa, because it seemed like a good place to escape failed love and my old shattered self. It was also the most distant point on the globe from LA. Soon after arriving, I settled into a small village near the Atlantic. And for the most part I've been content, living alone, far removed from my past. I own a cottage with an immense view of blue water, white sand, and wide-open sky. The sight and sound of birds early each morning is a tonic that protects me from feeling too alone.

These days I'm a consultant. Because of the time difference between here and LA, I work mostly at night, when I might otherwise think and worry over things I can't possibly change. Mine is a solitary life. I am the only American in this village, and yet I don't miss my countrymen, with their massive cars, their fast food, their insatiable need to consume and possess. If I'm in a shop and I hear an American accent, I'm careful to keep quiet until that person has gone.

It's a wonderful thing not to have to sneak down stairwells during the day. It is also wonderful to have the first hours of daylight to walk on the beach. Lately I've been gathering driftwood and have piles of it in my garage. So far I haven't done anything with the wood, but one day I hope the right idea will come, along with a strong dose of strength and resolve. For now these lost fragments of wood are like pieces of a puzzle yet to be formed.

I never again saw the woman with hair — not in the flesh, anyway. For almost a year I had visions of her when I slept. Nothing bad ever happened in my dreams, unless you count the time all the hair was shaved from her head. Lately the dreams have returned, and I sometimes wake from sleep wondering if I'm expressing a subconscious desire to return to a place that can never again be my home. Sometimes, to fend off these dreams, I try to stay awake.

Of course the trouble with not sleeping is you find yourself making desperate deals with the man upstairs. When it's dark and cold and you're weary, you find you are willing to lower your sights. Sometimes I convince myself that I might be able to find and be contented by regular love with a regular Sally with regular hair, a woman for whom I won't feel the mad passion of youth and to whom I won't propose by blurting out, "Marry me," one morning when I'm swept away by honeysuckle and the previous night's moon. On especially cold nights I stay under the covers, envisioning my regular Sally and me living in a regular house, working regular jobs. Even our wedding would be regular, taking place one fine summer day with violins and vows and old ladies weeping. Eventually we would have children — two daughters, perhaps — to raise and protect. College funds would be started, music lessons arranged. Evenings I'd read stories to our girls while my wife soaked in the tub. Years would pass, and I'd prepare my girls for what monsters lurk in the outside world. Of course I'd want the best for my daughters. I'd want them to immerse themselves in fulfilling jobs from which they would never wish to escape. And I'd hope that they would find people to love. I'd want for them a life no worse than mine.

But then morning returns, and I find myself wondering where lives and dreams join, and where they diverge. Daylight is like a wise friend, forcing me to call off any and all deals made with God during the night. But just before daylight I listen to what sounds like geese flying over, geese who honk uncertainly, as if they didn't know where they were going, only that they must go. Strangely, their indecision somehow puts me back on course and fills me with hope. I am soothed by these geese — soothed to imagine them flying all the way to California, back to LA, perhaps taking up residence in the Hollywood Hills. They will be locals in my old haunt, pursue my old paths, live among my friends. But what I envy most is their splendid luck at each finding one true companion for life. Even after the sun has fully risen, I keep my eyes closed, imagining that there will always be geese in my life. As long as I keep my eyes closed, the sky will be forever filled with geese; and they will fly with sureness and grace, dropping from their mouths single strands of hair that, like lovers whispering promises in the night, always have something wondrous to say. ∎

The Boy With Blue Hair

by CHERYL STRAYED

Years after I'd last seen him, I called him up. Which meant first I had to call his mother, a woman I'd never met. In another lifetime I'd written her number in my address book beside her long, unfamiliar name.

"Hello," she said, picking up the phone on the second ring three thousand miles away. I hadn't expected her voice to sound the way it did, so sweet and expectant and frail. He'd told me about her when he and I were lovers: How smart she was, and successful. How she'd been the valedictorian of her Ivy League college class and then had forged ahead and earned her PhD.

"Yes," I said, as if she'd asked me a question, and then I stammered out what I had planned to say more gracefully: who I was, what I wanted. It had taken some courage to call. No, *courage* isn't precisely the right word. It had taken a glass of wine and a single-minded bravado, coupled with a willingness to risk piercing this stranger's heart.

"He lives in San Francisco now," she interrupted me, understanding immediately the apprehension in my voice. "I'll give you his number," she added, her words slow and steady and intentional, as if we were speaking in code.

And we were. She wasn't just telling me where her son lived these days. She was telling me that he wasn't dead.

I'd met him on his birthday, seven years to the day before my phone call to his mother. I was twenty-five, and he had just turned twenty-four. I was separated from my husband but not yet technically divorced; he was using heroin but not yet technically a junkie. He walked up to me in a bar and put his hand on my wrist as I wrote in my journal. "Nice," he said, outlining the sharp edges of my tin bracelet with his delicate fingers. He had neon blue hair cut close to the scalp and a cartoonishly violent tattoo that covered half his arm, though his face was in precise contradiction to those disguises: tenacious and tender — like a kitten wanting milk.

That night we had sex on his lumpy futon on the floor and talked until the sun rose, mostly about him. He told me about his smart mother and his alcoholic father and the fancy school where he'd gone to college. The following afternoon we drove around, circling a parking lot until he spotted his drug dealer's car.

I hadn't known him twenty-four hours, and yet I felt inexplicably bound to him, as if we had traveled together on a long, hard journey and would never part. Deep down I knew otherwise. He was no one to me, a stranger, not even remotely my type. The men I'd dated previously, including the man I was still married to, were idealists and optimists, book lovers and acoustic musicians; men who, at least on the surface, were sincere and generous and kind.

He was nothing like them. He smoked heroin and did vicious, punk-rock things to his ears and nipples and hair. He drank big bottles of cheap liquor that he'd bought at convenience stores and named his car "Malice," so bent was he on demonstrating an ironic brand of destructive rage. Such poses would normally have repulsed me, but in him they compelled me instead. His entire being — the way he laughed, the way he fucked, the way he held his body as he walked down the street — was merciless and depraved, pitiless and pure, and in his presence I believed that I could be that way too. I *ached* to be that way, to shuck the weight of the life I'd been living. The life in which I'd struggled to resurrect my failing marriage and worked two jobs so I could pay my way through college. The life in which I'd taken care of my young mother while she was sick with cancer, and then, after she'd died, attempted to hold what remained of my family together. The life in which I'd held earnest jobs at nonprofit organizations and been a seriously aspiring fiction writer. By the time I met him I was about to buckle from the weight of responsibility, to burst from sorrow. He didn't care, didn't know, didn't even want to know about any of these things.

Which is to say that he was perfect. My luscious escape.

The second night I knew him, we went to a club to hear a band. I stood next to him on the edge of the dancing mob, getting jostled and thrashed by the occasional faceless body, high on heroin for the first time in my life. The music was a colossus of sound, so loud I could feel it beating like a heart beneath my ribs.

"I'm going in!" he shouted to me, though I couldn't make sense of what he'd said until he was gone, temporarily lost to me in the writhing crowd. *I'm going in too,* I chanted to myself, though I also chanted something else: *I'm not going to stay.*

It felt inevitable at the time, and still does. To me he was the darkness at the edge, the center of the flame, and the precise place I needed to be. It's times like those, when the ordinary becomes illuminated, that we are transformed, as by the wave of a wand in a fairy tale, and all that existed before is gone. He was that way to me then, at that moment in my life: exactly what I was looking for, though at the time I didn't know that I was looking at all.

He reappeared from the crash of limbs and grabbed me by the wrists. "Come on!" he shouted, though again I couldn't hear him. I didn't need to. I simply let him pull me in.

We spent the summer together having adventuresome sex, doing drugs, and wandering the city. We discussed poets that we believed nobody but us read, and listened to music only a small coterie of people knew existed. I wore little thrift-shop dresses and a button he'd bought me that said, APPLE PIE IS TOXIC, pinned to the strap of my bag.

In the end it wasn't much. A pranksterish half love that took on tragic undertones as he descended into the depths of heroin addiction and I came close to tumbling in after him. There was drama at my leaving, though it was more about my yearning for heroin than about my feelings for him. By autumn I was fifteen hundred miles away, having returned to the city where I actually lived, shaken and drained. By winter I'd come into the clear and continued on with my life, working at my job and filing for divorce, staying away from heroin and boys with blue hair.

Time passed, and he became not himself in my memory but an emblem of my youthful folly, my experimental daring, my authentic scrabble to find a way in the world. I was nostalgic for him on occasion, though not even remotely heartbroken. I wished him well in my mind, though I doubted in a far-off way that "well" was how he was doing. He was not an actual, potentially suffering person, not a boy I'd once known who had his own hopes and dreams, but a symbol of my own period of liberation and self-destruction. He was part of a story I got to tell, but not the story itself.

And then I saw him. It had been two years since our affair, and I had returned to live in the city where we'd met. I was standing in line for a movie, on a date with the man who is now my husband. I turned, and the boy with blue hair was there. His hair was no longer blue; his face was puffy and pocked and horrible looking. "Methadone," he explained, seeing the question in my eyes. We embraced and briefly spoke, though all the while I had the sensation that I couldn't quite land on who he was. I knew his name and who he'd been to me, but I couldn't believe this person was actually *him*. After a few minutes we drifted apart, back to our places in the movie line, as if nothing had happened. I stood with my future husband trying to conceal that I was trembling so badly I could hardly stand up. I started an inane argument with him, whispering fiercely so no one would hear. Furious with each other, we left the line and walked back to his car, where I sat in the passenger seat and wept.

"What's wrong with you? What's wrong?" he asked, his voice sweet now, no longer angry. I couldn't tell him, didn't know. Or I knew but couldn't find the words. Now I can.

What was wrong was that for the first time I'd seen my former lover for himself, not a reflection of me or an escape, not an adventure or a cautionary tale, not a cool symbol of twenty-something despair, but a person, stark and sick and broken, possibly beyond repair. And I'd seen my own life too, my *real* life, not the myth I'd created about the months I had spent on the dark side with him — "the bad boy I once half loved," as I'd taken to saying with a sardonic smile when I told people the story.

It was a beautiful thing, and painful, to turn and look and know, to see the truth and the lies, to witness the consequences rather than simply live the actions, as I had with him over the course of that summer. When I was with him, I had believed that I was trying, mercilessly, to uncover the truth, and that what was most true was whatever was darkest and most complicated and cruel. I didn't believe that anymore, as I sat in the car with my future husband after fleeing the movie line. And I didn't believe in half love either, or in truth without mercy, or in actions without consequences, or that apple pie is toxic.

I thought of him then, sitting in the darkened theater, watching a film that my future husband and I would never see, and I let myself love him entirely. I also loved the version of myself that had briefly passed through his life. It was a kind of growing up and the actual end of our affair, though it had ended in practical terms years before.

In the final days of our romance I'd seen an ad in the paper for an escort service that was hiring. I'd called the number and made an appointment for an interview that evening. I told him about it as I sat on the edge of the tub, shaving my legs. He thought it was funny and sexy and cool, the notion that I would sleep with strangers for money. I reasoned, falsely, that it was no different from my job as a waitress; that all work for wages was a form of prostitution anyway, so why not do the real thing and make it worth my while? The man on the phone had said that the job entailed "visiting" clients at their homes and hotel rooms. I would make one hundred dollars for every half-hour.

I examined myself in the full-length mirror before going out the door to meet the man who ran the escort service. I was wearing makeup and a black miniskirt and a pair of purple boots I thought befitted the occasion.

"Take your underwear off," my blue-haired boy coached, and then laughed wickedly as I bent to do it.

" 'Bye," I said to him, a small part of me hoping he'd implore me not to go, jealous or protective in a way he'd never been before.

" 'Bye," he said, an impish smile on his face.

I stuffed my underwear into my purse and walked out the door.

Once on the street, instead of getting in my truck, I continued walking past it. I was going to the store a block away, I told myself, to get a pack of gum. But then I sailed on by the store and down the side-walk. I walked past yards with lush flowers fading in the heat, past the summertime sounds of televisions coming from open windows and a woman playing fetch with her dog. I walked so far that my feet began to ache in the hot boots. Then I came to a cafe and went inside.

It was not the kind of place I frequented. A tad dated and old-ladyish, it had tiny iron chairs painted white and watercolors of ador-able animals on the walls and spider plants and ferns hanging in pots. I ordered a lemonade and sat drinking it slowly, thinking about my life.

I didn't know what I was doing. Didn't know I'd leave the boyfriend I only half loved within the week. Didn't know that he hadn't wrecked my life, or that I hadn't wrecked it myself. Didn't know that one evening almost seven years in the future, on the night of his birthday and the anniversary of our meeting, I'd pick up the phone and dial his mother's number and, a few minutes after that, his. I didn't know how it would be to talk to him then, across the miles and the years, his voice quieter and more melancholy than before but still edged with the crackle of the jokester he used to be. Didn't know the years he would describe to me, during which he'd sink entirely into the pain of addiction, overdosing and crashing cars, stealing from friends and trying repeatedly to get clean before finally checking himself into rehab and staying there until he'd shake heroin for good. And I didn't know the years I would describe to him, how I would sink into my own depths, grieving my mother and my ruined marriage, and then eventually pull myself up and out to find love again, go to graduate school, and write a novel.

I didn't know any of that then, that summer day when I should have been at my job interview to become a prostitute but instead sat drink-ing lemonade in an uncool cafe where I had never been and would never go again. But I did know a few things, and they came to me the way true things do: with the certainty and subtlety of a shaft of sun-light on the back of your head.

I knew that I liked the way the tree outside the cafe window looked in silhouette against the sky. I knew that I had to change my life. I knew that eventually I would rise and put my underpants back where they belonged. ∎

Evening Voices

by JEFF WALT

Mothers call the names
of their children
into the late evening.
Their hard voices echo
in the streets.
We sit on the edge
of the bed after sex,
in the silence
within the silence.
Happy words rush to my lips
but turn back swiftly.
I wish for the past, the days
we lived together and loved.
Remember hours spent wading
in the calm lake? The day you read
forever in my palm? You say
nothing exists beyond our
own breathing in this room,
but I know there is a chest of drawers,
a bureau and lamp, comfort
in the stillness cooled
by dusk's final breaths.
We are startled to hear your name
drift through the window,
some woman calling her son home
for dinner. Your body reacts:

the head lifts, the neck stretches
like that of some frightened bird.
Should you go to her — as if
the voice were your own mother shouting
through years of grief? Quickly
you pull me back onto the dirty sheets,
deep into the rage
of your lips and hands and tongue.

Ten Things

a short story by **LESLIE PIETRZYK**

These are ten things only you know now.

ONE

He joked that he would die young. You imagined ninety-nine to your hundred. But by "young" he meant sixty-five, fifty-five. What "young" ended up meaning was thirty-five.

In the memory book the funeral home gave you (actually, that you paid for; nothing there was free, not even delivering the flowers to a nursing home the next day, which cost sixty-five dollars, but you were too used up to care), there was a page to record his exact age in years, months, and days. You added hours; you even added minutes, because you had that information. You were there when he had the heart attack.

Now, when thinking about his life, it seemed to you that minutes were so very important. There was that moment in the emergency room when you begged for ten more minutes. You would've traded anything, everything, for just one more second, for the speck of time it would have taken to say his name, to hear him say your name.

Later, when you thought about it (because suddenly there was so much time to think; too little time, too much time — time was just one more thing you couldn't make sense of anymore), you wondered why he'd told you he was going to die young. The first time he said it, you punched his arm. "Don't say that," you said. "Don't ever say that again, ever." But he said it another day and another and lots of days after that. And you punched his shoulder every time, because it was bad luck, bad mental energy, but you knew he'd say it again. You knew then that there would always be one more time for everything.

TWO

He once compared you to an avocado. He was never good at saying what he meant in fancy ways. (You had a boyfriend in college who dedicated poems to you, one of which won a contest in the student literary magazine, but that boyfriend never compared you to anything as simple and real as an avocado.)

You were sitting on the patio in the backyard. It was the day the dog got loose and ran out onto Route 50, and you found him by the side of the road — two legs mangled and blood everywhere — and you pulled off your windbreaker and wrapped the dog in it while your husband stood next to you whispering, "Oh, God. Oh, God," because there was so much blood. He drove to the vet, catching every red light, while you held the dog close and murmured dog secrets in his ear and felt his warm blood soak your clothes. And when the vet said she was sorry, that it was too late, you were the one who cupped the dog's head in both hands while she slipped in the needle, and you were the one who remembered to take off the dog's collar, unbuckling it slowly and looping it twice around your wrist, and you were the one whose face the dog tried to lick but couldn't quite reach.

So, that night, out on the patio, the two of you were sitting close, thinking about the dog. It was really too cold to be on the patio, but the dog had loved the backyard; every tree had been a personal friend, each squirrel or bird an encroaching enemy. It was just cold enough that you felt him shiver, and he felt you shiver, but neither of you suggested going inside just yet. That's when he said, "I've decided you're like an avocado."

You almost didn't ask why, you were so busy thinking about the dog's tongue trying to reach your face and failing, even when you leaned right down next to his mouth. But then you asked anyway.

He looked up at the dark sky. "You're sort of tough on the outside," he said. "A little intimidating."

"Maybe," you said, but you knew he was right. In photos, you always looked as if you didn't want to be there. Lost tourists never asked you for directions; they asked your husband. It was something you'd become used to and no longer thought about or wondered why anymore.

He continued: "But inside, you're soft and creamy. Luscious, just like a perfectly ripe avocado. That's the part of you I get. And underneath that is the hardest, strongest core of anyone I know. Like how you were today at the vet. Like how you are with everything. An avocado."

At the time, you smiled and mumbled, but could only think about the dog, the poor dog. That was five years ago. What you remember now is not so much the dog's tongue, but being compared to an avocado.

THREE

He predicted a grand slam at a baseball game. It was the Orioles versus the Red Sox, a sellout game up in Baltimore on a bright, sunny June day, the kind of day when you look out the window and think, *Baseball*. But in Baltimore it wasn't possible to go to a game just because it was a sunny day; they were sold out months and months in advance — especially against teams like Boston, which had fans whose fathers had been Boston fans, whose kids were Boston fans, and whose grandkids would be Boston fans. He'd actually bought the tickets way back in December, not knowing what kind of day it would be, and it just happened to be that perfect kind of baseball day.

He'd grown up listening to games on the radio, sprawled sideways across his bed in the dark listening to AM stations from faraway Chicago, New York, St. Louis. He still remembered the call letters and could reel them off like a secret code. Now he brought his radio to the game in Baltimore and balanced it on the armrest between your seats, and the announcers' voices drifted up in bits and snatches, and part of him was sitting next to you eating a hot dog and cheering, and part of him was that child sprawled in the dark listening to distant voices.

The bases were loaded, and Cal Ripken came up to bat. Cal was your favorite player. You'd once seen him pick up a piece of litter that was blowing around the field and tuck it into his back pocket. Something about that had impressed you as much as all those consecutive games he'd played.

"What's Cal going to do?" he asked.

You looked at your score card. (He'd taught you how to keep score; you liked the organization and had developed a special system, with filled-in diamonds for home runs, a K for a strikeout, and squiggly lines to indicate a pitching change.) Cal wasn't batting especially well lately — the beginnings of a slump, you thought. "Hit into a double play," you said. Cal had hit into a lot of double plays that season, ended a lot of innings.

He shook his head. "He's knocking the grand salami" — meaning a home run bringing in all four runners. You'd never seen one in person before.

"Cal doesn't have many grand slams," you said — not to be mean (after all, Cal was your favorite player) but because it was true. You knew Cal's stats, and his grand-slam total was four at the time, after all those years in the Majors.

"Well, he's getting one now," he said.

After Cal fouled twice for two strikes, you glanced over at him. "It'll come," he said.

On the next pitch, Cal whacked the ball all the way across that blue sky.

Everyone stood and cheered and screamed and stomped their feet, and he held the radio in his hand and flung his arm around your shoulders and squeezed tight. From the radio by your ear, you heard the echo of everyone cheering, and you thought about a boy alone in the dark listening to that sound.

FOUR

He was afraid of bugs: outdoor bugs and indoor bugs; bugs big enough to cast shadows and little bugs that could be pieces of lint. Not "afraid" as in running screaming from the room, but afraid as in watching TV and pretending not to see the fat cricket in the corner; or walking into the bathroom first thing in the morning and ignoring the spider frantically zigzagging across the sink.

"There's a bug on the wall," you might say, hand outstretched, forcing him finally to look up and follow to see where your finger was pointing. You'd repeat: "There's a bug on the wall."

Still he'd say nothing.

"Do you see it?" you'd ask.

He'd nod.

So you'd grab a tissue and squish the bug, maybe letting out a sharp sigh, as if you knew you weren't the one who should be doing this. Or, if it were a big, messy bug like a cricket, you might try to scoop it up and drop it out the window. Sometimes, if you waited too long, the bug (silverfish, in particular) would scurry into the crack between the wall and the carpet, and you'd imagine it reemerging in the future: bigger, stronger, braver, meaner. Bugs in the bathtub were easiest, because you could run water and wash them down the drain. You learned many different ways to get rid of bugs.

He never said, "Thank you for killing the bugs." He never said that he was afraid of bugs. You never accused him of being afraid of bugs.

FIVE

He kept his books separate from yours. Certain shelves on certain bookcases were his; others were yours.

Maybe it made sense when you were living together, before you were married. If one of you had to move out, it would only be a matter of scooping up armloads of books off the shelves, rather than sorting through, picking over each volume, having to think. It would allow you to get out fast. Plus, with separate shelves, he could stare at his long, tidy line of hardcovers, undisturbed by your scandalous array of used paperbacks. He liked to stare at his books with his head cocked to the right — not necessarily reading the titles, but just staring at the shelf of books, at their length and breadth and bulk. You never knew what he was thinking when he did this.

After your wedding, when you moved into the new house, you said something about combining the books, maybe putting all the novels in one place and all the history books in another and all the travel books together, and so on, like that.

He was looking out the window at the new backyard, at the grass no one had cut for weeks and weeks. Finally, he said, "We own every last damn blade of grass."

"What about the books?" you asked. You were trying to get some unpacking done. There were boxes everywhere. The only way to walk through rooms was to wind along narrow paths between stacked boxes. There were built-in bookcases in the living room by the fireplace — two features the realtor had mentioned again and again, as if she'd known that you'd been imagining sitting in front of a fire, reading books, sipping wine, letting the machine take the calls. As if she'd known exactly the kind of life you had planned.

"I'll do the books," he said. But he didn't step away from the window.

It was a nice backyard, with a brick patio, and when you'd stood out there for the first time, during the open house, you'd thought about summer nights with the baseball game on the radio and the coals dying down in the grill and the lingering scent of medium-rare steak and a couple of stars squeezing through the glare of the city to find the two of you.

Again you offered to do the books; you *wanted* to do the books. You wanted all those books organized on the shelves; his and yours, yours and his.

"I never thought I'd own anything I couldn't pack into a car," he said.

You felt so bad you started to cry, certain only you had wanted the house, only you had wanted the wedding. "Is it so awful?" you asked.

He reached over some boxes to touch your arm. "No, it's not awful at all," he said, and it turned out that this is what you really wanted — not the patio, not the built-in shelves next to the fireplace, not the grass in the backyard, but the touch of his hand on your arm.

You did the books together, and suddenly something about keeping them separate felt right, as if now you realized that the books would be fine on separate shelves of the same bookcase, in the house you'd bought for the life you had.

SIX

He once saw a ghost. He was mowing the lawn in front, and you were in back clipping the honeysuckle that grew over the fence. Your neighbor — an original owner who'd bought his house for three thousand dollars in 1950 — wanted to spray kerosene and set the vines on fire, but you'd said no. You liked the smell of honeysuckle on June nights. You liked the hummingbirds flitting among the flowers in August. You even liked all that clipping, letting your mind go blank as you wrestled with the vines, cutting and tugging, yanking and twisting and pulling — knowing that whatever you cut would grow back by the end of the summer, that in the end the honeysuckle would always come back, maybe even if your neighbor burned down the vines.

It was that time of the early evening when the shadows were long and cool and the dew was rising on the grass; that time when, as a barefoot child, you would start getting damp toes. You half heard the lawn mower whining back and forth, back and forth, and you were thinking ahead to sitting on the patio and watching the fireflies float up out of the long, weedy grass under the apple tree. Then the lawn mower stopped abruptly; it needed more gas, you thought, or maybe there was a plastic bag in the way. When the silence lingered, you walked around to the front yard, curious, and found him leaning up against the car in the driveway, the silent lawn mower in front of him. The streetlight flicked on as you reached him; he held out his arms for a hug, and you felt his sweat, tacky against your skin.

"I saw a ghost," he said.

You pushed the hair back from his forehead and blew lightly on it to cool him down. His forehead was pale compared to the rest of his face.

He pointed over toward the big maple tree, the one that was so pretty each autumn. But nothing was there.

"What kind of ghost?" you asked. You still had your hand on top of his head, and when you removed it, his hair stayed back where you'd pushed it.

"Like a soldier from the Civil War," he said. "He was leaning against the tree, and then he was gone."

"Confederate or Union?" you asked.

He looked annoyed, as if you'd asked the wrong thing, but it seemed a logical question to you.

"It was a ghost," he said. "I saw a ghost."

"Did he do anything?"

"Maybe it was the heat," he said.

"Maybe it was a real ghost," you said. "There were Confederate encampments along here." There was a silence. A car went by too fast, music spilling from its open window. "That tree's big enough to have been here then."

"This is stupid," he said, and he leaned down and pulled the cord on the lawn mower. The engine roared, and he couldn't hear you anymore, and you watched him push the lawn mower across the yard. You saw nothing under the maple tree, just newly cut grass spit into lines by the lawn mower and shadows stretching slowly into the dark.

Now you're the one who cuts the grass. People tell you to hire a service, but you don't. When you're done mowing in the evening, you lean against the car and wait, but all you ever see are fireflies rising from the damp grass where you leave it long under the maple tree.

SEVEN

When he ate malted-milk balls, he sucked the chocolate off first. Thinking you weren't watching, he'd roll the candies from one side of his mouth to the other, making the sort of tiny noises you'd imagine a chipmunk would make, or a small bird, or something else tiny and cute. If he caught you watching him, he'd instantly stop. Sometimes, just to tease him, you'd ask a question to make him talk, and his words would come out all lumpy and garbled, pushed around the sides of the candy. "What?" you'd say, teasing. "I don't understand." But no matter how much you teased, he never chewed.

That's the way he was. He had a special way of doing everything. He developed a method of eating watermelon with a knife, cutting slices so thin the seeds would slither out, and setting aside the juiciest fillet from the middle to eat last. There was an order in which to read the newspaper: sports, business, style, metro, front page. The two of you never left a football or baseball game until the last second had ticked off the clock, regardless of a lopsided score or a ten-below windchill or being late to meet someone for dinner. He always carried a pen in his pocket and kept long lists of things to do and places to see on little yellow sticky notes inside his wallet.

If someone had told you about a person who did all these things, who imposed these rules on himself, you would've thought he was odd, annoying. But you found out piece by piece — like putting together a puzzle — and now you couldn't imagine your husband being any other way.

You watched him eat malted-milk balls one Easter morning (you'd made two little Easter baskets, setting them up on the kitchen table, each different because you and he liked different kinds of candy), the two of you reading the Sunday paper in his usual order. You were about to tease him, to make him talk around that gob of candy, to see if he'd bite down just this one time, but before you could say anything, he mumbled something to you, and you didn't say, "What?" because you knew exactly what he'd said; there were always more ways to say, "I love you," and through a mouthful of malted-milk balls on Easter morning was only one.

EIGHT

He hated his job for years. You lay in bed and listened to him grinding his teeth at night, unsure whether to wake him. You fantasized about waking him: "Let's talk," you'd say, and he would tell you all the things he was thinking; tell you exactly why he hated his job and how he really felt about the long, endless reports he wrote that no one ever read. You would offer sympathy, advice, kindness; you'd tell him to quit his job, offer to do his résumé on the computer; or maybe the two of you would just cry and hold each other tight.

But that's not what happened the times you did wake him. He told you he was fine, told you he was tired of complaining about his stupid job, told you to go to sleep. He used kinder words than these, but his voice was expressionless, like a machine that runs on and on by itself. And then you both pretended to be asleep, and then you knew he really was asleep, because he was grinding his teeth again.

You tried to bring up the subject during the day. "No job is worth this," you said when you called him at his office.

"I can't talk now," he whispered.

"Then when?" you asked.

There was a pause, and you heard his boss being paged in the background. He said, "My father worked for forty years on the line at Chrysler. You think every day was great?"

"This is different," you said.

And he said, "Nothing's different."

The conversation never went any farther than that. It was his boss; it was the nature of the business; it was turning thirty; it was stress; it was long hours; it was making enough money that most other jobs would be a step down; it was too much overseas travel; it was overly ambitious co-workers and unambitious secretaries; it was rush-hour traffic; it was sucking up taxpayer money to fund projects that improved nothing except the bottom line of the firm; it was living in an expensive neighborhood in an expensive city on the East Coast; it was a wife who wanted to be a writer and consequently was earning no money; it was needing his health-insurance plan because that was when you still thought you could have a baby together; it was being the oldest child, the responsible one; it was being raised in the Midwest; it was trying to prove he was as tough as his father and his grandfather — tougher; it was being brought up to despise weakness and whiners. You knew it was all those things, but you suspected there was something more that he didn't want to or couldn't explain but that you could help with . . . if only he would talk.

This is what you thought about on those nights when you pretended to sleep: You prayed for him to talk, even though you hadn't been to church in ten years. It felt strange to ask God to make a man talk. You thought about numbers: How many Monday mornings are there in a year? How many Fridays when he had to work late? How many quick lunches at a desk? What do you get if you divide x amount of dollars in his paycheck by y amount of unhappiness and multiply the result by a year, two years? How many times can one man grind his teeth in a single night?

"It doesn't have to be me," you told him. "Talk to anyone — a friend, your dad, a therapist, a bartender. Just talk. Please."

"There's nothing to say" was all you got from him.

The silence was thick and hard and invisible, like air before a storm. You waited and waited.

One night, you woke up and he wasn't next to you. When he didn't come back to bed, you got up and found him downstairs at the kitchen table writing on a yellow legal pad. A tiny moth circled the overhead light; you watched it instead of him. You asked, "Working late?"

He shook his head, kept writing, flipped the page over, wrote some more, and finally said, "I'm writing a movie."

He might as well have said he was being beheaded in the morning; it was that surprising.

The moth flew too close to the light bulb, then dropped onto the table next to him. You leaned in, brushed the dead moth into your cupped hand, threw it in the garbage, and went back to bed.

The next day, he told you the plot of his movie: a guy who hates his job goes to baseball camp to relive his childhood fantasies and wins the big game, not by blasting in a home run, but by bunting.

It took him months to write the screenplay. He thought he was going to sell it in Hollywood and buy a house with a pool and retire. By the time he realized that wasn't going to happen, it didn't matter, because there were changes at his job, new projects that he'd developed and was implementing, ideas that made sense, that made people pay attention. It wasn't the same old story.

You liked that he was happy at work. He talked to you about what he was doing, about his projects, about the results of his work.

The handwritten manuscript of his movie stayed on your nightstand.

NINE

The combination to the lock on the garden shed (0–14–5), where you keep the lawn mower, the rake, the snow shovel, the garden hose.

Every fall, mice took over the shed; you never actually saw them, only the traces they left behind — dry droppings like caraway seeds;

a corner chewed out of the box of grass seed; footprints crisscrossing the dust. He looked into poison. A neighbor across the street told him the right kind. "It shrivels their body from the inside," the neighbor explained, "so they dry up: no smell, no mess in a trap, no nothing. Clean and easy."

You didn't like mice. No one likes mice. But what kind of way to die was that, leaving nothing behind?

He set out the poison anyway.

Now, when you open the shed to drag out the lawn mower, you look for some sign of the mice, but he cleaned out the shed in the early spring, swept up all the droppings, hosed away the dust. You think that maybe you thanked him, but maybe not. After he was gone, faced with so much more to do than anyone could imagine, as if the world's to-do list had ended up on your own, you were relieved that cleaning out the shed wasn't on the list.

Now you're somehow disappointed that there are no mice, no way to know they were once here. You think, *They'll be back in the fall.* And you know that during the winter you'll keep the shed locked, that you just won't look. Then you can think, *The mice are there*, never checking to see if you're right or wrong.

TEN

You cheated on him. Once. Barely. Not enough to count, not really. But it was with his best friend, the one he'd grown up with, the one with the odd nickname you never quite understood, the one who met you at the emergency room and cried as hard as you did.

It happened in your kitchen at a party one night when you were drinking too much and your husband was drinking even more than you and, even though it was his birthday, you weren't talking to him, and he wasn't talking to you, but no one knew this except for his best friend, because you both acted how you were supposed to act at a birthday party. You were telling his friend your side of the story, why you were right, and he was agreeing, and the next thing you knew, you were kissing the friend — not a quick, simple kiss, not an embarrassed kiss, but a real kiss, lingering.

It was that sudden.

You thought about that kiss for a long time afterward. You remembered every detail — and that, as much as the kiss, was the cheating part, wasn't it?

The friend said he wouldn't tell, but he did. You didn't find this out until a couple of weeks after the funeral, when you were talking to him on the phone late one night because neither of you could sleep. (There were a lot of long, late nights; each time, you thought, *There couldn't be a longer night*, but it seemed the next one was always longer.)

"Yeah, I told him," the friend said. "It seemed like the right thing to do."

"What did he say?" you asked.

"He broke my nose," the friend said.

You remembered the broken nose, the funny story about walking into a ladder.

"I thought things were pretty much fine between us after that," the friend said, "because we were talking and joking again. But now I think there was something different. I can't say what." There was a pause. Then he asked, "What'd he say to you about it?"

There were so many ways to answer that question, so many lies you could've told this friend, but you picked the easiest: "He was furious. Absolutely furious." Then you faked a yawn, said you were getting tired and wanted to grab some sleep while you could. But you didn't go to sleep for a long time — OK, not at all — because you were trying to remember a time, any time, a minute, a second, anything, when there was something different between you and him. But there was nothing to remember, nothing.

That's how much he loved you.

And that's the thing you know most of all.   ■

My Fat Lover

by LEAH TRUTH

My lover is fat.

It upsets some people to hear me state this so baldly. "Doesn't it hurt her feelings?" they ask, as if the polite thing were to act as if I hadn't noticed that my lover weighs nearly three hundred pounds. Perhaps they think she hasn't noticed, either — that, upon reading what I have written, she will realize for the very first time that she is fat.

"You are the only person in my life who hasn't discouraged me or made fun of me," my lover tells me one morning over breakfast, crying. She's listening to *musica de trios,* traditional Puerto Rican ballads, and it's making her nostalgic. She remembers how her mother used to dance to this music, spinning with the broom through their little house. She remembers island breakfasts with *cafe termino medio* — half strong coffee, half warmed milk — French bread, and omelets filled with fried plantains. Then her face darkens as she also remembers how she was friendless throughout her childhood, ostracized all through her school years. "I weighed 180 pounds at age twelve," she confesses, as if this were an explanation. She tried to kill herself at sixteen.

There are few things harder than growing up fat.

What about growing up with a disability? you might ask. *What about growing up neglected, or on the streets?*

True, these other conditions are enormously difficult and arouse people's pity and discomfort. Yet they are not seen as the child's *fault.* Fatness is always the fat person's fault. As everyone knows, fat people eat like pigs. They smell bad. They don't bathe. They lack that revered American attribute, willpower. They are, quite simply, disgusting.

My lover showers every day. She has a closet full of stylish clothes in a wide range of sizes, reflecting her lifelong battle with the scale. She dresses well. She is scrupulously clean. But she grew up fat, and she is fat still. Not in a wheelchair, not on the streets, but the pariah of an entire culture.

E very taboo spawns a group of people who manage to eroticize the reviled, the feared, the forbidden. A disabled friend tells me there are people who are attracted exclusively to amputees. Similarly, I know there are "chubby-chasers" — people, most of "normal" weight, who are erotically excited by fat. A minor segment of the pornography industry caters to them.

I am not a chubby-chaser. Nor was I always, to use the politicized term, "fat-positive." I grew up in a family as red-bloodedly fat-phobic as most. My mother, who is five-foot-two and weighs just over a hundred pounds, was perpetually on a diet. My father's and my grandmother's standard greeting to all family members they hadn't seen in a while was "You look good — you've lost weight." At age sixteen, weighing barely a hundred pounds myself, I, too, dieted. Some days I'd eat nothing but a single doughnut. When I got to college, I made rules for myself in the dining hall: each night I could have a salad and an entree or a salad and dessert — but never all three.

Around the time our parents were splitting up, my younger sister, Jennifer, took to watching hours of TV each afternoon, her hand in a bag of snacks the whole time. By age nine, she'd grown chubby, a fact that did not go unnoticed in our house. "Baby fat," the family called it, fretting. Perhaps, as they claimed, they did not want her to suffer what fat people suffer. Or perhaps they just didn't want a fat — or even a pudgy — person in their midst. So, at age twelve, Jen began to diet, too. She ate maybe a Diet Coke with added Sweet-n-Low and a few green beans in an entire day. Many days, she ate nothing at all.

When Jen got down to eighty-five pounds, the family started noticing that this exercise of willpower had gone a little too far. Those were my mother's exact words: "I admire her willpower; she just takes it a little too far."

Jen was sent to a therapist, and she began eating again, but it was years before anyone realized what she did afterward. Her anorexia had become bulimia, a far more insidious illness. The incessant vomiting led to laxatives — eventually forty or fifty of them a day.

In the meantime, I had discovered feminist theory. My last year in college, I took women's-studies classes and read about the many kinds of oppression. I watched my sister; I made the connection. Furious, I resolved never to diet again.

"Leah, you're amazing," Jen told me afterward. "You're the only woman I know who can eat ice cream. . . . I mean, without throwing up afterward."

Fifteen years later, my sister still keeps no food in her refrigerator. Her dyed-blond hair is dull, like broken straw, and her skin has an uneven look to it, perhaps due to long-term vitamin deficiency. Yet, when I look at her, I see her as she was at fourteen. I remember the back rubs I used to give her on my visits home from college; the delicate, knobby feel of her spine beneath my hands.

It was around that age that Jen began going out with any boy or man who asked for her phone number. More than once, she was raped. Often, she told me later, she'd gone out with the guy only because she was afraid to go home, where there was a coffeecake in the refrigerator.

She felt safer alone with a strange man, a man who might rape her, than with a coffeecake.

I t was one thing to have a political stance against fat oppression. It was quite another, I found, to have a fat lover.

The problem wasn't with my first impression. I knew right away that I was attracted to her. Maybe it was pheromones. Maybe it was destiny. In any case, a feeling in my stomach told me I wanted to go home with her.

The problem didn't arise in bed. I wanted her, there was no question about that. My hands and mouth did not pass judgment on her flesh; they simply adored it, which is what they do best.

No, the problem came when I looked at her naked body after we had made love. The body I saw was not one I knew how to call "beautiful." My lover's belly was distended; her thighs were thick. Around her face, she had a double, perhaps a triple, chin.

As I began to fall in love, as it became clear that my lover and I could not stop touching each other, I struggled with this contradiction.

In the past, I'd had lovers who, like most people, disliked their bodies. It had been one of my talents as a lover to change those feelings. I'd praised their bodies, loving them with words as well as touch. Even after those relationships had ended, my ex-lovers had been grateful to me for that.

Now I wanted to do the same thing for my fat lover. Yet I could not tell her she was beautiful; the words would not form in my mouth. "I love your body," I told her instead as I kissed her, licking and stroking her flesh. "I love your body," I repeated like a mantra, to ward off the other feeling, the persistent, ugly remnants of my disgust.

Sometime in our first year together, I accompanied my lover to her doctor's office. When he asked her weight, she hesitated, then answered in a low voice, "Two hundred and fifty." She knew there was no point in lying — he'd weigh her anyway.

Two hundred and fifty pounds. The phrase reverberated in my head. It sounded grotesque, like a supermarket-tabloid headline. Out of habit, I recoiled.

When my lover had answered my personal ad, she'd told me she weighed 180 pounds. Not true; she'd actually weighed about forty pounds more. But 180 had been enough to tell me that she wasn't thin — that she wasn't, in the euphemistic parlance of personal ads, "fit." It had been a warning, in case I wanted to back out, sight unseen, as many people would have.

Later, as she gained more weight, my lover began to worry that there was a limit to how much fat I could love, or perhaps how much fat I could overlook.

"It's your essence I'm attracted to," I assured her when she finally confessed her fears. "It's what comes *through* your body. No amount of weight you could gain or lose would change my feelings for you." It was only as I said those words that I realized they were true.

"Oh," said my lover, visibly more relaxed. She had misunderstood me when I'd said I loved her body; she'd thought I loved it as an object, a fetish.

"When I say I love your body," I told her, "I mean I love *you*. Your body is just the part of you I can touch."

And somewhere along the way, the judging portion of my brain grew thinner and thinner until, like a fingernail sliver of moon, it almost disappeared. "You're beautiful," I told my lover then, because it was true.

L ater, as my lover's kidneys failed, I came to love her body in still other ways. Now that it had become a battleground, a locus of pain and discomfort rather than pleasure, I loved it in defiance, as if my passion could banish its ills. I loved it when it could not respond to me. I loved it perhaps in the same way that some women love "unavailable" men: *because* I could not reach it, even as I lay naked beside it. I loved her body with all the force and impatience of a hurricane.

After my lover came close to death and began the slow return to health with a new kidney inside her, she dreamed that she was shirtless at a party. Her large belly, fatter than ever, was uncovered and gashed with jagged pink scars.

"You're disgusting," a man told her, his face contorted with revulsion.

"I had a kidney transplant," she replied proudly.

"That's disgusting. You're so fat. I'd rather die."

"I'm sorry if you don't like it," she said, defending herself, "but this is my body — *mine* — and I love my life!"

P artway through writing this essay, I realized the topic is absurd. So the woman I love is fat. So I'm short. So what? Then I remembered a writing student I'd once had — a thin, blond, attractive woman who chain-smoked. One day, lighting a cigarette, she'd told me why: "I'd rather die of cancer than be fat again," she'd said.

A fter the kidney transplant that saved her life, my lover gained another fifty pounds. She'd gone months with no appetite, weeks with nausea that had forced her to live on just bread and applesauce;

so it was a joy when food tasted good to her again. Besides, the pred-
nisone she was now taking made her hungry all the time and changed
the way her body metabolized food.

It is also true that my lover is, in her own words, "addicted to food";
that she sometimes eats when she is not hungry; that she has ignored
her hunger so often — because she was dieting, or eating to fill other
needs — she no longer knows what it is to feel full. These things are
true of many thin women, as well.

From time to time, my lover declares she wants to lose weight. "I'll
never be thin," she says, "but I feel better when I'm around 240." Then
she fills our freezer with Weight Watchers breakfasts and dinners. I
want to help her achieve her goal, I tell myself, so I start making her
a salad each day for lunch and cooking fat-free vegetable soups. And I
catch myself beginning to watch what she eats. When she reaches for
the avocado and chips — she's always liked them in soup — I feel the
judgment growing in me again.

So I pay heed when my lover tells me that I am the first person
who hasn't discouraged her or made fun of her. She's forty-two years
old and on her third lifetime, having already survived two probable
deaths. She is a woman both brave and beautiful. She says I am the
first person who has ever loved her *at* her weight, not in spite of it. She
tells me this over the breakfast I've made: a crustless quiche with potatoes, apples, red onion, and smoked mozzarella. Cooking has always
been a way I nurture myself and the people I love.

I remember watching my sister refuse to eat. I think of the months
when my lover's failing kidneys made eating impossible. So tonight,
I think, I'll cook us a meal to celebrate our appetites at their most
joyous and untamable: maybe a garlicky Puerto Rican *asopao*, fresh-
baked corn muffins, and a salad of greens, pecans, feta cheese, and
pears. ∎

Blue Velvis

a short story by **THERESA WILLIAMS**

The charming and handsome serial killer Ted Bundy was executed on my birthday. Something about this fact brings birth and death full circle for me. I remind myself of this today, my birthday, as I am making dinner for my boyfriend, Lenny.

My mother brought me up to believe that you are supposed to give gifts on your birthday, not just receive them. She has always been a great believer in reciprocity. This dinner is my gift to Lenny, who took care of me in the weeks after I had my hysterectomy. My mother would be proud.

Lenny was not as good as my mother would have been at taking care of me, but he tried. Sometimes he didn't think about the little things you cannot do for yourself when you are ill. He did the big things, though, like feed me, feed my cats, cut wood for the winter, and fix things around my house. Lenny is always fixing things around my house.

One day I said, "Lenny, there's a crack in my bedroom wall."

This was after I had been in bed for about a week. The crack in the wall was driving me crazy.

"Where?" he asked.

"Right there," I said.

I live in a hundred-year-old farmhouse, which might sound homey and quaint, but it's not. My house has no style or grace, and it has a lot of problems. Lenny keeps saying the house will grow on me. I don't know about that.

Lenny examined the crack in my wall and said, "I'll fix it tomorrow."

The next day he came over with a big velvet Elvis painting and hung it over the crack.

"I don't want that ugly thing," I told him.

"Sure you do," he said.

"I want the wall fixed," I said.

"It is fixed," Lenny said.

"That velvet Elvis isn't fixing anything," I said.

"Elvis would be hurt if he heard you talk that way," Lenny said. "I paid three whole dollars for this."

And then, due to some mix-up between my brain and my mouth, I called the painting a "Velvis." I said, "That Velvis has got to go."

The Velvis became part of our standard repertoire of jokes.

I said, "That's not even Elvis. That's Elvis's cousin Velvis."

"Yeah," Lenny said. "It don't even look like Elvis."

And I said, "Yeah, and those people in Las Vegas, they're not Elvis impersonators; they're Velvis impersonators."

I happened to have on a blue nightgown, and Lenny sang, "She wore bluuuue Velvis."

A day or two later, I said, "Velvis. It sounds like a woman's body part."

"Don't let them take your Velvis," Lenny said.

"Why not?" I said. "They took everything else."

We made so many jokes about the Velvis painting that I started to like it. It is still hanging over the crack in the wall.

I have always been attracted to blue-collar men, men who work with their hands. Nothing represents potency to me better than somebody doing hard physical work.

Lenny is a jack-of-all-trades. He can build or fix anything. He has told me that the crack in my wall is just the beginning of this house's problems. "You don't fix somebody's big toe when their whole leg needs to be whacked off," he said.

That is why I have the Velvis and not a crack-free wall.

Lenny arrives for dinner at six o'clock, flowers in hand. Lenny always smells nice and clean. He tries to wrap his arm around my belly, but I do not let him. That's because I'm picturing in my mind what my scar looks like. Sometimes, when I go into the bathroom, or even in public restrooms, I raise my shirt and look at my scar, which appears garish and ugly in the harsh light. It divides me down the middle in a way that troubles me. I do not like the idea of being divided.

Lenny dresses in jeans and boots and always wears some kind of wide-brimmed hat. Some people, especially children, think he looks like a cowboy. I don't think he looks like a cowboy. That would be too much in the way of potency for me.

I take the flowers to the kitchen and put them in a vase, but, truth be told, my heart fell as soon as I saw they were carnations. I have never liked carnations, having seen too many of them at parades and funerals. It's silly, but somehow I was hoping he would bring me lilies. I have been thinking he would all day long.

The lilies in my garden were in full, fragrant bloom, mouths open, stamens trembling, their ruby throats showing, the day Lenny drove me to the hospital in Toledo for my hysterectomy. On the way to the car, I bent down to smell one, and my nose came away covered in pollen. It made us both laugh.

By the time I was able to shuffle outside after the surgery, the lilies had shed their blooms. I took one look at the bare stalks and cried into Lenny's chamois shirt.

They say that after a hysterectomy you have to learn to walk all over again. It's true. I am still learning, in a manner of speaking.

T here is no other way to say it: I have ten cats.

Right now, as I put Lenny's carnations into a vase, I hear the cats meowing at the door. They do not all stay in the house at once. I let a few in at a time, alternating among them. Tonight I have put them all outside. I do not want Lenny looking at my cats. He tells me I have too many. Sometimes Lenny tries to convince me to take a couple of them to the shelter. He tells me they do not kill cats at the shelter in Bowling Green. That is true about the shelter, I think, but I've heard that sometimes, when they get too many animals, they give them to other shelters that do kill them, or to labs for experiments.

Lenny tells me I am crazy to have ten cats.

An old gray tabby has been skulking around my place. He would make eleven, if I could get him to stay. He has a shaggy coat and shredded ears. I have often complained about him to Lenny because I don't want Lenny to know that I want the cat to stay. Sometimes, to make my act more convincing, I tell Lenny how mad I am at the old tabby, because he fights with the cats I already have.

Lenny tells me I should call animal control; they would come and catch the cat and take it away.

"Yeah, maybe," I say. "I'll see how things go."

The truth is, I have already partly beguiled the wild tabby with food. I picked him up once, and he did not seem to mind. He felt warm against my chest, and I heard a crackling sound within him, like he was getting fired up to purr. I felt his body poised to reverberate with pleasure. Then I brought him into the house, and the sound stopped. His heart beat fast. He jumped down and ran from room to room like he thought he was trapped. I let him out and have not seen him since. It has been a couple of weeks now. Maybe he does not trust me anymore.

When the tabby was still around, he once fought my cats while Lenny was here to see it. "Nora," Lenny said, "you really need to get rid of that cat."

"I know it," I said.

After a fight, the tabby would disappear into an old barn of mine. There he would lurk for hours, maybe days. Lenny complained that the tabby was terrorizing the other cats, but I secretly enjoyed the thought of him being there, sitting in the dark barn, waiting. I wanted to tell Lenny that a certain amount of terror might actually be a good thing, that it might keep you sharp and alive. But Lenny would probably have pointed out that it was easy for me to say; the terror was not after me.

I wait and watch for the tabby's return. Something in me needs to see him again.

Lenny is a dog person. I am uncomfortable identifying everyone as either a dog person or a cat person, but maybe there is some truth to it; all clichés were once fresh and true.

Lenny has two adopted greyhounds. He really loves those dogs. Lenny's greyhounds are skittish and take up a lot of his time, money, and energy. It seems like they are all he wants to talk about. Lenny has taught me everything about the abuse of greyhounds. He has told me how they are slaughtered when they can no longer race. He has described a place in Florida that was grinding dead greyhounds into food for alligators and other dogs.

It is clearly worthwhile to save as many greyhounds as possible. Yet I cannot understand why Lenny doesn't feel the same way about cats. It must be the truth behind the cliché.

B efore I serve the birthday dinner, Lenny brings in some wood for my stove from the pile he spent all summer cutting for me. Lenny takes a lot of pride in the wood he has cut, and so do I.

He says, "This place is lousy with cats." He tells me they are always getting under his feet.

Indeed, as Lenny stands there with his arms full of wood and the door wide open, Bubba shoots into the house between his legs. It has been a bitter winter so far, and Bubba hates the cold.

"Nora," Lenny says, "if I didn't know better, I'd say these cats are a psychological problem."

I am thinking, *My problem or his?*

Lenny does not always say things the way he means them. Sometimes he mixes up words with funny results. One time we were talking about human rights, and Lenny said, "This country won't really be free until people aren't discriminated against according to race, sex, or sexual performance."

I still rib Lenny about that one, but I am happy to be involved with such an egalitarian man.

I pour spaghetti noodles into the colander and say, "I don't have a problem, Lenny. It's not like I go out looking for cats."

"Well," Lenny says, "where will you draw the line?"

Why is it that people are always talking about "drawing the line"? Why are there lines and boundaries around everything?

"Think about it, Nora. You can't take in every stray."

"I suppose," I say.

"You never give a direct answer to anything," Lenny says.

I do not comment. Instead, I turn my attention to Bubba, who is rubbing against my shins. He stands on his hind legs and shoves his big head at me. Bubba has eyes like emeralds. He is a raggedy-ass mix of tabby and Russian blue. Somebody had him declawed, so I guess he had a family once. Now he tries to dig his phantom claws into the wood of my cabinet. His paws look crippled and useless. I bend down and pet him.

"All I'm saying," says Lenny, "is you can't go on like this. Ten cats. You have to agree."

I say nothing.

"Nora," he says, "you have to agree, right?"

The sauce is fine.

Really, it is a little off.

The wine has lightened Lenny's mood, and he pours us both some more and asks with a chuckle, "How's your Velvis?"

I tell him my Velvis is just fine.

He says, "You haven't let anybody take your Velvis, have you?"

We joke all the time about the Velvis now. It feels good making jokes that only the two of us get.

"Nobody gets their hands on my Velvis," I say.

"Except me," Lenny says.

Lenny and I have not had much sex since the surgery. We try, but it is terrible. Sometimes I wonder if this is the way people feel when they have lost an arm or a leg. I have always heard that those people sometimes feel sensation in the missing part, a phantom limb, but I do not feel anything where my uterus used to be. I do not think there is any such thing as a phantom orgasm.

Really, I can see how this whole Velvis thing might get to be too much.

The thing about Velvis is that he is an impersonator. Likewise, I sometimes feel as if I am doing an impersonation of myself. Not long ago, I dreamed there were two Noras and two Lennys. One pair I thought of as Nora and Lenny. The other pair I thought of as Vora and Venny. In my dream, Vora and Venny sat on a porch swing and rocked as they watched Nora and Lenny lying together in a brown field. Nora was dying, and Lenny was watching her die. Vora and Venny knew they could do nothing about it. They were sad. But as they rocked, they knew that whatever would happen, would happen.

Thinking about the dream always gives me a bad feeling in my chest, a sick kind of tiredness. This feeling usually spreads and makes my whole body feel like empty, useless rooms.

I say, "Do you like the spaghetti, Lenny?"

"It's great," Lenny says. He has eaten two big plates. He looks so innocent while he eats, so vulnerable and trusting. I do not feel worthy of his trust. Watching him eat the spaghetti makes me feel bad. I know it is not my best effort. I wish he would tell me, *Nora, this sauce sucks.*

I think maybe it was the generic oregano that ruined the sauce. I remember the day I bought it. I usually do not scrimp on spices, but that day I felt an overwhelming need to cut my grocery bill. More than that, I felt a kind of panic. The panic settled on me, heavy and cold, like a second skin. I felt lost in the store and was unsure which way was out.

Lenny sops his plate with homemade rolls. He has started talking about his greyhounds again. I made the rolls by forming the dough into long ropes, then slicing the ropes into pieces with a knife. The dough folded into itself as I cut. *Trying to heal itself,* I thought. As Lenny eats, I notice that the rolls look like amputated limbs.

I try to listen to Lenny talk about his greyhounds. I want to be like I used to be. I want to care about the plight of greyhounds everywhere. They are noble, suffering animals, I tell myself. Lenny describes to me how greyhounds are beaten and starved; how they are left in hot, airless crates for hours at a time.

I should feel sympathy for these animals because I, too, feel like I am running, running, running and getting nowhere. I do not have a full-time job. I do not have medical insurance. Since my surgery, I have been in debt. Like the greyhounds, I feel as if I am caged and beaten by life and made to run for others, having nowhere to go myself.

Yet I'm not sad about the greyhounds tonight. The stars are out, and they are pretty, and they are shining down on atrocities everywhere, but somehow I have lost the thread of why any of this matters.

Lenny and I finish our supper and go into the living room and sit next to the fire. We open the doors on the wood stove and watch the flames.

"You should be careful about sparks when you do this," Lenny says. "It wouldn't be hard to start a fire. This old place would really go up."

"I know how to use a wood stove, Lenny," I say. "I do it all the time when you're not here."

I say this even though I am thinking about the house in flames. A one-hundred-year-old house, destroyed by my carelessness.

"I know," Lenny tells me. "I'm just saying."

The fire snaps, and the logs groan. I think I might be starting to feel better. *This is not really a bad night*, I think. *It is my birthday.*

"Lenny," I say, "what's the worst thing that ever happened on your birthday?"

Lenny is stabbing at the wood with a poker. He likes to think he is influencing the flames in some way. He sees the fire as something he has to control.

"What do you mean?" he says. "My uncle got drunk at one of my birthday parties and beat up my aunt. That was pretty bad."

"Oh," I say. "That is bad."

"Nah," Lenny says. "It wasn't that bad. I got over it."

Everyone in Lenny's family has a drinking problem except Lenny. Lenny's ex-wife, Marina, also had a drinking problem, which is what destroyed their marriage. Before their divorce, Lenny's wife had a stillborn daughter. Lenny blamed it on her drinking. He does not like to think it might have had something to do with his exposure to chemicals in Vietnam.

Lenny told me once that he was there when Marina had the baby. I held Lenny's head in my lap as he told me that the room had smelled like death, that he knew the smell from the hospital in Okinawa where he'd recovered from his war wounds.

Lenny hates war. He even hates war movies. He says he is tired of death.

Even though I know he does not like to talk about such things, I say to Lenny, "The worst thing that ever happened on my birthday is they executed Ted Bundy."

Lenny says, "Nora, I don't know why you think about stuff like that."

I say, "I don't either."

The hickory logs are sweet-smelling. I think about my cats out in the barn, lying nose to tail, folded in on themselves like croissants. I remember how my uncle Will loved his cat Sam. Will was foulmouthed and irritable because he was sick all the time, and nobody would have anything to do with him except my father and Grandmother Bertie. Will lived with Bertie, and he loved Sam the cat because Sam didn't care that Will was crude, that his body was disintegrating, that wherever Will sat he left a pile of dead skin on the floor.

"How do you feel tonight?" Lenny says.

"Tired," I say.

"Really?" Lenny says. "I mean: really, are you all right?"

I think about it. I do not want to wear him out with my problems.

"I really want to know," Lenny says.

I feel I should tell him something. "Well, I don't feel all that great," I say.

Lenny gets up and grabs a couple of logs to put on the fire. I'm glad for the fire because it gives him something to do with his hands. Lenny is the kind of person who needs that.

"Sometimes," I say, "I just feel like somebody has hijacked my body." My hormones have been out of whack since the operation. Lenny has told me there are times when he thinks he doesn't know me anymore. This is too sad for me to think about very long.

Lenny throws the wood on the fire, and sparks fly out. They do not get on anything important. Most die out before they hit the floor.

"I really can't explain it," I say.

Lenny keeps busying himself with the fire. He pokes at it. He arranges the wood so there is enough air for the fire to breathe. He really has a good fire going — much better, I have to admit, than the ones I make.

Then he knocks the wood down, and it all lies flat and starts to smother the flames.

"What did you do that for?" I ask. "You really had it going great."

"Nora," Lenny says, "I have to tell you something."

The way he says this makes me think I don't want to hear what he has to tell me. I say, "You had the fire going just the way you wanted it, and then you messed it all up."

"Nora," Lenny says, "about two weeks ago, I caught that tabby, the one that was bothering your cats."

"Caught him?" I say.

Lenny puts the poker down. "I took him to the pound."

"Caught him?" I say again. "What do you mean?" I blink and shake my head. "To the shelter?"

"No, to the pound," he says.

"The pound?" I ask. "But why didn't you take him to the shelter?"

"Because the shelter was full. They wouldn't take him."

"But they kill them at the pound," I say. "He's probably dead already." My voice sounds thick, like it is rising up through blood.

"Yeah," Lenny says, his voice cracked and low. "Probably so."

Lenny's hands are on his knees, and he will not look at me. Smoke is curling from underneath the wood. It stinks. Lenny starts rearranging the wood again, but it is too late. He has killed the fire.

"Nora," Lenny says, "I knew you didn't really hate the cat. It . . ." He pauses. "It was wrong."

When Grandmother Bertie died, Uncle Will and my father went together to make the arrangements. When they came to the house that Will and Bertie had shared, they found Will's cat Sam dead in the road. My father buried Sam in the yard and talked to Will for a while before coming home to us, his family.

For the rest of his life, my father would think about how Will shot himself that night, and how that moment of desperation might have been avoided. I'm not saying Will killed himself over his cat. I am just saying that death always factors itself into your brain along with everything else. I am saying there are different kinds of deaths. I am saying that with every death, you are supposed to look for a new beginning, but not everybody can do that all the time.

My father sold Bertie's house, and sometimes he would go out of his way to drive past it. Sometimes he would sit in the car and look at it for a long time. Sometimes when we went out for a doughnut together, we would drive back by Bertie's house. My father and I would not talk. I would think about Sam. I would think about the bones of that cat buried in the yard.

It's past midnight. It is no longer my birthday. I am washing dishes. Lenny is talking about his mistake. He's having a hard time explaining. "Sometimes I do things like that. I don't know why," he says. "Sometimes I just feel like I've got to do something. Like I've got to take action. The last thing you needed was another cat."

He says he had to tell me because he does not want our relationship to be based on lies. His marriage was like that, and he is sick of lies.

"Even when I know what I'm doing is wrong, I still do it," Lenny says. "It's messed up."

He tells me he loves me.

I ask him if he would like to stay with me tonight, although I do not really want him to.

Earlier in the evening I did. Before this happened, I looked forward to us lying together in my bed, me and Lenny in the room with the Velvis. Me and Lenny spooned together in my bed. I would let him touch the scar, and he would say, like he always does, "Nora, I'm sorry this happened to you." When he touches the scar, he always says he feels the pain himself. This is what I thought my birthday would be like this year: Lenny and me and my two Velvises — one on the wall and one in the bed.

Lenny knows me well, and that is why he will not stay tonight. He says, "Well, you know, I'd like to stay, but there's the dogs." He tells me how the greyhounds are just too fragile. They will not understand being left alone all night. "Trust is very important to them right now," he says.

He tells me our lives will not always be this way.

After Ted Bundy's execution, the *National Enquirer* ran a picture of his dead face. You could see where the electrodes had scorched his forehead. His eyes were half open, and he seemed to be looking straight into you. It was the kind of photo that simultaneously intrigues and repels. The blank stare of the unseeing.

Looking at that picture, I thought how you cannot see your reflection in a dead person's eyes. But not many people could see that picture of Bundy, or any dead person, without seeing themselves. That is why the picture was so hard to look at.

I thought there was more that I was meant to see in Bundy's picture. I thought I was supposed to understand that there would always be terror in the world, that you cannot get rid of terror any more than you can get rid of good. That even if you tried to get rid of terror, it would always be there, staring you in the face.

I get into my bed and think that maybe I am living in a shadow, a shadow cast by Bundy's death, and it grows deeper and wider with each birthday.

I don't blame my doctor for anything. She did what she had to do. There are cases of women having hysterectomies who really do not need them. This was not the case with me.

When the doors of the operating room opened, I thought the room looked like a garage. Like an oil-change place or like an old garage I went to once with my father when I was little. I didn't have my glasses on in the operating room, so I really cannot say for sure how everything looked. But the room felt empty, the way places feel empty when people come and go and sometimes die there, but nobody actually lives there.

My doctor held my hand before I went to sleep. It felt like a sweet invitation, the way she held my hand. ■

Box Step

by **TODD JAMES PIERCE**

After the fight,
my mother sits
in her room,
staring out the window,
wondering where my father
has gone, though she already
knows he is driving
along thin mountain roads,
as he often does
when he is upset.
She wonders why
he always says
he might leave,
because it upsets her so,
even though she knows
he doesn't mean it.
When he returns,
she won't look at him
standing there in his best
blue shirt, his hands clutching
a record he bought
on his way home. Only
when he plays it
does she turn to him,
surprised to hear the song

they heard so many years
ago, their bodies close
in a dark gymnasium.
And seeing him there,
seated on the sofa,
a man lost with words,
she simply tilts her head
and waits for him
to take her hand
and lead her
to the dining-room floor,
where they dance a slow,
sorrowful box step,
even though the song is fast
and their hearts are still broken.

Au Revoir, Pleasant Dreams

by **ROSEMARY BERKELEY**

After all this time, my father's routine has become ritual. At 4:30 P.M. sharp, he switches off a rerun of *All in the Family*, lurches forward to bring the dusty rose recliner to an upright position, tosses the remote onto the empty recliner next to his, and says cheerfully, "Got a hot date." (Indeed, the whole performance is carried out in a cheerful spirit. "If you're going to do something, do it right" is one of his mottoes.) He goes to the bathroom mirror, picks up a brush, and poufs his white hair in the spots where it's thinning a bit. He's a storybook-looking old man — weathered but not stooped, still tall and handsome, like Cary Grant in his eighties. He does the Royal Canadian Air Force exercises every other day and is able to muster what he calls "pep" when it's called for. Sometimes he sizes up his reflection in the mirror and turns philosophical, saying, "At this point in life, it's all about maintenance," or, "That's the best I can do." Then he takes the green bottle of Polo cologne from the cabinet and douses himself with it.

He is particular about what he wears — off-white turtleneck with matching cardigan, black slacks, well-polished black loafers — but he never dresses for the weather. In the winter, I must argue to get him to wear gloves. A hat is out of the question. If there's snow on the ground or it's raining, he leaves early. If I cause his departure time to be delayed a few minutes, he is mad. He must be there at 4:45. "She's waiting," he says.

The Manor is less than a mile away. We drive through Boston's Oak

Square and up Bigelow Street, lined on both sides with eighty-year-old houses, the property lines demarcated by chain-link fences. We take a left at the top of the hill, at the house Joe Kennedy II and his wife bought after Joe was elected to Congress in 1986.

My father was delighted when the Kennedys moved into the neighborhood; the Kennedy family was the equivalent of royalty to him, an Irish Catholic born in 1917, just two months after JFK. My father and JFK served in the same war and got married in the same year, both bachelors until the age of thirty-six. The similarities end there, though. Dad worked the night shift at the post office to support his six children, and I'm pretty sure he never even seriously flirted with other women. My mother would not have been as tolerant as Jackie apparently was. My mother would have said, "So help me, I'll pull your ear the length of my arm if you ever do that again. God forgive me."

For the first few months after the Kennedys moved in, Dad often said, "They haven't done a blessed thing to that house since they bought it." I think he expected a major overhaul. Then, in July, he said grudgingly, "Well, at least they stuck a flag out front." After the first year, Dad said, "They have a chow dog now. That thing must eat a lot." Once, at Christmas, when the Kennedys had electric candles lit in every window, he said, "Why do they need such a big house? All those rooms. It must get lonesome." I made a mental note to alert my sisters and brothers that Dad was feeling lonesome. My father would sooner put on a dress and parade up and down Bigelow than say, "I'm lonesome." He speaks in code, though we children cracked it long ago. "The dog wants a treat" means Dad wants a dish of ice cream. "It's no bother" means it is, but he wasn't brought up to complain.

We take a left at the Kennedys' house and ride the brakes down the steep driveway of the Manor. This is the back entrance, marked by three overflowing dumpsters and a white vinyl banner reading, LEADERS IN QUALITY CARE. The front entrance is fancier. There's a wooden sign and, in the summer, some annuals in pots, though the flowers never last very long. To enter the back way, we must go through a glass door, then press a red button high on the wall that buzzes us through a second set of doors.

I think of the back door as the "stage entrance," because from the second my father's hand hits that button, he is on.

It's supper time, and the residents who are able to sit up are out in the hall waiting for their trays to be delivered. There are three old ladies lined up in our path. My father bends over in a courtly fashion and shakes hands with each of them, saying, "How are you tonight, dear?" or, "You look beautiful this evening. Pink is your color."

"Where's my breakfast?" the third one demands of him.

"I'm going to make it for you right now, sweetheart," my father answers.

"No jello!" she hollers in a raspy voice.

"Hold the jello!" Dad yells toward the kitchen.

As we walk away, he says to me, "It's like running a gauntlet." We keep each other going with jokes. Banter is our defense.

It's a busy time for the aides, but still they pause to say hello when they see my father. They're mostly Haitian, with a few Jamaicans in the senior positions. They have many pet names for him: Big Daddy, Mr. B. "Oh, here come my sweet man," announces Bianca, whose hair is arranged differently every time we see her. This evening, it reminds me of a fountain in the Boston Public Garden.

"Bianca," my father says, "where have you been all my life?"

She hugs him. Then, hands on hips, head tilted to one side, she asks, "When are you gonna bring me another present?" My father frequently brings boxes of chocolates for the aides.

"I'm watching your weight for you, Bianca," he answers.

I roll my eyes and say, "Dad!"

But Bianca doesn't seem to mind. In fact, she points to me and says, "You have a good daddy," as if I've been disrespectful.

We reach the room my mother has occupied for five of her seven years at the Manor. "She has seniority," my father jokes. Her bed is by the window, but I have never seen her look out. The view is obscured by light-blocking vertical blinds and heavy pink curtains. Often, in the summer, I shut off the worn-out air conditioner and open the window for some fresh air. Once, in February, when Dad was home with the flu, I opened the window wide, whispered to my mother, "Let go," and tiptoed out of the room. I was hoping she would catch pneumonia and die. I cannot say to my father that I want her to die. What one must wish is that God's will be done.

Mom's current roommate is disconcertingly youngish, with long steel gray hair. "She crazy," says the aide who calls my father "Big Daddy." Still, everyone must be greeted, and Dad insists on singing out, "Good evening, Margaret," to the roommate every night when he arrives. Tonight Margaret spits into a plastic cup and shuffles out of the room.

As he walks toward my mother, Dad speaks in his radio-announcer voice: "Good evening, ladies and gentlemen and all the ships at sea. We have a lovely show for you tonight, broadcasting live from the Rainbow Room high atop Rockefeller Center."

I resist the temptation to say something deflating like "She's confused enough without you telling her she's in the Rainbow Room."

My mother used to be pretty, with honey-colored hair and a saucy walk. My father makes much of the fact that her hair is still its original color, gray only at the temples. "How are you keeping it brown?" he asks her sometimes, as if she were in control of her hair color. As if she were in control of anything.

She's usually dressed in someone else's nightgown. Despite our determined efforts — my sister Rita labeled all my mother's apparel in indelible black marker when she was admitted — the anarchists in the laundry room refuse to separate clothes by owner. When we buy her something new on Mother's Day, or her birthday, or Christmas, it soon disappears into the vast communal closet of the nursing home. Still, we persist. Tonight her top is twisted, and I can read the name "D. Rufo" on the back. I picture some other daughter labeling her mother's clothes the way we do.

"She's wearing some Eye-talian woman's clothes tonight," my father mutters, product of a Boston neighborhood where families were either Irish or Italian. To him, all Italians are the Other — not disliked, necessarily, but different. Then he says, "Hi, honey. How are you tonight? I've brought Ro with me. You're so lucky to be inside. It's bitter — and I mean bitter — cold out." Today, as during every other visit, he takes hold of her chin and tries to make her look at him. It's comical, almost, the way she moves her eyes away from wherever he wants them to be. "Just like trying to get a kid to smile for a Christmas photo," my father says. Occasionally she looks right at him and gives him a radiant, surprised smile. Once, she said, "You," when she saw him.

When he has finished saying hello, he expects me to say, "Hi, Mom!" and bend over and kiss her. I try, but I can't muster enough enthusiasm to satisfy him. In my head, I can hear him coaxing, "More feeling!" as he did when he coached me for a sixth-grade speech contest.

He sings, "Night and day / you are the one," and turns the crank that elevates the head of the bed. Then he lowers the bedside rail, props up the stuffed bear with the green velvet vest — which he is convinced comforts her — and says, "There you go, Mama."

Dad keeps a stash of flexible straws on a small table in the corner. The nursing home provides only straight straws, though bent straws at least offer a fighting chance to someone who can't move her head. Tonight one of the aides has used up the bent straws and neglected to tell Dad.

"Damn it," he says. "They've been at the straws again. If they'd just tell me, I'd know to buy more!"

"Was that the last straw?" I ask, and wait for his comeback. I knead my mother's shoulder because I've read that Alzheimer's patients respond to touch. She stares straight ahead. I hope she can't make sense of the image reflected in the mirror across from her bed. There's really not much here for death to take away: she sits all day unmoving, unable to so much as shift her weight. More than a decade ago, when the doctors were still telling us she was experiencing "the change" or "empty-nest syndrome," it was my mother's stillness that filled me with a sick certainty that something was seriously wrong with her. When she'd been healthy, my mother had been a dervish. But after her illness began, she would sit quietly and stare off into space, not doing anything, not noticing the room getting darker, not remembering even to switch on a lamp.

Dad doesn't respond to my joke about the straw. He's dusting off her TV with his handkerchief. The TV hasn't worked in years, but it adds to the illusion that there is a functioning person in this space. A person who could watch television.

"How about I run up to Star Market right now and get some straws?" I ask. Am I a peacemaker, I wonder, or am I just trying to get out of here?

"No, I'll go tomorrow," he says, sliding the empty box into his jacket pocket so he won't forget.

Ten years older than my mother, my father retired soon after she was diagnosed with Alzheimer's in her midfifties. Despite cautions from doctors that it would be taxing, Dad kept her at home for twelve years. Before that, he had never entered the kitchen except to grab his lunchbox off the counter on his way to work. Now the sight of him in the kitchen is commonplace, though he occasionally shows me something he has found in the back of a drawer — a whisk or a garlic press — and asks, "Honey, what the hell am I supposed to do with this?"

Maneuvering his wife into a shower or out of a car became second nature for him. He had a firm opinion on which brand of adult diaper was best and figured out how to get my mother to take her Metamucil. (Mix it with applesauce.) He learned the kinds of tricks that parents of young children employ. When my mother was still living at home, there was a TV nun, Mother Angelica, who looked freakishly like my long-dead maternal grandmother. Each time the nun's face appeared on-screen, my mother would lean forward in her recliner. Such was the effect of Mother Angelica that my mother would submit to having her hair styled, something that normally upset her, so long as Mother Angelica was on. Long after my mother had lost her ability to speak, her hair remained flawless. My father believes that appearances must be kept up, no matter what catastrophe befalls you.

Now he finishes tucking a towel under her chin and finds the radio station that plays Sinatra every night from five to six. The part of the brain that remembers music is among the last to stop functioning: I learned that at a support-group meeting. Dad hated the meetings and went only once. "I refuse to sit in a church basement and listen to a bunch of bellyaching strangers," he'd say, and raise the newspaper in front of his face.

"But you have to share your feelings," my sisters and I would plead with him. Our worries about our parents took the obnoxious form of a zealous determination to help Dad — to *make* Dad — cope. We backed off only after a social worker suggested that if Dad ever did get in touch with his feelings, he might not stop crying for a long time.

One of the quieter aides brings in dinner and says, "Oh, you've got your daughter with you tonight. Good for you." I smile and nod at her, trying to look like the source of comfort I used to be. For several years, I was intimately involved in caring for my mother. Then some impulse toward self-preservation prompted me to live overseas for two years, and to undergo therapy for two years after that. I finally reached the point of believing — or half believing — that the drama of my mother's illness should not be the centerpiece of my life. I still feel like a deserter whenever I'm home in Boston.

My father lifts the domed plastic lid off the main course, and together we study the puréed mess on the plate.

"Beef?" I venture.

My father tastes it, shrugs, and says, "You've got me."

Now his real work begins. If he coaxes her into eating most of what's on her plate, he can go home, watch the six o'clock news, microwave some popcorn, and be at peace. Because she's been in the hospital a couple of times already for dehydration, he begins with the juice. That usually goes pretty quickly. I prefer to stand at the end of the bed and disassociate myself from what comes next. He takes the glass of milk, drinks about half of it, then adds several heaping teaspoons of the purée, stirs, and says, "We have a lovely cocktail for you tonight, Mrs. Berkeley. It's one of the specialties here at our bar. You're going to love it." Then he lowers his voice and says, "Come on, Mama, drink."

When she complies, I wonder if it's in response to the hint of desperation in his voice. (If she refuses food, they'll insert a feeding tube.) I wonder, too, when my father began referring to his own wife as "Mama." On the phone, he'll say to me, "Mama was out of sorts yesterday." Even in meetings with her doctor, he'll say, "Mama is holding her own, don't you think?" Ironically, my siblings and I have stopped calling our mother "Mom." We now refer to her by her nickname: "Franny looks good." Or sometimes by just a pronoun: "Why doesn't she let go?"

The woman across the hall, the one my father calls "Cat Lady" because of the peculiar wailing sound she emits, is acting up, calling for her son, who never visits.

"Pat, Pat," Cat Lady yells, "where are you?"

"Come on, Mama, just a little bit more."

"Pat, can you hear me?" Her volume is impressive.

"Ro came all the way up from Florida to see you, Mama," he says, deftly whipping a spoonful of mush into her mouth.

"Pat, why don't you answer me?" Cat Lady wails.

"Ro is making me a nice chicken dinner tonight," he adds.

Cat Lady marshals all her strength and screeches, "Pat, where are you?"

My father straightens and calls out, "I'm under the bed!"

Cat Lady is silent.

My mother lifts her eyebrows, which excites us both. I squeeze her hand, and she squeezes back, faintly, but undeniably.

"Hi, Franny," I say.

He has missed only a few nights in the last seven years, always because of the flu or some family obligation. He used to let me come in his place when I was in town — it didn't count as missing a night if I was there. I would go three, four, five times a week, insisting that he needed a break. I'd arrive a few minutes after the food trays were distributed and make my way briskly down the hall, calling out a greeting to the aides but making no attempt to engage them. I would breeze silently by Margaret, give my mother the juice, offer food but not press her, pat her arm, say, "Love you," and be gone in under fifteen minutes.

I often fed her that way, with the efficiency and detachment of someone cleaning a fish tank for the fiftieth time. Sometimes, though, everything in me fell apart at the sight of her in that stupid bed, and she became my mother again. I'd stand a few feet away, wondering if she knew I was there, wiping my eyes on my sleeves and asking, "Why in hell did this have to happen to you?"

One night, as I drove up Bigelow, I began to dread seeing my mother. When I got to the Kennedys', I couldn't take the left. I drove around town for twenty minutes, looking at my old school and the supermarket where I'd cashiered in college. An image of Mom's dinner tray sitting on the bedside table flashed into my mind. "I just can't do it, OK?" I said aloud, banging the steering wheel.

If you'd asked me whom I was talking to, I would have guessed it was the God my father believes in, the one who always pisses me off.

I left town the next day. When my father got to the nursing home that night, one of the aides asked, "Where were you yesterday?" and he said, "I sent my daughter!" and she said, "No, sir. I fed that lady myself."

He told all three of my sisters that it was the worst thing I'd ever done to him.

After the meal comes the grand finale. In the bedside table, my father keeps a Tupperware container full of the kind of candy no one under the age of sixty would buy: after-dinner mints resembling tiny pastel pillows; green, sugar-coated jellies shaped like leaves; spicy gumdrops. He selects three pieces and lines them up on my mother's shoulder. Then he takes a Tums from a bottle in the bedside table. "Now it's time for a little treat, Mama," he says, sticking the first candy in her mouth.

I have argued against this procedure many times. She doesn't seem to want the candy; he has to press it into her mouth. She is on a puréed diet, so presumably there is some danger of her choking on a sugar-encrusted green leaf. Is she aware enough to chew? So far, yes. She chews and chews, holding up our departure. The second piece goes in. She chews thoughtfully, as if she's trying to place the flavor. I go to the window and open the blinds and stare out. Now the third piece. I can see my parents reflected in the dark glass. He strokes her cheek and says, "You look like a little squirrel." She's too engrossed in the act of chewing to look at him. Finally, he holds the Tums above her like the Communion host and says, "Very good, Mama. One more," and she obediently opens her mouth a bit.

After the Tums has been administered, he lowers the bed and tucks the teddy bear under her arm. He pulls the bedside rail up and puts the plastic dome over the tray. "Go to sleep now, Mama," he says. "See you tomorrow night."

I say, "See you, Franny. Love you," and precede him out the door.

He looks back at her and calls out, "This is Ben Bernie and all the lads, saying au revoir, pleasant dreams, think of us when requesting your themes."

"What's that from?" I ask as we make our way down the hall.

He waves at an ancient woman whose wiry hair is done up in lopsided pigtails and says, "Ben Bernie was a bandleader at the Totem Pole."

"The Totem Pole?"

"A place on the Charles River with big bands and dancing. It was nice. Small tables with a lamp on each one." He pauses, then adds, "I took Frances there once."

The sound of my mother's full name, a name none of us uses anymore, grips me for a second like a whiff of perfume that I haven't worn in a long time. Frances: A woman in a pretty dress smiling in the lamplight. A vision from a past I can only imagine, back when it was just the two of them. A vision strong enough, sweet enough, and enduring enough to keep him going now — to keep *them* going.

"There's something between those two," the night nurse once told one of my sisters. "She won't go until he's ready."

He calls good night to a couple of people. When we get to the food cart, he slides her tray, which he has brought with him, back into place.

"Thank you, Sweet Man," Bianca says, hurrying by with trays in both hands.

Almost to the door, we pass the three old ladies, who are now wearing their dinners.

"Good night, ladies," my father sings out to them, then bends to pick up a napkin from the floor.

A flash of anger makes me want to kick the exit doors open. I hiss at him, "That's enough," which is something my mother used to say to us when we were pushing her too hard: "That's enough." *Enough what?* I wonder, even as I say it.

I bang the red button and say, "I'll drive." My father doesn't answer. We both take a deep breath of outside air. I'm trying to calm down, but I have the car started and my foot poised over the gas pedal before he's even settled into the passenger seat. I tear up the hill and out of the parking lot and hang a right at Joe Kennedy's, past his flag, his chow dog, his too-big lonely house. I can see my father's foot pressing the brake pedal that isn't there.

I say, "Sometimes it's all just too much, you know?"

"You sound just like your mother."

"Good," I say, and I exhale hard. We are quiet for a moment, driving under the black sky. Then I add, "Mom would say it's too much."

Claiming my mother as an ally is a ruse. Back when she was healthy, we disagreed on everything — birth control and skirt length, the kind of guy I should date and the way I wore my hair. I picture her at her sarcastic best, hands on hips, telling me to kiss her royal Irish ass, laughing at the idea that I know what's best — for myself, for her, for anyone.

I admit that I don't know what's best, but I am clear about what I wish for as we head home to the dusty rose recliners and Tom Brokaw. My wish is for my father, who looks drained and grayish in the dashboard light. I wish that, when this is over, he'll be left with the memory of love's blessings, and not its exacting toll. ∎

An Hour After Breakfast

by **MATTHEW DESHE CASHION**

He says, "I know your tricks, old woman.
You're trying to starve me."
Because he has forgotten, again,
          that he has eaten.

But this morning, like every morning
for sixty years, she has warmed
his plate in the oven before loading it
with bacon, eggs fried in bacon grease
(skillet-flipped so spatula won't bruise yolk),
and slow-cooked hominy grits gotten from
farmer friends. She has refilled his coffee cup
and stood over him in prayer:
"Bless us, O Lord, and these thy gifts . . ."

Every morning for sixty years
she has prepared this morning meal,
preferring cereal, or nothing, for herself.

Now, still seated at the scene,
with bits of egg on his face,
he insists she is trying to murder him.
To prove her love, she has started
taking Polaroids. "Here," she says.
"This is you one hour ago eating breakfast."

He starts to sob. His big belly shakes
from sobbing. Which makes her start
sobbing too. She knows, had he been himself,
he would have thought to say, "Why,
this looks just like yesterday."
Had he, for one second, been himself,
he would have said, "Why,
that's not me at all."

The Empty House Of My Brokenhearted Father

a short story by **POE BALLANTINE**

It was 4 A.M. and I was walking home from the bar with another man's wife. I'd been in love with her since she was a little girl, but my good friend had snapped her up very young. I never had a chance. They'd been married ten years, had two boys, and were settled in a house in the town where I grew up. Her husband worked long hours, swam Olympic laps of beer. I'd been traveling, hadn't seen her in a long time. My parents had just separated, abruptly and disastrously, and I'd taken my father's side. My mother had left him for another man.

I had no intention of having an affair with her. I didn't sleep with other men's wives. I went to great lengths to find legitimate prospects. I was a cornball, a dupe, a Nice Guy; my romantic history up to this point had been one spectacular fade, wrong turn, superficial exploit, and exhaustive disaster after the next.

I drove a delivery truck for a bakery on the west side of Yuma, Arizona. In the evening two or three times a week I went to an old-folks bar where the geriatrics nodded over their drafts. "New York, New York" played over and over on the jukebox. The cigarette smoke tangled like the ghost of youth around the green EXIT lamp over the back door. I never stayed long. I wasn't afraid of what my father might do alone, but I know what the silence is like when you are hurt, like clock hands made out of razor blades. You need someone to talk over it, to tell you that it's really not this way.

One night she called the bar. The barmaid looked at me. "Yes, he's here." She came in a few minutes later. I ordered two tall goblets of beer. The barmaid watched us with a stern and envious fascination.

We met I don't know how many times before anything happened. I'd go home afterward and pretend we were just old friends who'd gone out for drinks. I would climb into bed and her perfume would linger like soft flames in my hair. I'd close my eyes and still see the luscious lines of her lips. She stayed with me many nights in my dreams.

One night at the bar she kissed me so hard the jukebox bogged and every head turned up from its beer. I reached down under the table and grabbed her hand; the self rattled loose and spilled out like coins from a broken bag. Frank Sinatra wheezed back up. The Nice Guy wandered like an amnesiac out the back door.

She had a car but we walked, an ethereal fog walk. It was only a few blocks to my father's house, the house I'd grown up in. The light came silver down from the streetlamp. The 4 A.M. pines looked silver-sprayed like fake Christmas trees. The streets were sprayed, too, the rooftops, the sky, everything dipped in a silver Cupid-arrow poison. Our arms were locked. It did not occur to me that we might make love. (Yes, it did.) She was the one who said the word, made the suggestion (love was not the word). It broke my terror like a filigree of fine shattering. I felt in some way, through my great unsuccess and trial of loneliness, that I was owed.

I was low enough then to be proud. I loved her. I had always loved her. Love and desire were the same. The Dogs D'Amour as a rule did not toss me too many bones. I wanted a girl of my own, to love and cherish and be faithful and true to. I wanted an ivy-tangled fence and a flannel robe and a pipe burning some fragrant Norwegian mix and the sound of honey I'm drifting home. I wanted someone besides my mother and father and Jesus to love me.

We found clever, bumbling places to meet — a car, a bar, the couch of a friend who was not home. Sometimes I took her into the empty house of my brokenhearted father. We thought no one knew, no one suspected. We got sloppy and ridiculous, like fat people eating spare ribs from a bucket; there were no boundaries but a laughed-at sacrament and two boys sleeping in NFL muslin and a father swallowed in an armchair, his cigarette making slow arcs in the darkness.

It went on like this. We sat in the car and kissed and drank VO from paper cups. I never thought how she might feel. I didn't consider the reasons and motivations of a woman who was trapped in a complacent, aging marriage. But one night she made a declaration. She decided she was in love with me. She said she wanted to run away with me. She would give up her family. We would start up somewhere else, a bungalow with a ripped screen door and a bird in the air conditioner. She would wait tables. I could be a mechanic in a bus depot. We would start all over, kill the serpent and make apple pie; we would build a little brick house with a den and a sliding glass door, and an apron with ducks on it, smell of meatloaf, burble of orderly life on rerun TV, a birdbath with blue algae in it, a Bible in the drawer — the same thing she had now, but ten years back, with ardor and antelope running against the sky: the time-travel dream of the science-fiction housewife.

She was speaking my language, except a paramour is not a fool. A paramour is an opportunist. I redirected her, gave a speech, a famous Nice Guy speech in defense of family and love and flags. I was full of beans but deep down I knew: if she would do it to him, she would do it to me.

"Let's run away," she said.

The moment was too cinematic. We wrestled on the front seat. The vinyl was a little cool and it made buckling, rumpling sounds, announcing the insignificance of the event. I spilled the orange juice. One of us hit the radio button and "Spirit in the Sky" blared out across the neighborhood. She had borne two children and she was not precisely the carved image of the seventeen-year-old in my memory. Sometimes I closed my eyes or just stared at her throat. Her throat was lovely as I made love to her in the jungle blue shadows of the animal kingdom.

Part of my chivalry comes from cowardice. It is easier for the physically undistinguished to wax spiritual. I had learned not to act like a sap, but a man cannot change his true nature. When we were through grappling on the front seat, there was nothing about us, only the awkward re-dressing. The morning light began to fill up the sky and she sneaked back into her house. I went home feeling crap-cheap, my shirt wrinkled. My father was snoring. I didn't want to sleep. I sat and thought, counseled with virtue. I knew that on the chain of being I was below octopus, yet I made no resolve to do anything about it. When you are stuck in a place and town and situation that are not worth it, you take what you can get. I looked halfheartedly for a way out, but there was no one else, nowhere else. The noble life looks fine on paper; it is becoming to the aged, hangs well in the robes of moral heroes, glitters brighter than war in ancient history, but I was a guy in Yuma who drove a bakery truck. Through the loss of another I slept like the meat-belly beast. The barmaid watched me with wonder. The rumor made me desirable: a glamorous wink in the modern eye. I was like literature, like TV, like romance itself. I was danger and reckless fashion. I could have been a criminal. I was a criminal. We all want to be chased and gobbled up by a larger thing: fame, danger, evil, wealth, art, romance, or God. Anything to keep from going home and seeing the five o'clock news.

In the morning the sun rose, warm and lush, and I had breakfast with my father. I cooked, made sure he got off all right. He read the paper, forcing cheer, keeping the radio on, the rain-tight architecture of music. He kept a close ritual of coffee, then work, dinner, his television shows and cigarettes. The newspaper stayed on the table open to the personals. He had opened them the first day she had left him, like the reflex of a man covering a wound after being shot. His face was gray from survival. He was a man and he could not allow himself to break. The despair stretched out. The music from the stereo could not fill the emptiness. Our conversations were automatic, clock talk. His single guiding hope was that she would return.

The thing called "romantic love" is too often some variety of predation. We jockey for position. Once love is established and identified it becomes the point of attack. I almost always knew how it would go, how long it would last. The one who fell would be the one destroyed. I never dreamed that she would be the one who would fall. In a few weeks I broke it off. I told her simply that it was wrong.

What happened to my father he had never believed would happen. He was fifty years old, settled, comfortable, secure. His children were raised. He had worked hard all his life and now he could relax. I understood why my mother had left him, but I still condemned her for leaving — for taking the easy way out. My father and I played cards and watched private-eye dramas on television. He looked in the personals, called once at something that looked right, but canceled soon after; it just wasn't in him.

One Sunday afternoon I heard him crying in the bedroom. I didn't know what to do with a father who cried. He had taught me all I knew, the important things: honesty, loyalty, firm handshake, the love beyond self-love, the duty of a man. Trust was his only religion and it was failing him and in turn it was the failure of the world.

The one thing a human being asks for on this earth is to be loved. Why should it be impossible? ■

Greed

by **KATHRYN HUNT**

At dawn a complaining crow awakens me.
You have already left our bed,
placing a kiss upon my cheek
before going downstairs.

I remember the cool wet mark
your lips left behind
and the sweetness of your skin,
before I drifted back to sleep.

Why am I so ungrateful
for the little pleasures,
always wanting more?

Suzy Joins The Sex Club

a short story by **ALISON CLEMENT**

"**S**uzy, we are too old to be controlled by our hormones," Ellis says to me.

I say, "Don't you realize that a thirty-eight-year-old woman has the same sex drive as a sixteen-year-old boy?"

"There is no scientific proof to substantiate that."

I hit my chest and say, "Here's your proof!"

He says, "Suzy, you know what I think of anecdotal evidence."

"Oh, fuck you anyway," I say.

He says, "I don't think this is a very productive conversation."

Later Ellis claims to have known right away, but I say, "Yeah, you figured it out, all right. After I told you about a hundred times." Even the kids knew before he did.

"Mom, is that the one?" my little girl asks me.

We are at table 3, which gives us a clear view of the kitchen.

"No, honey, that's Sam, the cook. Jimmy Lee is washing dishes."

We look over to the sink, and there he is, bent over a fifty-gallon aluminum soup pot, a cigarette hanging from the side of his mouth: the most charming man in the world.

"Anyway, there isn't any man as wonderful as your papa, and don't you ever forget that."

And I mean it, too: there isn't any man like my husband. The way I feel about Jimmy Lee has nothing to do with anything lacking in Ellis or anything missing from what we have together. Whatever there is between Jimmy Lee and me is just between the two of us. Nobody can understand it. Everybody knows how lucky I am to have a husband like Ellis, and they're always telling me so. I know it, too, but how can I explain to them what I can't even explain to myself?

Jimmy Lee started working at the restaurant last winter, right after he got released. I knew something was going to happen the first time I laid eyes on him. Sometimes you get this feeling about someone just by looking at them. Or just hearing their voice — you know it's a voice you've got to hear in your ear, a voice you've got to feel on your neck, a voice that's got to say secret things to you and call out your name in the dark. You know that just by hearing it one time. And partly it's the way he whirls around and catches me watching him and our eyes meet for one second. In that second he tells me he knows what I'm thinking, and I tell him that I know he knows, and he tells me he knows I know, and on and on forever in the one second it takes before I turn away and pick up a plate of food.

I say to Ellis that I think the dishwasher is pretty cute, and he says, "Oh, really?" because I'm always thinking someone is pretty cute.

People tell me I'm an idiot for saying anything to Ellis about it. They say it's just plain meanness on my part. Everybody thinks they know what happened, like it's happened a million times before. But for me it's all new, like I invented it myself, so I have to make up the rules as I go along.

One night I stand at the beer cooler, which is right next to the sink, and say, "I think you're pretty hot, Jimmy Lee," which is totally unlike anything anyone would expect me to say — but he doesn't know me, so he doesn't know that.

He wipes his hands on his apron and says, "Oh, yeah? What are you gonna do about it?" He looks at me so hard that I blush and look away. Then he takes one finger and puts it on the soft skin at the bottom of my neck, and he traces a line straight down my chest.

"Meet me tomorrow," I say. I'm thinking, *We should talk*. I'm thinking, *I should clarify things* — when I know there is nothing to clarify. "Meet me at four o'clock at the ice-cream parlor on the corner of Oceanside and Fourth." Just like that, like I've done it a hundred times.

If there is any mystery in what we are doing, Jimmy Lee is unaware of it. I start explaining about Ellis, but he puts his fingers to his lips.

"Shhh," he says. Jimmy Lee knows when to press forward and when to back up. He knows where to put his hands and how to press his hips. We're leaning against the wall of the ice-cream parlor, staring into each other's eyes like we've got this big thing, like we're in love or something, and I'm thinking, *He's probably an asshole.* It registers with me, but it registers far away, like a phone ringing in the apartment downstairs. Like something that doesn't have anything to do with me.

Jimmy Lee slips his hands under my T-shirt, traces the outline of my lips with his tongue. I open my legs, and he moves in between them. When I draw his hips into me, I can feel his outline against my belly. I put my hands on his face as he kisses me, touch his lips with my fingers.

"**J**immy Lee!" the other waitress says when I tell her about it. "Are you out of your mind?"

"Life is a mysterious thing," I say in my defense.

How can I explain those hands on my belly, those hips against my hips, that voice in my ear? Whatever has gotten into me has gotten in deep and won't let up. I can't eat. I can't sleep. Jimmy Lee's body is out there somewhere, like a wolf on the hillside with its head back, howling. I have only one appetite. Ellis notices that, but he doesn't notice anything else.

Maybe it isn't Jimmy Lee. Looking at him I wonder, *How can all this be about Jimmy Lee?* Maybe he was just in the right place at the right time. Maybe it just hit me and there was Jimmy Lee, bent over the sink. Like a whooping crane opening its eyes, I was stuck with the first thing that came into view.

I look at my kids and my husband and think of all the things we are together, and I think, *Isn't it odd to be willing to risk all this so I can fuck some guy who washes dishes and whispers nasty things in my ear? Isn't it a mystery?*

Jimmy Lee is an alcoholic. He lives in an old motel with weekly rates, and he just got out of jail for robbing a convenience store. He tells me these things right away so I don't have to be surprised.

I shrug. I don't care about any of it — what he does or says or thinks, the way he lives, what he knows or doesn't know: none of it matters. The thing between us is in our blood and bones, in our skin. There's something pure about it that nothing else can touch. It is as pure and sweet as a mother's love for her newborn baby. Nothing can turn me away from it.

One night the owner calls to say he is sick and can I stay and close the restaurant? I say sure, and I'm thinking, *Now I can be alone with Jimmy Lee.* Suddenly I have a secret agenda. Though it's only eight o'clock, I turn over the sign on the door and shut off the outside lights. I tell the guy at table 6 that we're out of crab, because it takes everybody at least an hour to eat crab and I don't have an hour. I start sweeping the floor, just to make sure everybody gets the picture, and I don't offer anyone dessert. I refuse to make eye contact unless people are ready to pay. So the cook cleans up and leaves, the customers pay their bills and leave, and I don't care if they complain to the boss tomorrow and I get fired, because the only thing that exists for me is what is right in front of me, and nothing else.

I lock both doors and go to the kitchen. It's a hot August night, but the back window is open and a little breeze blows in off the ocean. I sit on the table we use for cutting fish and say, "Come here, Jimmy Lee."

I pull my knees apart so he can slide in close. He pushes my skirt up my thighs.

"Whew, you are wet." He puts his mouth to my ear. "What does that mean?"

I giggle. "It's my Pavlovian response to you," I say, looking into his face. I realize then that I am about to risk everything to fuck a man who has never heard of Pavlov.

That night, I ask my husband, "Would you divorce me if I fucked another man?"

"Why would you want to do a thing like that?"

He has a point. Things between us are hot. They're so hot that it made me start looking around. Can you understand that? Things between us are so good that it set off something in me, and I want more and more. So it's a compliment, but no one understands that.

Meanwhile, I'm talking to everybody I know about it. And every woman my age is going through the same thing. Every one of them is feeling the way I feel. And how do I feel? Like I'm in a convertible driving eighty miles an hour down a two-lane highway without a scarf on my head, wearing lipstick, playing the radio full blast. Maybe that's how people feel right before they totally fuck up their whole life, but I don't care. I don't want to feel any other way.

"I feel like I've joined a secret club," I tell Ellis. "It's like when you have a baby and you realize there's a secret club of women who nod to each other on the street, who meet in line at Safeway and talk about their episiotomies. They're strangers, but it doesn't matter, because they belong to the same club. When I got a dog, I realized there's a secret dog club, too. And now I'm in the secret sex club. I can tell by somebody's face if they're a member. And it's not like you can just fuck someone and it will go away. That's just throwing gas on the fire."

"You're having a midlife crisis," Ellis says. Like that makes it less than what it is.

"All right, then. I'm having a midlife crisis. Then let me have it."

They give it names like that to make it seem foolish. The erotic impulse is so frightening that we have to dress it up in a pointy hat and crooked nose so we can forget its power.

I say to Ellis, "I don't know how my feelings can have so little to do with any other part of me. It's as if they have a life of their own."

"Fuck your feelings!" he shouts. "I've had enough of your feelings!" I start to cry, and he says, "OK, I'm out of control. I apologize. I'm beside myself. I've stopped making sense." For Ellis making sense is very important. "You've got to decide," he says.

So I apply the brakes. So what if the top layer of my skin is peeled back and all my nerves are exposed. I make a hard turn to the right. I quit my job. I stop remembering how his hands felt. I stop touching my lips, remembering. I run five miles a day. I run looking straight ahead, forgetting about Jimmy Lee. ∎

On Catching My Husband With A Cigarette After Seven Years Of Abstinence

by **PATRY FRANCIS**

It is not the smoke that
   coils around your head
in the garage where you've
   retreated with coffee and the *Times*
for an early morning butt
   that so startles me.
No, it is merely your expression,
   the tacit admission
       we seldom dare to make:
that there is always
   a life we hold in secret —
unknown, ungovernable,
   fiercely unpossessed.

Small Things

a short story by **SUNITI LANDGÉ**

The desire for a man other than your husband begins with the smallest favorable comparison.

A single pleasing action by an otherwise total stranger can qualify him as a good human being, a good man, a good husband. It may simply be that this other man does not complain about your curtains' being drawn against the sun. (Your husband insists that they be open at all times, even though the sun gives you migraines.) Or this other man — whether visitor, friend, or relative — does not mind that your curry has *goda masala* in it. (Your husband has forbidden that spice, because it was used at your mother's house, not his.) Or that this other man, unlike your husband, is indifferent to the fact that your coffee table, with its sharp corners, is not placed in the center of the rug but near the wall, so that your baby can crawl around without hurting herself. (Her father's logic is that the more she knocks her head on its corners, the faster she will learn to avoid it.)

Small things. Not a family history of serving in high places in the government, nor owning businesses, nor inherited wealth. All of these your husband has in plenty. At this point in your life, after three years of marriage, the small things have become the basis for your opinion.

And you, when pleased by the small things a man does, accept that other man's jokes, his compliments. It is as if he has opened a secret door inside you, and you don't know where or how you let him in.

But there he is, a smiling man from Calcutta, an engineer. Married. With a sweet wife of his own. They have recently moved here to Bangalore, but the wife returns home often.

"The air here is too damp for her," the engineer says. "She gets pains in the knees and ankles."

You are surprised: Calcutta, by the sea, is no drier than Bangalore in the rains — in fact, it is just as humid.

"She is very delicate in her health," he adds, still smiling. His teeth are very white under his black mustache.

Later, you learn that his wife is an only child and has never before lived outside of Calcutta. She speaks mostly Bengali and is very shy about her English. She smiles a lot. Her husband calls her "Mishti," because her face is round like a *rasgulla*, and sweet, too. You can see she has that eastern fullness to her face, the slight upward slant to her eyes, the flat, broad lips. Yes, she is sweet to look at.

"He is only a mechanical engineer," your husband has informed you, "from an unacclaimed college in Indore. And he has no MBA."

"Which college did you qualify from?" you ask him, this smiling man from Calcutta, this Mr. Chatterji.

He made applications to sixty schools, he explains, covering most of Bengal and northern India. His teeth show in a wide smile. You notice the way his cheeks fold up in his face when he laughs — not quite dimples, but easy creases — and the way his eyes shine behind his square, dark-framed glasses.

"My father had lost all hope for me," he goes on. "He had even approached the dean of Jabalpur College for admission, because he knew him personally. But no luck. Then someone dropped out at the last minute at Indore, and I was in! I was two marks short of the cutoff test score." He looks embarrassed after his long explanation. Everyone is looking at him.

"What was the name of your college?" you ask. You want to know it, the name of that unacclaimed college.

"Indore Engineering College." He shrugs his shoulders and smiles. "Have you ever wondered why people are so short on imagination when it comes to names for colleges? Agra Medical College, Agra. Goa Medical College, Goa. Indore Engineering College, Indore."

You all laugh.

You are sitting in the drawing room. Mishti pulls her sari up over her ankles and sits down on the carpet. She pushes the coffee table aside and leans back against it. Her ankles look healthy to you. She opens her palms and invites your child onto her lap. "Aay," she says, nodding her head. Your child stops and stares at her. Drool drips from her chin onto the carpet. Your husband gets a napkin and wipes it off the rug. Then, with the same napkin, he rubs the baby's chin. He shakes his head at the dark patch on the rug. *Charcoal* was the word your sister-in-law used to describe the rug's color when you first bought it. She said the color was charcoal, not dark gray, as you had called it. *Charcoal.* You appreciate the accuracy of the word. *Charcoal.*

You pick the baby up and sit her on your knee. She struggles off and crawls toward the coffee table. Mishti puts her hand over the sharp corner as the baby comes toward her. The baby goes to the other side and pulls herself up. Mishti watches, keeping the corner of the table covered.

"Nice table," Mr. Chatterji says.

"Pure teakwood," your husband says. "A gift from my uncle." He looks at you.

Your family gave ugly presents — mainly stainless-steel cups and kitchen utensils with the names of the aunts who gave them engraved on the side: MRS. KAVITA FROM SULOCHANA MAUSHI, 1982.

Your husband does not eat or drink from stainless-steel utensils. He says he can't see what he is drinking from a steel cup. Everything looks dark in steel, he says. In restaurants, he asks the waiter to bring him a proper teacup.

You have set the table with china plates, napkins, forks, and knives, although you question the need for knives and forks, as your guests are Indian and will eat with their hands. Your husband's uncle, who was once chairman of the Indian Tobacco Company under British rule, always ate with a knife and fork, and it has become a family tradition, a mark of advancement, of progress.

When you first learned this, you were surprised. "Your uncle ate *hilsa* fish curry with a fork?" It takes you half an hour to negotiate two pieces of that fine-boned silvery fish — half an hour of carefully pulling bones as sharp as needles from the white and fragrant flesh of the Ganges *hilsa*.

"His cook knew how to debone it," your husband said.

The tablecloth is maroon and black with a stylish, modern design of jagged lines and concentric circles. It matches the curtains. All were wedding gifts, planned and coordinated among your various in-laws.

The baby has been put to bed. Everyone sits down to eat: rice, *aloo dum*, chicken curry, *rahu* fish *jhaal*, capsicum dry vegetable, tomato chutney — all are arrayed on the table in ovenproof casseroles. The desserts are lined up on the side table. You remove the lids from the bowls and start serving your guests: first the rice, then the curries.

Your husband complains that the rice is not steaming hot. This is true. It has gone cold and lumpy, having sat in its bowl for the last hour while you tried to get the baby off to sleep.

"The curries are hot enough," says Mr. Chatterji. "Who can eat boiling-hot food?"

His wife says she once burned her tongue on chicken-corn soup in a Chinese restaurant and then couldn't enjoy the rest of the meal. She pours the fish curry over her rice and begins eating with her hand. "Very good," she says, pulling the bones out with her fingertips and laying them on the edge of her plate. "Very fresh fish."

Everyone eats with their hands.

"So, do you travel much?" the engineer asks your husband.

"Not so much now. In the first year, I went all over Mysore — Shimoga, Belgaum, Mandya."

"Mandya?" Mishti says. "Isn't that where wild elephants destroyed the fields?"

It was in the news.

"What do people expect?" says your husband. "If they cut down the forests, this is what will happen." Your husband disapproves of people who cut down trees. He believes they are irresponsible, even if they need the wood to cook their meals.

Mishti seems not to have heard him; she is thinking of something else. She reminds her husband of a story she read in the news, about an elephant who trampled a man's scooter because he blew his horn at the animal.

The engineer laughs. "Oh, yes, I remember. There was this cartoon in the newspaper," he says, turning to your husband. "The scooter driver looked very frightened." Mr. C. opens his eyes wide and lets his jaw hang down. Everyone laughs except your husband.

"They can be quite dangerous," your husband says, once the laughter has stopped. "Sometimes they can kill you." He makes a crushing motion with his hand, as if it were the trunk of an elephant strangling someone. He looks as if he would like that to happen: for wild elephants to kill the people who cut down forests.

Then Mr. C. tells a story about a monkey at his office on the outskirts of Bangalore, where the thick banyan trees are alive with scrawny brown monkeys. Mostly they leave you alone, he says, unless you feed them. Once, he made the mistake of leaving his lunch in the basket of his scooter, and when he returned, it was gone. He never even found the lunchbox.

Mishti shakes her head and smiles. "That is not the only lunchbox you have lost," she says.

"I don't have to pack lunches," you say. "He prefers hot food at the cafeteria."

"Well, anyway . . . ," Mr. C. continues. There was this monkey at his work. She sat on the roof of his office all day. He saw her when he arrived that morning, and again in the evening when he left. At first, he thought she might have been sick or hurt, because she stayed apart from the others, who swung in the trees nearby. When he came back the next day, she was still there. She sat on the roof in the sun, and when it rained, she took shelter under the eaves. She couldn't have eaten or drunk in the time she sat there. It was then Mr. C. noticed that she held a baby; its head drooped off her arm. A dead baby. Stiff, still, silent.

On the third day, Mr. Chatterji was anxious to get to work to see what had happened to the monkey. She was still there, holding her baby, staring straight ahead of her. Sometimes she groomed the baby's head for lice for a brief spell, then went back to staring.

At the dining table, where the four of you are eating, there is silence — a silence of the careful pulling of bones from fish with finger and thumb. As you eat, you think how it might be to love this man from Calcutta, this man who watched a monkey grieve for three days on the roof of his office. He is quiet, food drying on his fingers, on his plate. He mixes some rice and vegetables with his fingers, bends forward, and places the food in his mouth. He is looking at the vegetables, the green peppers. You have the idea that he looks at the food you have cooked the same way he did the monkey with the dead baby.

You spoon some vegetables onto his plate, because it is nearly empty. He waves his hands over it, meaning *Enough*.

"What *masala* have you put in here?" he asks after another mouthful.

"No *masala*," you say, stealing a glance at your husband, who dislikes the way you cook green peppers. Your cooking style is west coast, Bombay, different from his family's Bengali cooking.

"No *masala*," you repeat, "just a little *besan*."

"It's very good." Mr. C.'s cheeks crease into a smile again, as he looks at you through his dark-framed glasses.

You wave your hand, dismissing his compliment. "Probably because it is a new taste for you."

You have scored a point here. Your husband has lost a point. You hope he has not noticed, because if he has, there will be trouble: *No one could eat that awful green mess you cooked. Next time, clear the menu with me before you embarrass me in front of people like that.* You watch your husband's face. He is playing with a fish bone, tapping it on the edge of his plate. There may be punishment later: words, silence, other things.

"Everything tastes better at someone else's house," you say. Your laugh swells in the silence. The sweet wife nods. She can never eat her own cooking, she says. Her mother's, her mother-in-law's, anyone's is better than hers.

You avoid the wife's eye (and your husband's) because you are thinking about this man and how you are a little in love with him. In love with the way he looks at things: at mourning monkeys, at your cooking, at you. You think how easy it would be to love this man who is not your husband.

And that is what you have done for the last two years, with different men, for the same reasons. For the way one shares an orange with his wife on a park bench. For the way another reads jokes aloud from the newspaper at breakfast. For the way this one enjoys your green peppers. You wonder if you are crazy, wicked, wild, what? What are you? You don't know. But at that instant, when you avoid your husband's eye and serve more peppers to your guest, you know your husband understands your treachery. He understands that infidelity that does not involve opening your legs, but opening your mind, the entering of another man through some hidden door inside you, and you don't know which one, where, how. And he, your husband, to whom the door closed long ago, can accuse you of nothing. Nothing.

"Go get the dessert!" His voice startles everyone. "It's getting late. We don't want to hold our guests up." He lowers his voice when he realizes that everyone is looking at him. "She has no time sense," he says to the engineer in the dark-framed glasses. "First the rice is cold, and now this."

You push back your chair to get the sweets.

"Did anyone feed her anything?" your husband asks.

No one appears to have heard his question. Mishti drinks her water. The engineer goes to wash his hands. You lay out the desserts on small plates.

"Did anyone feed the monkey anything?" your husband asks again.

"What?" your guest says, as if he did not understand.

And you think the same: *What?* Though later, when you look back on it, you will realize that your husband is not a bad man. He also felt for the monkey; that is clear from his question.

"Did no one offer her any food?" he asks once more, looking from one person to the other in exasperation.

"Would you like a *gulab jamun*, or a *rasgulla*?" you ask your husband, holding out the dessert tray.

"It never occurred to anyone to offer her food," the engineer from Indore Engineering College, Indore, says, shrugging his shoulders.

Your husband shakes his head in disbelief at the stupidity of people. He reaches for the *rasgulla* you have offered him. Everyone eats in silence.

That night, your husband wants to get inside you. He grips your wrist, and though you want to resist, you don't, because he is your husband. Afterward, in compensation, he asks if you want water. You are not thirsty, but he insists that you have some anyway, and you do, a little sip to freshen your mouth. Your husband watches you, but you are thinking of a dead monkey and trees and offices and a man in black-framed glasses watching from below. You smile at the thought of this man in black-framed glasses, and how his face creases when he smiles, and how his eyes shine, and how the sun looks in his hair as he watches the monkey. How beautiful the sun. ■

Her Shoes

by ALISON SEEVAK

I was wearing sandals the afternoon
we ran into your wife downtown.
No pantyhose because it was August and I was 22,
the weight of the world not yet upon me.
I remember how you dropped my hand in time,
suggested the cafeteria, where the three of us ate lunch.
I do not remember how you introduced us,
only that she wore pumps, brown leather, stiff.
I had a chef salad that afternoon.
And when I saw the two of you step out of line
with the daily special on your trays,
meatloaf, mashed potatoes, gravy, even in that heat,
I knew that I had been kidding myself.
You would never leave her.
I looked at your wife's feet under the table.
What I saw was that one day I would be 35, too.
A woman who would wear shoes
that fit just fine in the store.
They wouldn't bother her until she wore them a few times.
But by then, she really couldn't bring them back.
It would be too late.

And Passion Most Of All

by **MICHELLE CACHO-NEGRETE**

"**M**y life is leaking out of me like the water from this garden hose," my friend says, and wiggles the spray nozzle at me. A trickle of water darkens the sleeve of her sweater. Some shrug of shoulder or downward turn of lip betrays my reluctance to surrender hope. She shakes her head and warns, "Shape up. You don't have much time left to reach the stage of acceptance."

She lifts the hose to her lips to drink. Water drizzles down her chin and comes to rest in a shimmering pendant against her throat. "Rubbery." She grimaces and tosses the hose to the ground. A widening rainbow begins to arc around the nozzle. My friend's shoulders relax, her eyes lose focus, and she meditates on the transformation of water and light into some glistening new thing.

A certain stillness has replaced the restlessness that's characterized her as long as we've been friends. I check my watch — one hour until her doctor's appointment — and stretch out in a lounge chair, one of two shaded by a sugar maple in blazing regalia. Despite the dry autumn, the grass is lush. My friend waters diligently, mourning each flowering annual as its season for life passes. Russet and gold have overtaken the soft green of summer, but mums spike up purple, yellow, and white in their raised beds. Three of her rosebushes are studded with tiny, hard hips, prepared for winter, but the fourth, a cottage rose, in stubborn disregard of the cold nights, is flooded with pink buds even as the petals of spent blossoms curl and drop. The tenacity of the bush delights her, and she feeds it against all advice that it be encouraged to go quietly dormant.

"The roses and I are in a contest," she said when I arrived. "Which of us will hold out the longest." When I didn't respond, she cocked her head at my silence and said, "Get with it." Her eyes were hard. I knew then that she was going to be relentless and wouldn't give up until I acknowledged the truth.

The hose gives a final, hissing spurt as she twists shut the faucet on the side of the house. I close my eyes and try to meditate using a mantra she taught me. She insisted I'd enjoy meditating, but my mind scurries from the book I'm writing, to my husband's upcoming business trip, to problems with my psychotherapy clients. The lounge chair beside me creaks, and I open my eyes. She's moved it over a foot into the late-morning sun, and she rests there now with closed eyes, her pale face slathered with sunblock. Her hipbones jut out against her dark jeans. Her silver hair has grown back in the short curls of Roman boys in old frescoes. As if she knows I'm looking at her, she reaches over and pats my hand.

"Shouldn't you move out of the sun?" I ask.

She shakes her head. "I'll have lots of time to be in the dark."

I packed my car with Maine icons for this visit: soap and moisturizer from Tom's of Maine; photographs of the coast; real maple syrup; a ceramic crow from a gallery in Portland; an L.L. Bean vest; a poster from the Portland Museum of Art. In honor of our history of junk shopping, I added an exotic gypsy scarf, gaudy dangling earrings, six mystery books, and two cashmere sweaters from the Salvation Army. My husband watched as I layered it all on my back seat. "Hug her for me," he said. He hesitated, then added, "Tell her I'll see her soon."

I nodded, but we both knew it was a crapshoot.

She ran out to the driveway when I arrived, and glowed when I threw open the car's back door and began to fill her arms with gifts.

"That's all?" she said. "Are you sure you didn't forget anything?"

After dinner each night, we watch reruns of her favorite shows. In the darkness of the living room, images flicker across the screen, and time accordions back into itself: Alan Alda is maturely handsome rather than time-ravaged; William Shatner is not yet camp. We have returned to an era before polluted air and water, extinction of species, and glacial melting. We're back in a long-ago time when only other people died.

This morning my face in the mirror was drawn, eyes already saying goodbye. Time is slipping away from me. "Why her?" I whispered to my reflection. My mother, my brother, my first husband's grandparents and aunt, two other friends, and a writer I knew: all dead. Also Andre Dubus, François Truffaut, Raymond Carver, Janis Joplin, Jimi Hendrix, Billie Holiday, and millions more, known and unknown.

Nobody survives life.

At breakfast, my friend ate a spoonful of oatmeal and examined me. "You look like shit."

"Thanks," I answered. "I'm going to meditate on that."

She laughed and said, "Let's go sit in the yard after I water."

In the lounge chair, my friend opens her eyes and looks at my watch. "Time to go." She threw her own watch in the trash when she learned she was dying. "Time is relative," she said. "A day with my son when he's home from college is shorter than a second; a twenty-minute wait for the results of a test is longer than a year. Dying will take as long as it takes."

My friend stands in a single, graceful motion, and I realize she's been practicing how to move as if she were still healthy. She stops beside the cottage rose and beckons to me. "Let's go. I don't have forever." Her fingernails and toenails are painted the same vibrant pink as the roses. She flashed them at me when I first arrived — she was wearing sandals despite the chilly fall weather — and said, "We're having a girly party later, and I'm polishing yours."

Our friendship had begun when we were both young mothers, and now she was offering an escape to an adolescent past we hadn't shared. "OK," I agreed, "but I refuse to watch *Gidget* and drink Coke while you do it."

So now my fingernails, too, are bright pink.

"Don't worry about those," my friend says as I carry the lounge chairs to her porch.

"It might rain," I protest.

"Where?" she asks. "In India?" It's true: we haven't seen a cloud all week. She bends to sniff one of the roses. Pain floods her face, and she places a hand against the curve of her back. My throat knots with sorrow. She looks up to hurry me, sees my expression, and quickly plunges her nose back into the petals. I clear my throat and say, "Let's go."

Once we're belted into the car, she turns to me, squares her shoulders, and says, "Ready?"

I nod, and we grab the handles that open our windows. "OK," she says. "Ready, set, . . . go!"

We both crank furiously, but she opens her window first. She raises her hands in a gesture of triumph. "Winner and still champion. You buy lunch — again."

"I'll win next time," I say as I back out into the road.

"Ha," she scoffs, and leans out the window. The brim of her green cap snaps in the wind. As the car picks up speed, she pulls her head back in to say, "You're running out of time to win."

Relentless, I think, then answer, "There's the trip back home."

"No," she says quietly. "We both know I'm going to be first." She leans out the window, but not before I catch a glimpse of the fear in her eyes.

At the oncologist's office, we sit in the waiting room, which is painted blue and pink like a nursery. Thin rays of light sneak in through closed blinds and rest on the flat beige carpet. The radio plays music you forget even as you hear it. Vapid watercolors break up a stretch of wall. The only other patient is a gaunt man with eyes like the last, lingering coals of a fire. He sits across from us wearing a crisp white shirt and paisley tie and restlessly fingering an issue of the *New Yorker.* A heavy sweater and fedora lie beside him, and his gray hair is the length of new spring grass. His expression is wry and a little bitter.

My friend cocks her head at the Muzak and says, "Steely Dan would drop dead if they heard this version of 'Dr. Wu.'" The man laughs. "So, is this where you come to loosen up?" my friend says to him, and I realize by her tone that she's flirting.

"Yes, and what's a nice girl like you doing in a place like this?" he asks. He's wearing a wedding band. So is my friend.

"Where else can you get a cocktail with this kind of kick?" She shimmies her shoulders provocatively. I'm astonished to see him give a quick, self-conscious shimmy back.

The man's name is called, and he rises, makes a drinking motion, and pretends to stagger through the door to the doctor's office. My friend burps noisily, as though she's had too much to drink, and the receptionist looks up and smiles vacantly.

Once the man is gone, my friend says, "I should have at least one affair before I die." She sighs, but her eyes gleam.

I swallow hard and glance at her shocking pink nails. "Hey, we've only got one life to live."

Her laugh tells me I've said the right thing, a feat that's getting harder to accomplish.

As the wait drags on, my friend fidgets and whispers loudly, "Who has this much time to kill?" The receptionist blinks rapidly but doesn't look up. My friend stares out the window, and I memorize her profile. I miss her already. My first marriage, my children, my younger son's surgery, my divorce, my present marriage — I imagine it's impossible for an event to occur in my life if she's not there to witness it.

She turns to me and says, "I felt that."

"Where is all this telepathy coming from?" I ask.

"I'm practicing channeling," she answers. "First on the receiving end, later on the sending."

"Are you going to be this relentless the whole visit?"

"It depends on you," she says. "It may need to be the whole visit."

The magazine she has put down lies open to a quiz with the title "Do You Have the Courage to Dream Big?"

"Let's take it," I suggest.

We roll our eyes at each inane question about decorating your house, choosing a car, changing makeup. The gravity of the tone suggests that meticulous attention to such trappings is essential to achieving harmony.

The final question is "Are you excited about every new adventure?"

"I lose," my friend says, and closes the magazine.

I'm struck hard by the bleakness in her voice, and I grab her hand. Just then the doctor's door opens, and the other patient steps out, buttoning the sleeves of his shirt. He's paler than when he went in and looks uncertain of where he is, until he sees my friend. He sits down and says, "I need to wait, just in case I have a reaction to the injection."

The nurse calls for my friend. As she passes the man, her long leg brushes his knee. "Is that all you're waiting for?"

His eyes lighten, and he answers, "Maybe not all." He watches her vanish behind the closed door, then turns to me and smiles. I'm suddenly self-conscious about my fingernails, as though I haven't earned the right to wear such a brave shade of pink.

We sit silently, turning the pages of magazines and watching the play of light on the carpet until my friend swings open the door of the doctor's office. She sees the man and asks, "No bad reaction?"

"Oh, that," he says. "I forgot about that. I'm just hanging out and soaking up the ambiance."

She puts a hand on his shoulder and asks, "Can you tear yourself away from the music and join us for lunch?"

He immediately stands, pulls his sweater over his head, adjusts the fedora, and cocks an arm for each of us. "Let's go," he says. "I'm dying of hunger."

My friend laughs and takes his arm. "We're going to a little organic restaurant I love."

"Perfect," he says.

Outside, milky clouds drift across the sky. The sun is bitterly bright for early autumn.

"I'll follow you," he says, and he opens his car door and slides in. "Drive slowly." I nod, and my friend pats his hand on the steering wheel. When he looks at her, the expression on his face is so stark and naked that I turn away.

On the road, she watches his car in the side mirror and leans out the window to wave. When I stop at a red light, she applies lipstick and face powder, pursing her lips at how dry and flaky her skin is. I feel my heart break.

We eat winter-squash soup and endive salad at a table beneath a picture window. Sun filters through gauze curtains. The restaurant is quiet; we've come between lunch and dinner. Each table has a small rose.

When we first sat down, my friend leaned over to sniff our rose, then announced with disappointment, "They're scentless."

"You like roses?" the man asked.

"I love them," she said. "I have one still putting out blossoms, as if it hasn't figured out summer's over."

"A fighter," he answered.

Throughout the meal, they laugh and talk in a complex language of medications, treatments, and experimental programs. It's not a graceful dialect, yet they speak it as if it were a Romance language. My friend eats with more appetite than I've seen her show in a while, nodding enthusiastically and waving her fork in the air to make a point. The man pushes his plate away and rests his face on his hands to watch her.

They have a lot in common: She reviewed books in her "former life," and he's an avid reader. She's a computer whiz, and he was a science teacher. They both love museums. His wife owns a business and travels all the time; ever since my friend received her "sentence," as she calls it, her husband, an executive for a computer company, has been working late and is always at a conference somewhere.

"He's buying new suits and watching his diet," she says as she takes a last forkful of salad, then pushes her plate away. Her mouth twists. "He and I have both grown thinner, only not together. I hardly miss him anymore." She takes my hand.

The man looks at us sadly, then reaches across the table and squeezes both our hands. I'm a little bit in love with him, too, the aplomb with which he handles himself.

They discover more commonalities: They both take their sleeping pills and painkillers sparingly. They both refused a second round of chemotherapy, believing it wasn't worth the misery just to have a few more months. They both employ a regimen of vitamins and herbs prescribed by the same neighborhood naturopath.

"Hell," my friend says, "I've never felt better in my life." She leans toward the man seductively, a mannerism left over from a time when she still had breasts. Leaves tremble outside the window, and shadows flicker over her.

"And you look great," the man says, leaning forward. "I can't believe you've ever been more beautiful."

Their fingers meet across the table. There is something glowing inside her that I haven't seen for years, a feverish light that ignites her. I suddenly imagine a miracle, something beyond medical science. I know she would laugh derisively at me if she knew I had such thoughts.

We order coffee, and my friend takes hers with cream, a luxury she never allowed herself before. She and I order chocolate cake. The man gets apple pie. They exchange tastes of their desserts. There is a haze around them of midafternoon light, their skin as translucent as rice paper, blue veins as delicate as map lines. Everything is slowed down. It seems to take an hour for his pie-laden fork to reach her lips.

The man insists on paying the bill. "It's our first date," he jokes. He generously includes me.

Outside they exchange telephone numbers and then graze cheeks. The man leans over to kiss me, as well. "See you," he says.

"I hope so," I answer honestly.

He walks to his car, waving over his shoulder. His stride is a little stiff but still fluid: a man traveling a path between the middle and end stages of a terminal disease. My friend watches him go.

Back in the car, she rolls her window down before I'm even in my seat. "Hey, no fair," I protest.

"Sometimes you've just got to cheat," she tells me.

At the house she laughs at the lounge chairs that I folded neatly on the porch and holds her palm out mockingly, feeling for nonexistent rain. I'm preparing herbal tea when her husband calls from Washington, D.C., where he's attending a conference. She holds the cordless phone in one hand and with the other picks up a spoon and plays a row of glasses on the counter.

"Nothing's changed," she tells him. "No, nothing's worse, and nothing's better." She's quiet. Then, "No, had lunch with a man we met at the doctor's office, the three of us." She's quiet again, then stares directly into my eyes and says briskly, as though reciting a weather report, "The same as mine, hopeless." A muscle twitches in her jaw, and the spoon speeds up, bouncing between glasses. "Nothing," she says, and stops tapping. "Some noise from outside." After a moment she tells him, "No, don't call. I'll be asleep by then." She plays the glasses again, gently, a crystal symphony. "Yes, goodbye."

She hangs up and turns to me. "Bastard," she says. "He's getting impatient."

We sit in the yard, wrapped in light blankets, drinking tea and watching the sun leave the sky. The phone rings, and my friend goes inside to answer it. When she returns, her eyes are thoughtful. "Would you mind if I went out for a while this evening?" she asks. The blazing sunset casts an orange aura around her.

I feign shock and say, "Do I know this boy? Don't get into the car if the driver has been drinking."

"I promise," she says. Then she fiercely embraces me. I feel her tears against my cheek, and she trembles. I rub her back and think of her husband, absent and remote almost since her illness began. I suddenly hate him and know he is no longer a part of this equation. She has friends who love her, women who will rally around her and do anything she asks. But there are needs that friends can't meet. She is counting on this man, and he is counting on her. Time has collapsed, like a building falling in on itself, and what could take weeks to develop in ordinary time has transpired in an afternoon.

I suddenly want her to die before the man does. I don't want her to suffer his vanishing and be left behind to wait for her own end.

I've reached acceptance at last.

"Is this a good idea?" I whisper to her.

"Because I'm married?" she asks bitterly.

"No."

She steps away from me and studies my face. "Yes," she says, "you're finally there. And yes, it's a good idea."

I feel an unexpected flash of jealousy when her car pulls out of the driveway a half-hour later. I promised her I'd try to meditate, but I can't sit still, and I wander around her house, as worried as I was when my children went out at night. I touch her things, as familiar as my own: The old table we bought at a yard sale and lugged home, carrying it between us, putting it down every few minutes. The ridiculous crystal chandelier we found at Goodwill. A photograph taken when we were both still married to our first husbands, our faces earnest and unlined; a picture of a time before illness. There are books we both own, records we've shared: Miles Davis, John Coltrane. I walk from room to room crying, knowing that when she is gone I will never see these rooms, these things again.

Feeling edgy, I pour a glass of wine. My mind is whirling too fast for me to read. I climb into bed with a second glass and click on the television: a rerun of *Star Trek*. I want to be "beamed" out of this reality. I fluff the pillows and settle down, listening anxiously for her car in the driveway. *Don't be an idiot,* I admonish myself. An automobile accident would be too ironic.

I n the morning I find my friend drinking coffee at the kitchen table, a bouquet of roses in the center. I kiss the top of her head, and she smiles up at me. There's a softness to her features, a luminosity to her skin. She seems younger in the gentle morning light, the woman I met when we were twenty-something. I pour a cup of coffee, sniff the roses, and ask, "You had fun?" It's a rhetorical question.

"When was the last time you sat up half the night talking and necking and making stupid jokes?" she asks dreamily.

"Too far back to remember." I take a sip of coffee.

My friend giggles at some private thought, and the sound is so delightful that I giggle, too.

Last year, in a phone conversation, she said wistfully, "I miss passion most of all." Now she is experiencing not the frantic carnality of young adulthood, nor the comfortable familiarity of middle-aged partners, but the thrilling kisses and hand-holding of a teenage crush.

She takes my hand. There's fear in her eyes, but also something else: a brief staying power that has made time bend in some crazy, forgiving way, like a Möbius strip, a geometric anomaly with no beginning or end. Past, present, and future are melting together. Events of long ago are happening even as we remember them. And her smile is so alive, so radiant that I stop time right here. ■

Prayer For Your Wife

by KATHLEEN LAKE

That she blondly beam
like the lantern of my silence
When she steps out onto the wide
veranda, that birds gather for her
in the snow   That she sleep
like sea foam   That the whites of her eyes roll
startle-bright as the unbroken steed
That she never lose speed
That she wonder about me
That she bleed
with you for the planet   That you uphold her
when storms come   That the o of her womb be red,
and fertile as the sound of Barbados
That you honor where she curves
toward you, and where away   That she play
by the fire   That she never drop the pitcher
full of blue stars
on Sunday morning   That she laugh, that she always know
what is true   That she bold and delirious grow
next to you   That her body be a welcome
That she wake up praying
That her fingers leave a brush of greenery
in all the corners   That air be ample
That dust forsake her
That she wear heavy wisdom like a light

silk veil   That she wrap herself in being
your chosen   Every morning,
that you be the first thing
she sees   That her eyes wash clear
That she remember all
her choices   That she fill herself
at the deepest wells   That she lift herself
into dancing blind   That she balance fruit
on her head like a juggler
That her toes flash like tetras
That she smile in the mirror
That you smile
on each other as the shade smiles
up at the tree
That she not feel like me
That all three of us should be free

Everything I Thought Would Happen

by **ASHLEY WALKER**

In July 1971 my father's heart exploded, and, faced with a comfort-less, parent-snatching universe, I said to my husband, "We need to move out of this city. I'm afraid of becoming one of those assholes who wear aviator sunglasses and scream at cabdrivers." In fact, I already *was* one of those assholes and had been for quite some time. Still, I was growing jumpy with life in Boston and uneasy with the hard edges I had gone to such trouble to get. My husband smiled mildly and agreed, then disagreed, and finally agreed again, and we set off for Iowa in our vw. He didn't want to go, and I didn't care if he did nor not, but we weren't ready to face that yet.

We left for Iowa because we both knew that after you'd labored in the city until you felt as charred as a bad steak, it was time to go live a simpler life with the ducks and bunnies. The hippie wisdom then was to grab land in Nova Scotia and farm it, or build a geodesic dome out of old car parts in the Mojave, or grow dope in Oregon, and, however you could manage it, save your immortal soul and mortal ass.

It was a generational idea — that we could peel ourselves away from a lousy capitalist society and hammer together a utopia out of notions from Marx, Rousseau, Esalen, Stewart Brand, and the movies. We believed we could do it at a moment's notice; all we needed was to pack up the van and head toward some trees. We had an untested faith that a cleansing dunk in nature could launder away soul sickness. We would be transformed. Easily.

My husband and I made our quarrelsome way west from Massachusetts to a solid, square house in the middle of an Iowa cornfield that backed up to thick woods. As we curled together in the unfamiliar, pitch-black nights of the country, we heard shotguns booming in the darkness outside. Our neighbor to the right looked like Mammy Yokum and poured her garbage straight out the kitchen window. When the plains winter howled like a big animal and licked at the cracks around the doors and windows, people across the way piled up hay bales around their rusty trailers. Someone a mile down the road nailed a rotting deer head high on a telephone pole, and someone else got hauled off for child molestation. One night, I drank six boilermakers in a row and heaved them up into a bush near our house. My vomit froze on contact and hung there until late March.

We tried out the local customs. I boiled cow heart on our undependable electric stove — which housed a mouse family in the lid drawer — and sliced the rubbery stuff up to make big, resilient sandwiches. Like the natives, I made "finger jello" by combining twelve packages of Knox gelatin with one package of Jell-O. Iowans seemed to prefer foods with the texture and bounce of erasers. Meanwhile, in hippie-approved proletarian style, my husband drove a forklift on the graveyard shift. Amazingly, he still had enough energy left over to crank up an affair with a large, depressed woman in his free-clinic therapy group. He and I both wore waffle-weave long underwear around the clock. Enveloped by our identical parkas, we searched for the VW buried in stiff, dirty snow; we stamped sullenly in the cold, jabbing at icy mounds with a broom handle. Once a week, we got together a collection of wrinkled bags and sifted odd, purplish grains at the New Pioneer Food Co-op. I cooked groats and made heavy, chewy breads that had an obscure, soapy taste.

By seven o'clock each evening it was like midnight on an ice floe outside the black windows. Exhausted from doing unfamiliar things we hated, we'd sag together in our cold living room, tired of the weather — which was as unrelenting as bad news — too irritable even to fight with one another. Each night, my husband worked on a novel about an Indian basketball player in Lone Wolf, Oklahoma; the entire book consisted of a single internal monologue by the Indian narrator as he stood at the free-throw line. As winter deepened, the Indian's thoughts got crazier. Guiltily, disloyally — correctly — I suspected the book was unpublishable. As I wondered why I was saddled with an adulterous husband who was a terrible writer to boot, my self-pity bloomed moonily.

My mind wandered back a million years, before I'd been married, to my life in Washington, D.C. There, I'd clatter to my low-paying fashion job wearing a pink mohair dress and alligator heels, my fake Sassoon bob tied back with pink grosgrain ribbon. The dress had been paid for on layaway, the shoes had been warehouse discount, and I'd cut my hair myself, but in the city the illusion worked and I was as much a part of the place as the pigeons at my feet. Sometimes I'd go out with a government wonk as young and badly paid as I was, and we'd drink whiskey sours until 2 A.M. in a piano bar overlooking the glittering city, where everyone was still awake. In Iowa, thinking back on that time, it seemed as if I'd been a character in a story about someone else.

As I tossed wads of paper for my cat to retrieve and listened to my husband typing his rotten book, I decided my abrupt move to Woodstock Nation was symptomatic of a deep character flaw running through me like a fault line. The problem was I treated the world like a cafeteria, selecting a little of this, a chunk of that, a small dish here, a piece of pie there, certain I could make something tasty out of what existence offered me. Too greedy to discriminate, I bounced from choice to choice driven by conflicting and cloudy notions of duty and romance, making decisions variously as a wife, a painter, a hippie, a grad student. I found it easier to paste labels on myself than to consider what on earth I was doing.

With no television, few books, and, for all practical purposes, no husband to distract me, I couldn't run away from my moods. Nor could I escape by bustling around the house doing extraneous chores, as I sometimes had in the past; our landlord, a kind, hyperactive farmer, had not only laid carpet and installed paneling but, inexplicably, surrounded the tub, sink, and counters with brick. There wasn't much for me to do other than hose off the surfaces now and then and wonder why the inside of my house looked just like the outside.

Alone in the cold, bricked-up living room, I was thrown back on myself, and all the thoughts I'd tried to silence returned uninvited. *I don't belong here* echoed over and over in my head, faithfully, clearly, repetitively. *I don't belong here.* By *here* I thought I meant the country. I would never feel any fondness for the red-faced hunters who strapped hulking deer carcasses on their truck hoods; I would never like our sly, gap-toothed neighbors squatting contentedly amid old car parts; I would always dread finding all the dead varmints my cat lined up on the doorstep night after night; and I would always hate the freezing drive into town and feel like weeping when it came time to leave.

Late at night I heard another, graver voice: *I don't love him.* I'd heard that voice before, but hadn't wanted to listen. Questions boiled up inside me: *What were these years all about? Where will I go? Who will ever love me? Will I ever love anyone? How could I make a mistake this big?* As it turned out, my bout in the Iowa gulag gave me what I'd hoped to find by fleeing to the country, although not the comic-book version I'd imagined. By saying to myself steadily and resentfully, *No, not this, not this,* I gradually came to know what I wanted. Cold, boredom, and the hatefulness of my life wore me down to a more honest nub.

Had we not been so cooped up and isolated, I don't know if I would have realized the truth so speedily. In cities and college towns, we'd been distracted by our busyness, which was of a particular, urban sort: *going out.* We were always going out, he and I: to film festivals, poetry readings, demonstrations, lectures, dinners, friends' houses, bars, exhibits, vigils, rallies. In the country, on the other hand, it appeared the objective was to *stay in*: from the snow, the wet, the bad roads. Once in, we were faced with each other and our own disinterest. Perhaps if we'd been real rustics and not weenies, we would have sharpened tools, quilted, made jelly, or cleaned our guns. Instead, we adopted rotten habits.

I drank. Having discovered a warm bar where construction workers, hippies, and art students hung out, I wandered in as often as I could and drank beer after beer, chattering pointlessly. At home I smoked dope, and from time to time in my studio I took speed: purple hearts, white crosses, Christmas trees, crank.

As for my husband, he went nuts methodically. Businesslike, he roamed from biofeedback to hypnosis to regression to massage before settling into a therapy group. Every so often he would break out in a wild, hollering rage and storm around the house waving his arms, blaming me. We stayed even. I was prone to drunken outbursts in which I shattered dishes and screamed accusations at him. *You you you you you*, we both ranted. *If it weren't for you* . . . Our art was dragged into the uproar. He brought home depressed women from his group to have them read his ghastly novel while, across town, I made quaky sketches on bar napkins.

I wasn't happy with the drama reverberating around us. My drunkenness and his nuttiness seemed bogus — like badly written parts we'd been given at the last minute. Back then, I believed marriages ended only for large, horrific reasons: gambling with the grocery money, an affair with the paperboy, an unexplained disappearance to Mexico. It seemed too petty, too ordinary to say I was just sad, I didn't care, and my life was dreary. It wasn't much of a story. It was the kind of revelation that would be greeted only with indifference. So rather than telling the truth — that I irritated him and he bored me — we played with booze and madness like two children left alone with a box of kitchen matches.

Still, our lives went on. He worked in the factory and I painted in my freezing studio above the WeeWashit Laundromat. The images I made then were flat, sharp, bladelike forms I called *Iowa Weeds*. I claimed to have gotten the idea from the meadow outside our house. Actually I didn't think about the meadow at all, except about how I'd like to burn it off and pour a concrete slab for parking. What I really thought about was a city. I'd never been to this city, but I could picture it. It had big, curving freeways with triple lanes of traffic that rose on pylons and circled in intricate, scary cloverleafs. The buildings were made of green glass that reflected the light like sunglasses. At night, from overhead, city lights glittered red and yellow for miles on either side with the cheeriness of costume jewelry. The city roared with trucks and with planes coming in to land and with the perpetual sound of traffic. The city was crowded, crammed with people I'd never have time to meet, whom I'd never know, people who were black and brown and red and yellow and white, who chattered over the din of traffic and led lives as complicated as mine.

The image bewildered me. I'd never lived in a city like it. The East Coast cities I knew — Boston, New York, Washington — were as comfortable as flannel. This city of my waking dreams was like Oz, remote and glittering. It scared me. It wasn't a city with subways, pizza by the slice, and parks where old men played boccie. It was a place where I'd have to drive a big car in murderous traffic, where I'd find a job in a remote glass building, where I'd be alone. It was a cruel place, and I was haunted by it.

In my everyday world, I was tired of drinking and tired of buying dope from my hearty Swedish dealer. I despised the cold and slush. I hated the gray-brown grass that poked through the snow outside my house. Mostly, I felt crappy about having married someone I didn't love. It seemed like the worst thing I'd ever done, and I decided the only decent thing to do was leave.

I composed a short, brisk speech that made no mention of love or the lack of it but merely suggested that we were going different ways. One night, while we ate dinner, I recited it to my husband. He looked at me with cold, flat, fishy eyes and didn't speak. I rambled on nervously about how we wanted different things and we weren't making each other happy. I said I thought we ought to separate.

When I'd finished, my husband told me I was sneaky, that he'd had no idea I felt like this, that out of nowhere I'd bopped him on the head with it. Silently, I agreed with him, but for different reasons; I *had* been very sneaky lately, in unpredictable ways.

For one thing, I was shoplifting. I'd stolen three eye shadows just that week. I observed my own behavior curiously; it seemed as if chunks of me were snapping off. *This must be what's meant by a breakdown,* I thought. Parts of me I'd always taken for granted were chipping away like the edges of a shoreline. I'd never cheated on a test, never lied on my taxes, never stolen anything. I was astonished how easy it was and how little it bothered me.

After I'd brought up the idea of a separation, we entered a DMZ of the heart. Mostly, we were carefully polite and didn't talk much beyond inquiring whether the other wanted butter or had slept well. It was as though we were two lone riders on the high plains who'd stopped to talk, eyeing each other squintingly, about to wheel off in opposite directions. We didn't know what to say now. We'd been married ten years, and we'd already said a lot, most of it hurtful.

One night, sitting in my bricked-in bathtub under the yellow overhead light, I began to cry noisily like a child. Hearing me, my husband raced into the bathroom and knelt by the tub. "It's just so sad," I wailed, my face red from the steam and tears bouncing down my cheeks. "We've loved each other so much, and now it's all *gone*." My husband knelt by the brick edge of the tub and cried too — loudly, even histrionically. *Has he always been such a bad actor?* I thought. At that moment, there was a twang in my skull like a guitar string breaking, and I felt myself go cold inside. Suddenly the room seemed too bright, illuminating in embarrassing starkness my blotchy skin, my knees poking up like a couple of undiscovered islands, my hair lank and ratty. I abruptly quit crying and patted my husband's hand while he wept shining, phony tears. "Hey, it's OK," I told him, wanting him to shut up. "It's OK."

Our encounter in the tub haunted me for years afterward. Of course, I was the one who was a phony. I was crying because it seemed sad I'd spent so many years pretending to feel what I didn't feel. I was crying because there was no payback.

After that, selling my belongings seemed like a reasonable thing to do — selling them little by little, selling what I was sure would not be missed, saying nothing. We stopped being polite. I existed in icy reticence, squirreling away money, hiding out in my studio, hunting for an apartment in Iowa City. At home, my silence became even more pronounced. In response, my husband began to yell. He hollered steadily from the time we got up each morning until I left for the day. When I returned each night, he was still roaring, the splintered bits of whatever furniture he'd destroyed that day scattered around the house. He bellowed nonstop, not even pausing to sleep; I'd lie in bed with pillows tight over my head like earmuffs, out of ideas. After several days of this, I drove into town, leaving him to destroy the house, his shouts and crashes echoing in the distance.

I drove straight to the mental-health clinic and stalked into the office of my husband's psychiatrist. I'd never met him before. He was spooky, his skin the color of Roquefort, his hair and beard yellowy white. Wrapped in a wrinkled black raincoat, he looked like a prune. His young girlfriend was folded into a z shape on the couch, looking moist and plump. She stared at me blankly, chewing her lower lip, while I beat on the doctor's desk with my skinny fists. "When is this silly son of a bitch going to get well?" I shouted. "All he does is break up the furniture and yell. Coming here has just made him a better nut. He knows more ways now to *be* a nut and more reasons *why* he's a nut." I ripped open my parka. "I weigh eighty-nine pounds. He's making *me* nuts, too. Are you going to cure him, or what?"

"Oh, my," the doctor said mildly. He lit a Kool, drew on it hard, and coughed. "I had no idea. No, I didn't know he was like that at all. No, indeed."

"So what should I do?" I asked him, really wanting to know.

"I think," the doctor told me carefully, pausing to tap the ash from his cigarette, "I think it would be a very good idea for you to leave him. Would you like some Valium?"

Now my life began to move very quickly. A friend who was leaving town offered me her apartment, another friend let me borrow his truck, and, after we'd divided our belongings straight down the middle, I left my husband forever.

I lived in town, had a series of apartments, a series of jobs, a series of boyfriends. Nothing was stable but my habit of painting every day. During off hours, I applied for jobs out of state. For some reason, the jobs I applied for were nearly all in Texas. The University at the Permian Basin had an opening in the art department year after year. I loved the name. Saying the words *Permian Basin* to myself, I imagined the taste of salt in my mouth, palm trees, gulf waters, and large, leaping fish. There was also another picture in my head: of a perfectly round, hot sun high up in a sky as hard and blue as enamel; of brown, stubbly grass; of a horizon stretched like a pencil line dividing sky and earth. It was a picture from the paperback cover of Larry McMurtry's *Movin' On*, which I'd read sometime back. It had made me want to travel around photographing rodeos.

As it happened, I moved to Dallas to teach for six months. Flying into Dallas–Fort Worth at night, I looked down at the shining lights scattered below me while a drunken cowboy kicked the back of my seat with a pointy boot.

"Wassa pretty gal like you doin' in Texas?" he asked over and over while I gawked.

As the plane dipped lower and lower through the bruise-colored sky and the boot whammed into my seat again and again — "Wassa li'l gal like you gon' do here?" — I finally said, "I think this is where I'm going to live."

It turned out I was right. I came to Dallas and never left. Unlike with the country, everything I'd imagined about the city was true, and everything I'd thought would happen did. ■

Self-Storage

by **LEE ROSSI**

I

I lift another old box
from the locker
tape crackling to splinters
arrow pointing THIS SIDE UP

I open the flap
to a jumble of letters
stamped with likenesses
of Luther and Erasmus

letters I wrote
my first wife
when, for the sake of our
careers, we lived on
separate continents

II

I read the lies I wrote then
my "loneliness," my "need for you"

all the partial truths

I filled the pages with

and I remember the nights
I danced with others

pressing my hand
on the curve at the waist

where the bell that is woman
opens to sound

and echo —
my deepest hunger then

this secret sharing
skin of mouth, skin of breast

long unbroken skin of back and leg
wholeness of the body

my secret joy

III

I trudge downstairs
Sisyphus in reverse

waddle outside
to the dumpster

heave the box onto the lip
of the heavy metal bin

lift the lid, fragrance
of orange peel and coffee grounds

rotting lettuce, leaves, crankcase oil
tip my past into this
lovely marinade

give my sins
to the earth

The Kitchen Table: An Honest Orgy

by **DENISE GESS**

Food was just a pretext.

> — *Carlos Drummond de Andrade, "The Table"*

My estranged husband calls from Paris to tell me that if I were there beside him, I'd be proud of his outfit. Bill actually uses the word *outfit*, and for some reason, although he doesn't fish, I picture him in fly-fishing gear. I imagine him casting lures as exquisite as exotic earrings into a cold stream, and I tell him this.

"No. I look like a Frenchman," he says.

"I'm glad, honey."

That "honey" slips out, skitters off my tongue. Although we've been separated for more than a year, we keep forgetting not to use such endearments. Bill reports on the weather, sounding as close as the next room. "People are in love all over the place here," he says before he explains the real reason for his call, which is to tell me my copy of our divorce complaint is on its way to me.

I'm in Philadelphia, Pennsylvania, and except for this vacation to Paris, he's still living in our house in New Jersey, which has sold. We're waiting for the settlement in mid-June before he, too, moves back into the city. Then, for the first time since we began dating, we will live eight blocks apart from each other, just as we used to, except now we have a history. Whenever we speak we are alternately stunned and sad that what remains — a kind of untarnished affection one reserves for an old friend — is both more and less than we expected after fourteen years. His copy of our divorce complaint arrived without warning just before he left for vacation. "I cried, seeing our names," he says. "'Plaintiff.' 'Defendant.'"

My own tears shock me. I know where he was sitting when he read those words: in his usual place at the kitchen table. He always sat in the middle. My daughter always chose to sit at the end near the long window that faced the garden. I sat at the other end, close to the stove and the wall phone.

I have neither the table nor the six unmatched, antique Hitchcock chairs I purchased one at a time whenever I found one in fairly decent shape. Little in this current apartment recalls that kitchen, except the black-and-white tile floor. When Bill says the table holds "so many memories," I'm surprised. Despite the plans we had for communion at that table, in reality he spent very little time in the kitchen, except in the mornings. We did maintain that ritual: cereal and coffee while he read the gossip page of the newspaper aloud to my daughter and me. Sometimes we'd ask to hear our horoscopes; invariably, his and mine would be off by a mile. "Figures," my daughter would say. "Water and fire." Then she'd arch one eyebrow, a gesture I envied. He is fire; we, mother and daughter, are moody, mutable water.

After I've hung up the phone, I hunt down a poem I've recently read again after some years. The poem is called "The Table," written by Brazilian poet Carlos Drummond de Andrade and translated by Elizabeth Bishop. My copy is underlined. When had I inked up the pages, taking note of this line: "Around the wide table . . . It was an honest orgy / ending in revelations"? No words I might struggle to string together this morning will resonate more, and no other object we own tells a story quite the way that kitchen table does.

We found the table at an antiques show in a remote south-Jersey town whose name I no longer recall, but I do recall my husband wanting something much less primitive, surely less scarred. Nevertheless, when I spotted the nineteenth-century farmhouse table with hand-carved barn-red legs and a modest pine-plank surface, I fell in love. Maybe the writer in me is attracted to damage and flaws, to the paradoxical beauty of ruin, but in less than a minute my desire transformed the battered farmhouse table into a monument of perfect imperfection.

I must have gasped, because Bill touched my elbow with his forefinger. This was our predetermined antique-hunting "caution" signal. I felt his hot breath in my ear: "He's seen." He meant the dealer had noticed us. I was then, and still am, quite incapable of concealing strong emotion — favorable or unfavorable. The dealer now knew that I loved the table, which would make bargaining difficult.

"Let's get a cup of coffee," my husband said insistently. Slipping off for coffee was a move that I had taught him: *You have to be willing to walk away from what you love.* Yet I never seemed able to take my own advice. As we edged away from the booth, the dealer began telling us that the table had also served as a barn work table; then, having heard me mention writing, he shifted his voice to a low, confidential tone and said, "If I remember correctly, the owner before the man I bought it from was a writer himself."

"He wrote what?" my husband asked.

The dealer scratched his chin. "Cookbooks, I believe."

We headed for the coffee concession. Over weak coffee served in styrofoam cups, my husband said, "I thought you wanted a round table." He had me there. The kitchen in our newly acquired eighteenth-century house was narrow and long, aesthetically better suited to a round table. But I had also learned, through trial and a few costly errors in furnishing our previous two houses, that there is no such thing as too big or too small or "wrong" when an object is cherished. I ticked off the list of our beloved pieces of furniture: Hadn't his grandmother's rosewood desk fit into the most unlikely spaces? And the club chair that I'd dragged with me from my first marriage — hadn't that always found its place?

He didn't argue. Either he was tired that day or — now that I think about it from this distance of the estranged wife — he was already settling into some private resignation, one as insidious as my private disenchantment. So we would buy the table. We finished drinking our coffee, decided on an acceptable price, and made our way back through the crowds. As we neared the corner booth, the dealer was enthusiastically talking up the table to another couple. I was relieved when I heard the woman proclaim with conviction, "It's too long," before she tugged her husband away.

We examined it again. It was pockmarked and scratched, and initials had been carved into it. Who were "D.H." and "C.A."? What boldness or recklessness had led them to make their marks here rather than on the trunk of a tree? As I ran my hand along its surface, I was delighted to discover a smooth depression in the left corner; the palm of my hand slipped snugly into that worn section, where, I decided, many other hands must have rested, gripped, slammed, and pounded the surface while negotiating the everyday struggles of family life. Surely it would serve us as well, humble us with its simplicity, and provide the setting for forming connections. This would be the table at which I could keep an eye on my daughter and stay in touch with her and her friends. This would be the table where Bill (who claimed to need and love and miss sitting in the kitchen) would linger with me in the mornings before going off to work, and where we'd find each other again late at night to talk. And, given its general appearance and long history, I had faith that any human accident — spilled juice, a hot dish that might leave a mark, a harsh word spoken carelessly — would be forgiven here.

I've always been as serious about creating a life with meaning as I am about creating a work that *lives*. What I wanted, what I believed *we* wanted and needed as a family, was a house where, as the architect Christopher Alexander puts it, "you can feel the weight of your own heart." That year, Bill's heart was under wraps. He had suffered three losses: his best friend, then his father, then his mother. I had committed to good times and bad, and in this crisis I wanted to provide comfort: *Come to me. I want you to come to me and rest here. Here is home.* But he never spoke of these deaths, which left me bereft of a way to reach him. Maybe it was naive of me, but I sank a lot of hope into that table as a stage for intimacy and believed that, after taking its place in the kitchen with the black-and-white tile floor, it would be our house's heart.

We brought the table home, and after a few days Bill warmed up to it. Rarely spontaneous, he now dug out his penknife and announced he was putting the knife in a kitchen drawer for brave and well-loved guests to use to carve their initials in the table, too. My parents were our first dinner guests, and my mother thought we'd lost our minds when we proffered the knife. A child of the Depression and a believer in lemon oil and glass-smooth surfaces, she likes her furniture unmarred, matched, polished. *Patina* is not in her lexicon. "You need to sand and paint it, not write on it," she said.

Her words struck a nerve. *Not* writing was what I had been doing for more years than I cared to admit, and I blamed everything outside of myself for this artistic crisis: not enough time, the wrong town, no office space, the wrong house — and no kitchen table. I actually said that at a faculty party when the host asked me how the writing was going. He was incredulous. No kitchen table? What kind of corkeyed excuse was *that*? I would have agreed, except that kitchen tables have always mattered to me. Tables. My life has revolved around them.

T hroughout my childhood, I reveled in Sunday visits to my paternal grandmother's house, where dinner was served at one in the afternoon. My mother would dress my siblings and me in our best clothes, and we'd usually arrive by late morning. Before I even entered the vestibule, I could taste the raw dough for handmade ravioli, and I knew that Little Grandmom had gone to early Mass at Saint Calista's Church, that on her way home she'd bought the ricotta cheese at Mancuso's, and that she was already in the kitchen rolling the dough flat on a bed of pure white flour.

She saved the best part for me: spooning onto the dough dollops of ricotta cheese that she had blended with whole eggs, sharp Parmesan grated by hand, parsley, and — her secret ingredient — the tiniest smidgen of nutmeg. With her skinny fingers riding mine, we folded the dough over carefully and then dipped the mouth of a clear, wide drinking glass in flour before pressing it down over the bumps to make cheese-filled rounds. We repeated the process until the table was covered in rows of swollen, fleshy coins. While she and my mother put the finishing touches on the ravioli, sealing the edges with fork tines, I licked leftover streaks of cheese from the pressed-glass mixing bowl. By then, the steam from the salted boiling water on the stove had fogged the lone kitchen window, clouding the view of the enormous snowball bush in the yard. Little Grandmom, who wore dresses on all occasions and her fancy voile apron on Sundays, would pull the short white step stool from under the formica table and place it close to the stove. Then she'd pat the top step: "OK, Den. Bring the oil." It was my job to stand on the stool to add "just a little bit" of the earthy-smelling olive oil to the pot.

But the food was only part of the fun. In that steamy kitchen I listened to stories: my grandmother's unvarnished disapproval of her soon-to-be son-in-law "the gambler"; what was happening to poor Antoinette across the street ("The louse left her nothing"); Grandmom's visit to Aunt Lena around the corner; did I want to go "up the street" and visit Aunt Annie and Uncle Nick after dinner? Life's important moments were about people: about feeding them, loving them, forgiving them, and — as I learned too soon — losing them.

In 1965 Big Grandmom, my mother's mother, as buxom and broad as Little Grandmom was petite and wiry, came to live with us. But no matter whose house we were in, the Italian traditions remained the same. Now my mother and I made the ravioli on our round, rock-maple kitchen table, and the relatives came to us to pay their respects, to keep their ever-hopeful eyes on my grandmother, whose body was slowly being ravaged by colon cancer. Although eating such a rich meal was impossible for her, we devoured the tender meatballs. Our eyes smarted when the peppery sausage hit our tongues, and we smiled when she said to my grandfather, "Joe, dip this in the gravy. I just want a taste." She'd tear off the heel of the crusty Italian bread, and he'd sop up the gravy with it, then feed it to her as if he were a groom feeding his new bride the first piece of wedding cake.

Those Sundays came to an abrupt halt two days into the new year in January 1966. How fitting the brutal gray skies and white snow seem now. The night the paramedics took her from the twin bed in the bedroom she shared with me, the hard-packed snow glistened under the streetlamp. Our cul-de-sac, always the last to be plowed in our subdivision, was riven with icy tire tracks. After the commotion, on my way back to bed, I passed the bathroom and noticed her denture container — a thin, pearly pink plastic — still on the sink. Without thinking, I grabbed it and ran outside in nothing but my blue nightgown, howling at the ambulance's red taillights, "You forgot her teeth!"

Afterward, my grandmother's absence became the most palpable presence in the house. I saw her in my mother's restlessness and her sorrow, which burst out at the oddest times: while my mother was baking a cake or cleaning the living room. I'd see my mother polishing the wooden arms of the chair my grandmother had often sat in, and before I knew it, she'd be polishing with lemon oil and tears. I started sneaking into the kitchen late at night. First I would reheat any leftover coffee in the pot; then I'd sit down at the kitchen table and write in my black-and-white marbled composition book, inventing people to fill the silent, empty space.

A year of secret nights passed before I began writing a series of Michael-and-Jennifer stories. In every story it was always August, and it was always hot. Jennifer, a long, tall blonde, often felt compelled to leave Michael despite a love affliction for him so silly and serious it could have been a Motown song. Although she never left him for another man, nevertheless, she left. She left to tend lepers in a colony, like a character in a Graham Greene novel; she left to become a brain surgeon; she left to heed her political call, her bohemian call, her healing call, but she did not stay behind for Michael's call — no matter what.

I tested my apprentice fiction on my mother while she stood at the kitchen sink washing dishes. I was supposed to be drying, but I ignored the plates piling up on the drainboard and read aloud instead. Though I was searching for a way to distract and entertain her, my mother regularly wept, her tears trickling into the sudsy water. Often she wept before I could get to the sad parts. One night she said, "Enough."

"What?"

"Can't she just marry him? Just once? Stop sending her to Africa."

"But she has this thing. Here," I said, pointing to my heart. "She *has* to go."

Looking back on those nights, I see that although my mother never doubted I would become a writer, she wanted me to do it under the umbrella of convention. And since I was a good girl to a fault, an acutely responsible firstborn, I bypassed adolescent rebellion entirely. I was a coward with an operatic mind, lacking the gumption for actual bad behavior. So I wrote. Early on then, the tension between the women I'd grown up loving (wives and mothers to the exclusion of all else) and the gypsy locked inside me was taking root.

It's no surprise that I continued writing at the kitchen table in my first apartment after I married my high-school sweetheart, and then at the kitchen table in our first house with my daughter playing on the floor beside me — domesticating my muse, no doubt, satisfying my desire both for a "normal" family and my work.

The night before Bill and I moved to the eighteenth-century house with the eat-in kitchen, I sat down to write a farewell journal entry to the house we were leaving; instead I wrote a prophetic passage heralding the future I could not imagine then: "If you don't write in this new place, you're going to have to face the fact that it's not the house or what is or isn't in it; it's something else."

T he divorce complaint arrives in a bulging white envelope. Because I've been warned of its arrival, I don't expect to come unglued. On it, I see our names and note that I never took Bill's last name. Oh, we claimed it had everything to do with hating hyphenation and the fact that I had already published two novels as Denise Gess. But the simple truth is we didn't like his last name with mine; it sounded strange to our ears and in our mouths, as ill-fitting and temporary as braces.

W e worked on our house until it was stunning enough to be part of our town's annual Christmas home tour. Fifteen hundred people walked through our house during the course of one long, cold day in December 1995. Why was it, then, as I stood sentry in my dining room, that I felt my heart winding down like an old clock?

What sticks in my mind is a comment made by one of the tour-takers, a heavyset woman in a blood red wool coat. When she stepped into the dining room, she gasped at the Christmas tree, one of three in the house. "Oh, it's so right," she said. And it was, down to its cinnamon sticks and popcorn strings and dried slices of orange and lime: appropriate, perfect, approved.

From the room behind her, I heard my husband telling ghost stories in a confident, booming, tour-guide voice. His pride bordered on hubris. I suddenly felt frightened rather than pleased by what we had created. I had fulfilled my mother's dream: a fine and secure life, albeit with a collection of country antiques instead of matched pieces from Ethan Allen. My grandparents, my links to everything old-world Italian, were gone, leaving me with only one question: *Whose life have I been living?*

As I'd hoped they would, love and children finally flocked to that table. Because of them — or, rather, because of what they opened up in me — the words began flowing. There was a man whose teenage son and my daughter were each other's first loves. Since I worked at home, our children were often with me. The man's office was nearby, making his initial impromptu visits at lunchtime seem natural. We sat at the kitchen table, of course. The first time he saw the table, he laid his hand in the deep groove. "I love this," he said.

After a while our conversations veered from the safe topic of our children to ourselves. He openly admitted to hating his own home, especially the kitchen, where no one ate together. Their refrigerator was a wasteland of condiments. And he admitted to feeling lonely and dissatisfied. "I feel I haven't made anything," he said. "You, though — you make something from nothing."

But I had not, and suddenly I wanted to for the first time in years. Within the span of a few months this new extended family began tracking through our back door. We always ended up in the kitchen, gathered around the table, reconnecting me to the tables of my youth, to a time when I'd felt safest and most loved, and to the part of myself that had gone underground.

These dual loves — our children's (sanctioned and expected) and ours (unsanctioned and unexpected) — existed within the fragile bubble of "friendship between families." Though he and I had enough sense not to sleep with each other, the error of finally declaring our feelings and two regrettable kisses forced us to make a choice: this could be a beginning or an ending.

We ended where we'd begun, a final lunch at the kitchen table. I told him: "There's this reckless, breakneck, bad-girl part of me, and you've brought it out."

"That's convenient," he said. "If not for the bad boy, the good girl would remain good? At least I can look you in the eye and tell you I'm not so nice." He wasn't. And neither, I realized, was I. His self-deception (which he called "sublimation") suited him, but I wanted to shuck off mine. My own words circled back to me: *You have to be willing to walk away from what you love.* But I was tramping across a landscape of minefields. Where was there to go now?

I scolded myself: *Make something.* So I returned to the table late at night.

N o one approved of my leaving Bill; indeed, I didn't approve. Yet once my hidden heart had revealed itself, I couldn't fathom locking it away again. "What do you think you'll find out there alone?" friends asked. I honestly didn't know. But writing demands the ability to continue to entertain possibilities, to take risks. It's what I love; apart from it, nothing — not even my daughter, who would soon go off to live her life, as she should — was truly mine.

Perhaps if I'd given myself time alone and not become a bride at twenty, I wouldn't have needed so much solitude at forty-six. What can I say? I am a slow learner. My best guess is that I must have been more fearful when I was younger. Watching my grandmother's slow death in my home, then living in the wake of my mother's tenacious grief, led me to cling to familial attachment in life, while my heroines risked adventures in my fiction. Now, in middle age, I wanted to silence fear.

C losing day on the house is fraught with delays and problems — the buyer's, not ours. We spend five hours in an airless room, sitting around a standard-issue conference table, drinking coffee.

Later that afternoon, home sale complete, Bill pulls up outside my apartment building in a van loaded with furniture, which we've divided between us. He's brought me the Hitchcock chairs. "I wanted you to take the table," he says, "but I didn't think it would fit in your kitchen."

A few days later, I call him. "I'll find a place for the table. Shall I buy it from you?"

He laughs. "No, no," he says. "The truth is I never wanted it." His relief is unmistakable. "You love it."

"I do."

"Now you are reunited," Carlos de Andrade Drummond writes, "in a wedding ring much greater / than the simple ring of earth, / together at this table / of wood more lawful than any / law of the republic."

This morning I sit at the table preparing to pay monthly bills — a task that makes me shudder these days. My daughter is away at college. I am alone for the first time in my adult life. Nothing is certain or secure. Whenever I visit her in New York City, I marvel at her poise as she whisks me through turnstiles with her Metro card. "My day job's going to be a psychologist," she says. Then travel. *Then* marriage.

One night on our way to a poetry reading, crossing Broadway at West 107th, I asked her if I had disappointed her, made her life too difficult by divorcing twice.

She didn't answer right away. When I looked at her face, she was smiling. "Mom? What did you want most in the world? More than anything else?"

My answer was easy "You and a book."

"See?" she said.

Still, sometimes, when I'm least expecting her, the little girl in her blue nightgown who stood howling in the snow rages through these rooms — a little ghost, a little warrior trying to stave off inexorable loss, waving her grandmother's teeth against the frozen sky. *Come now and calm yourself here at this table. Let me tell you a story.* I push the bills aside and lay my hand in that warm, worn depression. What rises up into my palm is a small miracle: not one body, not one kiss, not one sorrow — but all flesh, all kisses, all sorrows of the spirits who have gathered around it. I consider Drummond de Andrade's phrase "lawful wood." Hardwood. Enduring. ∎

Marriage

by **LOU LIPSITZ**

I was splitting wood,
oak and hickory,
with a wedge and a sledgehammer,
and somehow was not able to tire myself
regardless of how frustrating it
sometimes became.

My son watched. Now and then he
handed me the small ax.
He saw me try to split
those pieces of sweet gum that
someone had left in the woodpile
we'd inherited with the house,
and that I, in my ignorance,
treated just like the other wood.

He saw how, with these logs,
the wood opened but did not split,
how it grabbed the wedges
and, hard as I hammered, would

not let them free.
He saw two wedges stuck and
my useless, endless hammering,
and he asked, *Dad, what are we going
to do now?* and I, not knowing,
ashamed to admit defeat,
looking at him for a moment,
laid my heavy arms down.

My Marital Status

by **JAMES KULLANDER**

Six years after the event, I still cannot say for sure whether I am divorced or widowed. The question comes up whenever I am filling out a form that wants to know my marital status. All the other questions I can answer in seconds, but this one — which asks that I check *single*, *married*, *separated*, *divorced*, or *widowed* — always stumps me. I'll pause there at the dentist's office, insurance company, or bank, and, while the clock ticks and other people's children scamper at my feet, I'll reflect on what it really means to be married.

The event I refer to is the death of the woman who used to be my wife. Wanda was not my wife when she died in December 2001 at the age of forty-two. Not legally, anyway. She and I had met in the summer of 1980, married in the summer of 1984, and divorced in the summer of 1994. Before we'd gotten married, I'd made it clear to Wanda that I did not want children, and she'd told me that she could accept this. Yet, throughout our years together, it seemed she never put her longing to rest. I watched her study the infants our friends and family brought into the world, as if she were silently hoping I would change my mind. I didn't. I couldn't see the sense in my becoming a parent and said so. Wanda's mother, with her affable proddings, would ask me why I'd married her daughter if we weren't going to have children. That, she would say, did not make sense to her.

The discontent Wanda and I felt about each other's intractable positions eventually spread into the rest of our marriage and soured it. What Wanda's mother kept saying began to make sense to me: why stay married if I wasn't going to give Wanda the child she wanted?

I was forty; Wanda was thirty-four — still plenty of time for her to have a child with someone else. I talked to Wanda about it, we put ourselves through a year of psychotherapy, and finally the two of us sadly agreed that things just weren't working out.

After we'd split, our lives suddenly took far different turns, as if we'd been spring-loaded to take off in new directions. I began studying Buddhist meditation; went on retreats in Nepal, Thailand, and here in the States; and found myself at the feet of dozens of spiritual sages who invariably spoke of the impermanence of everything. I knew about impermanence, having ended a marriage that was supposed to last as long as we both would live. But somehow hearing it spoken by teachers I considered wise gave me solace. I also put myself through Union Theological Seminary in New York City and earned a master's in divinity.

Meanwhile Wanda launched herself into physical pursuits, becoming a luminary in the local contradance, zydeco, and swing-dance community — a scene the two of us had never set foot in when we'd been together. She occasionally invited me to dances at a local parish hall or rec center near our homes in upstate New York. Sometimes, when I missed her, I'd show up. I'd pick her out of the crowd and wave, and she'd scoot over and guide me onto the floor, where I'd hobble along under her patient instruction as some of her suitors looked on. I can keep in step to rock-and-roll, but to this music I was like a rusty engine that's reluctant to turn over. Wanda and I would laugh at how clumsy I was. Then I'd watch her dance with another man, the two of them seeming to glide across the floor.

The remorse I'd felt about initiating the divorce diminished when I saw Wanda enjoying life on her own. From time to time we'd talk on the phone and trade stories about our latest romantic escapades. It turned out she and I were better friends than we'd been spouses: happier, more candid with each other, and less prone to bickering.

I had not seen Wanda for several months when she phoned me in April 2001 to tell me she was having surgery to remove a large mass in her abdomen. As I penciled in the date on my calendar, she told me not to worry, said it was nothing. And off she went with her latest beau to a Cajun-music festival in New Orleans.

I have always liked Wanda's family, and they have always liked me. Even after the divorce, I was invited to holiday dinners, birthday picnics, and Christmas services at their church. Wanda was Chinese American: her father had emigrated from Beijing and her mother from Shanghai in the 1940s, both fleeing the communist takeover. They'd met in New York City, married, and moved to suburban New Jersey, where I met Wanda while working at a newspaper. I was a young reporter, and she was an intern in the paper's graphic-design department. A middle-class, Connecticut-raised WASP, I was charmed by Wanda's Asian beauty. Although she and her two siblings were as American as I was, her parents were still very Chinese, and their culture seemed exotic to me. Her mother spoke with an accent I found hard to understand. Her father showed me saw-tooth-edged black-and-white photos of the house where he'd grown up: a palatial estate in Beijing that had been confiscated by the communist regime and turned into a barracks for the People's Liberation Army. Wanda and her family seemed less tormented by the guilt, worry, and conflict that droned on in my family and friends, and this held a certain allure for me.

On the day of Wanda's operation I joined her mother, father, older sister Frieda, and brother-in-law Peter at the hospital. Wanda maintained her silly, often droll sense of humor throughout the pre-op. As the nurses rolled her on the gurney into the operating room, she held up the hand not tethered to the IV and cranked it side to side, like Queen Elizabeth waving from her Rolls-Royce. Several hours later we met with her surgeon. We learned that a softball-sized pelvic mass had been removed in a total hysterectomy. He appeared disconcerted; the tissue, he said, would be sent to a lab for a biopsy, and the results would take a couple of days. Wanda would remain in the hospital to recover.

One evening a few days later I walked into her room after a stressful day at the office. Wanda was on the phone, snapping at the hospital-switchboard operator — unusual behavior for her; Wanda was usually courteous to a fault. And she was glaring at the foot of her bed. The way I figured it, she had just been sliced open and was in pain. Of course she was irritable. Seeing me, she hung up and started to cry.

"I don't have good news," she said.

Whatever had bothered me at work that day fell away, and I rushed to her bedside and cupped one of her hands in mine. I imagined some infection, or perhaps she would need another operation.

"What is it?" I asked, caressing her long black hair.

"It's cancer," she said.

Ovarian. And it was serious.

I laid my head on Wanda's lap and sobbed.

In the years we'd been apart, Wanda and I had each had several lovers who'd come and gone, but neither of us had remarried, nor were we seeing anyone at that time. This gave us the freedom to be with each other without competing love interests at the margins. I spent hours with Wanda in the cramped living room of her apartment, which adjoined her parents' house, an hour's drive from mine in New York State, where they had moved a few years before. A hospital bed her maternal grandmother had used in her final years was set up there. I also accompanied Wanda and her sister on trips to Boston's Dana-Farber/Brigham and Women's Cancer Center, where Wanda was treated with punishing, nauseating rounds of chemotherapy that kept her down for days. It was an aggressive regimen. She had a rare and virulent form of cancer — clear-cell — and it was at stage IV, which meant that the cancer had gotten into the liver. Stage IV can be treated but is terminal; few live beyond five years. In the aftermath of these treatments, Wanda would sometimes call me to gripe about the pain or for comfort, often weeping.

I tried to appear strong in the face of Wanda's weakening condition and, to some extent, my own. I visited her, ran errands for her, and sometimes cooked for her while the earth tilted us into summer and then fall. The September 11 attacks left Wanda and her sister stranded in Oregon, where they had spent a week learning *qigong* from a renowned Chinese master, hoping this ancient healing practice might help Wanda get well again. A few days later, when Peter and I drove to the Newark airport to pick them up, we could see, across the New Jersey tidal marshes, clouds of smoke from the still-smoldering remains of the Twin Towers. With all the death and dying in the air, I was elated to see Wanda alive at the gate. We hugged, and for a moment I had the idea that everything was going to be fine.

For most of October, Wanda's condition remained relatively stable; her oncologist seemed encouraged by her response to the experimental brew of chemotherapy he'd prescribed, and perhaps to the *qigong*. Then one November morning Frieda called me.

"Something bad is happening with Wanda," she said, her voice distant from the poor cellphone connection. Peter had gone into the apartment to get Wanda, she said, and found her lying upstairs on a stripped bed in a spare bedroom, disoriented and barely cognizant. An ambulance was on the way.

"Jim's here!" exclaimed Frieda when I parted the baby blue privacy curtain at the emergency room. Wanda, stretched out on a gurney, looked at me. There was no spark of recognition. Her head stayed tilted to the left, and her eyes were wide, as if she were shocked by the condition in which she found herself. The sole movement in that tight space was Wanda's left arm, which slowly rose and fell like a machine, as if to push back from her face the thick black hair she'd once had. Doctors say hearing is the last of the senses to go, and I wondered if Wanda was listening as her family and I discussed her condition. I passed my hand lightly over her head to let her know I was there.

Wanda was admitted for observation and a battery of tests to determine what, exactly, had gone wrong with her brain. I spent my days and nights at the hospital while a handful of office colleagues took on a good portion of my work. I had barely noticed the changing of the seasons that year, and when I did finally notice, it was through the sealed, grimy window of Wanda's fourth-floor room. The tops of the trees had gone bare, and the people on the broken sidewalks had thick clothes on, their shoulders hunched against the cold and puffs of steam coming from their mouths. I wanted so much to be out in the world; I wanted Wanda to be out there, too — on the street, making plans, living life.

Wanda had a room to herself, and the night nurses let me stay past visiting hours. With the very real possibility of death hovering near, the world outside the window became increasingly irrelevant. The lines between day and night, the known and the unknowable, were beginning to blur. Even the fact of our divorce seemed to get erased.

I tried to get some rest in two tangerine-colored chairs I'd pushed together, but I never could sleep sitting up. To distract myself, I slipped on the headphones of the portable cassette player we'd brought for Wanda. (We'd thought music might comfort her.) I pushed the PLAY button. Van Morrison's "Carrying a Torch" came on.

Wanda had made the tape, labeled "Mellow Music," several weeks earlier. She'd put the Van Morrison song on it, she'd told me, because it reminded her of us. Sometimes we'd joked that when we got old and feeble, we'd shack up together in a nursing home. Now, delirious from insomnia, I gazed at Wanda's wasted form in the pale gray light and listened to Van Morrison beseech his lost lover to "reconnect and move further into the light." It was as if everything under me — the earth itself — had been pulled away, and I was plunging through a dark space, nowhere to go but down. I felt that by not wanting children and initiating the breakup of our marriage, I'd committed a heinous crime, and now I was being punished. Selfish bastard that I was, I'd stayed involved with Wanda even after we'd split up, perhaps thwarting her chances to get remarried and have the child she'd wanted. I'd read that not having children can increase a woman's risk of ovarian cancer — so that, too, was my fault.

Early the next morning, I was awakened by the sound of Wanda gurgling on vomit. After being admitted, she'd been given a morphine patch to ease her pain. I'd voiced a mild objection, having been told that, because she was "narcotic naive" — Wanda hardly even took aspirin — morphine could make her nauseous. Now I ran down the waxed hallway to tell the nurse that my "wife" was throwing up. It was the first time I had called Wanda my "wife" since we'd separated. I wanted the nurse to take my plea for help seriously, and somehow I thought that using the word *wife* would do the trick. But there was another, less calculated, reason: as I had vowed nearly twenty years before, I still cherished Wanda as if she were my wife, in sickness and in health.

The nurse came and wiped green bile from Wanda's chin, and, despite my misgivings, I agreed Wanda should keep the morphine patch on. A few minutes later, though, just as I thought Wanda had drifted back to sleep, she started heaving again. I called the nurse back, and this time I took it upon myself to peel the morphine patch off Wanda's pale, blue-veined chest.

"She doesn't want morphine," I snarled, as if it were the nurse's fault it had been put there in the first place.

I'd been awake barely a half-hour, and already the day had taken its toll on me. Left alone in the room, I climbed into bed with Wanda. I thought that if she couldn't see or hear me, perhaps she could feel me. The rubber-coated mattress crinkled under my weight. Her emaciated form lay still as I curled against her, fetal-like, and nuzzled her neck. Wanda fell back to sleep, and after a few moments so did I. It was the first time we'd been in the same bed together in eight years, and in a strange way it felt like home. When her family doctor showed up later that morning, I was startled awake and felt intruded upon, as if he'd barged into our bedroom.

A couple of days later, tests revealed that the cancer cells had wormed their way into Wanda's skull, causing the brain tissue to swell. The neurologist described the condition as "impossible to treat."

So that was that. Her words were like a door gently closing, the lock quietly clicking into place. Wanda's family and I were drained of all the hope that had buoyed us through the previous six months — and there'd been plenty, I realized the moment it was snatched away. Wanda was brought home in an ambulance and put back in her grandmother's hospital bed to die.

I don't know when the idea first occurred to me, but I began to consider asking Wanda's family if we could hold a remarriage ceremony. I could not give Wanda back her life or undo the divorce. I couldn't even offer my help: the errands had all been done; the trips to Boston were over. Love was all I had left to give, and the ceremony would be a declaration of that. It would not be a legal marriage; Wanda was incapable of consenting. But I believed she would have wanted it. There had remained a sort of low blue flame of love between us, the kind Van Morrison sings about in the song on Wanda's tape. Wanda and I — and also her family and I — still carried that torch for each other.

At first I was reluctant to make my request, for fear her family might be upset. But the idea of us carrying to our graves the broken promise I had made to Wanda in our first marriage ceremony — to be together "till death do us part" — troubled me. When I timidly mentioned the idea to her family, they were thrilled; they'd been thinking the same thing but had been unable to bring themselves to ask me.

The family's minister came to the apartment to perform the ceremony. I spoke of the love that had kept Wanda and me and her family connected through the years. The minister read from the Song of Solomon ("Love is strong as death") and Ecclesiastes ("For everything there is a season"). Then he read some vows for me to respond to with "I will" and "I do." I wondered whether Wanda heard any of it. Could she see the small circle of friends and family members who had gathered round us? When it was over, Wanda's mother opened her arms to me, and we held one another tight, both of us weeping. Wanda's younger brother, whom I hardly knew, suddenly embraced me and said, "Welcome back."

During the night, I kept vigil, sleeping fitfully and dreamlessly in a twin bed perpendicular to Wanda's. Her breathing had grown labored and painful to listen to: somewhere between a snore and a wheeze. Each night her condition deteriorated, and she often gasped as if being strangled, which maybe she was as death tightened its grip.

In the predawn hours of December 6, five days after we'd brought her home from the hospital, Wanda's labored breathing awakened me, louder than ever. Spit that looked like strained peas pooled in the corners of her mouth and on the collar of the thin cotton hospital gown. Normally squeamish about bodily excretions, I'd tended to Wanda's without a second thought. Her mother and I had already changed Wanda's soiled undergarments several times, both of us noticing how her right foot was turning ever deeper shades of purple from lack of circulation. I had little reaction to all of this. Perhaps I had closed down, or perhaps I was opening up. Buddhists speak of how, if you can train the mind not to get attached to human suffering, you can benevolently enter any "hell realm" of existence like a swan with wings spread, swooping down on a lake. I now got up and wiped Wanda's chin with a handful of tissue, then passed my hand over her head, trying to comfort her. Her eyes were wide and fixed on something beyond me, beyond all of us.

I climbed back into my bed and fell asleep. When I woke again, a cold gray December dawn was showing through the tops of the skeletal trees outside the windows. This time it was not Wanda's breathing that had awakened me; it was the silence.

I rose, felt my bare feet hit the shag carpet, slipped on some clothes over my briefs and bare chest, and knelt by her bed. She was cold and hard to the touch; rigor mortis was already setting in. It seemed she was still staring at whatever she'd been staring at earlier, and I had to put a hand over her eyes to close them because her eyelids kept going up like the weighted eyes of a doll. When I lifted her left arm — the one she had repeatedly passed over her head — to put it under the covers, it felt as stiff as a downed tree limb. I slipped from the stubborn fingers of Wanda's right hand a set of sandalwood Buddhist *mala* beads I'd given to her as a talisman against evil spirits. I stuffed the beads into the left front pocket of my jeans; I would carry them always as a way to remember her. Then I read aloud the Twenty-third Psalm, as I had planned to do, from the Bible that I'd used in my years as a seminarian: "The Lord is my shepherd, I shall not want . . ."

I slipped into Wanda's parents' kitchen to deliver the news, feeling like some dark angel. Her mother was making coffee and didn't hear me coming. As I floated toward her, I uttered the heaviest, gravest words I've ever said to anyone: "Wanda's dead."

"Oh. OK," she replied. That was it. I'd expected her to fall apart, but she didn't. Nor had I, come to think of it. We hugged lightly, as if I might have been going off to a day at the office. I think we were in shock. No matter how close someone you love is to death, there is nothing so final as a corpse in your midst.

A couple of hours later a gray panel van arrived from the funeral home, and two men lumbered out to retrieve Wanda's body. If I'd had any sense, I would have backed off and let the men do their job, but I was not yet ready to abdicate my responsibilities to Wanda. I helped lift her body off the hospital bed and onto a gurney, bedsheets and all. I'd prepared to lift a heavy weight, but Wanda's frame was so insubstantial, so eaten up by cancer, I could have picked her up by myself. One of the men had put a pale blue corduroy body bag on the gurney, and I zipped it up over Wanda the way you would a child's parka on a winter day. Wanda disappeared, and I realized this would be the last time I'd ever see her.

As I helped wheel the gurney out to the van, I suddenly insisted that the body be moved headfirst, and the driver obliged. Years earlier I'd read about an ancient Hindu tradition: you carry a body feet first at the start of its trip to the funeral pyre, so the spirit can remember its earthly life; for the second half of the journey, you turn the body headfirst, to help facilitate the spirit's departure from its material existence. After the van had pulled away, I turned to Susan, a friend of Wanda's and mine whom I'd called that morning, and I collapsed into her arms and fell apart.

Later that day at the funeral home, as we prepared the death certificate and obituary, I asked whether I could accompany Wanda's body to the crematorium. Wanda's family wanted her cremated so that, come spring, we could gather and each fling a handful of her ashes wfrom the sharp gray shoulders of Shawangunk Mountain, which you can see in the distance from the back deck of Wanda's apartment. I knew it was an unusual request, but I didn't know what else to do except see my grief through to the end, if there was one.

Consent was granted, and Susan accompanied me. No special arrangements were made for us. In fact, we were treated as a minor inconvenience. In my car, Susan and I trailed the funeral-home van past strip malls, warehouses, and office buildings to a lovely cemetery with a palatial mausoleum. The crematorium, however, was a square, squat cinder-block building at the end of a narrow paved road, where you'd expect to find a maintenance shed. Inside, a huge black furnace stood like the machinery of Oz. The van backed up to the open garage door, and I was shocked to see a long corrugated-cardboard box emerge. Two attendants indecorously dressed in jeans and T-shirts — they were maintenance workers, after all — clumsily hoisted the box onto an assembly line of rollers about chest high. Before Susan and I caught up to what was going on, the furnace door was lifted, and the box with Wanda in it was gliding toward its open maw. Susan and I reached out just in time to tap the box goodbye before it rolled away. The furnace door was lowered, a switch was thrown, and the woman I'd loved in the flesh for twenty-one years went up in smoke.

As Wanda was efficiently transported into the ether, a man in a dark suit — he must have been management, perhaps showing up as a last-minute courtesy — told us the heat inside the furnace could reduce a corpse to ash in minutes. Was this supposed to be some sort of comfort? My mind reeled. I tried to reconcile this small, shabby scene with photos I'd seen of the towering, flower-strewn funeral pyres along the Ganges River in India, and all the ancient, complex rituals for honoring the dead. While the man prattled on, Susan and I stared at each other with raised eyebrows and finally, by some silent agreement, decided that it was time to go.

On the busy road at the edge of the cemetery, cars and trucks streaked by, windshields glinting in the morning sun. Susan and I started toward my car, but something made us look back, as if the tips of our noses were tethered to the grim place we'd just left. We both saw in the windless blue sky above the crematorium chimney a blurry streak of heat and ash: Wanda's ashes. It should have shattered me, but instead I was struck by the bizarre collision of events — these final moments of Wanda's corporeal existence, the gruff handling of her remains by the maintenance workers, the blather of the manager about the furnace heat — and I began to laugh. Susan joined in, and soon we were both pitched over, warm tears wetting our cold cheeks. The two of us nearly fell on the frozen pavement, so disjointed by the pain and hilarity of it all that we could hardly stand. We caught ourselves on the trunk of my car, bent over like a couple of marathon runners, come at last to the end of a long and exhausting race. I knew then I was going to be all right. I felt Wanda laughing with us, the three of us gathered in the arms of the big, fat, grinning Buddha, howling at the absurdity of this mortal coil, as if that was all there was to us. And even if it was, so what?

For weeks afterward I was awakened on dark winter mornings by the smell of bacon frying in my house, where I live alone. Some Sunday mornings, in the home Wanda and I had shared, she'd cooked bacon for breakfast. Waking up now to the smell of bacon when no one was cooking anything was eerie but comforting. I considered all the rational explanations for the phantom aroma, but my nearest neighbor was hundreds of feet away, and all my windows were sealed against winter's cold. Maybe I was just imagining it. No matter, I thought. When it came to coping mechanisms, an imaginary one would do just fine.

One hot summer night a few months before Wanda had died, I'd shown up at a dance fundraiser her friends had put together to help pay her medical expenses. Wanda and I were outside the parish hall on the lawn. We could hear the band playing a Cajun reel through the open windows, and Wanda asked if I wanted to dance. I said, as usual, that I didn't know how. She took my hands and placed them on her shoulder and waist and showed me the steps. It seemed like trigonometry to me, and when it became clear that I was never going to get it, we fell into each other's arms for a long hug.

When I smelled bacon cooking in my house, it felt as if Wanda and I were still doing some sort of dance, and she were still taking the lead.

A part of me died with Wanda, a part I was glad to see go: my resistance to love. I'd often put distance between myself and others as a way to keep from feeling trapped or getting hurt. I'd delivered wearying criticisms of people I'd thought were less than perfect — as if I were any better than they were. Living like that had been a long, hard battle with many casualties, the most wounded sometimes being me. I think that during all those silent-meditation sessions; in all the time I'd spent listening to the wisdom of renowned teachers, theologians, and sages; in all the millions of words I'd read in profound spiritual tracts, I'd been trying to learn how to love. But no amount of meditation or yoga or studies of scriptures could have given me that. Wanda's death put me in touch with one of the highest orders of human existence: to love others as though we are all dying all the time, because the plain truth of the matter is that we are. For a long time I didn't know how to articulate this new feeling, even to myself. Then a couple of years ago I heard k.d. lang sing a Leonard Cohen song in which love is described as "a cold and broken hallelujah." And I thought, *Yes, that's it.* In this love I found rest from a sort of homesickness that had afflicted me all my life.

It was not long before my days reassembled themselves into a more or less familiar shape, which was a sort of relief. But I began to forget how, in my hour of grief, I'd cherished my existence and the people around me. Years later, it sometimes feels as if I have to reach across a great psychic distance to get in touch with the way I felt then, as though it lay beyond the curve of the earth.

I have not remarried. From time to time I wonder if I will ever again feel for anyone else what I felt for Wanda in our final months together. And if not, then what? Sometimes someone will ask me if I regret not having children. No, I say. And yes. I don't know whether being a father would have sustained the love I felt as Wanda died. Parents I know have told me that this is what having children does to you: it opens your heart. One mother said that what you feel bringing a person into the world is akin to what you feel seeing someone out of it. Perhaps I didn't have children with Wanda because I was afraid of feeling too much; I don't know. What I do know is that I miss Wanda's features — her brown eyes, round face, delicate frame, and silly sense of humor — some of which appear in the children of her siblings, some of which would no doubt have been replicated in our children. And maybe if Wanda and I had brought a child or two into the world, it wouldn't be such a struggle for me now to recollect the love I felt when she was dying.

So my pen hovers over the little boxes on those forms. My own internal compass tells me I'm widowed. Even if we'd never had that remarriage ceremony, I still would have felt married to Wanda when she died. Our divorce did not end our relationship, and, for me, her death made it even more lasting and unfathomable.

For a while after she'd died, I checked "widowed," hoping the clerks would notice it and tease a story out of me. It was like a little flag I waved. I wanted sympathy, to be seen as more than just another client, customer, patient, student. I was also hoping to trigger a discussion of a similar loss on their part so we could commiserate, like strangers in a snowstorm, and I could give voice to the huge, uncertain emotions swirling inside me.

Legally, however, I am not widowed. So, reluctantly, I check the "divorced" box. But what is a marriage if not the depth of feeling you have for each other? It's only the love between two people that's real, that lasts. Everything else just comes and goes. ■

The Song Of Forgiveness

by GENIE ZEIGER

I imagine forgiveness comes to us like a far-off song, and when your body is seized by that distant music, you can't fight it; your hips begin moving, then the rest of you, even if you can't really hear the damn melody, don't recognize the tune. . . . What I mean to say is: I want to forgive my ex-husband. I don't want to die hating, or even resenting, him. We will never make love, never even kiss again. Never So where is that song of forgiveness, reputed to be so sweet?

All this is coming to me now because his mother, my former mother-in-law, is dying. I haven't seen her in fifteen years — the same fifteen years it's been since I saw him, except for that chance meeting seven years ago at Coughlin's Market, next to the produce. I was shocked at what time had done to his dear face. "You look gray," I said, meaning I saw new white hairs I'd never touched. "I look great?" he asked. "No, *gray*," I said, and he immediately countered with "And you look old." Flustered, I muttered something about how real living should show; how if you didn't really live, you might still look twenty-five — all of it bullshit to drown the deep-down, dirty hurt in my chest. He always did that, hurt me. And I took it, along with all the good things he did for my heart — not to mention the gold earrings from Florence, the thick silver necklace, the Icelandic coat that came with its own special brush.

His mother once sent me twenty dollars for Christmas, and I bought a bunch of little gifts for myself. One of them was a mug with bunnies on it; they were having sex, really going at it. "The fucking-bunny cup," my kids called it. Most mugs break, get lost, are tossed out, but not this one. It's like new except for the dark stains at the bottom that Clorox won't touch, just like his stain that time won't touch, because whenever I think . . . No. No dreams, no thoughts of him. It's over. I get into the car and that goddamn Nanci Griffith song starts in my head again: "And if I miss you / Well, you know what they say / Just once in a very blue moon."

He has gone to get his mother and bring her to die at his house, once ours, two towns away. I hear this news from my daughter the day after I finally sent him a note, figuring I'd try to forgive him on paper. I made it short and gracious, thanked him for the time we shared, admitted it was probably the finest time in my life — not that I'm not happy with my new husband, as I hope he is with his new wife. Of course, now he probably won't get the letter until he returns with his mother, and maybe in the interim his new wife will read it and throw it away and loathe me even more than I imagine she already does.

Still, I feel the Florence Nightingale in me waking up again, as she does when I read news of great troubles in the world, such as in Rwanda or Bosnia. I imagine myself bedecked in white, entering that house, which was once mine, to serve his mother in her dying. I imagine how I'd read her Psalms (I'm good at reading aloud), how I'd look into her eyes in that house I haven't been in for so long: the house he built for us, where I had my own small room with a white carpet. Maybe his mother will die in that white-carpeted room, just across the hall from the room where we slept and made love, where once lightning almost killed me. Maybe I will attend her.

Get real, I tell myself. His mother will die without me. She will be with him, and his new wife, a nurse, will undoubtedly attend. Perhaps I will visit once, when he's not at home. Yes, I'll arrange that. I will walk through that door into our palace of heaven and hell, up the stairs that our puppy Maggie used to fall down, and into the bedroom that contained the largest dream of my life.

Once, when we were young and going through one of our toughest times, I said to him, "We'd better work it out, or we'll come back and torture each other again in different guises." I was thinking about the psychic who'd told us (and whom we'd half believed) that in a former life I had been a famous male poet and he had been my wife. I'd neglected him terribly then, and now he was paying me back with his narcissism and disregard. Who knows? Still I pray: O gods of all the earth, I praise you for your power to damage and repair. Our fires haven't purified us yet. In the meantime, what will we do? O what in the world will we do?

He calls me early one morning to tell me his mother has arrived and would like to see me. He thanks me for my letter, apologizes for not answering, explains how difficult it has been. The conversation is surprisingly relaxed, as if it were a continuation of one we had yesterday. I stare out the window at my garden, where the tulips are up, tall and yellow. I tell him I'd love to come over. Then immediately I begin to panic at the thought of seeing the house, his mother, and him all at once. I call back the next day and ask apologetically if he could make himself scarce when I visit. He says he'll try, but he's not comfortable leaving her alone, so he'll have to be there at least long enough to let me in.

The driveway to our old house is a familiar serpentine curve, and sumac still intrudes on the long, narrow garden. The chicken coop has been converted into a toolshed, but the small stream beside it gurgles as it used to. The trees have grown taller, casting the house in shadow. The hosta has been moved from beside the front door to a skimpy flower garden under the kitchen window. There is green mold on the sill.

I knock and enter the mud room. Through the window of the door, I see him in the kitchen. The shadows of the tall trees are everywhere. He waves me inside. As I step into the kitchen, I hear Marian, my former mother-in-law, call my name. It is all oddly Shakespearean, and at the same time utterly ordinary. Not knowing what else to do, I give him a cursory hug, then call to Marian, "I'm coming!"

She is in bed in the corner of the living room. She stretches her arms up toward me, fingers moving quickly in a hurry-up gesture, as if she were playing a harp just over her head. I bend to hug her; the flannel of her pale pink shirt is soft on my cheek. She is warm and sweet smelling, and I think: *Death does not smell this way.*

We hold hands as I sit on the edge of her bed, and she speaks of how she is ready to die. She is lucid and glowing, her hair thick and lively. The cancer in her stomach, she explains, takes away her appetite and gives her pain, but the morphine helps with that. "In the meantime," she purrs, her eyes moistening, "I'm so glad that you two have become friends again, so happy. . . . I was so sad when you split up. I just didn't understand it; you two had so much in common."

The couch he and I bought together in New York is behind her head, its green upholstery faded. The lilac I planted just outside the window is about ten feet tall now, the branches spindly, a few stubborn blossoms at the top. *It's just too dark here,* I think. Then I kiss Marian's hand and read her a Psalm, exactly as I imagined.

The next day, my ex-husband calls to say how hard my visit was for him, how he felt frazzled and upset, how it reminded him of the old days when he was always at a loss to deal with my emotional needs.

I listen quietly, then thank him and say, "Well, we sure have improved our ability to communicate."

"I should hope so," he says.

A week later, he and I kneel beside her. She is obviously near the end. The death mask is in place, her breathing labored. "I want to go home," she mumbles. "I want to go home." He is stroking her brow, and I notice that his free hand is around mine. We tell her she is going home.

Once she grows quiet, he turns to me and says, "This has been so stupid." He means, I realize, our fifteen-year silence, and everything behind it.

"Painful and stupid," I say. "As far as I'm concerned, it's over."

He nods in agreement, and we squeeze each other's hands, then turn back to tend his mother. And just like that, I know forgiveness has arrived. ■

Bleeding Dharma

by STEPHEN T. BUTTERFIELD

I t's your anniversary. She's been losing weight for weeks, carrying on about how to celebrate, and hinting that it might be time for you to buy her some new lingerie. All afternoon you miss her, counting the hours until she'll be home. You play the CDs you both like and plan things to say to her; you'll ask about her latest academic success, and what she thinks of your new painting. She has been promising you hot sex all weekend. You look forward to the little rituals you share each night when she comes in: playing with the dog, telling jokes, sipping coffee, recapping the day.

When she still hasn't arrived at three in the morning, you call the state police, but there are no accident reports. You pace around and around, still playing the CDs and trying to stay interested in your painting, but the minutes drag on. Why hasn't she called? (You would never do this; you call her daily whenever you're away and give her your complete itinerary.) You become angry, then terrified, and the first trickles of grief begin to flow from the crack that is opening in your heart.

She comes in at 4:30 and spends half an hour in the bathroom without speaking to you, and you know why she is washing. She walks upstairs to the bedroom and announces that she has found someone else, she has just spent the night with him, and she is moving out. She blames you.

You howl in anguish, curse, weep, tear your hair, follow her around while she packs. You ask her, *Why? Why?* and learn only more and more horrible things: that she has not loved you for eighteen months;

that she has only pretended, deceived you, mocked you, kept up a front, repeated your love rituals in order to go on taking your money while beginning a new love affair behind your back, using your support and your car — and it was him she lost the weight for, not you. She drives away and leaves you alone with this new knowledge, in a house you shared with her for five years.

It is the worst wound you have ever received, and you've had plenty. It is hideous. You feel as if you have been bitten by a cobra and your whole system is filled with poison. The only important question is whether you will survive.

The survivors of wounds like this laugh; you have laughed, and have been a survivor, too. But you're getting old now — you're fifty-three — and you had no idea that it gets worse with age. You thought the wounds of your youth had toughened you. Uh-uh. Because on top of the loss, the grief and anger at having been betrayed, and the knowledge that you yourself left someone who loved you in order to be with her, there is the humiliation that you could not see it coming, that you were so gullible, so easily used by a younger woman. You fear that you will despair of ever trusting anyone enough to try again, that you will sink into darkness, alone and unloved, prey for the scavengers that haunt the fringes of the pack, waiting to pick off the old and the sick.

Because you have some meditation skills, you begin to watch the pain. It is not like a nail in the foot — something you can point to and say, "If only I could pull that out, I would get better." It is nowhere in particular, although gradually it begins to localize in the chest, in the region of the heart, a diffuse sensation of bleeding, bleeding, all the time, your lifeblood draining away into space.

The house you shared with her is like a prison, a torture chamber; you hate the rooms, you hate the views, you hate the dishes, you hate the bathroom, you hate the vanity shelf and the mirror that you hung for her there. And you hate the bed — especially the bed.

Her belongings are still around. You will be finding them for months, maybe years. You will be getting her junk mail, coming across her old love notes in your books. You will be reading your journal entries about rolling on the floor with her and yipping like puppies, about her riding you into explosions of joy, about your longing for her when she went away for a week and how you watched her footprints fill up with snow. It's your house, and she has managed to take it from you and turn it into hell.

The wound goes deeper; the venom begins to corrupt and weaken your will to live. You don't want to live through this. You don't want to be here. You don't want to have veins, a beating heart, circulating blood, eyes, ears, lungs, limbs — you don't want any of it. Above all, you don't want to have a cock, to feel again the desire you felt for her.

You once thought life was a gift, but not anymore. You committed yourself to the idea of helping others, but, if this pain is life's bottom line, what kind of help can you give anyone? The best help you can think of is carbon monoxide. It is much better never to have existed. You want to be nothing, nothing at all. You have said many prayers, and now your deepest, most fervent prayer is to be made into nothing, as if you had never been. The best advice you can give anyone is: die; and if you happen to get reborn, kill yourself instantly, and keep doing it.

First you try willing yourself to drop dead, but your heart goes on beating. So you put a plastic bag over your face, but before you lose consciousness your hands fight to tear it off and your lungs defeat you, gulping long drafts of air: your body wants to live. It is like your dog, who licks your face and wags her tail while you roll on the floor weeping and howling and praying for God to strike you dead. Your dog licks the tears off your cheeks. What will she do after you are gone? Who will feed her? Who will take her for walks, play games with her, hug her, groom her, clean her ears? When you were suicidal as a young man, you stayed alive for the sake of your children. Now it has come to this: you are hanging on to the stub end of your existence for the sake of a dog. Yet whenever death finally comes, you will face the same agony: What about my dog? What about my family, my house?

So why not do it now? Why keep creating these false dreams of happiness that always dissolve, always? Make a will, write your last letters, and ask a friend to adopt the dog. You are still young enough to choose the time, the place, the method. If you wait too long, these choices will be taken from you, and there will be nothing left you can control, not even your bowels.

You begin to write suicide notes. In the process, you find yourself meditating on the nature of emotional pain, and the nature of life. Speaking the unspeakable is a kind of pleasure; putting your torment into words, something of a challenge. Amiri Baraka titled one of his works *Preface to a Twenty-Volume Suicide Note*. What a perfect description of the writer's dilemma: he wanted to die, but he didn't want to come to the end of the note. Once we come to suspect that life is not worth living, we bravely walk out over the shark-infested sea on a plank made by our own words, prepared to leap into the abyss. But we keep generating more words to delay reaching the end of the plank.

So you write letters — to your friends, to her friends, to her. You make a fool of yourself by mailing them, because you know that, if you didn't, the pain would suck you down. You do the things people are supposed to do during crisis: contact your local mental-health agency; reach out for support from your family and friends. But their powers are limited. They cannot sit with you all the time and hold your hand. They cannot bring back the dream world you have lost, or restore your youth, or give you a reason to live. And they cannot save you from the nights.

The nights are the worst. For the first three, you don't sleep at all; then you sleep in fits, an hour here, two hours there. You are not interested in food. Strangely, the dog stops eating, too. She sleeps beside you, on the floor next to the couch. You pat her as always, massage her body, stroke her muzzle, hold her paws, whisper her name, and this giving of affection nourishes her. And, unaccountably, it nourishes you, too. You begin to eat again, more for her than for yourself, and soon she is begging you for tidbits and eating ravenously.

Your children call regularly and come to your house, not to borrow money or ask for help, as before, but to see how you are doing. Your son describes to you painful episodes in his life that you knew nothing of, and you receive him into the brotherhood of the scarred. You collapse weeping in front of your daughter, whom you rejected because your ex-partner didn't like her. This is the first time you have ever allowed her to see you weak and wounded, and she holds you and weeps. Your every interaction with these human beings you fathered has changed. Now you need them, instead of their always needing you.

Maybe you could live a little longer just to enjoy this new kind of dialogue with them.

Now there are breaks in the wall of grief, occasional moments when you feel you can move around a bit without praying for death — enough to notice that inside you there is a sufferer who remembers your former life and roasts in flames of anger, betrayal, and loss; and there is a watcher, a questioner, who does not judge but merely reflects. The sufferer says, "I want to be nothing. Please make me nothing." And the watcher responds, "What are you now, other than nothing?" The sufferer says, "Then please stop this pain. If I'm nothing, why is there so much pain?" And the watcher says, "What is it like? Where is it located? What triggers it?"

It is triggered by memory, by nostalgia.

What happens?

There is a memory of something pleasant, then a sense that it is gone forever, and then anger and a feeling of betrayal, because it was an illusion even at the time it was happening, because I believed the experience was shared, and it wasn't; I was being exploited.

What has become of that belief?

It's gone. The illusion is gone.

And the exploitation?

That's gone, too.

Then where is the pain coming from now?

From the memory of the passion. From clinging to that memory. From wishing I had it back.

From clinging, then.

Yes, precisely: from clinging.

Clinging to an illusion.

Yes, a mirage. A beautiful mirage.

The wound goes on bleeding, and the blood is love: for the dog, for your children, for this strange dialogue with the watcher, a Buddha figure sitting on his rock. During the day you clean the house, rearranging the furniture to make the rooms look different, removing everything of hers, reclaiming the space inch by inch. While you work, you still think about suicide, about methods and the business that must be resolved before you depart, but you also think of ways to depart other than killing your body, which has been your faithful dog and does not deserve your aggression. You could put the house on the market and relocate.

You go up and down the stairs, up and down, removing her things, cleaning out her room, stripping it back down to the room it was before you ever knew her. It is not such a bad room: you built it for meditation, opened it to the sky, and the skylight and windows are still there, and the old barn-board walls that have belonged to you since childhood. It is a good piece of construction. Like your own mind, your heart.

You mow the lawn, remembering how she used to wave to you from the house and walk toward you wearing her wide-brimmed white hat, and the memory hurts; all memories of her hurt. They trigger that hideous rumination, which brings back the desire to die, which reopens the dialogue. You heave the loaded grass carts off the machine and suddenly realize that you have not been this strong for ten years. You have been severely lung-impaired, unable to climb stairs without frequent stops for breath, but now you are running up and down the stairs to remove her belongings and heaving loaded grass carts around, and you begin to laugh. You lie down in the grass and shout at the sky, "I'm getting stronger! I'm not dying! She didn't kill me; she made me stronger!" You laugh in triumph, and at the irony of it — you can't stop laughing. When your laughter changes suddenly to tears, you realize you are having manic fits.

Now you are grieving in a manic cycle. On the upswing, you feel as if you have finally let go and the pain has stopped. But soon another memory pulls you down into a closed catacomb of depression, and you see no point whatsoever in being alive. But the watcher is still there. The watcher is in every twist and turn of your mind, no matter how bizarre, crazy, or painful, no matter how tortured you are by feelings of abandonment and loss. And, always, there is the dialogue.

Can you enjoy the beauty of the mirage without clinging?

No, I can't, because I'm not a rock like you.

A rock like me? Who do you think weeps and laughs?

But aren't you an illusion, too? Is there anything that is not illusion? What does it matter that everything is illusion if I suffer anyway?

It doesn't matter, except to help you wake up.

Wake up to what?

To this.

If I let go of everything because it's all an illusion, then why should I live?

There is no reason why you should live. Why do you?

And you meditate for a long time on that question, as if it were a koan: if you say there is a reason to live, then you are clinging to illusion; if you say there is no reason to live, then you are denying the beauty of the mirage. Why live?

For the time being, you live only for the dialogue, and the koan. They transmute the pain, but you don't understand how or why. The dialogue and the koan are you. There may be no other time but this time. There may be nothing else.

So you dust off your shrine, carefully cleaning and polishing the water glasses and the crystal that symbolize the clarity of awakened mind, the dharma text, the brass bell, the incense dish, the rice offering bowl, the candleholders. You light the candles, do your Buddhist rituals, recite your mantras and invocations. You had almost forgotten how. You don't know yet whether this is better than the plastic bag over your face, but at least it leads to more dialogue; the other would simply still your voice — like cutting out your tongue because someone tells you to shut up. You practice, formally, for the time being, for the first time in three years. And, for the first time ever, perhaps, you have heard the dharma, heard and understood.

She owes you back rent. ∎

Committed Relationships

by ERIC ANDERSON

If I'm in your way, just knock
me down. I don't mind; I've been
on the floor. Our dog used to lie
on the rug under the table. I've been
the rug, and what's under the rug.
Not just the dust, but the floorboards
and the underside of the floorboards,
which is the top of the basement,
which is my kind of height. I can get lower.
I've been the basement in the dark
months with only the cold
light slanting through. I've been
the silver light on the cement. Remember
that handprint we found, a child's hand,
pressed into the concrete? There
was a name and a date.
One of the fingers was missing.
I've been as low as the shadow
in those shallow knuckles. I'm above
the dirt, but just barely. You could say,
"Excuse me." I'll move sideways. I've been
sideways. I slipped past the plaster
and slats, such a slight movement
you never even heard me,
breathing in the walls of the house.

The Year In Geese

a short story by **RITA TOWNSEND**

Late Winter

I don't see eye to eye with the large white geese now sharing our hilltop, home to three neighbors and myself. For one thing, the endless days of rain have made them ecstatic — and why not? Every day their watery home grows larger, adds another wing, while I become morose and resentful, watching the margins of my outdoor living space grow smaller, mud and goose droppings at every step.

It's bad enough, isn't it, that I live alone in this tiny cottage surrounded by families? That Tom has plowed the orchard to within a yard of my door so I can't even walk there without hip boots, but since he is the owner and has no need to listen to me, I am left voiceless? That the lover who once made this a sanctuary is gone and will not even answer my letters?

Now the rain falls day in and day out, the road down the hill is studded with stop signs where it's fallen away to one lane, and I must tiptoe each day through the leavings of this ecstatic pair of geese. That's another thing about them: this mating for life. While I like it in concept, particularly against the stark backdrop of my own unmatedness, in practice it seems hazardous — especially for Mrs. Goose, whom Mr. Goose never lets out of his sight except when she's walking a step behind as he, long goose neck protruding in front of him, stalks the pond's perimeter. He does all the talking, the most you hear from her being an occasional pale echo of his vociferous honk.

Spring

Alleged spring, in any case. The rain will not stop, nor the cold. The few blossoms the trees have put out are soggy and pale. Days and weeks slide by, and the space Laura occupied in my life is empty. No, not empty, for I think of her, dream of her, know her scent better than my own, hope still for some mending. Not empty but silent.

My niece LeeAnn visits, and I tell her the story of the geese, how they once lived ten miles farther down the coast at Pinto Lake in Watsonville, but for some reason last fall Mrs. Goose disappeared, and Mr. Goose struck out in search of her. They both ended up at Wildlife Rescue, where their rapturous reunion made it clear they were mated. I've often imagined that reunion, their eyes wide with joy on seeing each other, their piercing cries, probably a great flapping of wings.

My landlady, Paula, Tom's wife, frequents Wildlife Rescue and brought them home to the pond. I never thought to ask why they weren't returned to Pinto Lake. Thinking back, though, to the way Mr. Goose began to claim his territory, I see that he might not have been an ideal park resident. He swaggered around what I began to think of as his compound, managing to make his waddling goose gait imperious. Every few steps, and certainly when any other living thing approached, he thrust his beak to the sky with an earsplitting honk, almost always followed shortly by a big dollop of teal green poop dropping behind.

And he charged whatever appeared in his path — children, dogs, cats, adults, and cars — his neck becoming a sort of missile launcher, thrusting at least two feet in front of him, tipped by the fiery orange bill. All the kids began carrying sticks wherever they went, but almost everyone got bitten at least once anyway, on the back of the leg or the butt while in flight.

LeeAnn and I have just escaped one of his car attacks — he actually pecks at the sides of the car once you have evaded him, jumped into it, and begun up the driveway — when we begin discussing names, something more personal than "Mr. and Mrs. Goose." Actually, I've begun referring to him as "the Terminator," so after some discussion we settle on Arnold, which seems perfect. I'm not sure how we come up with Cissy, but it strikes the right chord as a feminine counter-point to Arnold. So the geese have become, to me at least, Arnold and Cissy.

Early Summer

Occasional days of rain continue as the tireless El Niño gradually gives way to the usual summer coastal fog. The trees are not yet fully leafed, and plums that were ripe by this time two years ago are still hard green knots. Still, the new bunnies and quail are making forays out into the grasses of the orchard. The pond is home to over-nighting wild geese, mallards, coots, and an occasional egret, and the symphony of the bullfrogs is in full force, making me believe in summer, though I can't see or feel it.

Arnold and Cissy have settled in a bit. Though Arnold is only mini-mally less aggressive, they do spend more time now wandering the farther reaches of the compound, floating on the pond, and diving for whatever it is they dive for — heads shooting straight down until only tufted white bottoms and peachy feet are left waving in the air. Thus, there is somewhat less time for deafening honks and making us run for our lives. I've accepted the trade-off of goose poop for not having to mow the little patch of weedy grass in front of my cottage, which they keep cropped. I talk to them as I go about chores outside. "Hey, Arnold, Cissy, how's it going?" And I stop sometimes just to admire their preened beauty: both stark white, with strips of fawn brown down the backs of their necks.

On a July morning I wake long before dawn to find the room radi-ant with moonlight. I walk from window to window, each made lumi-nous by the glistening limbs of the almond tree, the vivid jade off the pond. And I realize how I've longed for her light through this winter and spring with unclouded night skies so rare, and into this sum-mer closed in by fog. Drenched in her absence, I could not remember what was lost. But in her presence now I recall the clear, warm nights of my first summer here, how I stalked the night windows and even moved my bed to be where the moon- and starlight would touch me as I slept.

Longing. And how my longing has worn Laura's face, her long body. Confessing now how much more deeply I let her in than I believed I had. Yet not knowing, really, how much the longing and loneliness is for Laura and how much it only wears her face but opens wide beyond her — to all that I won't name, even to myself.

Late Summer

Arnold stands outside my front door. His sharp cries echo off the pond, slice through the hot Labor Day air again and again until I yell at him, "Arnold, stop it! Go away!" He eyes me through the screened window, his body shudders slightly, and he raises his head to repeat the earsplitting call, his harp-shaped breast pumping in and out.

Cissy disappeared suddenly two or three days ago, and Arnold is inconsolable. *It's a dangerous world that you and I inhabit, Arnold,* I think. The heads of the sunflowers, which lifted toward the sun only days ago, have been lopped off and thrown onto the compost pile. While Paula shelters several baby squirrels in her house, bottle-feeding them around the clock, yesterday her cat Milo caught a wild one to torture before eating it for lunch. I momentarily considered leaving it to its fate, then locked Milo in my cottage until the baby had run, its brushy red tail waving, back to the trees.

Arnold seems to listen now, and I think I do hear some sound from the other end of the pond. I hope it is Cissy. I first thought that she'd become confused, or fed up, and had lifted into the early-morning air with the wild geese who often spend the night on the pond. But domestic geese aren't much for flying, so it seems unlikely. Paula thinks she may be nesting somewhere, but it seems too late in the year for that. I've already given up hope of seeing Cissy and Arnold followed across the water by ten or twelve little goslings. Anyway, if she were somewhere nesting, Arnold would not be so disconsolate, and he seems to grow more so daily. Our unspoken fear, of course, is that a coyote has taken her.

In the early morning a day later, I wake to the screaming (there's no other word for it) of some small animal and bound to the door to call my cat Reuben, who appears instantly. I step out onto the porch to look into the moon-washed clearing, scanning the pond and the garden: no movement, no sound. I take in a dim Orion, Venus off by herself, three or four other stars visible in the washed-out sky, then step back into the house and walk to the bathroom. Twenty feet from the window there, half in and half out of the shadow of the pear tree — the coyote, watching me. Moonlight brushes the surprisingly lush fur of its rising and falling breast. I feel I should shout or knock on the window to scare it, but I don't. I only watch as it turns and trots through the orchard toward the brush at the edge of the clearing.

I go back to bed and dream of Laura, of unexpectedly finding myself in the same office building with her and hiding so that she won't see me. She walks directly to me anyway, and we look into each other's eyes without speaking. Then she is sitting down and I am walking behind her. I reach out to touch her but pull back my hand, remembering that I am not supposed to touch her now. The urge is like a fire in me.

Awake again, I feel Arnold's cries echo inside me. I lie in bed, covered only by a sheet, and my heart lies above me like the torn-open animal I imagined earlier somewhere out in the weeds. I cover it with my hand, and the warmth eases the pain, comforts me.

Early Autumn

Arnold's grief has been unflagging. Because I work at home much of the day while everyone else is gone, he now, like the neighbors' dogs and cats, tends to focus his attention here. But while the others maintain a respectable distance, at least until they see a door open, Arnold comes right up on the porch, knocking and demanding. I know I've brought this on myself. There is something about his ceaseless lament that draws me. The days shorten and cool, and as the slanted sun throws its deep shadows around everything, my own losses pull at me. Listening to Arnold trumpet his grief to the heavens day after day, I have wanted both to comfort him and to join him.

At first I just stood near him and talked softly: "Oh, Arnold, I am so sorry Cissy is gone; yes, I know you're sad." He quieted then. Tentatively

I reached a hand toward him, and he wove his long ribbon neck away to avoid me, looking quizzically up, but did not step away. I reached again, beyond the orange bill, behind the round eyes, and slid my hand lightly down his delicate downy neck. He stood absolutely still. I could almost feel a sigh in him, and I passed my hand again and again down this fragile stem of life, then out onto the fan of feathers across his back, the narrow spiny ridges and silken expanse. I was entranced, and Arnold, for once, was silent.

But the silence lasts only as long as I am with him. As soon as I come back into the house, the honking begins again. It is the first sound I hear on waking and lets up only intermittently until sunset.

My office is just off the small covered porch at the back of the cottage, where Reuben often sleeps on a carpet remnant. But now Arnold has discovered me here. Sometimes I gradually become aware of a light knock-knocking on the glass and look up to see him two feet from me, pecking at the French doors. Or I am roused from concentration by a terrible racket on the porch — hissing (goose and cat), yowling, wing-flapping, pots and water bowls turning over, and barking when the dogs get into the act. The upshot, generally, is that Reuben is gone and Arnold is stationed at the door, pecking at the glass and honking till it vibrates my bones.

Sometimes when I leave the house, I have to shoo Arnold off the steps to get out the door, and often have to warn him with a kick in his direction when he comes at me, because I've ignored or challenged him. He's back to attacking the car as I leave, and each time I am amazed at just how outrageous he is. Also, there is something in his attitude now, the way he wants to keep me in his sight, that is an uncomfortable reminder of the way he treated Cissy. A small, and I suppose silly, suspicion grows in me that Arnold has taken me as his new mate.

Midautumn

L aura and I ran into each other at a workshop two weeks ago. So strange to be near her — her dense physical presence drawing me. We said a sort of shocked hello in the morning, at lunch sat at a table with other people, but near each other. By evening I could stand it no longer, and we found a room to talk alone.

We argued, but to me it felt like arguing that went somewhere, went through. Finally, things were being said. Before leaving she asked me for a hug, and it was long and close.

The next day, though, Laura called me, angry again, saying that I had tricked her into feeling that something was different, that it was safe. But because she had felt anxious when she woke up that morning, she knew it had been a trick, something I had done to her. Anything I said was just more treachery. I am not allowed to have a voice.

Arnold's voice, on the other hand, is unrelenting. This afternoon, yet another altercation on the back porch interrupts my work, and this time I go out to drive him away. The dogs come bounding over, and I encourage them to chase him, then feel like a betrayer. But ten minutes later, just as I am settling back into work, Arnold is on the front steps. After another twenty minutes of yelling out the window at him, I am losing my mind. I push open the screen door, which forces him off the narrow steps, but he goes no farther.

I go down the steps and begin to kick in his direction, yelling at him to get the hell away from me. Arnold backs off about a yard, then rams his neck straight out and, with a venomous hiss, comes at me. I have no way to defend myself — he's already too close to kick — and fear grips me. I do the only thing there is to do: reach out and grab his neck. Arnold stops instantly, and we are eye to eye. Images and emotions pour through me: my mother wringing the necks of white pullets, Laura's eyes the day I admitted that sometimes I did not like her, the mixture of rage and tenderness in me.

I use my other hand to turn Arnold's body around, letting his neck swivel within my fingers, and then release him, giving a little kick to his butt to send him away from me. Arnold walks to the middle of the driveway and sits down. I have never seen him sit down. He is smaller, and quiet, shaking his neck and moving it around.

Overcome with remorse, I can think only of the feel of his neck in my hand, the frail vertebrae and tendons, think only that he trusted me, allowed me to touch the most vulnerable part of him. I cannot decide if what I did was a reasonable act of self-protection or an unreasonable act of treachery. I move toward him on the driveway: "Arnold, are you all right?" He rises and moves away from me into the grass near the pond.

I come into the house, sit down, listen to the silence, wipe away tears, finally go to the window and see that Arnold is sitting again, still adjusting his neck. Unable to bear the thought that I have injured him, I go out and very slowly approach him, talking. "Arnold, I am so sorry if I hurt you, but you scared me. You're driving me crazy. I don't know what to do for you. . . . I don't know what to do for either of us."

The following morning Arnold is up and walking around but sticking fairly close to the pond. By afternoon he's trying out a few honks, and the next day he is pretty much back to normal, though he keeps some distance from my cottage.

A few days later I stop by the post office to pick up my mail and find the letter I've been dreading from Laura. I sit reading it in the car. She says she wants no further contact with me.

I come home tired and bereft. Arnold is waiting for me in the driveway and waddles beside me toward the door. I stop and look at him, sighing: "Arnold." Knowing I shouldn't, I reach and let my fingers touch that softness. He doesn't even flinch.

Late Autumn

I couldn't leave well enough alone. Now Arnold is back to his old behavior, and I am contemplating on a daily basis saying to Paula that he must either have a new mate or a new home or something. He is putting me over the edge. Then Tom is home one day, in and out of their house with workmen, when suddenly the air is filled, not with Arnold's shrieks, for once, but with Tom's curses: "Damn it! Damn it! He bit me! Shit, did you see that? He bit me!"

This is the second time that Arnold has gotten Tom, and I'm not surprised when I learn it will be the last. Late that day Paula tells me she has Arnold in the back of her car, where Tom put him. After she picks up the kids, she's going to take him back to Pinto Lake. I am enormously relieved and try not to think of Arnold squatting somewhere in Paula's car, his soft whiteness against gray vinyl. I don't go to say goodbye.

Early Winter

T he rains have come back, and after a dry fall, the pond has begun to grow again. While there have been some hard rainstorms, La Niña — if that's who we have now — is kinder than her brother and breaks them up with days of sun, though she also brings nights of hard frost and air that keeps its bite throughout the day.

It may be that the cold has made the coyote more desperate. Two weeks ago he dug under the fence of the chicken pen and killed two of the three brown hens who've lived there peacefully and safely for the last two years. He injured the third, who occupies the pen now all on her own, hiding at the back unless I call her out to feed her greens left in the garden.

A month after Arnold's departure, I finally go to Pinto Lake on a sunny midafternoon to visit him. The first thing I see is a gigantic pair of geese preening themselves at the grassy edge of the park. They are larger than Arnold and Cissy, with black and brown backs, coarser voices, and bills that are shorter and of a deeper orange color. I never doubted that I would recognize Arnold, or he me, but I am surprised I can see these differences so clearly.

Three young girls arrive with bread and immediately clamber, squealing, to the top of a picnic table as literally hundreds of ducks, gulls, and coots swarm toward them. The two geese wander over, too. One of the girls throws chunks of bread to duck after duck while the male goose, standing patiently right beneath her, bobs his head this way and that, following each thrown piece. I find myself silently urging her to throw one to him, but she doesn't.

Skirting willow, sycamore, and pine, I walk the accessible perimeter of the blue lake nestled among coastal-range hills. My eyes graze the landscape, the inlets of water, the unreachable boundaries of the lake for Arnold's hefty snow-whiteness. I listen among the quacks, shrieks, and caws for a piercing honk and can neither fathom nor deny my disappointment at not finding it.

Ten Days Before Christmas

Reuben gets me out of bed in the predawn. When I open the front door to let him out, the moon is slipping toward the eastern horizon, the whole of her pale, round face illuminated by the fiery crescent burning at one side. The barn owl hoots twice; otherwise it is silent.

A deep sigh rises and falls in me. *It wasn't silence that I wanted,* I think. *Does anyone understand that? It wasn't silence I was looking for.* ■

Smashing The Plates

by **ALISON LUTERMAN**

I'm smashing the plates with a hammer. *Boom!*
The blue plates and the yellow ones from Goodwill.
It's to make a mosaic. *Pow!* I'm smashing them
On the cement floor of my friend's warehouse.
I thought you loved me. *Boom!*
And perhaps you did.
The red plates and the green ones, bought at yard sales,
Someone's discards. This one has such a pretty pattern
  of flowers
On its border, it seems a shame — *Boom!* —
To break it, but there it is, in jagged ceramic pieces.
I kneel on dust, wrap in a towel and smash
Something that once carried rice or greens or meat
To a hungry mouth. We are so rich in this country
We can afford to break —
Pow! Bam! — whatever we want.
Whatever we are bored with.
You held me in your arms and told me you loved me.
One tear leaked from your eye as you said it.
Did you forget?
I am stacking up the gold plates, color of pumpkin
  harvest,
And the shiny midnight blue. I don't like white.
I have never liked white,
The color of silence.
Crash! Pow! It's like smashing tiny bodies

Wrapped in swaddling,
As if you couldn't bear to see their faces,
And suddenly I understand how men might want to murder
What they can't bear to look at.
Where is the home for my heart? *Crash! Pow!*
We are going to make something beautiful
Out of all of these pieces. My friend is sorting them
Into plastic containers while I kneel and smash.
Was it the face of my love you couldn't bear?
Men go blind when they look at the sun
Directly. I know I will never
Have answers to my questions, and what's done —
Smash! Bang! — cannot be undone.
I know we will find some beautiful use
For all the pieces.

Finding A Good Man

by JASMINE SKYE

L ast summer, when trouble started heating up in the apartment building next door, it occurred to me that I was a potential statistic: a single woman in a ground-floor apartment on the wrong side of town. Exhausted from lying awake till all hours with my ear cocked for the faintest sounds of forced entry, I decided to do something.

So I got a dog. Barney was a middle-aged, raggedy black cocker-spaniel mix with a gray muzzle, legs like lacquered canes, and paws the size of oven mitts. He was talented: knew how to sit, stay, and "go lie down." He could also, as a neighbor's kid discovered, shake a paw — something I'd never have figured out, because I wouldn't have risked embarrassing him by trying. Barney conscientiously set to work warding off evil — a task that consisted mainly of barking at the couple upstairs, whose telltale smokers' coughs unrolled every day in the hallway like a suicidal lovers' duet.

For the first month after I brought him home from the pound, Barney crept into my bed at night and wedged himself tightly against my back. Asleep, he shivered and wept and shook, caught in the grip of nightmarish memories. I soothed and quieted him, stroking his body and murmuring, "It's all right. . . . You're safe now. . . . Safe." Some mornings I'd turn over and find him lying beside me with his head on the pillow, nose pointed toward the ceiling, like a husband.

I have not been in a relationship with a man for more than a year now, a situation that has resulted in a dangerously high increase in my doughnut consumption. I eat doughnuts each time I realize, with fresh pain, that the men I'm attracted to are completely out of reach: monogamous, left-leaning, gentle-spirited, broad-shouldered carpenters with a love for the works of minor poets — and, inevitably, a family.

I see this type of man in hardware and grocery stores. He's dazed from sleep, and his hair resembles a cornfield after a flying saucer has landed. He shuffles slowly down the aisle, work boots untied, children hanging off him like Christmas-tree ornaments. He's like an old sofa you can lie down on without worrying about spilling food. But there's also an air of thoughtfulness about him, a sense that he's going over lists and calculations in his head as he stands motionless, staring at the items in the sale bins. He's the type who speaks infrequently, and when he does, your ears prick up, because you imagine any ideas that have taken so long to develop are definitely worth considering.

On Saturday night, this guy gets cleaned up to *GQ* level and stands in line at the movie theater with his wife, who is usually tall, slim, and self-contained. She believes that, without her, this man would lose his sense of direction and become just one more dreamy, cosmic, hairy-chested innocent wading through a sea of inchoate emotions. She imagines that she helps him to realize who he is and what he wants.

He allows her this illusion.

The city where I live is small, historic, picturesque — a city of century-old limestone buildings and annual boating events. It has one good university, five penitentiaries, and two factories: one manufacturing plastics, the other aluminum. In a nationwide almanac, my city is listed as being a good place for senior citizens to retire. Single, educated women outnumber comparable men here by about four to one.

How I ended up here is not very interesting, nor is the reason I continue to live here. I have a handful of friends, but no one I would miss terribly were I to be transplanted to some other city tomorrow. I stay because I'm a reclusive painter, because this place is familiar, and because I can't think of anywhere else to go.

For the past few years, I've looked for love in the personals. Almost without exception, the men who place ads list sports as their number-one hobby. They want a woman who is (surprise!) also into sports and is "happy" or at least "easygoing." There are those seeking a "slim" woman and others looking for someone "queen-size" or "height-weight proportionate." I once read an ad by a man who said he'd take any woman who wasn't "too ugly to look at or too stupid to talk to." Then there are the cheaters: the sly, bored, unhappily-married-but-powerless-to-leave-her men looking for a "discreet relationship."

Dispirited, I barely glance at the men-seeking-women ads anymore. I stick to creating my own, which I hope convey something in utter contrast to the meat market that surrounds them.

I met my last boyfriend through the personals. Tall, soft-spoken Curtis was a farmer who walked naked in his fields to feel the warm summer air caress every part of him. He was the most complicated man I'd ever met: beautifully articulate, emotionally expressive, and clinically depressed.

Curtis had answered several women's ads at the same time, he confessed, and I was the only one who'd called him back. Almost immediately, he told me about his depression.

"That's OK," I said. "I think I'm agoraphobic. I'm looking into it."

"Really?" He brightened. "My dog's agoraphobic." He told me how he'd rescued it from a neighbor who'd kept it shut up in a barn for the first six months of its life.

Curtis said that meeting me was a gift, and that it cured him of wanting to be a tree — stationary, uninvolved. He requested that I give him a ring to let other women know he was taken. I picked one designed by a jeweler friend of mine. It seemed made for Curtis, with flowing, interwoven strands of silver — like water, like roots. I said it was OK that he couldn't afford to buy me one.

It was a potent attraction. For three months, we made love fiercely, marveling at our amazing good fortune at having found each other. Then the hints of trouble I'd been ignoring came more clearly into view: Curtis talked only about himself and was rarely interested in the daily workings of my life. He called a former lover a "dragon-breath bitch." When I told him I was thinking of writing a story about us, he offered as a possible opening line "Pine trees are the architects

of their own destinies because of the space they create around themselves." And then he actually said, "I want someone in my life without
that person affecting my life." And finally: "I'm sick of you."

I don't know when he left the ring I'd given him in the dark blue velvet box in my desk drawer. I hadn't noticed that he'd stopped wearing
it. For a long time afterward, whenever I had to go into that drawer,
I'd tell myself that I really should move the ring someplace where I
wouldn't have to see it. But I couldn't bear to touch it. I think I needed
periodically to experience the shock of finding it, a tangible reminder
of my phenomenal lapse in judgment.

I retreated from the personals and focused on trying to be single
with integrity. I devoured all the books I'd accumulated from yard
sales but never gotten around to reading, took a yoga class, and got
together with my women friends for videos and popcorn. I alternated
between feeling relief at having myself back again and grappling with
the low-grade depression that always accompanies my not being in a
relationship. My friends preached to me about how happy, fulfilled
people attract love, and emotionally needy people repel it. Be self-
sufficient and industrious, they advised, act as if you don't need anyone, and you'll attract someone who'll love you as an independent
equal. Of course, most of the women who imparted this advice were
in relationships themselves and therefore not stuck for someone to
massage their backs at night.

My single women friends weren't much better. Most of them had
gone without relationships for years, like camels without water. Some
were perpetual students, full of enthusiasm, with an insatiable desire
to learn. "The world is such a fascinating place," they'd say. "There's so
much to do that there's just no time for the emotional demands of a
relationship."

I, on the other hand, crave those emotional demands, though I admit I approach relationships irrationally. As I begin to fall in love, it's
like an ego death. I lose myself to the intoxicating drug of lovesick-
ness. I barely eat or sleep, and something inside me explodes with
creativity: even before the possibility of sex is on the table, I have
accurately sketched, from memory, the face of the man who has me

enthralled and richly celebrated him in a poem, which I've then likely set to music. When I love a man, I want to portray something of his beauty to the world — or maybe just to myself.

My friends tell me I'm too intense, that in a past life I was probably a medieval troubador, writing sonnets for my lady, wearing her colors into battle. I'm at my most hopeful and believing when in love. True, it dissipates after a while, becomes something familiar, sedate — but that's agreeable, too. I love the comfort and companionship of doing a crossword puzzle together over breakfast, or going on yard-sale excursions, or driving to the ocean. I'd even settle for just helping each other fold the laundry. I'm easy to please where love is concerned because, to me, being alone is just running errands, remembering to floss, and making sure the recycling goes out on the right night. It's having no one to consult at the video store who actually has a stake in which movie I choose. It's watching people make love in those movies and feeling as though they're the ones leading a normal life, while I'm living on a piece of celluloid. Being alone is spending too many nights in a row sharing doughnuts with my dog.

A year after the Curtis fiasco, I placed another ad. The first man I met was Andy, who on the phone had the voice of a DJ playing exotic world music from a moonlit, tropical location.

In reality, Andy drove a van for a maximum-security prison, transferring violent criminals clad in hand and leg irons to special-handling units. In his spare time, he liked to work out at the gym, cook, and read supermarket novels. Though forty years old, he looked as if his mother still picked out his clothes. When we went out to a restaurant, he wore his baseball cap throughout the meal and neglected to pull his sweat shirt down over his blond-haired potbelly. He answered my questions in monosyllables and asked none of his own. I tried to reconcile that beautiful voice with the entirely ordinary man sitting in front of me, but it was as though he were part of some real-life ventriloquist act.

So as not to appear too hasty in my judgment, I invited Andy back to my apartment for tea. He sat on my couch with the baseball cap still glued to his head, the odor of his spicy aftershave circulating on small updrafts of air. Barney fawned all over him as if he were an emissary of God. When I pointed to a bulletin board displaying photographs of my paintings — as if to say, "There's my soul" — Andy squinted at it for a second without bothering to get up, and then gave, I'm positive, a mental shrug of boredom.

The next man I met was Joe, a fifty-three-year-old master mechanic and right-wing Christian fundamentalist. He was all man, with the rugged, intelligent face and powerful bearing of a Celtic druid. He called women "gals" and men "fellas" and began sentences with "I seen." He talked mainly of his work — the technical details of repairs he'd made, the trucks he'd seen jackknifed on the highway, the one sitting in a pool of titanium dioxide, or something like that. He described these things as though recounting ancient battles, and I drank in every word with a sense of accomplishment, as if I'd been the one to repair the trucks myself.

I was smitten by Joe's cheerful ability to fix anything that broke down, and by his chivalry in general. He joked about his right-wing politics and Pentecostalism as if they were just offbeat ideas he was flirting with and the jury was still out. He brought me wine and steaks for dinner and inspected my art with a passable attempt at interest. It was enough.

After our second date, I was able to imagine us together — me pared down to my pioneer essentials, Joe like a character out of *Braveheart*. Granted, we probably wouldn't be able to discuss books or paintings or films other than haltingly, but at least he would be loyal, dependable. Over time, we would develop things in common. I fell headlong into this fantasy as I waited for him to call. Five days of confusing silence ensued. Finally, I called him. He'd been up all night, he said, working on two trucks that had jackknifed, one of them driven by "a nigger — I mean, a Negro."

After Joe, my friend Melanie decided to take me in hand. "Forget the personals for a while," she instructed. "Let's go to a singles dance." There was one coming up at the Holiday Inn.

I didn't see how that could be an improvement. In fact, the idea sounded hugely unappealing, an even more pathetic and awkward lonely-hearts situation. But Mel said it was fun. She called ahead and found out that we should dress the way we did for work. Although I worked at home in paint-spattered plaid shirts and ripped sweat pants, I basically understood what that meant.

The prospect of going to a dance was daunting to me. I spent so much time in solitude and silence that I hardly knew how to behave at large, noisy gatherings. I worried that my attempts at small talk would taper off into embarrassing silences. To avoid this outcome, I skipped work the day of the dance and instead practiced being in public by shopping for an outfit that would make me look as though I had a "real job." I selected a paisley blouse and a short, dark jumper, which I tested in the dressing room, lifting my arms above my head to make sure it wouldn't ride up too far if I happened to dance with any tall men.

Studying my reflection in the mirror, I saw a thirty-seven-year-old woman, never married, childless, with a smooth, unlined face and long, dark hair, carrying about fifteen extra, doughnut-laden pounds. The word *wholesome* came to mind. I looked as though I should be either the mother of a brood of preschoolers or an outdoorsy type, hiking ruddy-cheeked in the woods — not someone about to enter a world of lonely divorcées with their teenagers and mortgages. I was a renter with no car, no savings, and no particular plans in life other than to save my soul and maybe find true love, or at least become comfortable with isolation.

I was vaguely embarrassed walking through the door of the Holiday Inn lounge with Mel, who was the picture of calm, casually conversing with the woman selling tickets. Several pairs of eyes followed us as we found a table from which to begin our own surveillance of the room.

Mel draws a lot of looks. She has classic, timeless features, like an icon from the realm of art or religion. She's how I imagine Joan of Arc — tall, slender, bobbed auburn hair, serious brown eyes gazing out from under delicate brows. Once, when we were sitting in a restaurant, I joked that she should pass on to me whatever guy happened to be stalking her that week. Her face split into a grin, and the man at the next table was so captivated that he accidentally lowered his newspaper onto the candle flame, catching it on fire.

At the dance, she resembled a gracious visiting dignitary, sipping a ladylike amount of white wine while I socked back three beers in a row. Because I almost never drink, I expected it to hit me hard, but I barely noticed any effect.

The DJ looked about seventeen and played a mix of seventies hits and country-and-western tunes of the two-stepping variety. The volume was low, probably because most of us were over forty — some over fifty — and we reminded the DJ of his parents. I visited the bathroom at regular intervals, just to keep moving. A heavyset woman with bleached-blond hair, wearing expensive, tailored clothes, leaned across our table to tell us that the men liked to be asked to dance; they were often too shy to do the asking themselves. I nodded understandingly and swallowed another mouthful of beer, knowing that nothing could induce me to ask anyone.

When a man finally asked me to dance, I was unnaturally calm, completely steady. His name tag said RICK. He was a few inches taller than me, thin, and trembling. My hands were warm and dry — one in his hand, the other at his waist — and I almost began to murmur soothing sounds to him, as I would to a frightened child or an animal. *How unbelievable it is,* I thought, *that two complete strangers can join in an intimate embrace on a dance floor.* I knew what it had cost him to work up the nerve to ask me, and I felt a sense of compassion. But I didn't have a clue what to say to him. When the song ended, I bowed slightly, said thank you, and returned to my seat.

Rick kept asking me to dance. In the course of the evening, I learned that he'd driven a school bus for eight years and had recently gone back to school to learn to be a cook. He was thirty-eight, and, although he liked the Beatles better, he had bought a ticket to the upcoming Rolling Stones concert because he'd never seen them play and thought he should. He wanted to know if I was into hockey.

"Not really," I said apologetically.

"That's OK," he responded, a little too quickly. He had a nice voice, not too high or too low, and an open, caring quality that I liked. But something in me couldn't quite believe that his pleasant companionship would be enough. It wasn't enough, I realized, to find a man I could stand to spend as much time with as I did with my dog.

What I really wanted sounds so clichéd and seems so far beyond my reach that I can hardly bring myself to voice it: I wanted to find a member of my own tribe, someone who spoke the same language. I wanted not just another dizzying infatuation, but something meaningful and true.

After the dance, I went home to Barney, who is still fascinated by everything I do. He watches me operate the electric juicer as if preparing for a day when he'll be called upon to make my morning elixir. He studies me fresh out of the shower, naked and combing the tangles from my hair. Sometimes I'll look up from reading a book and meet his gaze across the room: still, dark, and contemplative, as if I'm the most soul-saving thing he's ever seen in his broken-down life. ■

Eight Love Poems

by SPARROW

QUESTION

Can two nations
fall in love?

LOVE

Love
is the
first
word
we don't
say to
everyone.

A PHRASE ONE NEVER HEARS

"My lover and I are doing our taxes."

SUNLIGHT

Sunlight
loves to fall
on a bed.

TWO PROFESSORS

When two professors
fall in love,
their students rejoice.

NAMED

We are all named
out of love — for
an uncle, a cousin,
a dead violinist.

Often we forget
the love in our names.

THE MOON

The moon loves
snow, because
it reflects.

TEN COMMANDMENTS

The Ten Commandments
do not
mention love.

The Date

by **BRENDA MILLER**

When I return naked to the stone porch,
there is no one to see me glistening.
> — *Linda Gregg*

A man I like is coming for dinner tonight. This means I don't sleep very much, and I wake disoriented in the half light of dawn, wondering where I am. I look at my naked body stretched diagonally across the bed; I look at the untouched breasts, the white belly, and I wonder. I don't know if this man will ever touch me, but I wonder.

I get up and make coffee. While I wait for the water to boil, I study the pictures and poems and quotes held in place by magnets on my refrigerator. I haven't really looked at them in a long time, my gaze usually blank as I reach for the refrigerator door. But this morning I try to see these objects clearly, objectively, as if I were a stranger. I try to figure what this man will make of them, and so, by extension, what he will make of me.

He'll see pictures of my three nieces, my nephew, my godson. He'll see my six women friends hiking in a slot canyon of the San Rafael swell, straddling the narrow gap with their strong, muscular legs. He'll see the astrological forecast for Pisces and a Joseph Campbell quote that tells me if I'm to live like a hero I must be ready at any moment, for "there is no other way." He'll see Rumi: "Let the Beauty we love be what we do. There are hundreds of ways to kneel and kiss the ground." He'll see me kayaking with my friend Kathy in the San Juan Islands; me sitting with my parents in the Oasis Cafe in Salt Lake City, the three of us straining to smile as the waitress snaps the photo; me standing on the grounds of Edna St. Vincent Millay's estate, my arms around my fellow artist-colonists, grinning as if I were genuinely happy.

Who is this person on my refrigerator door? I try to form these bits and pieces into a coherent image, a picture for me to navigate by as I move through my solitary morning routine of coffee, juice, cereal, a few moments of rumination before the stained-glass kitchen window. But I've seen these fragments so often they've come to mean nothing to me; this collage exists only for others, a persona constructed for the few people who make it this far into my house — into my life. "Look," it says. "Look how athletic, spiritual, creative, loved I am." And my impulse, though I stifle it, is to rearrange all these items, deleting some, adding others, to create a picture I think this man will like.

But how can I know? How can I keep from making a mistake? Besides, I tell myself, a mature woman would never perform such a silly and demeaning act. So I turn away from the fridge, leave things the way they are, drink my coffee, and gaze out the window. It's February and the elm trees are bare, the grass brown between patches of snow. Tomorrow is Valentine's Day, a fact I've been avoiding. I think about the blue tulips I planted in the fall, still hunkered underground, and the thought of them down there in the darkness, their pale shoots nudging the hard-packed soil, makes me a little afraid.

I'm afraid because I'm thirty-eight years old, and I've been alone for almost three years now, having dated no one since leaving my last boyfriend, who is now in California marrying someone else. Sometimes I like to be alone; I lie on my bed at odd hours of the day with a small lavender-filled pillow over my eyes, like the old woman I think I'm becoming. At times like these, the polish of light through the half-closed Venetian blinds seems a human thing, kind and forgiving, and my solitude a condition to be guarded, even if it means remaining unpartnered for life.

But other times I gaze into my bedroom and see no comforting light, smell no lavender. Instead, the empty room feels like a reproach — dark, unyielding. Unable to move beyond the threshold, I stand there paralyzed, panic gnawing beneath my skin. I try to breathe deeply, try to remember the smiling self on my refrigerator door, but that person seems all surface, a lie rehearsed so many times it bears a faint semblance to truth, but not the core. I cry as if every love I've ever known has been false somehow, a trick. This loneliness seems more real, more true than any transient moment of happiness.

At these times I want only to be coupled, to be magnified in a world which too often renders me invisible. In my parents' house, an entire wall is devoted to formal family photographs, arranged in neat symmetry: my parents in the middle; my older brother, his wife, and their two children on one side; my younger brother, his wife, and their two children on the other. When I lived with my boyfriend Keith for five years, my parents insisted we have a portrait taken as well, and we did: me in a green T-shirt and multicolored beads, Keith in jeans and a denim shirt, the two of us standing with our arms entwined. So for a while my photo, and my life, fit neatly into the family constellation.

Then Keith and I split up, but the photograph remained on the wall another year, staring down at me when I came home to visit for Hanukkah. I know my parents kept it up out of nostalgic fondness for Keith. "You have to take that down," I finally told them, and they nodded sadly. Now a portrait of myself, alone, hangs in its spot — a nice photograph, flattering, but still out of place amid the growing and changing families that surround it. Whenever I visit, my eight-year-old nephew asks me, "Why aren't you married?" and gazes at me with a mixture of wonder and alarm.

A man I like is coming to dinner, so I get out all my cookbooks and choose and discard recipes as if trying on dresses. I want something savory yet subtle, not too messy, and not too garlicky, just in case we kiss. I don't know if we will kiss, but just in case.

I don't know much about this man. He has two young daughters, an ex-wife, a hundred high-school students to teach every day. He writes poetry. His hair is the same length as mine, curling just below the chin. I don't know how old he is, but I suspect he's younger than I am, so I need to be careful not to reveal too much too fast.

It will be our third date, this dinner. From what I've heard, the third date's either the charm or the poison. I have a friend who, in the last five years, has never gotten past the third date. She calls me at 10:30

on a Friday night. "Third-date syndrome," she sighs. She describes the sheepish look on her date's face as he delivers the "Let's just be friends" speech, which by now she has memorized: "You're great. I enjoy your company, but (a) I don't have a lot of time right now; (b) I'm not looking for a relationship; or (c) I'm going to be out of town a lot in the next couple of months." My friend tells me, "I just wish one of them would come right out and say, 'Look, I don't really like you. Let's just forget it.' It would be a relief, in a way."

I listen to her stories with a morbid fascination, as if she were a traveler returned from some foreign land to which I, thankfully, have been denied a visa. But then we hang up, and I turn back to my empty house: the bed whose wide expanse looks accusatory; the pile of books that has grown lopsided and dangerous. I stare at my fish, a fighting fish named Betty, who flares his gills at me and swims in vicious circles around his plastic hexagon, whipping his iridescent body back and forth. My friend Connie tells me this behavior indicates love, that my fish is expressing his masculinity so that I might want to mate with him. In my desperation, I take this as a compliment.

A man I like is coming to dinner, which means I need to do the laundry and wash the sheets, just in case. How long has it been since I washed the sheets? There's been no need to keep track. It's just me here, after all, and I'm always clean when I go to bed, fresh from the bath; nothing happens in that bed to soil it. When I lived with Keith, or Seth, or Francisco, I washed the sheets every week, but then I had someone in the laundromat to help me fold them when they were dry.

Today, as I dangle the dry sheets over the laundromat's metal table, I realize that I've never really dated before. I've always been transparent as a door made of rice paper: approach me and you can see inside; touch me and I open, light and careless. It's difficult to remember the beginnings of things; was there always this dithering back and forth, this wondering, this not knowing? My first boyfriend and I took LSD and sat in a tree for five hours on our first date. We communicated telepathically, keeping our legs intertwined, sinewy as the branches of a madrone. We were eighteen years old.

Such a date, now that I'm thirty-eight, seems foolish, ridiculous. Now I have to weigh everything: to call or not to call; whether to wait three days, or five, or six; whether to ask everyone who might know this man for information, then form a strategic plan. I shave my legs and underarms, make appointments for a haircut and a manicure, all of which will make no difference if nothing happens. I think about condoms and blush and wonder if he will buy any, wonder where they are in the store, how much they cost these days. I wonder about the weight of a man's hands on my shoulders, on my hair. Marilynne Robinson, in *Housekeeping*, writes that "need can blossom into all the compensations it requires. . . . To wish for a hand on one's hair is all but to feel it."

I want to believe her, so I wish for the hand. I close my eyes and try to picture this man's hands, to feel the soft underside of his wrist against my mouth. A man's wrists have always been the key to my lust; something rouses me in the power of a hand concentrated in that hinge. And yes, I feel it. Yes, my breath catches in my throat, as if he has stroked his thumb against the edge of my jaw. My body's been so long without desire that I've almost forgotten what it means to be a sexual being, what it's like to feel this quickening in my groin. It's all I need for now: this moment of desire unencumbered by the complications of fulfillment. Because craving only gives rise to more craving; desire feeds on itself and cannot be appeased. It is my desire, after all, my longing, more delicious than fulfillment, because over this longing I retain complete control. This arousal, breathless as it is, lets me know I'm alive. That's all I really wanted in the first place.

A *date*. The word still brings up visions of Solvang, California, and the date orchards on the outskirts of town, the sticky sweetness of the dark fruit. My family drove through the orchards on summer car trips, hot and irritable in the blue station wagon. But when we stopped at the stores with giant dates painted on their awnings, we grew excited, our misery forgotten. My mother doled out the fruit to us from the front seat, her eyes already half closed in pleasure. The dates — heavy, cloying, dark as dried blood — always made the roof of my mouth itch, but I ate them anyway because they came in a white box like candy. I ate them because I was told they were precious, the food of the gods.

I lied. I changed everything on my refrigerator, my bulletin board, my mantelpiece; I put up a letter announcing a prize, took down my nephew's drawing because it ruined the aesthetics. I casually added a picture of myself on a good day, my long legs tan, my skin flawless as I pose in front of a blazing maple bush on Mill Creek. I try to suppress an unbidden fantasy: a photograph of me and this man and his two daughters filling the requisite place on my parents' wall. I know this is a dangerous and futile image, but it lodges stubbornly in my head.

I call my friend every half-hour or so with updates on my frame of mind, asking for reassurance that I am not a terrible person, asking questions as if she were a representative of the dating board: "On which date does one start holding hands? Kissing? If I ask him out again and he says yes, how do I know he's not just being polite?" If there were a guidebook, I would buy it; a class, I would take it.

Yesterday I discussed this imminent dinner with my hairstylist, Tony, as he bobbed my hair. Tony and his boyfriend are essentially married, but he's had his share of dates, and he gave me both sides: "Well, on the one hand, you've got to play the game," he said, turning the blow-dryer away from my hair, "but, on the other hand, you need to show some honesty, some of the real you. You don't want to scare him off. This is a good lesson for you: balance, balance, balance."

Tony is my guru. When I came to him the first time, I told him my hair was in transition: not long, not short, just annoying. "You can't think of it as a transition," said Tony, cupping my unwanted flip. "This is what your hair wants to be right now. There are no transitions. Right now, this is it."

Yesterday, Tony cradled my newly coiffed hair in his slender fingers, gazed at me somberly in the mirror. I smiled uncertainly, cocked my head. "Good?" he asked. "Good," I replied. Satisfied, he whisked bits of hair off my shoulders with a brush. "Don't worry," he said. "Play it cool." I nodded, gazing at myself in the mirror, which always makes my cheeks look a little too pudgy, my lips a little too pale. Whenever I look at my reflection too long, I become unrecognizable, my mouth slightly askew, a mouth I can't imagine kissing, or being kissed. I paid Tony, then walked carefully out of the salon, my head level, a breeze cold against my bare neck. In the car, I did not resist the urge to tilt down the rearview mirror and look at myself again. I touched my new hair. I touched those lips, softly, with the very tips of my fingers.

A man I like is coming to dinner. In two hours. The chicken is marinating and the house is clean. If I take a shower and get dressed right now, I'll have an hour and a half to sit fidgeting in my living-room chair, talking to myself and to the fish, whose water of course I've changed. "Make a good impression," I plead with Betty. "Mellow out." He swims back and forth, avoiding my eyes, butting his head against the plastic hexagon. I call my friend: Do I light candles? A fire in the fireplace? Use the cloth napkins? She says yes to the napkins, nix to everything else. I must walk the line between casual and formal, cool and aflame. Perfume? Yes. Eyeliner? No. I remake the bed, realizing only now how misshapen my down comforter is, all the feathers bunched at one end. The cover, yellow at the edges, lies forlornly against my pillows, and my pillowcases don't match. Skirt or pants? I ask my friend. Wine or beer? My friend, a saint, listens then finally says, "Why are you asking me? I never get past the third date!" I freeze. Suddenly, I want to get off the phone as quickly as possible, as if her bad luck might be contagious.

A man I like is coming to dinner. He's late. I sit on the edge of my bed, unwilling to stand near the front windows, where he might see me waiting. My stomach hurts and is not soothed by the smell of tandoori chicken overcooking in the oven. Like a cliché, my hands are sweating. I lie back on the bed, not caring at this point if I mess up my hair or wrinkle my green dress, chosen for its apparent lack of effort. Pale light sifts through the Venetian blinds at an angle just right for napping or making love. If I had to choose right now, I'd choose a nap, the kind that keeps me hovering on the edge of a consciousness so sweet it would seem ridiculous to ever resurface. My lavender eye pillow is within reach. My house is so small; how could it possibly accommodate a man, filling my kitchen, peering at my refrigerator door?

On my bedside table is the *Pillow Book* of Sei Shonagan, a tenth-century Japanese courtesan, a woman whose career consisted of waiting. In that expectant state, she observed everything around her in great detail, finding some of it to her liking and some not. I idly pick up the book, allow it to fall open, and read, "When a woman lives alone, her house should be extremely dilapidated, the mud wall should be falling to pieces, and if there is a pond, it should be overgrown with water plants. It is not essential that the garden be covered with sagebrush; but weeds should be growing through the sand in patches, for this gives the place a poignantly desolate look."

I close the book. I look around this apartment, this house where I live alone. My room feels clean, new, expectant. Right now I want nothing more than to stay alone, to hold myself here in a state of controlled desire. But if this man doesn't show, I know my house will quickly settle into the dilapidation Sei Shonagan saw as fit for a single woman; the line between repose and chaos is thinner than I once thought. Despite all I've tried to learn in these years alone — about my worthiness as an independent woman; about the intrinsic value of the present moment; about defining myself by my own terms, not someone else's — despite all this, I know that my well-being at this moment depends on a man's hand knocking on my door.

The doorbell rings, startling me into a sitting position. I clear my throat, which suddenly seems ready to close altogether, to keep me mute and safe. I briefly consider leaving the door unanswered: I imagine my date waiting, looking through the kitchen window, then backing away, shaking his head, wondering. Perhaps he would think me crazy, or dead. Perhaps he would call the police, tell them there's a woman he's worried about, a woman who lives alone. Or, more likely, he would drive to a bar, have a beer, and forget about me. The thought of his absence momentarily pleases me, bathes me with relief. But of course I stand up and glance in the mirror, rake my hands through my hair to see it feather into place, then casually walk out to greet this man I like, this man who's coming to dinner. ■

The Word

a short story by **ROBLEY WILSON**

O n the weekends she stayed with him, the first sound she heard
in the morning was the meowing of his cat. The people in the
apartment next door also had a cat, only theirs was put out overnight;
his was strictly an indoor cat, black and nearly a dozen years old and
just beginning to turn fat. The next-door cat always came to its owner's
front porch and yowled to be let in. His crouched in the bedroom window, peering down, and the two cats carried on a conversation until
the next-door cat went inside.

"It's an aubade," she said to him one day.

"What's that?"

"A morning song." She turned her face toward him and kissed his
neck, feeling the sleep-warmth of him radiating from under the blue
sheet. " 'Aubade for Two Felines.' "

"What time is it?" He always wanted to know the time, as if time
mattered.

S he'd known him now for nearly a year, knew by heart the stories
of his bad marriage and worse divorce, and of the lovely house in
the country he'd had to forfeit. Of course, the stories were all as seen
through his eyes, so she tried to take everything he said as if she were a
confirmed skeptic. But she was not a skeptic; she was in love with him.

She could never get him to admit that he was in love with her. "I've
decided to be fond of people," he said. "I'm too old to love them."

Sometimes she said, "It's her, isn't it?" meaning the ex-wife, meaning that she had soured him on love, meaning to give him an excuse

for again not declaring his love for her — even though they practically lived together.

Other times she said, "But I love you; I don't mind saying the word to you," meaning she wished for reciprocity, for mutual declarations, for at least the idea of love, whatever it had to do with the two of them.

Whichever way she put it, he changed the subject. She despaired of ever hearing the word.

One day something changed. It was his birthday, and the champagne they drank to celebrate had gone to his head; his eyes glistened and his speech was slurred and he would not look at her, but only at the cat asleep in her lap where she sat under the bay window.

"That cat," he said. "He used to be an outdoor cat. Had six acres to hunt, stayed out most of the time, except on really cold days in January. He hunted rabbits and pheasants and field mice, and one day he brought home a rat. He must have gotten it near a neighbor's trash pile. Birds, bunnies — you name it. He was always bringing his trophies home. That's cats."

"So they say." She held the cat in her lap and listened to the man; she watched his face. His demeanor was solemn, intense.

"He's healthy as a horse now, that cat. I only have him at the vet's for his annual shots. But all the years I was married and we lived on those six acres, he was at the vet's over and over. He'd get into fights — other cats, raccoons, maybe a skunk or two — and his wounds would abscess. He always had to take pills, get shots, have the abscesses lanced. And worms. He was always getting worms, especially tape, from the stuff he ate in the wild."

"Poor kitty," she said, petting the cat's wide brow and stroking its tattered ears.

"You pay a price for being free," he said. Now he looked at her. "I think I've finally learned that."

She felt the old cat purring under her hands. *Ah,* she thought, *so this is how he says it.* ■

Under The Apple Tree

a short story by **LAURA PRITCHETT**

When Joe left me sitting under the apple tree and started to walk across the meadow toward my trailer, he looked back and waved, and then walked on, and then he did a complete circle with his arms out, like he was embracing the world. That made me laugh, because he was so happy and willing to show it. I was leaning back against the tree with most of my clothes back on, and I blew him kisses as he went on his spinning, cheerful way. Then he reached my dirt driveway, where he'd left his truck, and he climbed in, honked his horn, and left.

We'd just made love, and we'd both come twice, and my body was feeling full and tired. The contrails from the flying sparks of orgasm were just starting to fade as I picked twigs out of my hair and wiped a smudge of dirt from my forearm and let my mind think thoughts like *The only thing grand enough for a human life is to love* and *This is where wild and gentle get sewn together* — the sort of thoughts that make perfect sense at a time like that, and only at a time like that. I considered the fallen red apples and the yellowed leaves, and I guessed that I was in love — that, in fact, I was more in love than I'd ever been. And I simply took notice of that feeling and concentrated on the sharp, rotting smell of the apples and the slant of sunlight on my bare feet and the ache in my thighs.

After some time, I walked to my trailer, spinning around myself, and went inside and fell on my bed and closed my eyes and replayed the whole thing: our lovemaking, and my orgasms, and his, and our mumblings, and his eyes. And then my mind wandered on to less romantic thoughts, such as: perhaps my rear end is not attractive from behind, because it's dimpled with fat, which is too bad, because I like that position; and perhaps I had said a stupid thing or two, which was also too bad, but entirely predictable. I brushed away the bits of earth still smashed against my spine and rubbed my head where it had hit the apple tree, and I considered the violence of love.

Joe and I have the exact same hair color — a brown so dark that it's almost black — only his is curly and mine hangs straight to my waist. Also, both of us have gray in our hair: Joe's near his temples and mine throughout. I love it when he takes my hair and starts to braid it, which he knows how to do from braiding harnesses. And I love pushing my hands up through his hair and feeling his soft scalp. Thinking of our hands in each other's hair, I made myself come again, because I was curious to know whether I could accomplish three, which I'd never done before.

When my body stopped pulsing, I decided that orgasm is the greatest physical pleasure in life, and I wondered if Joe felt the same way. I wondered how he saw the world, through what lens. I imagined I *was* Joe. I tried to be in his tall body, looking at himself in the mirror, touching his own stubbled jaw, seeing his graying hair and brown eyes. I imagined how he might stare down his fears and hopes and hurts. I tried to feel his breath move in and out. I tried to imagine how he might close his eyes and become aware of his body and perhaps be aroused, feel alert and alive. Doing this made my heart hurt a little. Joe was a good man, and for some reason his goodness made me feel raw. I found myself thinking, *Don't trust him. He will hurt you.* But I turned those thoughts off and kept them off. Instead of tempering my feelings for Joe with those judgments the brain continually makes, instead of balancing love with *Joe-lacks-such-and-such-a-quality* thoughts — all those strategies the mind uses so that it loves less and therefore *feels* less — instead of doing those things, I stared at the ceiling of the room, with my hand still between my legs, and I felt Joe and knew Joe and experienced Joe as much as I could at that moment in time, despite the very real danger.

I live too hard, and I know it. I drink too much, I smoke too much pot, and I've continued to date men after they've hit me. Every once in a while I get into trouble because of this, but over the course of my life I have come to believe that it's worth it. My body and heart are getting worn out faster than they should, but I won't regret this life as much as some people want me to, because at least I feel alive.

One thing to know about me is that I severely dislike stingy people. By this I mean not only penny pinchers, but people who aren't generous with their "Thank you's" and "I'm sorry's"; people who spend too little time thinking about others, too little energy loving; people who get through life by giving as little as they can. I do not like miserly hearts.

Which is probably why I like Joe so much, because he is, at heart, generous. For example, he's willing to walk away from his new lover and tell her goodbye in the most charitable way he can, by spinning and holding his arms out to the world, announcing: *Life is good. That was good. I love you.* That is something. Really, that is something.

I am a housecleaner, and I sell pot on the side. My goal is to make a living while working as few hours as possible, so I can spend the rest of my day drinking, or reading, or getting high, or now, increasingly, with Joe and his body, or with my thoughts about Joe and his body. The only other interesting thing I can say about myself is that I've always been fascinated by sex — which is not to say that I've engaged in a huge amount of sexual activity, but rather that I have paid attention to sex as a topic. I know about *The Hite Report* and *Deep Throat* and Candida Royalle porn. I know what Freud and Foucault have to say, and I know the most basic truth about enjoying sex, which is that it's part instinct, but it's mostly a learned activity. It can't be learned with just anybody, though, and I'm beginning to think that's what's going on with Joe: I am learning from him. That is why the thought of losing him scares me. He's going to open me up, make me understand and feel, and then he will get in his truck and drive out of my life, back to his horseshoeing and hunting and woodworking and all his other activities that do not include me.

So I'm hoping we can both be generous with each other for at least a while, long enough for my body to understand this new feeling. I want to have the body knowledge of what it is like to be this happy.

W innie is my one friend, and my only neighbor way up here on this mountain. She has short hair, which she dyes blond, and she's married with two kids who are always coming over to my property to pick apples. Winnie exercises and eats right. In many ways, she is the opposite of me. That's part of why we're friends: so we can each see the road not taken, and we can enjoy the scenery along that road without having to walk it ourselves.

The apple tree stands midway between our two houses, with about an acre of land on each side. My lot is bigger than Winnie's and more overgrown with raspberry bushes and milkweed and mountain mahogany and grasses. I tell Winnie's kids to watch out when they come to pick apples, because there's a bear around. Its scat is all over the place: big, apple-seed-laden piles. In fact, Joe and I had to search to find a place under the tree that was free of the stuff. I haven't actually seen the bear, but I can smell the vinegar scent of its urine, the rank odor of its body, and I imagine it's pretty fat by now and ready for winter. Winnie keeps an eye on the kids, but sometimes they escape out of the house — when she's trying to put bread in the oven, for instance. These kids were meant for the outdoors, and I think that's great, but I worry about the bear.

Winnie's marriage is a typical one, which means that sometimes it gets rough, but then it gets better. As far as I can tell, there's not a lot of passion, but there is that blend of patience and knowledge and affection that marks long marriages. Except for the boredom part, it seems pretty appealing. The boredom would kill me, though. Winnie's house is very organized. She lines up cans in one cupboard and plastic containers in another. She makes lists. Sometimes I envy the clean edges of her life, how marriage and motherhood seem to be enough to hold her together, although I don't completely understand her for this very reason.

Winnie thinks I'm amusingly wild, and I like regaling her with stories. So when she came over that day for our usual five o'clock margaritas, I told her about Joe and me under the apple tree. Winnie's kids, five and six, were playing in the grass, and Winnie and I sat wrapped up in blankets and drank our strong drinks and watched the sun set over the mountains. I told her about how Joe's kisses had a certain pull to them, how his hands had a certain knowledge, how his fingers listened. I told her that it was startling, at this age, suddenly to be experiencing such orgasms: orgasms that came so easily, the muscle contractions spreading through my body with unexpected force; but orgasms that, despite their force, were grounded in tenderness. I had never believed that being with a man could seem so safe and gentle.

Winnie rubbed her fingers over her lips in a thoughtful sort of way and said, "Jeez, Gretchen, I wish I was having sex like that."

She meant it too. I could hear it in her voice. So I said, "Well, a lot of days I wish I had kids."

We like to lust after each other's lives. Come right down to it, neither of us would trade what she has, but still, there's that occasional yearning.

"I haven't kissed someone new in thirteen years," she said.

"I don't have anyone to sleep with me at night," I said. "Not most nights."

"Well," she said, "we could all use more than one life."

We sat for a while and ate some of her homemade bread with havarti cheese and the last of this year's raspberries, the sweet kind that grow over by the property line between my land and hers.

"Can I ask you something?" I finally said. "When you have an orgasm during sex, you're telling yourself a story in your head, right? You're imagining another scene, other than the one that is occurring, right?"

"I think that's probably true," she said.

"Can you have an orgasm without it?"

Her eyes moved across the pasture, as if the pasture were the landscape of her brain and she were examining the horizon for memories. "I don't think I can. I think I need the story. I'll have to pay attention next time, to be sure." She stuffed some bread in her mouth and looked up at the sky.

"Because I couldn't. Come. Without a story," I said. "But then, with Joe, I suddenly can. I mean, it's ridiculous!" I told her I knew it sounded like I was doing a disservice to womankind by granting the man too much credit, by having too much pleasure, by exaggerating the possibilities. It was also just the beginning of an affair, not the part that tests and tries you. I knew that too. "But I just want to be happy right now," I said. "I want to store these moments up for later."

"That sounds smart," she said. "Have another margarita."

"I've had bad sex before," I said. "Plenty of it. Bad sex, mediocre sex, OK sex. But suddenly this. It has to do with how *there* we are. It's a whole different way of being, really. And it's confusing my body. I just didn't expect it." I stabbed the knife into the havarti and looked at her.

She said, "Maybe you should figure out a way to make this work. And just so you know, married sex can be good too. It can be great."

"I believe it." I said this like I meant it, which maybe isn't true, but I'd like it to be.

Winnie looked at me and bit her lip, and I could tell she was reminding herself of all the things she *didn't* like about my life, so that she could confirm her choices. As part of righting herself, her eyes veered off to her kids, as if to say, *There. That's what you have. There they are.*

"Can I ask you one more thing?" I said. "These stories in your head, they have some violence in them, don't they? At least sometimes?"

Winnie raised her eyebrows and said, "Gretchen," in that tone of voice you use with a child who's gone too far. But then she backed away from it and sighed. She's very patient. That's another thing I like about Winnie: her great capacity for finding fondness for people, even after they've irritated her. Now she found her fondness for me and said, "Probably. Well, yes."

I said, "I think most women link violence and arousal. Some buried evolutionary remnant or cultural leftover. It's true for me. Or it *was*, before Joe. But here's what I'm getting at; I was thinking about this while I was cleaning today: Humans are going to evolve. Someday, when you and me are long gone, humans will change for the better. This violence, it's going to disappear; it's just not going to be inside us anymore."

Winnie gave me an endearing look and said, "Gretchen, that's very optimistic of you."

"I know," I said.

"You seem very young today," she said. "It's lovely. Your cheeks are flushed."

"It's ridiculous, I know," I said. "I'm thawing. I'm evolving. And I'm sorry I sound this way, but I can't help it. I don't know what to do, because he's a good man, and I'm in love."

Joe has one strange quirk, I've come to find out: he will make love only outdoors.

"I can't breathe inside," he told me.

"It's more comfortable inside," I said. "There are things like beds and blankets and *heat*. Winter is coming."

He shrugged. "I can *do* it. I'm *capable* of it. But I don't like it, not as much."

So I immediately started thinking of ways to meet his request: Blankets I could pull from the shed and wash. Sleeping bags. Perhaps a little tent.

Now we were under the tree again, mostly naked, but Joe's green flannel shirt was thrown over my back for warmth. I was on top of Joe, and he was inside me. We had stopped to catch our breath and let our heartbeats calm, and he noticed, while he was flat on his back, that the bear had recently clawed the tree. The bark had been shredded away, leaving long, pale streaks of tender wood. What had happened, he surmised, was that the bear had gotten all the apples within reach, then had climbed to get the ones at the top.

"See, if we weren't outside right now," Joe said, "I wouldn't have seen the bear's claw marks. These leaves wouldn't be falling through the sky. And I couldn't watch the way the light hits your body. And they're all very beautiful."

That made me shy, so I laughed and said, "Schoolkids, that's what we sound like."

He said, "I know. It's great."

He leaned up to kiss me, and his hands went to my breasts, and his lips moved to my throat, which made my back arch, and then the nerve pathways traveling between my mouth and breasts and pelvis were all activated, and then his hands were on my hips, rocking me harder now, and there was a long period of me feeling good, so good that I had to hit the ground with my fist and could not help but moan and thrust my body into Joe's with a violence that would have scared me had it not been matched by an equal tenderness. I was telling my body to come, come, and I was afraid I was going to go numb, but then the *inside* of my body broke out in a sweat — that's what it felt like — and I heard myself making noises that seemed a little out of hand, and then an image flooded my mind, of Joe walking with his arms out, embracing the world, and I thought, *Oh, yes, just let yourself do this,* and he made his own animal noise as he came, and we both sounded like the wild creatures that humans can sometimes be.

For a long time Joe ran his hands over my back and front and thighs, and he told me about bears. This time of year, he said, a bear will spend almost twenty hours a day foraging. Now that they've switched from summer flowers and grasses to berries and apples, they have to work harder to get the calories they're going to need for winter. Bears mate in the spring, but they have delayed implantation, which means the fertilized egg floats freely in the uterus all summer and implants in autumn. Joe said, "Black bears are solitary and intelligent and curious, just like you," and he kissed me. "One of these days," he told me, "we're going to see this bear."

When he was done talking about the bear, I talked about women and sex, since that's what was on my mind. I told him that the reason women can come more than once is that after orgasm, a woman doesn't return to an unaroused state, but rather to a preorgasmic level of arousal. Though I'd been aware of the female orgasmic capacity before I'd known him, I had been unable to have more than one. I said this was probably good for his male ego, but that wasn't why I was telling him. I had my own selfish interest in the topic. I told him that these orgasms made me feel strong, and also that they smoothed over all the hurt in my life. I told him that I had recently decided that good orgasms took some concentration, some imagination, and a little spark of craziness. They also relied heavily on a feeling of safety and generosity.

Joe sat there, head propped on one hand, the other touching my body.

I said, "Do you have to be somewhere? Do you need to go?"

"No," he said.

"I don't believe you," I said. Then I added, "The more orgasms a woman has, the stronger they become. The more she has, the more she *can* have."

He seemed curious in the best way, willing to listen without expectation or judgment.

I said, "I just think you should know all this."

He said, "I think I should too." Then he leaned over to kiss my nose, and we made love again, and the only time I spoke was to whisper that I wanted *him* to feel good, too, and that he needed only to tell me what to do. Then I listened as hard as I could with my body. He was on top of me this time, and when he crumpled down on me and buried his head into my shoulder, I wrapped my arms around him and traced his back with my fingers.

While we were resting this way, a gunshot sounded from somewhere in the valley: hunting season. A flock of geese took off honking into the sky. I moved Joe aside so I could sit up. The world — the songbirds and mice and deer — seemed to stop, braced for danger, alert and waiting. I hugged my knees close to my body and breathed out and stared at the sky.

"You startle easily," he said.

"I know," I said.

Joe sat up beside me, and we stayed that way for a long time in silence. Winnie would be bringing her kids home from school soon. Since the apple tree is in full view of her house, we had to take her schedule into consideration. We waited until the last minute, then gathered up our things. After Joe climbed into his truck, he jumped right back out again to kiss me one last time, mumbling something about "Good God, I'm forty-two," his eyes sparkling, and then he drove away.

Joe shoes horses; that's his main job. He drives a truck with a propane forge and an anvil stand and a bunch of tongs and hammers inside, and all of this is so heavy that the back of his truck tilts down. HAPPY HOOFER FARRIER SERVICE, his truck says. There are a lot of horse people around here, so he keeps busy enough. He stops at my house between calls. At first it was just random, him stopping by to see if I was home, but now we plan ahead.

Joe doesn't talk about his past much, but I somehow get the idea that he's always been pretty shy, which is why he prefers to work with horses and not people. I'm fairly certain that Joe's experience with women has not been *that* extensive, because of this shyness, which is surprising given how much he knows intuitively about a woman's body — or *my* body, at least.

Joe spends a lot of time looking at my body, with his hands and with his eyes, and it pleases me to be with a man who really pays attention to me. We've only been seeing each other for a month, but there's the potential for a long-term relationship here. Neither of us has ever had one, and the idea makes us uncomfortable, so we haven't talked about it, but I can feel us both wondering where this is going. Should we make an agreement to hang on? No, maybe this relationship should remain suspended in the present. Talk of the future could wreck it. The truest thing I can say about me is that I've got this reckless need to live free and alone. And Joe, in his own way, does too.

When I came home from cleaning houses the other day, the kids were out by the apple tree, winging fallen apples around. I watched them as I unloaded my cleaning supplies: the bucket of rags, the bottles full of chemicals, the vacuum. I'd cleaned three houses in record speed. It's amazing the sort of energy that love can give you. I went inside and wrote myself a note to buy a new can of WD-40, because it's the best for taking off sticky residue. I flopped on the couch and tamped some pot into my beautiful green pipe but didn't light it.

Though I'd been happy all day, now I was sad: extremely sad, even tearful. Perhaps I'd been feeling too happy lately, and the pendulum in my body was swinging back. Or maybe I was getting my period; it's hard to tell because they're irregular these days. Or maybe it was because Joe was in Denver at a horseshoeing convention, and even though we had put no restrictions on each other, I was afraid he might be attracted to someone else — a smart, beautiful veterinarian perhaps. Or maybe it was simply that I knew I wouldn't see his truck winding up the drive anytime soon. On top of that, the sound of Winnie's kids yelling outside reminded me that it was too late for me now — I was never going to have any children — and the fact that I didn't really want any didn't alleviate my sorrow much.

Being lonely is not necessarily bad. In fact, sometimes I think the good feeling I get from being with Joe is possible only because of the basic human condition of being lonely. Plus, learning to live alone is an excellent way of staying grounded and safe and avoiding the jerks of the world. As I've gotten older, I've gotten better at being alone. And loneliness is good because it gives you time to consider other people's lives. I can, for example, consider Winnie and her particular brand of loneliness and wonder if marriage doesn't create more loneliness than it wards off. I wonder if the institution of marriage will evolve as humans evolve, and I wish I could be around to see it.

I was thinking now about the future for Joe and me. I tried to stop myself, but I couldn't resist going over the possibilities. Of course our relationship would end at some point in time, the way most relationships end, which is to say one or both persons drift off. It takes too much energy — too much bravery, really — to say goodbye, so usually there's just a silent withdrawal, hardly perceptible until it becomes obvious. You quit being so generous with yourself. Joe will quit going out of his way to stop by, and I won't go out of my way to rearrange my cleaning schedule. And strangely enough, this lack of giving will make us feel trapped, and we will want our freedom again. Then we'll offer each other a tired, sad smile, because somewhere inside we'll know it's over — or at least that the most alive part is over.

Because I read a lot — I wonder, rather egotistically, whether I read more than anyone else on this mountain — I know who the Roman poet Ovid is, and one beautiful thing he wrote is "If you seek a way out of love, be busy; you'll be safe then." So I sat on the couch and lectured myself: *Do* not *do that. Do* not *get busy.* Instead, I decided, when Joe and I were through, I would sit around and smoke pot and let the great wilderness of the inner life take over, as it should.

Because it was a gloomy day, I knew Winnie would be making brownies — chocolate helps her get through the gloom — and I knew she'd bring me some, because she's not stingy, and something about that made me want to go and play with her kids. I stashed the pipe for later and went outside and found them under the apple tree. They were wearing puffy coats but no hats and gloves, and Zoe had a clear line of snot running from her nose to her lip. They were crouched down, staring at two grasshoppers, who were — no joke — having sex.

"Look, Gretchen!" Zoe smiled up at me. "These grasshoppers are wrestling!"

"Indeed they are," I said.

"Just like we wrestle!" said the boy, whose name is Michael.

"Sort of," I said.

"There's a lot of bear poop under your apple tree," Zoe said disapprovingly, as if I were responsible for it. "We poked at it with a stick. We think the bear ate ten million apples to have so much seed in its poop."

"That seems about right," I said. Then I said, "Are you two happy?"

They looked up at me, faces flushed, as if wondering whether I was stupid. Michael didn't say anything, but Zoe said, "Yes."

And that's when we heard it. A *huff, huff* and then another *huff, huff* and then the smell hit me — a terrible smell, really — and I said, "Oh, kids," about the same time that the bear appeared out of the raspberry bushes. I thought, *Damn, this bear was supposed to come when Joe was here,* but I said, very calmly, "Don't worry, kids. It will go away," and then I addressed the bear: "Bear, go away. Go away, bear."

But it did not go away. It was walking on all fours toward the apple tree as if it had not seen us, although surely it had. It seemed very calm. Its fur was dark brown, darker in the head region, and its ears were round, and its nose curved upward just a bit. It took four more steps and then sat back on its butt, and I saw the row of nipples that ran down her belly.

Zoe let out a small noise of fear, and Michael was frozen in place, but I could tell he was about to scream or run, so I said, "Kids, don't move. Do *not* move. Stay right next to me." And then I shuffled them behind me. "Bear," I said, "we are not going to hurt you, and you can have the apples. If you hurt us, I will hurt you back."

The kids were starting to cry, and so was I, actually, although I think it had more to do with my previous sadness than with fear of this bear. The bear was making me miss Joe, and I kept telling myself,

Jesus, Gretchen, don't think about Joe now. Now is not the time. I said, more firmly and loudly, "Kids, I want you to know one thing. This bear will have to fight me before she gets to you. And let me tell you, I can put up a big fight." Then I started talking to the kids about some cockamamie plan my brain was developing, something about us all backing up slow, and if she charged, they should turn and run. No, I would put them up in the tree and guard them. But no, that wasn't a good idea, either. So I told Zoe and Michael that I could tell, with my grown-up knowledge, that the bear wasn't going to attack, that she was a big sweetie. It was just ridiculous, the things I heard coming out of my mouth. While I was talking, the bear got bored and started walking in our direction, but a little to the right. All she wanted was the apple tree.

I looked around for sticks, but there weren't any, only a few bruised and wormy apples scattered about, so I bent over slowly and picked up three at my feet. I guessed that I could throw pretty hard and had good aim, and no creature really wants to be pelted with apples, so I knew that the apples were going to save us, and then I felt calm and safe, which gave me enough time to pause and consider the bear. She was sitting and huffing again, as if trying to decide whether the apples were worth it. Her need for those apples was strong, though. I decided that I liked her, because she was stubborn and perhaps lived too hard. If I hadn't had two kids behind me, grabbing so hard at my shirt that they were strangling me, I might have stood there and considered the bear for quite a while.

"All righty," I whispered. "We're going to back up now. Are you ready? If she comes, I'll throw apples at her and punch her in the nose, and you two keep backing up, no matter what. OK?"

As we backed away, the bear lowered her head, and her nose twitched, and then she moved forward rapidly, right at us, and I heard myself say, "Oh God oh God oh God," and my right arm cocked back with the apple, ready to pitch it at her face, and my other arm went back and low, to shield the kids, and then I said, very loud, "Bear, your egg is implanting and you're going to have a baby and you will not hurt us!" Suddenly I was angry with her, and my face flushed, and I thought of the time an old boyfriend had struck me across the cheek, and my head had flown into the corner of an open car door, and the blood had run down through my hair and down my cheek, and then I thought of Joe and his hands running across my back and how when I had an orgasm with him my body began to shake, all wildness, and there was no story in my mind. My mouth opened on its own, and I made a wild noise, a noise that basically meant *Get the hell away from me and these kids,* and the bear stopped short.

As I told Joe a couple of days later, the bear held her ground and watched us go inside. The kids and I stood at my kitchen window and saw her climb up the apple tree, where she stayed for some time. "That's one of the few times I've backed away from danger," I told Joe. "I prefer, generally, to move forward. It's safer that way."

We were lying side by side, partly naked, under the apple tree, and it was starting to snow — tiny flakes that reminded me of campfire ash, perhaps because they reflected the gray of the sky. They were blowing sideways, and it was very cold out, and I kept pausing during my story and saying, "This is ridiculous," and Joe kept saying, "It sure is," but we didn't move.

Joe had piled our coats and clothes on one side of us to make a wind barrier, and he used his body as another, but still I was freezing. I was also filled with nervous energy, maybe because I was thinking about the bear, or maybe because I had come to the point where I felt the need to unleash my words upon Joe. In any case, I talked for a long time. I told Joe that Winnie had hugged the kids and promised me a lifetime supply of brownies. I told Joe that Winnie's marriage had gotten to that place where imagination and willpower fail, and that she and her husband were both feeling like they were each other's prisoner. But probably at some point they'd stop feeling that way, and then it would get better. I told him we'd probably ramble through the same cycle ourselves, if we stuck it out. I told him that our lives seemed to be getting caught up together, and that from time to time I considered the beauty in that. I told him that I loved him, and that when we broke up, I would look back on this period as the "time of Joe," and that I believed that a few good memories could sustain a person. I told him that I nearly cried with love for him every time I had an orgasm, because when the body loses its limitations, the heart does too. I told him he was the best lover I'd ever had, and that new things were happening to my body, that the violence was getting worked out. I told him that no matter what happened with us, he should know he had created a new and better version of me.

He held me to him and listened and hugged me tighter now and then. Sometimes he said a word or two to show agreement, or simply to acknowledge that he was listening, and then, when I had wound down, he told me that he saw no point in forecasting the end of us, although he understood the impulse, and that he too had recently wondered what there was to live for besides love. Our conversation went around and stopped and started and circled back, and I felt as if our bodies and our words were grapevines, and then I felt the foolishness of that, and then I let go of feeling foolish.

It was during a lapse into silence that we heard the fall of feet in new, wet snow. Joe and I raised our eyebrows at each other as if delighted to be caught, and then turned toward the noise. It was Winnie. She had a big brown blanket under one arm, and a silver thermos under the other, and in her hands she held a tinfoil-covered plate.

Joe pulled a shirt over his hip, so that he was covered, but I stayed where I was. When Winnie stood above us, she did not blush or look to the side, but smiled as if pleased with us and for us. She handed the thermos and covered dish to Joe, and then she flung out the blanket in the air, where it hovered for a moment before she guided it down on top of us.

"Joe," she said, "it's nice to meet you."

He reached up to shake her hand. "Winnie, the pleasure is mine."

"Have a brownie," she said. Then, to me, "Gretchen, I'll be over at five." And she turned on her heel and started back across the snow.

"Joe," I said, as I watched her go, "I want you to stay. Maybe that's selfish. But I want to be with you. Once, I looked at you and thought, *Here's where gentle and wild get sewn together,* and now I want to believe that most of life can be that way, if we let it."

Joe scratched the gray curls at his temple and said, "I'm scared too." He shrugged and smiled, as if that was all he could say, and that said everything.

I breathed out a long gust of air, and my teeth began to chatter. We pressed our bodies together under the blanket and drank Winnie's coffee and ate her brownies and watched as the snow blew sideways. When we were done, I looked over at Joe. His eyelashes had melting flakes in them, and I stared at the drops and said, "This is ridiculous, Joe. It's *cold* out here. This is the craziest kind of love story, I'll tell you that."

We got dressed then, and we ran for my trailer, our hands thrown out to the world.   ■

I Am Not A Sex Goddess

by LOIS JUDSON

Butt plug. Butt plug. I've been walking around muttering these two words to myself for days now, like a six-year old experimenting with a new curse. (It even sounds like an insult: "You're nothing but a dirty butt plug!") I savor the way the words pop crisply from my lips: the hard *t* of *butt* and the guttural *g* of *plug*. Until a few days ago, I didn't even know what one is.

To me, a nurse who occasionally has to deal with incontinent patients, "butt plug" sounds like something to be removed every so often to allow for drainage: unpleasant and tedious and not at all sexy. Most patients do not like nurses inserting things into their anuses (ani?). But maybe some of them do. Maybe their grunts and wiggling are expressions of sexual arousal, not discomfort. What do I know? I don't even know the plural of *anus*.

This has come up because of Donna Mae, who happens to be a nurse, like me, but whose real vocation is sex goddess. When we are idle at work (a frequent condition on a psych unit), she will begin to talk about sex. It was from her that I learned there was such a thing as a butt plug and that I have been neglecting my sexual partners' *ani* my entire life.

Lest you peg me as a repressed woman: I learned about orgasm at the tender age of six, when I was sitting on a half-deflated soccer ball and rocking back and forth. I came of age in the sixties and was never squeamish about oral sex or Kama Sutra positions. I have had relationships in which sex was important — at least, at the beginning. It always seems to fade in importance, and my long-term bonds have been based more on feelings of security and affection. I've never been drawn to those *Cosmopolitan* articles that promise "Ten Sex Tricks Men Love" and "How to Keep Hot Sex Alive." I'm more interested in how to keep bugs off my potatoes.

If you saw Donna Mae sitting at the nurses' desk, you might not realize she was a sex goddess. For one thing, she is heavy. Though she's also tall — I'll give her that — she packs a lot of weight onto her six-foot frame. She is what I think Southern men used to call a "big-legged woman." That may have been a compliment down South, but here in New England big legs are not considered an asset. Further up on her frame, Donna Mae has massive breasts. I think a new bra size had to be invented for her. She is not young but is moving tentatively into her fifties, like me.

The clues to her goddesshood are subtle: Her hair is a unique shade of blond highlighted with auburn streaks and always carefully coiffed and sprayed into place. Her fingernails used to be incredibly long, like the nails of a Mandarin dandy, until our head nurse told her she had to cut them in the interest of hygiene. She still drums them on the desk when scanning the area for male prey. She wears a lot of makeup and sometimes applies it at the nurses' desk without a mirror. And she has green eyes, an asset of many a romance-novel heroine.

Donna Mae was hired a couple of months ago, and I met her during a change of shift. I had not talked to her for more than a few minutes when she said, quote, "If a man manipulates my nipples just right, I can have an orgasm from that alone." She paused and then added, "I have a voracious sexual appetite."

I can't recall exactly how the subject of orgasms came up. I think we began by talking about back pain, and then breast size as it relates to back pain, and then breast-reduction surgery as a cure for back pain, and then the fact that during breast reduction the nipple is excised and moved to a new location, which would, naturally, involve the disruption of nerve pathways. From there we went merrily on to erogenous zones and orgasm. There is apparently something about me that invites such confidences, as if people can look at me and tell I have loose boundaries.

Some women might not have risen to Donna Mae's bait. Some women would have replied, "Oh, that's nice. The roads were a bit slick when I drove in. Be careful driving home." But not me. Good fences make good neighbors, but bad boundaries make for more-interesting conversations.

Which isn't to say I wasn't somewhat taken aback by her declaration about her nipples. I was silent for a moment. Then I said, "Really? My breasts are as numb as an old boot."

Donna Mae's presence did not go unnoticed by the males who work at the hospital. She fell like a rock into the placid waters of our ward, and the ripples eddied out as far as the police force and maintenance staff. The building workers began to linger in our vicinity, and their presence had an electrifying effect on Donna Mae: Her back straightened. Her lips actually plumped, as if she had erectile tissue in them. Her lids lowered, and she looked at said male, if he was even slightly eligible, with the stare of a cougar sizing up a young deer. It was not long before she and one of the police officers were exchanging sexy e-mails that zipped, as if lubricated, across the dingy halls between them.

I may have encouraged this: In the first few weeks we worked together, Donna Mae had filled our empty hours with tales of her estranged lover, the recently divorced owner of a large horse farm. Donna Mae had met him because she has a horse. She also owns a souped-up Mustang convertible. Donna Mae likes to possess the accouterments of the sex goddess and will go into debt to buy them. She does not even use her Mustang for day-to-day transportation, but breaks it out on sunny summer days for the impact she makes when ensconced in its black leather seat. And she does not ride her horse anymore but keeps it as a sort of prop.

At any rate, Donna Mae told me that on her first date with the horse farmer, she'd pushed him up against his truck in the parking lot of the restaurant, torn his pants down, and given him the blow job of his life. She described the act to me in unnerving detail, depicting him as a hapless hayseed, undone by the suddenness of her attack. She told me of her momentary surprise at encountering his foreskin: she was used to circumcised men and worried he might not be up to her fastidious standards of cleanliness. But she had gone too far to stop. With a flick of her wrist she pulled the foreskin back and wrapped her lips around his —

I might be able to finish writing this scene if I read pornography, but I don't. I read mostly historical nonfiction. Right now I am reading about Cabeza de Vaca, a Spanish explorer who lost almost all of his men as he walked the length of the New World, from Florida to Mexico, in the sixteenth century. Cabeza de Vaca probably fell into bed, or perhaps into the rushes, with several Indian maidens, but I am fairly sure that their sex did not involve butt plugs, cock rings, and the like. This is not something I would have contemplated before I met Donna Mae. She has opened my eyes to a panting, lubricious world out there.

The horse farmer dated Donna Mae for several years but never proposed. Finally she told him he'd better give her an engagement ring or she was going to leave. It struck me as odd that marriage would be the ultimate goal of a sex goddess, but there you have it. He demurred, and she left, her heart broken. As she poured out the history of her lost love, I didn't need to say much more than an occasional "Mmm." I even read some historical nonfiction while she talked. But Donna Mae would get irritable if I didn't appear to be listening to her at all, and at some point I got fed up and said, "The best way to get over someone is to find someone else."

It was shortly after that that she began to have sex with the police officer. She told me about their encounters in detail, of course. Apparently he had a large penis, which was a plus in her book. He also shaved his pubic area, which was nice for her because she liked to take his balls in her mouth while she stuck her finger up his anus, which caused him to scream with delight. She said he also enjoyed it when she applied her vibrator to the area between his anus and his testicles while nuzzling his nipples.

When I admitted that I had never done these things to a man, Donna Mae looked at me in a pitying way. Then I told her I'd never owned a vibrator. She was aghast.

Let's face it: I am not a sex goddess. In fact, I am probably not a particularly exciting lover, which might explain why my partner, Peter, and

I have sex so infrequently. I have my excuses: I'm going through menopause; I'm on antidepressants that sap my libido. Peter is getting on in years and doesn't seem that interested either. We're happy to go to bed and cuddle a bit and not feel alone in the world, then yawn and turn away and go to sleep.

But all Donna Mae's talk got me thinking, and one morning over coffee I asked Peter if he'd like me to put my finger up his butt. He looked alarmed and pointed out that he had hemorrhoids. I knew this, because he anoints them every morning with Anusol, and his droopy white BVDs are stained with the unguent. Donna Mae says real men do not wear white BVDs. Once Peter purchased some patterned boxers, which I thought looked cute. I was not, however, moved to throw him down on our bed and ravish him.

Another morning, after a long conversation with Donna Mae at work the night before, I asked Peter if he thought I should get a vibrator. He said he didn't want to compete with a machine.

Nevertheless I did order a vibrator on the Internet. It came in a plain brown box and was called the "Rabbit." It was purple and stuffed with fake pearls that ground against each other when it was turned on. It also had a pair of "ears" that reached up from the base of the dildo part and landed in the vicinity of the clitoris. Peter wasn't home, and I decided to give it a test run by myself. Squatting near the TV with my cat looking on, I had an orgasm in about thirty seconds.

I've concluded that no man can compete with a vibrator unless he can rotate his body 360 degrees in midair and have a seizure at the same time. Technology has rendered men unnecessary for orgasms. What men are good for is what I already had from Peter: intimacy, companionship, a warm body.

Not long after that, Peter and I tried the Rabbit out together. First he had an orgasm the old-fashioned way, and then we fired up the "love machine," as he calls it. This time I wasn't able to have an orgasm. I felt as if I were riding some desperate little animal, which killed the mood. I think Peter was secretly pleased.

Since then the Rabbit has lived under the bed. Peter has continued to come to bed each night and fall asleep in ten seconds flat. Sometimes I cuddle up to his stout body and smell his underarm, the scent of which never fails to please me. Perhaps there is something to this idea of pheromones. His scent alone used to set me itching. I divorced my husband for Peter, and in the months leading up to this dastardly betrayal, Peter and I would spend hours at a time necking. (He would not sleep with me until I'd ended my marriage.) We had a secret spot on the bank of the river where we used to roll around on the pine needles and tantalize each other with tastes of the delights to come. He used to talk dirty in my ear, which was a revelation to me. I'd never had a man do that before.

Maybe when my meno is fully paused, or when they come up with antidepressants that don't act as Novocain for the nether regions, or when I've learned to like myself more, we will return to the regular sex we used to enjoy. But I will likely never go down that road of pornographic videos and cock rings and butt plugs. I know this is probably a result of my Puritan background. People say that sex is about joy and love, but to me it feels faintly bestial, a frightening urge to which I'd rather not give in. Isn't that why Buddhist monks eschew it? Could several million Buddhist monks be wrong?

When Donna Mae talks about sex at work now, I listen with a half smile and sometimes try to tell her how I feel, but this seems only to drive her to greater heights of hyperbole, as if it were her mission to awaken the sleeping sex goddess in my soul. Talking to her is like looking at pictures of a country I once visited and to which I have no wish to return.

I suspect there are many people like me who no longer see sex as an important part of their lives, but we're ashamed to admit it. We're told in books and magazines and on talk shows that people should be sexually active right up until their death. The idea makes me slightly squeamish. When I'm eighty — *if* I'm ever eighty — I expect my shape, despite yoga and a high-fiber diet, to be sad and droopy, the odd bumps and wrinkles progressed past the power of cosmetics to soften them. Sexual striving, with its undignified explosions and tremors, will have passed away, and I do not expect I will miss it. All I will ask of my body then is that it carry me to my garden and back, and that it allow me to hold a grandchild or two, and that it let me see and smell and taste a few seasons more. ∎

Blowing It In Idaho

by STEPHEN J. LYONS

I t's 6 P.M., wine hour at the Hotel McCall in central Idaho. I grab a bowl of tortilla chips and a glass of chardonnay and stake out a spot on the back patio overlooking Payette Lake. A seaplane circles and dips over the silvery blue whitecaps. The lake is bathed in gauzy autumnal light. No postcard, no poem, no million-dollar advertising campaign can convey this quality of light and shadow and dusky color.

Tourism is down this time of year in McCall. Boats lie in dry dock. Cafes close early. The streets are deserted — except for the locals, who emerge smiling to briefly reclaim their territory. They proudly display bumper stickers that say, "Welcome to Idaho. Now Go Home," "Native of Idaho," and "Idaho Is What America Was." I came to northern Idaho eleven years ago and stayed mostly for the landscape and the light, and because I don't know where to go from here.

A couple sits down and obscures my view of the lake; I have to look directly between them to see the water. I guess their age at mid- to late twenties. Neither wears a wedding ring, so I imagine a romance still in that dreamy stage of denial, each participant concealing any disconcerting baggage or irritating tendencies, such as drinking milk directly from the carton, or not replacing the toilet-paper roll. I know that stage well. It lasts about a month and is followed by a stage of relief, then a stage of loss, then a stage of dread.

While the man fetches two glasses of wine, the woman moves his empty seat closer and hikes her skirt up two inches past her knees, releasing millions of pheromones across the state. Somewhere a stallion whinnies. I forget about the lake.

The woman's bra shows through her white blouse. I can see the outline of a nipple. Her dark hair is pulled back like a ballerina's and held in place with a sterling-silver clip. Sheer stockings cover her thin, shapely legs. Earrings dangle and graze the tops of her shoulders. The straps of her leather sandals twist up her ankles like snakes. Tonight, she is as pretty as she will ever be in this short lifetime. And tonight she would like the man she is with to be sweet on her and make love to her in the most tender way imaginable.

The man returns with two full glasses of pale amber wine. He sits and scoots his chair back to its original position to give himself more leg room. The woman pulls her skirt back down and looks sourly at him. He doesn't notice. He wears hemmed khaki shorts with a belt, and a blue-and-white-striped shirt, like the Beach Boys used to wear. They open books — big, thick paperbacks, the kind you buy on impulse in checkout lines and read in the bathtub. He places his free hand in her lap, where treasures lie. I know what that feels like, that warmth coming up through the material. The furnace. Worthy goal of all mammals.

Payette Lake's color is softer now, impossibly soft, like an impressionist watercolor. The plane is a speck in the distance. The temperature suddenly drops. The hotel windows rattle from the vibrations of logging trucks gearing down to make the ninety-degree turn onto Main Street. The woman shuts her pulp novel, sips her wine, and begins talking: "It's always going to be like this. I'll never be satisfied!" Her companion swallows a yawn and nods politely. Suddenly I'm tired, too. She continues: " 'Lou,' I said, 'stop it! Go away! We're going to McCall, and that's all there is to it.' " She crosses her legs — not a good sign. I wonder who Lou is: Boss? Boyfriend? Stepfather?

Shadows lengthen across the water as dusk sets in. The plane is gone, but I can still hear the logging trucks, removing America's forests, tree by tree. I think of Gary Snyder's description: "the work of wrecking the world." The aspens and brush along the shore are beginning to turn yellow. The mountain air is chilly but still hints at summer. The man's book must be six hundred pages long. The title is printed in flashy, embossed letters. He's barely paying attention to the woman's conversation, to the lake, to the subtle shift in seasons. He is oblivious to her romantic overtures in this, one of the most romantic places in North America, and I want to kick him for it. She should dump him, lose the makeup and the nylons, release her tight hair, and wear cowboy boots and vintage skirts; get a large male dog with a nasty disposition; learn to play the piano; move up the highway to Lake City or Donnelly, to a cabin behind the taxidermist's shop; grow sweetly eccentric and talk to herself all the time. I want her to hunt elk with a bow and arrow; come down from the mountains into town only once a year to sell pelts and handmade quilts; bathe exclusively in hot springs; and slowly, in the time it takes to grow a hundred-foot cedar, forget these foolish men who bring her to these sacred places and then die.

The man holds up his book as if it were an Idaho garnet, turns it over and over in his hands. He explains the plot: espionage, illicit sex, political machinations, and Middle Eastern terrorists. It takes him — I look at my watch — two minutes and seventeen seconds. The woman feigns interest and looks to the lake, which is now the color of coal. She is contemplating her options.

A flock of silent mallards skims low, and the first bats flutter out. In a moment the couple will disappear into the warm, glowing belly of the hotel, where they may or may not make love. So much depends on the man's attentiveness, and so far he is blowing it. I know more than a little something about that myself.

I've reached middle age a seasoned veteran of romantic conflicts. I've inflicted hurt with the best of them and, more importantly, been knocked down to size a few times too. I'm nobody special in this regard. Unless you live in a monastery or a convent, you arrive in your forties with similar scars. Say it's the heart that's been hurt, if you like, but the damage is more widespread. You feel it in your cells, in the follicles of your hair.

I have walked away from love in favor of lust and selfishness. I have left a lover who begged me with every fiber of her being not to go. I have said things in anger that cannot be taken back with flowers, apologies, or even the distance of decades. In turn, women have hit me, thrown frying pans at my head, threatened suicide, stalked me like serial killers, and demanded that I pay for their counseling after the breakup.

Maybe it's a result of age, or of finally marrying the right woman, or of having a cast-iron skillet fly past my skull, but I realize now how precious the connection is between a man and a woman — and how fleeting life is in general, much like this short time in fall, before Idaho's first snow. I want to ask the young man seated in front of me, How many opportunities do you think you will have in this lifetime to watch the lake turn colors in this season between seasons? Five? A dozen, at most? How many women will ever want you the way she wants you right now, at this moment? Why are you reading at a time like this?

The long shadows fall across the patio, bringing with them the chill of early evening. Chairs scrape the concrete. The man and woman rise and walk toward the golden light of the hotel. Her tight hair has come undone. His shorts are wrinkled in front. Upstairs, a warm room with quilts on the bed awaits them. Fluffy pillows. Soft lamplight. Cool sheets. Cabin lights begin to blink on across the lake. The intervals between logging trucks lengthen until the destruction grinds to a temporary halt. Stars and planets appear in the clear sky. The sounds of night take over. I could sit here until dawn, listening for coyotes. Precious. Fleeting. Every bit of it.   ∎

The Woman In Question

by **TOM IRELAND**

Here I am on the western shore of Lake Michigan, thinking about a certain woman who is fifteen hundred miles away, more or less. Nothing certifiably romantic has happened between us, but I can't stop thinking about her beautiful laugh.

I recently called to ask if she wanted to come visit me in Sturgeon Bay, Wisconsin, where I'm on sabbatical at my sister's vacation home. She sounded interested but had a work deadline in a couple of months and other plans after that.

"Then I might have to find some excuse to visit you there," I said.

"Yeah?"

"My cat probably misses me. He lives pretty close to you, come to think of it. The people renting my house are taking care of him while I'm away."

"What's his name? Sorry. I'm not trying to change the subject."

"That's OK. His name is Max. Some relation of Max Factor had him when he was a kitten."

"Max is a good name for a cat. Better than Factor, anyway."

"Maybe I left a burner on at my house."

"Soup's probably hot by now."

"Oh, my God, the soup!"

By the end of the conversation we still didn't have a date, although we clearly intended to have one at some point in the misty future. Two months? Three? Much too long — at least from my perspective, sitting here at the lake with the sea gulls. However long it takes before I can see her again, I'll be waiting, though waiting is something I promised myself I'd never do. Why wait for something illusory when you can have what's in front of you right now — the dead-flat lake, an inch of cold tea in a cup, this heavy solitude? Waiting is nowhere, but Sturgeon Bay, Wisconsin, is someplace real and specific, with many appealing aspects yet to be discovered. Last year at this time, I was waiting for my year off to begin, so I could do more or less what I'm doing right now, minus the waiting.

There wasn't much going on when I got here in May. The summer people hadn't arrived yet. A week passed before I saw anybody walking on the beach — a woman bundled up in foul-weather gear who obviously couldn't wait to get back inside. I had to call the septic man to pump out the holding tank; he came and went without introducing himself. When I went for a haircut at Joe's Barber Shop, Joe didn't even ask what kind of haircut I wanted; he'd been giving the same one to every customer for thirty-four years, and he knew how it was done. I thought of checking out the local pub, but people don't go out much around here on weeknights, and what would they have to say to an outsider who doesn't even like to fish?

One sure way to avoid waiting would be to get in the truck and drive back to see her, except then it would look as if I didn't have anything else to do and was driving back just to see her — which is to say, it would look too much like what it was. Better yet, I could fly out there tomorrow or the next day and take her to dinner. A plane would cross in a matter of hours the distance it took me four days to drive coming the other way. I traveled back roads and stopped often to eavesdrop in roadside cafes. In Oklahoma I found a recreational area next to a duck pond and put up my tent. It was early in the season, and the only other camper was an unemployed sheet-metal worker from Minnesota who was going fishing while he waited out the economy. He'd once been on a charter boat that had sunk in a storm on Lake Michigan. Thankfully, nobody had drowned. He asked to be remembered to the skipper, Vince somebody, from Sturgeon Bay, if I ran into him while I was here.

Dinner for two is a possibility. But what if it doesn't work out? What if she's bored to death by my rapturous descriptions of Wisconsin in the early spring, the music of love-drunk frogs pulsing in the swampy woods, those little flies that swarm over the clearings like smoke? What if she decides, as a result of our long-distance date, that I'm not potential boyfriend material, the way that other woman did: the anesthesiologist from Florida, who flew out to see me for a long weekend and left the next day, remarking bitterly on the way to the airport that my dog needed a bath? Then I will wish that I'd stayed here thinking about the woman in question instead of traveling all that way to be disappointed.

Taking everything into account — the distance between her and me, the newness of our friendship, her deadline, and the fact that my cat has not troubled himself over me for one second since I walked out the door nine months ago — I write her a letter saying I've decided to tough it out here for "a while" and do what I set out to do: write, read, ride my bikes. I don't let on that I will be waiting all that while to see her again, nor that I have been unable to stop thinking about her since we met. She writes back saying she is happy for me but "sorry" for herself, a sentiment that causes me to reconsider: it wouldn't do for a woman like her to be sorry on my account.

Most people my age have outgrown this kind of thing, and just a year and a half ago I started to think that it was happening to me, too — that I'd finally used up my lifetime allowance of love and was entering an era of more-sensible pursuits: writing, mountain climbing (while I'm still able to climb them), making more and better friends of either sex. What a relief to be liberated from the whole tragicomic struggle of wanting and not getting, or wanting, getting, and losing, which could all easily be avoided by not wanting in the first place!

I would find better things to do, become less selfish and more productive. Love is too damn much trouble, far too demanding of time and energy. Just think what I might accomplish in the postlove era. I could dedicate myself to doing good works with the same intensity that I'd once dedicated to love. I'd shine so brightly in my liberation that women would be unable to resist me.

Then, while visiting friends in New York City, I sat next to the woman in question at dinner. We drank wine and ate sushi. She was so lovely, so warm, so rich in her attention to everyone and everything that I knew there would be consequences for me of one kind or another: soaring bliss or abysmal misery; probably both. On the way uptown in the cab to drop her off, I mentioned that I was "looking for something to do" in New York for the next few days before flying back to Wisconsin, and if she wasn't "all booked up," would she be interested in doing something with me? She was. Notebook and pen leapt from my shirt pocket, and I wrote down her number. At that instant, somewhere on the nighttime streets of the Upper West Side, my resolve to live a life of virtuous independence went straight to hell.

We went to the Metropolitan Museum of Art to study the influence of the Spanish painters on the French painters. She studied the paintings, and, from a respectful distance, I studied her — a paintable woman if there ever was one. She disappeared into the galleries, which made perfect sense: I'd dreamed her up, and now she had returned forever to the kingdom of dreams. No, there she was in front of *The Annunciation*, a dubious look on her face as she regarded the cherubs piled up like wood shavings around Mary, who was just then receiving the word from on high: "Guess what? You're pregnant."

We spent the day getting lost and unlost in the museum, which was part of the fun. Having asked a guard how to get to southern Asia ("Turn right at the Medusa," he said), I placed a hand affectionately but paternally on her shoulder, as if to show the way. It was awkward, but everything I said or did, no matter how confused and clumsy, was a source of shared amusement. Walking back across Central Park in the warm afternoon, we saw an eight-foot-long yellow-and-white albino python, someone's pet, lounging on the new green grass. I couldn't decide if the grass was so green because the python was so yellow, or because this woman had mysteriously opened my eyes to the color of things.

Two days later we sat on the steps of the New York Public Library and talked for an hour or more before going inside to see the sonnet exhibit. Then she wanted to eat oysters in Grand Central Station, so we walked east. I was so engrossed in our conversation about the meaning of the name "Wurlitzer" that I almost walked right past the station and might have kept walking all the way to the East River had she not gently suggested that Grand Central might be that building right across the street. (I grew up in New York and drove a cab there. I know Grand Central Station when I see it.)

Later, heading downtown in the subway to visit Ground Zero, she asked for my address in Wisconsin.

"Are you going to write me a letter?" I asked, like an idiot.

"Then you don't want to give me your address," she stated.

"No — I mean, yes!"

Her postcard, which arrived a few days after I'd returned to Wisconsin, was what gave me the courage to call and ask her for a date. Spending time with me in New York had been "delightful," she wrote. But exactly *how* delightful? The card didn't say. Had she been as delighted as I'd been, or was she just being polite, like when you write your aunt to say how delighted you were to get the fruitcake she sent for Christmas? And what about this "Love," capitalized, followed by a comma, above her signature? Was it the same kind of love that people always signed letters with, or was it a hint of something yet to come?

She and I continued to write and talk on the phone at long intervals. Sometimes as many as three or four days went by without a word in either direction. When I tried to make plans to meet her later this summer, she said she wanted to take "one thing at a time." What was the "one thing" she had in mind?

It wouldn't do to call on weekends. She might be seeing someone, and she'd know that I wasn't. Once or twice I thought of the dark-haired Bulgarian waitress in a neighboring town, to whom I'd said, "You don't look like you're from around here," as she'd served up the breaded-whitefish special, but more as a way of diverting my attention from the woman in question than from any significant interest in the Bulgarian waitress.

There were times when I could hardly remember what the woman in question looked like, but even then I remembered too well how it had felt to be close to her. And I remembered who I had been when I was with her: a man I'd immediately liked and wanted to know better. Nothing seemed to take my mind off her for very long. Not the long bike rides on country roads, intended to make me so hungry and tired that I could think of nothing besides food and sleep. Not the pileated woodpecker that flew across the road during one of those rides, a giant compared to any woodpecker I'd ever seen before, and a bird that not even the natives saw often. Its dazzling red crest brought an unconscious shout of amazement out of me. Then it was gone into the trees, and in no time at all I was thinking not of the miraculous woodpecker, but of the woman fifteen hundred miles away who was working on her deadline and probably having stimulating social encounters without me.

Maybe the trick was to give in to the waiting, rather than gainsay it or call it something else: "caution," "maturity," "strategy." Maybe the waiting was really the thing that I'd been waiting for. For two weeks, I consoled myself with the thought that if, by some impossible chance, she walked through the door and threw herself into my arms, then this delicious hunger, this feeling of longing for her, would be gone. Too bad that longing, especially when one is in the midst of it, always seems such a poor substitute for what is longed for. No question, it had been far nicer to eat oysters with her that afternoon in Grand Central Station and hear her beautiful laughter than it was to sit here and think about it.

Then came a paltry excuse: some people I didn't know — a Lutheran minister, his wife, and their dog — were coming to stay in this house on Lake Michigan, where I'd been so conscientiously waiting and thinking. They were wonderful people, I was told; their dog was a wonderful dog. It was a big house, three bedrooms and two baths. We could all share it happily for the two weeks they planned to stay.

I called the woman in question and told her about these rowdy Lutherans who were about to ruin my peace and quiet. "Wisconsin is starting to get to me, anyway," I said. "I'm eating bratwurst and saying, 'You betcha,' to the checkout ladies at Econo-Foods. So, if you're going to be around in three weeks or so, I'd like to take you to dinner."

She agreed. Neither of us acknowledged in words what we both knew: that I was planning to cut short my retreat by six weeks, load up all my gear, and drive fifteen hundred miles just to take her to dinner.

In my next letter, I added recklessly at the end, "When can I start saying inappropriate things to you, like how beautiful you are?"

She wrote back, "Plus or minus fourteen days."

I replied, "Sorry, can't wait that long. You are astonishingly beautiful."

As soon as I'd mailed the letter, I knew that I'd spoken too soon and said too much, even though what I had said was obviously true and, besides that, true to what I felt. The word *astonishingly* repeatedly slipped my memory in the days that followed. It was too painful to be reminded of my clumsy come-on. How beautiful had I said she was? Astoundingly? Devastatingly? Outrageously? For days I mentally dredged up the letter and subjected it to withering review. What an ass! Why had I felt the need to say anything? There would have been plenty of time to tell her how beautiful she was when I got there, when I was actually beholding her beauty.

A few days later she replied with a postcard: William-Adolphe Bouguereau's painting of two young angels embracing. It was close to two in the afternoon. I stood in sunlight next to the mailbox on Lake Michigan Drive. Birds were probably singing in the woods; I can't really recall. On the back of the postcard was a message: "I loved your letter & I want to kiss you: I want to kiss you."

There are still a few days to go before I leave. Four, exactly. The things that I've been doing up to now to wait out the waiting — refinishing doors for my brother-in-law, driving into town at every opportunity to check my e-mail at the library and pick up some bananas, watching the NBA playoffs and the Italian bike races on television, obsessively cleaning and lubricating my bikes: things done to take my mind off other things and trick time into passing more quickly than it would have passed otherwise — are now performed like a dance, to music. The waiting has turned into something more like patience.

Things in the refrigerator will have to be eaten: the purple asparagus bought from an angelic blond farm girl at a roadside stand. She said some people thought the purple was a little sweeter than the green. I still haven't done anything about the copper teakettle that suffered a meltdown and lost its spout that night I was talking on the phone with the woman in question and forgot about the water heating on the stove. The house is clean enough, but I'll clean it anyway and water the potted flowers that won't be watered again until the Lutherans arrive. Then, come Tuesday, I'll get up early in the morning and drive like mad to her door. ∎

This Day

by JOHN HODGEN

Today hell has finally frozen over.
Mephistopheles glides by, double-runnered, huffing,
a spark in his eye.
Today God is getting new frames,
has lost count, momentarily, of the angels and pins.
A sparrow falls, dusts himself off, spits, gets back up again.

Today is my lucky day. Heybobareehoh.
I am plumb loco with luck, He Who Walks Backwards,
the one left alone in the wagon-train ambush,
tetched in the head, maize boy, too much in the sun,
the one who holds on to the overturned lifeboat,
who crawls like a worm from within the mass grave.

I am high man on the totem pole.
I walk from the plane wreck, stand up in the fusillade.
There is no bullet that bears my name.
I will never be taken alive.

Today it is for other men to be broken into boys,
for others to saw at their legs to survive.
I am Jack be nimble. The world can shut its trap.
My friends, my brothers are the heavy hearts.
The mark is on them.
They are scathed, fall chickens, good joes petered out.

No blood is daubed like unction on their chambered doors.
The man going through their rubbish outside
has brought them his sorrow, some vagrant plague.
They are the flies someone actually hurts.

Today the moon makes eyes at me.
Today I know the exact intensity that a woman brings
to the brushing to the left of the rivers of her hair.
When I hold her, the woman, the moon, I see in her eyes
the reflection, the waving arms of the dying and the drowned.
I make love to her anyway, lucky stiff, lucky bastard,
lucky as all get-out and hell.

My Accidental Jihad

by **KRISTA BREMER**

Early one morning in September, when our house is pitch-dark and the entire family is still asleep, my husband, Ismail, sits upright at the first sound of his alarm, dresses quickly, and leaves our bedroom. Later, after I've woken up and made my way downstairs for a cup of coffee, I find him standing at the counter, stuffing the last of his breakfast into his mouth, his eye on the clock as if he were competing in a pie-eating contest at the fair. The minute hand clicks forward, and, on cue, Ismail drops the food he's holding. I'm momentarily confused. My husband and I usually sit down together over our first cup of coffee, and he rarely eats breakfast. Then I realize: Ramadan has begun.

For the next month, nothing will touch my husband's mouth between sunup and sundown: Not food. Not water. Not my lips. A chart posted on our refrigerator tells him the precise minute when his fast must begin and end each day. I will find him in front of this chart again this evening, staring at his watch, waiting for it to tell him he may eat.

Ramadan is the ninth month of the lunar calendar, the month during which the Koran was revealed to the Prophet Mohammed through the angel Gabriel. Each year, more than 1 billion Muslims observe Ramadan by fasting from dawn to dusk. In addition to avoiding food and drink during daylight hours, Muslims are expected to refrain from all other indulgences: sexual relations, gossip, evil thoughts — even looking at "corrupt" images on television, in magazines, or on the Internet. Ramadan is a month of purification, during which Muslims are called upon to make peace with enemies, strengthen ties with family and friends, cleanse themselves of impurities, and refocus their lives on

God. It's like a month-long spiritual tuneup.

My husband found fasting easier when he lived in Libya, surrounded by fellow Muslims. Everyone's life changes there during the fast: people work less (at least, those who work outside the home), take long naps during the day, and feast with family and friends late into the night. Now, with a corporate job and an American wife who works full time, my husband has a totally different experience of Ramadan. He spends most of his waking hours at work, just as he does every other month of the year. He still picks up our son from day care and shares cooking and cleaning responsibilities at home. Having no Muslim friends in our Southern college town, he breaks his fast alone, standing at our kitchen counter. Here in the United States, Ramadan feels more like an extreme sport than a spiritual practice. Secretly I've come to think of it as "Ramathon."

I try to be supportive of Ismail's fast, but it's hard. The rules seem unnecessarily harsh to me, an American raised in the seventies by parents who challenged the status quo. The humility required to submit to such a grueling, seemingly illogical exercise is not in my blood. In my family, we don't submit. We question the rules. We debate. And we do things our own way. I resent the fact that Ismail's life is being micromanaged by the chart in the kitchen. Would Allah really hold it against him if he finished his last bite of toast, even if the clock said it was a minute past sunrise? The no-water rule seems especially cruel to me, and I find the prohibition against kissing a little melodramatic. I'm tempted to argue with Ismail that the rules are outdated, but he has a billion Muslims in his corner, whereas I have yet to find another disgruntled American wife who feels qualified to rewrite one of the five pillars of Islam.

People say that for a relationship to work, a couple needs to have a shared passion. My husband and I do have one: food. Years ago, when we first met, we shared other passions, such as travel, long runs on wooded trails, live music, and poetry readings. But now that we have two small kids, those indulgences have fallen by the wayside one by one. No matter how busy our lives get, however, we have to eat. On days when it seems we have nothing in common, when I struggle to recall what brought us together in the first place, one good meal can remind me. Ismail is an amazing cook. I remember in great detail the meal he prepared for me the first night we spent together: the walnuts simmering slowly in the thick, sweet blood-red pomegranate sauce; the chicken that slipped delicately away from the bone, like silk falling from skin. The next morning the scent of coriander ground into strong coffee filled his small apartment as he served me olives and fresh bread for breakfast.

Our love heated up like a sauce on the stove, our lives slowly blending together, the flavors becoming increasingly subtle and complex. I'd watch him prepare a bunch of cilantro on the counter, carefully separating the stalks with patient attention, gently plucking each leaf from its stem. He could toast pine nuts in a pan while carrying on a conversation with me and not burn a single one, magically rescuing them from the heat just as they turned the perfect shade of brown. Using his buttery fingertips, he would separate paper-thin sheets of phyllo dough without tearing any. He always served me first and studied my expression closely as I took a bite, his face lighting up in response to my pleasure. When he took his first taste, his eyes closed halfway, and a low moan of pleasure escaped from his mouth. There in the kitchen, all the evidence was before me: he was patient, attentive, thorough, economical, generous, creative, and sensual. I was ready to bear his children.

But when my husband fasts, our relationship becomes a bland, lukewarm concoction that I find difficult to swallow. I'm not proud of this fact. After all, he isn't the only one in our house with a spiritual practice: I stumble out of bed in the dark most mornings and meditate in the corner of our room with my back to him, trying to find that bottomless truth beyond words. Once in a great while, I'll drag him to church on Sunday. Whenever I suggest we say grace at the table, he reaches willingly for my hand, and words of gratitude flow easily from him. He has never criticized my practices, even when they've been wildly inconsistent or contradictory. But Ramadan is not ten minutes of meditation or an hour-long sermon; it's an entire month of deprivation. Ismail's God is the old-fashioned kind, omnipresent and stern, uncompromising with his demands. During Ramadan this God expects him to pray on time, five times a day — and to squeeze in additional prayers of forgiveness as often as he can. My God would never be so demanding. My God is a flamboyant and fickle friend with a biting wit who likes a good party. My God is transgendered and tolerant to a fault; he/she shows up unexpectedly during peak moments, when life feels glorious and synchronous, then disappears for long stretches of time.

But Ramadan leaves little room for dramatic flair. There is no chorus of voices or public celebration — just a quiet and steady submission to Allah in the privacy of one's home. For some Muslims who live in the West, the holiday becomes even more private, since their friends and colleagues are often not even aware of their fast.

During the early days of Ramadan, Ismail deals with his hunger by planning his next meal and puttering around the kitchen. In the last half-hour before the sun sets, he rearranges the food in our refrigerator or wipes down our already-clean counters. At night in bed, as I drift off to sleep, he reviews each ingredient in the baklava he intends to make the following evening. "Do you think I should replace the walnuts with pistachios?" he whispers. In the middle of the workday, when I call his cellphone, I hear the beeping of a cash register in the background. He is wandering the aisles of our local grocery store. "I needed to get out of the office," he says matter-of-factly, as if all men escaped to the grocery store during lunch.

The last hours before he breaks his fast are the most difficult and volatile time of day for him. Coincidentally, they are the same hours at which I return home from work. I open the door and find him collapsed on the couch, pale and exhausted, our children running in circles around the room. Ismail is irritable, and his thoughts trail off in midsentence. I dread seeing him in this state. I count on my husband to speak coherently, to smile on a regular basis, and to enjoy our children. This humorless person on my couch is no fun. Every few days I ask (with what I hope sounds like innocent curiosity) what he's learned from his fast so far. I know this is an unfair question. How would I feel if he poked his head into our bedroom while I was meditating and asked, *How's it going? Emptied your mind yet?*

One balmy Saturday in the middle of Ramadan, we go to hear an outdoor lecture by a Sufi Muslim teacher who is visiting from California. The teacher sits cross-legged under a tree on a colorful pillow while the sun streams down on him through a canopy of leaves. After a long silence, he sweeps his arms in front of him, a beatific expression on his face, and reminds us to notice the beauty that surrounds us. "If you don't," he says, "you're not fasting — you're just going hungry."

I take a sidelong glance at Ismail. He is looking very hungry to me these days. I guess I imagined that during his fast a new radiance would emanate from him. I imagined him moving more slowly, but also more lovingly. I imagined a Middle Eastern Gandhi, sitting with our children in the garden when I got home from work. In short, I imagined that his spiritual practice would look more . . . well, *spiritual*. I didn't imagine the long silences between us or how much his exhaustion would irritate me. I didn't imagine him leaping out of bed in a panic, having slept through his alarm, and running downstairs to swallow chunks of bread and gulp coffee before the sun came up. I didn't imagine his terse replies to my attempts to start a conversation, or his impatience with our children.

I thought I understood the rules of Ramadan: the timetable on the refrigerator, the five daily prayers. But I didn't understand that the real practice is addressing a toddler's temper tantrum or a wife's hostile silence when you haven't eaten or drunk anything in ten hours. I was like the children of Israel in the Bible, who once complained that, despite their dutiful fasting, God *still* wasn't answering their prayers. The children of Israel had it all wrong: God doesn't count calories. The fast itself only sets the stage. God is interested in our behavior and intentions *while* we are hungry. Through his prophet Isaiah, God gave the children of Israel a piece of his mind:

> Behold, in the day of your fast you seek your own pleasure, and oppress all your workers. Behold, you fast only to quarrel and to fight and to hit with a wicked fist. Fasting like yours this day will not make your voice to be heard on high. (Isaiah 58:3–4)

Ismail tells me that in the Middle East, Ramadan is a time of extremes: There are loving gatherings among family and friends at night, and a tremendous public outpouring of charity and generosity to those in need. Meanwhile, the daytime streets become more dangerous, filled with nicotine and caffeine addicts in withdrawal. People stumble through the morning without their green or black tea, drunk so dark and thick with sugar that it leaves permanent stains even on young people's teeth. Desperate smokers who light up in public risk being ridiculed or even attacked by strangers. The streets reverberate with angry shouts and car horns, and traffic conflicts occasionally escalate into physical violence.

Our home, too, becomes more volatile during Ramadan. Ismail's temper is short; my patience with him runs thin. I accuse him of being grumpy. He accuses me of being unsupportive. I tell him he is failing at Ramadan, as if it were some sort of exam. I didn't ask for this spiritual test, I tell him. As if I could pick and choose which parts of him to bring into my life. As if he were served up to me on a plate, and I could primly push aside what I didn't care for — his temper, his doubt, his self-pity — and keep demanding more of his delicious tenderness.

And then there is my husband's unmistakable Ramadan scent. Normally I love the way he smells: the faint scent of soap and laundry detergent mixed with the warm muskiness of his skin. But after a few days of fasting, Ismail begins to smell *different*. Mostly it's his breath. The odor is subtle but distinct and persists no matter how many times he brushes or uses mouthwash. When I get close to him, it's the first thing I notice. I do a Google search for "Ramadan and halitosis" and learn that this is a common side effect of fasting — so common that the Prophet Mohammed himself even had something to say about it: "The smell of the fasting person's breath is sweeter to Allah than that of musk." Allah may delight in this smell, but I don't. I no longer rest my head on Ismail's chest when we lie in bed at night. I begin to avoid eye contact and increase the distance between us when we speak. I no longer kiss him on impulse in the evening. I sleep with my back to him, resentful of this odor, which hangs like an invisible barrier between us.

The purpose of fasting during Ramadan is not simply to suffer hunger, thirst, or desire, but to bring oneself closer to *taqwa*: a state of sincerity, discipline, generosity, and surrender to Allah; the sum total of all Muslim teachings. When, in a moment of frustration, I grumble to my husband about his bad breath, he responds in the spirit of *taqwa*: He listens sympathetically and then apologizes and promises to keep his distance. He offers to sleep on the couch if that would make me more comfortable. He says he wishes I had told him earlier so he could have spared me any discomfort. His humility catches me off guard and makes my resentment absurd.

This month of Ramadan has revealed to me the limits of my compassion. I recall a conversation I had with Ismail in the aftermath of September 2001, when the word *jihad* often appeared in news stories about Muslim extremists who were hellbent on destroying the United States. According to Ismail, the Prophet Mohammed taught that the greatest jihad, or struggle, of our lives is not the one that takes place on a battlefield, but the one that takes place within our hearts — the struggle to increase self-discipline and become a better person. This month of Ramadan has thrown me into my own accidental jihad, forcing me to wrestle with my intolerance and self-absorption. And I have been losing ground in this battle, forgetting my husband's intentions and focusing instead on the petty ways I am inconvenienced by his practice.

Ramadan is meant to break our rigid habits of overindulgence, the ones that slip into our lives as charming guests and then refuse to leave, taking up more and more space and stealing our attention away from God. And it's not just the big habits, the ones that grab us by the throat — alcohol, coffee, cigarettes — but the little ones that take us gently by the hand and lead us stealthily away from the truth. I begin to notice my own compulsions, the small and socially acceptable ones that colonize my day: The way I depend on regular exercise to bolster my mood. The number of times I check my e-mail. The impulse to watch a movie with my husband after our children are in bed, rather than let the silence envelop us both. And the words: all the words in books, in magazines, on the computer; words to distract me from the mundane truth of the moment. I begin to notice how much of my thinking revolves around what I will consume next.

I am plump with my husband's love, overfed by his kindness, yet I still treat our marriage like an all-you-can-eat buffet, returning to him over and over again to fill my plate, as if our vows guaranteed me unlimited nourishment. During Ramadan, when he turns inward and has less to offer me, I feel indignant. I want to make a scene. I want to speak to whoever is in charge, to demand what I think was promised me when I entered this marriage. But now I wonder: Is love an endless feast, or is it what people manage to serve each other when their cupboards are bare?

In the evening, just before sundown, Ismail arranges three dates on a small plate and pours a tall glass of water, just as the Koran instructs him to do, just as the Prophet Mohammed himself did long ago. Then he sits down next to me at the kitchen counter while I thumb through cookbooks, wondering what to make for dinner. He waits dutifully while the phone rings, while our daughter practices scales on the piano, while our son sends a box of Legos crashing onto our wood floor. Then, at the moment the sun sets, he lifts a date to his mouth and closes his eyes. ■

The Stranger

by **MICHAEL HETTICH**

You wake before dawn beside someone
you don't recognize, a dark woman who snores
from her belly as though she were churning inside.
It alarms you at first, though you're drawn
to the shape of her ears, her neck, the way
her long black hair drapes across the pillow,
and you move over a little, naked and cool
under the covers; you nudge her so you can
observe the other parts of her more closely.
The room is still half dark, so you listen to the tick-
tock of your windup alarm clock, which tells you
this is the bedroom you've slept in for years,
every evening winding that silly contraption
she gave you before you were married — so you would
remember her love each time you wound it
and set the alarm. Or else it will run down,
she said, and stop somewhere in the middle of the night,
and you'll just keep sleeping.
But who is this woman beside you?
Could this be your wife? She's beautiful, maybe
as lovely as your wife is. And when you get up
and wander through the bedroom,
you notice that everything's
just as you left it, familiar as your own
middle-aged body: the old dog asleep
on his towel in the corner is the same mutt you got

for your children when they were just children; the house
is full of your children's absence as you roam,
picking up books and notebooks and trinkets
they've left behind on their visits. But it's still too early
to get up. You're tired. You should go back to bed,
lie down beside this beautiful woman
who will become your wife again
in a few hours when the alarm pulls you
from dreams back into the man you've been
for so many years now it's hard to remember
who you were before you became him.

Blue Flamingo Looks At Red Water

a short story by **KATHERINE VAZ**

That bus is going to slam into my daughter. In my stop-action memory, everything lies bare a grace note before the accident. The school bus grinds forward stupidly, a yellow hippo. Henry is at the crosswalk, waiting for me as I turn the corner. He is not holding Mary's hand.

I'm forever saying, *Remember to hold on to her.* She bolts toward the cat across the room, the crocus past the fence. She unfastens from me, too, and I have to catch her. In my arms she grows vehement and fights like a fish. We chose the name "Mary" because it is plain-spoken, classic, but after she was born, I looked it up: It means "rebellion." Even while she floated inside me, her thigh bones twitching like fire-making sticks, producing her fiery skin, she was already a grace note ahead of becoming herself, rising out of the skeletal place where our names store their forgotten meanings.

My hand goes up in a half-wave, half-jabbing motion to indicate that he must get a grip on her. (Only the stop-action reveals that the warning comes before the greeting.) We are going across the street to Belinda's Crafts, because Mary loves tempera paints. Henry is tired from long hours at Ketchum & Doherty, where he is a paralegal. He has recently completed the task of threading his father, who is riddled with Alzheimer's, into an open spot at Sunrise Homes. I have just finished teaching my geography seminar at Redwood University. After visiting Belinda's, we plan to stop at Jun's for Korean barbecue. Mary is five years old. She considers the wet green seaweed a wonder.

For a fraction of a second (not available to the naked eye: I detect it only when I run the film on its slowest speed) Henry takes in a pretty blonde going down Jasmine Street and then turns to wave at me while I scream, "Mary!" She can't wait. She wants to be at Belinda's; she's on to painting the next picture.

Memory has lifted away the sound of the impact; horror first thrusts itself into my nostrils: the brew of rubber, the ether of exhaust. I smell rather than hear the wail of the woman driver. It's all milk and oil. She's fat and lurching about, like the dybbuk of the bus let loose from its host body. Henry jumps back. It's just a twitch, an instinct, because then he throws himself forward, but I'm there first. I run with that voidance of time that puts you in the place you can see before you should land there, so I'm ahead of Henry (how could that happen?), leaning over her. He's reaching around me; tall as he is, he makes a shell for me to tuck myself inside, but I'm the animal with her probes out. Thin red stripes cover Mary, as if she wants to keep this clean and neat, but then there's an explosion of blood with my hands in the middle of it.

Henry must have pulled me away; I must have stood up. Because everything else is gone now. It is only later that Mary's voice finds me: *Blue sky. Yellow bus. Me in red, Mother.* I had been teaching her that, out of the primary colors, all pictures can be made.

I'm slower than you are, Isabel, Henry likes to proclaim, and he is. Slower to get out of a car, to add up sums, to get ready for a party, to remember. I loved it once, that slowness. It used to embody care, the tea-ceremony approach to living; care in arranging items in the trunk of a car; care in brushing my hair, slowly, until it knocked me out; slowness in kissing me.

I want her ashes buried at sea. Cold penetrates me while I sprinkle her over the San Francisco Bay. I'm wearing an apricot dress and my stockings with the black dragons, the ones Mary adored. Mary in the fire, then Mary in the water; Mary red, then Mary blue. Where is Henry? He's on the boat, but I don't see him until we're back in our tiny bungalow for the wake and he's setting out meats and hardened bread slices, fingers of carrots, a knife stuck in mustard. I'm quaking from the chill. Henry reaches for me, and I shudder. My colleagues and neighbors are not bad people, but the weight of trying not to say, "If there's anything you need . . . ," causes Lucille, an assistant professor, to ask, "Isabel, aren't you part Mexican?" I know what she means: cha-cha-cha happiness, cha-cha-cha grief. Why aren't I screeching? We've seen them on newsreels, those women with their ululations, writhing like octopuses atop coffins. But after "Mary!" there isn't anything left to yell.

What's pounding the cage of my insides is a whisper. Henry is on his third beer. I can tell the thought that comes out of me hits him a glancing blow, because his head rears back and he opens another beer: *Can't you remember anything? I told you not to let her go.*

I walk outside. A bird of paradise guards our lawn and the Joseph's coat roses. I say aloud to no one, "You forget everything."

In the fable, the barber who sees that King Midas has sprouted the ears of a jackass crawls outside, digs a hole, and whispers into it, "King Midas has the ears of a jackass!" He covers up the hole.

The barber is stunned when the plants exude the chant "King Midas has the ears of a jackass," grass echoing to grass, until the whisper goes inside everyone and bursts from their mouths.

The guests leave, and there's only Henry and me, two middling souls, bloated and weary. Even in the three months before Mary died, we made love only twice. A run through a dragon on my stocking makes it appear beheaded. The whisper blows in from the wide outdoors, where I left it, and scrawls itself in the air, in plain view.

Henry disappears for one day. His own whisper erupts: *You sit there without a word of comfort. It could have been you.*

In Henry's absence, Simon and Lana, my friends from the art department, arrive with a videocassette of *The Terminator*. They are married and work together on kinetic sculptures, winning grants to bring discarded bits and pieces of scrap metal to life and then drinking up the outraged howls. Lana favors velvet dresses and mud-caked army boots. "Isa-bella-donna," says Simon, hugging me. The three of us laugh ourselves sick at Arnold Schwarzenegger's murder of the entire planet.

I am alone in bed in the afternoon when Henry returns. He stretches out next to me, and I don't release the new whisper, but it's that fast into the earth and through the trees, exhaled by the leaves: *I can't touch you.* We even hold hands — a sad little unity, but the only one we have, because we both hear the words at exactly the same time.

The arrival of Jacob Meyers at our bereavement group one Saturday morning causes a shifting, a tremor of discomfort and excitement. Even in a basement room at Redwood University, there is a ranking and collating, an assessment of celebrity, a hierarchy stuck over the wet mess of pain. Jacob Meyers is a famous attorney and a single father whose eleven-year-old girl, Dawn, was tortured and left disemboweled near the highway outside Sacramento. Betty, whose infant died after his insides refused to grow, scurries to get Jacob some coffee. She has given up asking me where Henry is. He says, "Those people didn't know Mary, so I don't want to know them." I am not beyond admiring that sentiment.

Jacob takes the cup from Betty. He's tall and hesitant, dark and sharp featured, and where most men seem to be a head and hands and clothing, he is a body barely contained by what he is wearing. He was in the search party that found Dawn, and he offers a detail that we did not read in the newspapers. Betty gasps, and hands fly to mouths when he says, "A rabbit had jumped onto Dawn." Dawn, though brutalized, was still offering a living thing a place to rest. I understand for the first time that line "Every angel is terrible." I burst out with "She was lovely!"

My words cleave the room. Coffee quivers seismically in people's styrofoam cups. Betty may swoon, and Andrew, whose son died of cancer, might strangle me. Right as I am about to apologize, Jacob says, "Yes, thank you." Desperate to find the words that will destroy the grotesqueness, he says, "It was like her, what she did, holding on to something alive. That's it; that's Dawn."

The meeting does not last long. The group disperses, and I see Jacob in the hallway, lingering and looking at me as I walk toward the ladies' room. His hand is on the water fountain, but suddenly it is too much for him to bend over for a drink, and I put my hand on his inclined back and say, "I . . ." I keep my hand there.

It is such a short distance to lean into him as he rises to meet me.

We open our mouths against each other to deliver the words coming from our throats.

We go to the Pine Resort Motel on the Redwood Highway. I hold on to his arm while he drives, and he pulls me toward him in a way that almost lifts me off the seat. Inside the room, I stay lifted up. That is the marvel of him. The carpet is worn in spots down to its beige grid; an aerosol scent of lavender makes a dome over a staleness of smoke. He presses me against the wall to kiss my neck, and my hands are all over him, and I say, "Wrap my legs around you," and I am thoroughly in the air. I used to try to guess: is it the man trying to crawl into the woman's hide, or the other way around? With Jacob gliding in and out of me and me pouring wet down the front of his thighs, I see that it's both at the same time. All that desire rammed up against cauterized nerve endings, deadened in order to get us through the day. *Is everyone like this?* I wonder — and still do. I think: *Yes. Flail off my skin. Kiss me until I feel teeth. Crack open my chest.*

We collapse together and sleep, and then, still holding on to each other, we go into the bathroom and take turns peeing, like an old married couple. I touch the underside of his penis, the liverish patch where the doctor's knife miscut him when he was a baby. It is time to go home. Out in the light, we blink. The highway and the rushing cars, blue and red and yellow: the landscape faint but filling in. Where am I? What's here? Where is my daughter? I want to talk to her — not about this, but about our need to watch out for each other, since I'm given to bolting, too.

Jacob leads me to his car and opens the door for me. I don't want to climb in and make this be the end of us. When his hand sweeps the hair out of his eyes, it is like that first gesture we make in the morning, coming to, recalling ourselves. My head rests against his shoulder. His hair is a disaster area. I like his tallness, his dark eyes. I like all that he is, down to the history of himself that even he doesn't know. I put my hand on his chest, and the tremors are still going through him: the remainder of loving me, the great, fine habit of the body to retain the memory of its finest hours. His fingers go through my hair to my scalp. "I didn't hurt you, did I?" he says. "I don't mean to hurt you."

There's only us, with throbbing stars crowning our veins. The sky looks as if it's been swabbed with erasers. I'm blindingly, out of my skin in love. "It isn't hurt I'm feeling," I whisper. He kisses the spot where the water pours out of my hairline, as if there were a fissure there.

"I'm so sorry, sweetheart," he says. "It is. That's what it is." He adds that I'm pretty, that he likes the light in my eyes, and says, "I won't forget this. I won't forget you." Today is the day that everything else must fit itself over.

I elicit a promise: Will he call me every year on my birthday — to see how well we manage to fit time over today?

He says yes, he won't forget.

As he takes me home, we agree, yes, nothing is better than when joy curves so far around it sucks on its own sorrowful tail.

But in the night, knives come at me and worry the body's slits: eyes, asshole, ears, cunt, mouth, nose, nipples, navel, pores, leaking everywhere. Henry comes home late from work, while I'm asleep, and wakens before I do the next morning. He calls from work to say, "Were you drunk? You wet the bed. I thought that was my job, wet dreams."

I say, "Getting drunk is your job," and hang up on him.

How can you go on? That's the implied question whenever an outstretched hand hovers over my skin, worried that a mere touch might detonate me. People don't mean to be cruel. They're just not as lucky as I am. No Mary or Dawn to reveal to them that memory only seems locked in the past to disguise how it streams forward. I live in a constant thrill: What will Mary do next? Life twists the paths begun in childhood: her vehemence might turn into a romantic fervor, doomed and hidden. She comes to me with her eyebrows — black and heavy, like mine — plucked into a thin line, the result of a lifelong project of badly taming herself. Why does it persist, this invented memory of Mary wearing a mortarboard and graduation gown, this perpetual finding her on the verge of something? It seems to grow out of Mary in her water wings in the backyard pool. I ask Henry if he thinks Mary would have been as good a swimmer as he is, and he stares at me before he says, "She already was." Henry's grief has a sadder twist: he can't dream her forward, so he has left her stuck in time.

It works backward, too, memory; it revises the past we foolishly think can never be altered. I was born in Mexico City and lived there until I was seven. My father, Inocencio, was an electrician who played the harp. I would ride with him in traffic while he transported his harp, a Veracruz *jarocho*, on a bicycle we'd bought from the baker, with enormous side baskets. We wobbled past buses with riders hanging out of the doors, past swerving green cabs. Once, we rammed into a man steering a red toy wagon filled with piglets. A friend with a chestnut cart liked to pelt us with uncooked chestnuts when we passed his corner, which made my father roar with laughter and almost crash as we headed into the Alameda Central, with its booths of miniature Kings of the Orient and Snoopy dolls, maize leaves, clay whistles, and amplifiers. My father kept shouting, "Here we go, Mechita!" My middle name is Mercedes, and he found my nickname there, because I was thin and quick-tempered, and *mecha* is also the wick of a candle. I recall being fearless.

This is my native country for me: father, harp, baker's bicycle heading through traffic, people with their lives dangling every which way. A fullness reigned there: cracks in walls sprouting ivy with wood spiders hanging from the leaves; a perilous, decorative, brimming disaster taking a long time in front of a mirror to put on its hat; everyone trailing bits and pieces, everything bendable or easily shattered, like vertebrae.

Mary lived only the years she would have remembered little of as an adult, so I invite her in to revise what I think I know about my own early years. She insists that my father is not shouting, "Here we go!" but, "Hold on!" The past changes, thanks to her: I'm clutching my father's guayabera shirt until I feel skin, because I must hold on, and I'm holding on, holding on, danger spilling past me, holding on to my father and to the daughter not yet born, Mary Gomez Eisenberg, my name tucked into the middle of her.

My father died not in traffic, but in his bed, of heart disease. My Texas-born Irish mother moved us to San Francisco, where she had a sister. Henry had a Jewish father and a Norwegian mother, and when we were first married, we joked about his mother's native gods in their severe costumes. Mary was our prediction of a new hybrid rule. We did our part to free the world of its obsession with tribal purity.

On my first birthday after the accident, Jacob Meyers calls and says, "Tell me what you're doing."

I am putting away a box of Mary's paintings that I have recently taken down from the walls. (I haven't kept her clothing or furniture, things another child could use.) My favorite is the one I call *Blue Flamingo Looks at Red Water*. The blue flamingo is looking at its reflection in a red pool. The water is giving its tones to the bird, and the bird has lent its color to the water.

"I'm looking at her paintings," I say.

"That's good," he says.

He tells me he is writing a book.

On my second birthday after the accident, Jacob Meyers calls and says, "Have you found Henry again?"

They are only now returning to me, people orbiting around objects — streets, strata, names, all of which should matter to me, a teacher of geography: Foraging with Simon and Lana in the junkyards for bizarrely shaped iron. Henry as I watch him go out the door with his orange bag of swimming gear, on his way to the Olympic pool on the corner. Henry going gray while slumbering in his chair, the night still young. (How could I have married a man twelve years older without imagining this time would come?) The town, Redwood, white-hot in summer, the flanks of dogs marinated with the oil of the wild mint, the red plastic cups in the gutter from the kegger parties, town versus gown, California's affection for giving its streets self-loathing names: Yale, Harvard, Cornell. Henry sitting at Roma Cafe, denying that he is gazing at girls. But when I study his corneas, the images are stuck there, scrapes of sexual fandango. The forty-year-old geography teacher who gave up the dream of being a photographer and the fifty-two-year-old paralegal who was never a lawyer; the late bloomers, late parents, mildly, slowly — with Henry's slowness — sliding toward erosion. The second glass of wine topped off heavily, so that the next glass can be thought of as a third and not a fourth. The game show after the evening news, eroding further into an addiction to police shows. Ending a marriage isn't easy. You hack it to pieces, but the pieces sprout into tiny replicas of the marriage, bleeding on your shoes.

I go to our bedroom, a bursting-at-the-seams place, books and clothing piled on the floor, T-shirts over the backs of the rickety chairs that Henry saved from college and never replaced. (That I never replaced, either.) Henry lies asleep, kneading the sheet in his hands the way people do in hospitals right before they die, as if retreating under a winding cloth. His tight grip on the sheet alarms me, and I kneel on the bed, tugging the covers away from him. I shout, "Henry? Henry!" He fights for the cloth — white with sprigs of violets, my selection, not his; how many men lie down every night in the woman's choice? — and I fight back and succeed in pulling it away. There is a cushion of beer under his skin, up and down the length of him. It's a light and foamy thing, the beer simply pooled beneath the surface without any digestion, pausing only to wick anything alive out of his hair, which used to be blond but now is straw. Here's the answer to why his eyes have yellowed.

"Oh, Henry," I say, my palm on his chest. He pulls me to him, and that quickly I am below him and he is inside me, clinging so ferociously I can't move. "Henry?" I say. He's crushing me. I don't have a sensation of my chest, only of my bare rib cage, a carcass picked clean by ants. It's not Henry's face pressing all over mine, but the skeleton inside his face; it's the bones I feel as he suffocates me with kisses. I have an image of the jangling man from biology class, hanging by a thread to teach us femur, clavicle, butterfly plate of pelvic bone. I kiss him back because I am too sad not to. He thinks all is forgiven — and it is, because I am suddenly aware that this is what I've been building toward: I want to cut the last tie that will keep me from slipping into indifference. Because this isn't love; this is a determination to reinstate love through impact. I want him to release me. I struggle, and that is enough of a response for him to moan my name. I am crying. He kisses away my tears. Still he holds on; his pressure won't relent. I stroke his back with my hand. And I take back, frightened, the notion of indifference: if it is not love, it is compassion soaking into me, and that, after all, is not far from the thing itself, though we may never get back to it.

In the morning we rest against each other without speaking. He buys me new walking shoes, and I train climbing roses, tea-sized crimson, up the front of our bungalow. He gives me blank books with elaborate covers depicting antique maps or Victorian clocks. That's the old Henry, as he was when I first met him: generous, suffering a hundred details on my behalf, taking two hours one day to correct my timing of frog kick to breast stroke in the pool; me generous right back, thinking up ways to thank him.

His oddest gift now is an intensification of his silence. Every now and then, he flinches. He tells me that he's reliving the sensation of impact. His frame takes the hit of it. It is what I am missing about Mary: he goes to it and winces, while I pull up short. I can't go where he's going, but because it's some recollection of Mary, I try to draw closer to it. The doctor said that Mary hadn't felt a thing. Mary feeling nothing? What is that split second like, to have your body crushed, your head slammed against metal? What is the enormity of that pain? The bus a mastodon against the bobbling wind chime of a child's skeleton.

I don't know how to rescue Henry from this. I would like to supplant the sensation of impact with sounds of sad beauty. At the music store, I find a CD of the Portuguese fado singer Mísia. Fados are the traditional songs of fate, mournful; a singer risks disappearing into the heat of them. Mísia has a Louise Brooks–style bob haircut and full lips and is said to bring a modern sensibility to this music of the past.

Henry thanks me, inspects the CD, turns it over in his hand, sets it out in view, but does not play it.

He hangs paper fish on the patio and calls it the "Inland Sea." My arm around his waist, I say, "Thanks, Henry. It's pretty." I don't mind that the wind comes in and shreds the fish. We watch pieces of the lobster being carried away. Red dots will land on far places, and no one will guess that the specks are lobsters from an inland sea. Would a person taking a ferry on the bay know that they are riding over my little girl? I stop. For the first time, I can identify a moment — watching the lobsters — when Mary (or is it Henry?) has given me relief from contemplating her.

But it is Henry who clings more and more to the relief of not dwelling upon Mary: too much imagining of the impact has shattered him, and now the pieces of him are going sailing who knows where.

I say, "Remember when I took this photo?" Redwood no longer has any redwood trees, but there was once one so huge that, when they sawed it down, they polished the stump into a dance floor. We went to a fancy party there. We dressed Mary in her green shift, and I let her wear my clip-on shell earrings and red lipstick. I snapped a picture of her blowing kisses, surrounded by women in evening dresses and pearls and men in suits who had come to whirl around on top of the chopped-off neck of the King of Trees. Henry had disappeared into the crowd.

"Sorry," he says. "Was I there?"

We drive to the Yuletide Farm for a Christmas tree. Henry takes Road 102; it's as if the valley heat defeated any imagination for naming the byways. (My student Maureen's essay comes to mind: "How Terrain Determines Our Degree of Hope.") The landscape's redness is brought out by the rain, as if storms have flayed away the pale skin. The Persian-rug colors, gold and crimson, are interrupted only by an apiary, a dairy. Milk and honey. (Matthew, another student, who is taking geography because he wants to map the real world — the erosions, depths, rings, and upheavals — writes about the effects far inland of California's crumbling coastline.)

I am happy; we used to bring Mary to the Yuletide Farm, and she'd stamp her feet and dash into the thicket of trees. "Remember the time that Mary climbed one of the firs?" I ask.

"No, Isabel, I don't," Henry says, impatient, and I am so furious that we end up leaving our saw in the car and selecting a tree that's already cut down. In silence, we tie it to the top of the car in the traditional slaughtered-deer pose.

Is it willful erasure, an attempt to acquit himself of her? Often his *Sorry, no* angers me, and other times I experience a guilt that leaves me thinking, *To each his own way.* If Mary had selected me and not him to keep reliving the sensation of her last moment — how wearying. No wonder he's exhausted. Then, now, always: he wants her to *stop.*

But he starts saying, *Stop,* to me, too.

On the third anniversary of Mary's accident, I ask Henry what's on his mind. To me, the square of the day sits on the calendar like a jack-in-the-box with its hair-trigger latch: out springs Mary.

"I'm thinking that maybe you think too much, Isabel," he says.

He goes beyond the great three lost items — keys, glasses, wallet

— and now misplaces events. I ask him to make a reservation at a restaurant, and he neglects to do it. I leave out the papers he needs to bring to work, and he overlooks them. *Now, what was that fellow's name again? Now, when was that? Was that Thursday?* The refrain drives me into the bathroom, where I shut the door and splash water on my face to keep from shrieking. He jots down lists before going to the grocery store, and then he forgets the list but brings back something he knows I'll like.

I remind him to call Sunrise Homes every week to get permission to take his father out for their Sunday breakfasts. I collect magazines for his father, and then Henry leaves them behind. He has been visiting his father several times a week; are sympathetic symptoms afflicting Henry? His dad's Alzheimer's has not yet removed the memory of his son, and of course Henry should cling to that slender tie as long as possible. I walk outside to cool off: *You forget everything* is still written in the air where I first spoke it, circulating on the breeze that stirs the last hanging fragments of the Inland Sea.

At Simon and Lana's, Simon asks Henry if he remembers the night with the coyotes.

"No," says Henry, his voice low and tired.

I'm startled. It has honestly gone out of his head.

"Sure you do," says Simon.

Lana, cutting the strawberry torte, pauses with the knife and says, "Henry, that was six months ago."

"We were at my brother Patrick's ranch, out in Death Valley," says Simon. He shoots a glance at me, but I have to look away. I stare at their sunflower-patterned tablecloth, dizzy.

"We'd been drinking a lot of beer, and Patrick led us out to piss around the perimeter of the ranch, because he'd heard the scent of humans keeps the coyotes away. We laughed about getting skewered on the cactus spines, remember?"

"Sort of," says Henry.

My foot swings out and knocks a leg of the table. Lana stops cutting the torte. I'm not going to be able to contain myself. I can recall that evening down to the low-lying wildflowers, a vibrant purple. Henry and I made love that night with a howling like the furious animals held at bay around the ranch's borders.

"How can you forget that?" I say, more harshly than I should.

"What?" he says.

"Jesus Christ!" I shout. "Can't you remember anything?"

Henry is red and subdued.

Lana says, "Shhh, it doesn't matter."

"It does," I say.

"All right," says Simon. "It's been a long evening. I didn't mean to —"

"You're fine," says Henry. "I'm fine."

I'm going to strangle on the words: *No, you're not!*

When we say goodbye, Simon whispers, "Don't worry. It's good to see you both out and about again. That's all."

But it isn't all. In the car, I say, "Henry, what is with you?"

He explodes. "*Nothing.* Nothing is — what did you say? — 'with me.'"

"That's right. *Nothing* is with you," I say, and he stares straight ahead. Instead of asking him what's wrong, I start to cry and say, "I'm sorry, Henry."

"For what?" he says, and smiles at me sadly. He squeezes my knee. He absolves me so readily, as if my outburst has already fled and gone from him, the images dissolved in his head.

When Jacob calls me on my birthday that year, I say, "Tell me what's new with you."

He has finished his book. It is not a rehash of his "case"; he won't offer up Dawn for public scrutiny. It's a novel based on his childhood in Idaho, where the Snake River vanishes into a terrace of land. He is becoming who he is now by revising who he was. His law practice is doing well. He is getting married to a violinist who teaches poetry in the schools. Her name is Emily.

"Jacob," I say, "I'm so glad." Because it amazes me. At any diminished point, with its impetus toward further diminishment, *life pulls up*, fresh and strong, turning away from the wall.

He asks, "What's ahead of you, Isabel?"

I freeze. It's as if I lift my head and look at the approaching years: why have I been so frightened to see Henry? I think I know; I think I've known for quite a while. I figured that, after Mary, our account with tragedy was so overdrawn that it would leave us alone. But time has trickled on to a new present, a new dilemma, even if I have not been ready to name it.

"I don't know what's ahead," I say to Jacob. "I think I'm afraid to say."

"Will you take care of yourself?" he asks. "Will you take care of Henry?"

Henry arrives home that night with my birthday present: a gift certificate for scuba-diving lessons. My affection for water is romantic; I've mentioned that I would like to make it real. He has kept this in mind.

I kiss him. Women often ask about men, *What has he done?* when they know they must ask, *Who is he?*

He extracts the Mísia CD from the heap near our disc player. "I love this album," he says. "Remember how we made love while this played in the background at the ski cabin four years ago?"

Surprise courses through me. Instead of saying, *Henry, are you out of your mind? I bought that for you a short while ago. How can you forget?* I am quiet.

He goes on with his reverie: It was the weekend we like best, our annual winter trip to the mountains, when everyone else vanishes inside to watch the Super Bowl. The scenery of pure snow clears away until there's only him and me, and maybe some others. But mostly it's him and me, and the world packed up in white, ready to be stored away, as if then, truly, it would be just the two of us.

I close my eyes. He thinks I'm shaking from the memory, so he touches my face. Fifty-two is young, but I can guess the end that is in store for him. He has turned toward old age. He is not forgetting Mary to avoid pain; he is entering a new pain that is famous for not stopping. As befits Henry, it is happening slowly, and that is how I will lose him, instead of full-force and swiftly, as we lost our daughter. I have been too horrified to see what is true. The dead body of a little girl is not a painting. It is not beautiful. And loss of memory can be a physical fact; death strolling in when we weren't looking, grinning, taking its time. Taking its time in telling us that it has come to stay.

Henry has a surprise for me. He knows that on my birthday I like trying something a little frightening or new. We run two blocks to the civic-center pool and steal over the fence, like high-school kids. He brings my suit, goggles, and towel but forgets my cap. I tell him not to bother going back for it.

He wants to teach me the butterfly, a stroke I've never mastered. It requires a person to sweep her arms outward, as if trying to toss her body into its own embrace, right as it's time for the next thrust forward.

"Like this," he says, telling me to hold on to his neck. I stretch out full length along his back. "Don't let go," he says. His hips arch and descend, and mine do, too; it's supposed to look obscene, he's told me, as if you're humping the water. When he pauses at the wall and asks if I'd like to try it alone, I say that, left to myself, I would drown.

"Then hold on," he says, and I put my arms around his neck and lie on his back again. His muscles know so perfectly what to do that they no longer need reminding. His legs pound in the dolphin kick as his arms circle. I liked this about him the first time I saw him, before knowing his name.

We haul ourselves out and sit, shivering. Henry puts his arm around me, along with the towel. The moon is smeared into a white glaze. He says, "Are you going to leave me, Isabel?"

Our hearts are working hard — his from swimming the distance, and mine from the effort of making the new motion. The body sends its tired blue blood to the heart, where, in the divided chambers, hidden but ceaseless, the work goes on, minute by minute, cleaning it to red again. Bless its repetition; bless that old washerwoman, the heart.

Because I have not answered, he asks again merely by saying my name.

"Isabel?"

Bless Mary's blue flamingo, speaking to me across the years: blue washing its reflection in red water.

"You're always talking about what Mary did," he says. "I only remember who she was. I'm sorry."

"Don't be sorry," I say.

"Her black hair, like yours. Her impatience, like yours. Her hands covered with paint. The way she called out for me and expected me to come running."

I know what is to come with Henry as he drifts farther into forgetting, but not whether I have the fortitude to bear it all the way to the distant finish. I've neither set him free nor loved him enough nor looked clearly at his dying memory. I have been letting go of him with brutal slowness.

"Isabel," he says, "remember our time in St. Louis?"

The two of us are riding a riverboat on the Mississippi. One dance floor offers rock-and-roll, another ballroom dancing. A third features big-band music and older couples reliving that odd sensation of being festive during wartime. The sunset flattens a replica of itself onto the river: red sky onto blue water, then blue-black night sky looking at red water. Stars shrunk to the size of water bugs are painted on the surface. We have not been married long. Neither of us is a dancer, but we both know how to move through water; we met and fell in love while swimming, and here we are still — carried upon this river.

We stumble across something marvelous: The first deck is reserved for a large group of people in wheelchairs. They have come with spouses, who hold their hands and wheel them in a dance while the music rises up from the other floors: Bach and then the Stones and then some country western. Everyone is content to veer without hurry. The faces of those being wheeled are lifted toward the lit-up eyes of the dance partners guiding them around.

"I remember," I say to Henry. "I'd forgotten."

As the Mississippi moves below the different styles and times stacked one on top of the other, we play that game of whispering: Would you love me if I couldn't walk? Would you kiss me if my hair fell out and I went blind? Would you still want me?

Would you love me if I forgot my name and yours? If I forgot my past and everyone in it? You would have to remember for me that we promised never to leave this behind, this wanting to die of happiness as the wheelchairs circle. The river is slow, and the boat is slower. The porthole windows let in the air as the bands play. Already, before we know her, our daughter comes to greet us with her wild imaginings, because the water is scarlet. The heart is halved. The sky was red and will wash blue by morning. We pass by the lighted cities that we will never visit, with their storehouse of invisible lives and lovemaking in unknown rooms, with the blue and the red and the river without letup making its mysterious sounds while slowly bearing us on. ∎

Sixteenth Anniversary

by **TESS GALLAGHER**

for Raymond Carver and for Chris Morgenroth,
Quileute Nation

August 2, 2004

You died early and in summer.

Today, observing the anniversary
alone in a cabin at La Push,
I wandered down to the gray-shingled
schoolhouse at the edge of the sea.
A Quileute carver came out of a low shed.
He held classes in there, he said. Six
students at a time. He taught me
how to say "I'm going home"
in Quileute by holding my tongue in
one side of my cheek,
letting the sounds slur past it, air
from the far cheek
a kind of bellows.

I felt an entirely other
spirit enter my body. It
made a shiver rise up in me
and I said so. The carver
nodded and smiled. He

said he taught carving
while speaking Quileute.
I imagined that affected
the outcome, for the syllables
compelled a breath in me
I'd never experienced before.

He showed me a rattle
in the shape of a killer whale
he'd been carving. The tail
had split off, but he said he
could glue it back. He let me
shake it while he sang
a rowing song they used
when whaling. My whole arm
disappeared into the song;
the small stones inside
the whale kept pelting
the universe, the sound
raying out into the past
and the future at once,
never leaving the moment.

He told me his Quileute name,
which he said didn't mean
anything except those syllables.
Just a name. But I knew he
preferred it to any other. "I'm going
home," I said, the best I could
in his language, when

it was time to walk on
down the beach. Fog
was rolling in so the rocks
offshore began to look
conspiratorial. He offered
his hand to shake. Our
agreement, what was it?
Wordless. Like what
the fog says when it
swallows up an ocean.
He swallowed me up
and I swallowed him up.
And we felt good about it.

You died early and in summer.

Before heading to the cemetery
I made them leave the lid up
while I ran out to the garden
and picked one more bouquet
of sweet peas to fan onto your
chest, remembering how you
beamed when I placed them
on your writing desk in
the mornings. You'd draw
the scent in deeply,
then I'd kiss you on the brow,
go out, and quietly close
the door.

We survive on ritual, on
sweet peas in August, letting
the scent carry us, so at last the door
swings open and we're both
on the same side of it
for a while.

If you were here we'd
sit outside, accompanying
the roar of waves
as they mingle with the low notes
of the buoy bell's plaintive warning,
like some child blowing
against the cold edge of a metal pipe.
I'd tell you how the Quileute
were transformed from wolves
into people, though I'm unsure
if they liked the change. I'm
not the same myself, since
their language came into me.
I see things differently.
With a wolf gazing out.
I can't help my changes any more
than you could yours. Our life apart
has outstripped the mute kaleidoscope
of the hydrangea blossom
and its seven changes.
I'm looking for
the moon now. We'll have
something new
to say to each other.

Green

a short story by **COLIN CHISHOLM**

The man kneels in her garden. All around him it is growing, so green it infuses the air with light. Which calms him. Which soothes him. Which passes the time.

His knees are dirty, the soil so deep in his skin he can't wash it out. Earth fills his fingernails, darkens his hair. He digs with his hands, parting the soil each time as if he may never do it again. As if this time could be the last.

He plants catmint, spearmint, and peppermint because he likes their smells. He plants columbine, wild iris, bleeding heart, forget-me-nots — hearty plants, plants that will grow in the shade.

He's been gardening for a week, ever since Katrina's mother gathered up her daughter's belongings and flew away into the gray-blue sky.

Katrina had been talking about the garden for years, as long as he'd known her. Some women dream of white weddings, or sandy beaches, or new diamond rings; she dreamed of spinach and lettuce, garlic and tomatoes, and tall native grass in the spring. Each day, the man looks out the window above their bed and sees that there is more to be done, that her garden is green but not green enough.

He remembers Katrina's vision (though she wasn't religious) of a lighted tunnel leading to God. She woke from her drug-induced hospital sleep and touched his hand and said that the tunnel was a garden, its floor a soft carpet of moss. Ancient maples lined the path, their gnarled branches arching overhead, thick with leaves.

If someone asks, he can't say how long the work will take. A new beard grows on his face, leaf shards dangling from it like crumbs. He eats little. He wakes in the morning, sees her garden through the window, and rises, still dressed, from their bed. His clothes smell, but he doesn't notice. He hasn't changed his socks in days. He isn't thinking about socks.

He pushes open the creaky screen door to the garden and begins digging and planting, weeding and pruning. Friends say he is losing weight. When they stop by with food, he regards them blankly for a moment, then continues working in her garden, protected on all sides by walls of raspberries and caragana and drooping lilac trees.

They chose the house because of the garden, though it was a wreck when they moved in. That was in September. All winter long, she came home early from the office each day and worked in her garden until dusk, preparing the beds, clearing away dead foliage, rearranging rocks, and sketching a plan for springtime. She was a planner, a scribbler, a list maker. He used to tease that her lists included such items as "brush teeth," "sleep," and "eat."

There were no children, never would be. She didn't want them, and he didn't mind. The vasectomy irritated him, but that was more than she'd had to say about the abortion. It had been years ago, and they rarely spoke of it.

In ten years, they'd lived in five different tiny, run-down apartments — all they could afford while he was in graduate school and she shuffled papers at a law firm. Wherever they lived, she planted a garden, no matter how small: in the alley; behind the garbage shed; in a cardboard box by the kitchen window. When they moved, she'd gently dig up her favorite perennials and take them with her, all the while talking to them in a voice so tender he did not recognize it.

He did all the driving because she couldn't keep her eyes on the road; she was always turning to look at wildflowers. Once, she'd nearly run a man over. He wondered sometimes if she wasn't a little crazy. She admitted the possibility herself.

Now he obsesses over the dandelions that pop up in her soil whenever he turns his back for a moment. He tries to tolerate them, because she did, but his sense of order is too strong. He hates the yellow heads so soon turned to seed, their random, rampant growth. He dreams of their slippery roots slithering deep beneath the garden until the flowers and vegetables are choked and overgrown. He grinds his teeth in his sleep.

When the university hired him, he and Katrina began looking for a house. They quickly found this place, set far back from the street, the garden overgrown and wild. The columbine was still blooming, and the yard smelled of mint, licorice root, rich compost, rain. While the real-estate agent showed him the inside of the house, Katrina wandered outside to pull weeds from the flower beds. Bees swarmed thickly overhead in a tree she could not name. Its small pink flowers were shaped like clogs. She called it the "pink-clog tree."

The house was old; the stone foundation was cracking. From the bedroom window, he saw her crouched in the garden, playing in the dirt like a child. With her hand she pushed away a strand of hair that had fallen in her face; her finger left a stripe of dirt across her cheek. He knew then that they would buy the place.

The man transplants flowers from pots in the house to the garden, as she taught him. He touches the roots tenderly, the same roots she handled over the years, moving the plants from place to place. Some people move their furniture, but she had no love for furnishings. Their bed was just a plywood platform atop cinder blocks. Except for the plants, the house was nearly barren: no photographs or paintings on the walls, a few rickety stools scattered around an old card table in the dining room, and, in his study, a desk and hundreds of tattered history books stacked on the floor. The kitchen was utilitarian and smelled of garlic. They had a total of three forks, two spoons, and five dull knives. The countertops were always gritty with dirt from Katrina's potting, and all around hung evidence of the encroaching natural world. The man joked that Katrina wanted the house to deteriorate such that, one day, garden and house would merge.

The man hums as he works, the same song over and over again. He can't name it, but he remembers the sound of a wooden flute and a violin. It's as if the tune is the theme song for a movie he is in. He hums while down on his knees, his hands plowing the soil beneath the pink-clog tree. He sees a single teardrop fall and melt into the dark humus. The bees dance on the clogs as the throaty flute song wafts away on the wind.

She told him the news in the garden while she was weeding the spinach bed. "I have a lump," she said, her voice quiet and distant, as if she were talking to the wrinkled green leaves.

The wild iris and forget-me-nots are invading the vegetable garden. He was never as big a vegetable fan as she, so he doesn't mind. He waters the beds and tills in wildflower seeds. A patina of moss envelops the brick stairs at the back of the house, threatening to spread into the garden. He does nothing to stop it. He likes how it feels under his bare feet. He remembers how she wiggled her toes in the damp velvet growth. He remembers her tunnel to heaven.

At dawn, she'd put water on to boil, slip into her plastic sandals, and wander through the garden, never hearing the teakettle shriek. He'd rush to quiet it, pour the water over her black tea, add a dash of cream and honey, and bring it to her in the garden. She'd smile and thank him, her eyelids still puffy from sleep. She slurped as she drank — "very unladylike," her mother would say, but it never bothered him. She slurped and walked among the rows, imagining her future flowers and carrots and peas. She touched the turning leaves of the maple tree, her skin dappled with yellow-green light.

She denied that she snored at night, though he swore he didn't mind. Now he finds it difficult to sleep without her sound. He tries to imagine it, but it's never quite right. He wonders what else he will forget.

Katrina's left breast was removed three days before their first Christmas in the house. The day he brought her home from the hospital, a thin crust of snow covered the ground. She didn't speak. She watered her plants and repotted a fern. She showed him the scar across her chest, bruised the color of eggplant, and he kissed it.

"I'm sorry," she said, and he cried with her.

It's springtime now in her first real garden. No more cardboard boxes and cramped, tangled roots. Next to the old gray fence, he plants her bleeding heart, which she kept alive all winter in the bathroom's south-facing window, along with a dozen other favorite perennials. She'd take long baths in scalding water, her small right breast bobbing on the surface like a lone buoy, steam rising and gathering like dew on the leaves of her plants.

Around the bleeding heart, he places a ring of river-smoothed stones.

In February, they took her right breast. Her surgeon looked like Gandhi. He swallowed slowly when he told them, "Six months. . . . I'm sorry."

For the first time, the man imagined their aborted child, a girl with her same lips and ringlets of dark hair, those faraway eyes. She would be seven years old, he thought. And he wanted her.

"At least I'll see the garden," Katrina said. "I'll plant the bleeding heart and see the pink clogs bloom."

Now the soil is rich and waiting, full of earthworms and beetles. Digging, the man finds bits and pieces of a child's life: a plastic toy soldier, a broken wheel from a Tonka truck, spent firecrackers, and, next to the maple tree, a small rusted box filled with nickels and pennies. Yellow columbine and purple asters bloom alongside the house. A hummingbird sips from the feeder that she hung from the old lilac tree.

She died the last week in April, one day before his thirty-sixth birthday. The garden was just beginning to turn green, the morning chill still sharp. On his birthday, he took her spade from the garage and began digging. Rain fell, and the ground softened. He put aside the spade and dug with his hands. He dug all day, until it was time to fetch her mother at the airport. He looked at himself in the mirror: he was covered in mud. He smelled the dirt on his hands. The smell was hers.

He cried in the shower because it washed her away.

When the garden blooms, he is awestruck. Most of the flowers he cannot name. On his knees he smells them, spreads their petals to see the delicate fluted canyons of their insides. The wild irises smell like snow, the poppies like honeycomb. He sneezes and remembers her sneezing in the garden, her face squeezed tight. He likes the tiny flowers best, their transparent pink and blue petals, their leaves like lace. They grow in tight bunches on the shady north side of the house, alongside the ferns. They tremble and sway in the slightest breeze.

When he stops going to work, the chair of the history department visits, ducking under the untamed caragana branches that arch over the entryway. She is pretty, her lips like two halves of a ripe fruit.

"You've been granted a leave," she says, "until the fall. Is there anything I can do?"

"I'm not coming back," he answers, his voice hollow but certain. "I have too much work to do."

He doesn't see her go.

He tastes a poppy seed, a petal, a leaf. A smudge of yellow brightens his nose. He decorates a spinach salad with the poppy's orange petals, slivers of mint and parsley. He leaves it for the deer.

Katrina's mother was terse and unforgiving; she blamed him for not having married Katrina, though it was Katrina who had shunned marriage on principle. She picked through Katrina's things like a raven while he dug up the season's first dandelions.

She demanded Katrina's ashes. The night before she left, he stole a handful from the metal urn, grains of bone and teeth between his fingers.

Each day, he lives their life again. He sees their first meeting at a college soccer game. She wore cutoffs and ran barefoot, her white skin against the rain-green hills. They fucked (she called it this, despite his protests) in an old tree fort down by a dirty trickle of a creek. Afterward, they watched the stars, and she told him about growing up on military bases in Texas and California, how dry it was, and about her father's plastic lawn. She spoke of the garden she would have one day.

Her mother flew into the gray-blue sky with the urn.

With every planting, he adds a flake of her. Under the bleeding heart, a chip of molar; beneath the columbine, a bit of bone. The flowers take. They thrive under the rain of her as he stands, palms up in the afternoon storms. He feeds them like fish, sprinkling the ashes and watching the stems rise to accept her. The flowers bloom, again and again. ∎

Hello, Gorgeous!

a short story by **BRUCE HOLLAND ROGERS**

Long ago, in his twenties, he had been something of a Romeo. He met girls at his job in the shoe department of Mervyn's in Denver, Colorado. After he'd knelt in front of them and squeezed to feel the bones of their feet through the thin leather, it was no trouble at all to ask the girls for their phone numbers at the cash register. He went to church every Sunday and met girls there, too. Even better, he would stroll across the college campus looking for pretty faces. Some girls showed him their engagement rings, said they had a steady guy, or just told him to get lost. He didn't mind. Sometimes he struck up a conversation even after he had already spotted the diamond ring. He just liked talking to girls.

He did more than talk, but not much more. Those were innocent times. A date consisted of meeting at a soda fountain or maybe riding the bus to see a movie at the Oriental. A walk to her door. A few chaste kisses. An early good night. College girls had dorm curfews. Working girls had parents or roommates who expected them home by ten.

That was all right with him. He thought about sex as much as any young man, but he was a gentleman and would have been ashamed to get a girl in trouble. Besides, his biggest thrill was meeting someone new. Three or four times a day, at least, he would see a girl and just be unable to stop looking at her. *Hello, gorgeous!* he would think. If he had two dates in the same day — one in the afternoon and another in the evening, after he had left the first girl at her door — it wasn't because he was inconstant. He was, in fact, constantly enchanted.

His life changed once he had saved enough to buy a car, a used Bel

Aire. Then he could take girls to drive-in movies or to park by Sloan's Lake to watch the stars. He grew serious about one of the girls. In a year he was married and had a son. A year after that he was selling cars instead of shoes.

He wasn't unhappy, but he also didn't stop noticing other women. His wife said it embarrassed her, the way he stared. So he did his best to change. If he caught himself admiring another woman, he would deliberately turn away and say the Lord's Prayer under his breath. By the time he was thirty, he had cured himself of his old habits.

Through the decades that followed, he was steady. He worked hard, but never on Sundays. He bought a bigger house. The cars in the driveway were always new. He didn't think he was unhappy. He didn't think about happiness at all. He had responsibilities.

At some point, he broke his own rule and started working on Sundays. There was college to save for. His wife could take the kids to church. By the time he was fifty-five, he had put two sons and a daughter through college. That same year, cancer took his wife. It was that sudden.

The house was silent as only an empty house can be. Coming home from work, he would turn on the television even before he had his coat off, just to fill the room with voices. He'd make himself dinner in the microwave, then watch medical dramas.

"Dad," said his eldest on the telephone, "it's been three years. You should get out. You should meet someone."

"By 'someone,' you mean a woman."

"You should travel, anyway. You have plenty of years ahead of you. See some sights! What good does it do you to sit around moping?"

He went to Greece because the travel agent said it was a bargain. On the flight over, he read magazine articles about the first signs of stroke and the best diets for beating cancer. He looked at his Greek phrase book. He practiced saying, "I need a doctor," in Greek.

The resort hotel was full of Dutch and French tourists. He ate breakfast, lunch, and dinner in the dining room alone, listening to conversations in languages he didn't know. He walked around the pool once or twice in his street clothes. Women of all ages sunbathed topless, but it made no impression on him. He went down to the beach and sat under an umbrella for a while, watching the ferries move along the horizon. By breakfast on the third day he was already tired of the food they served.

He rented a car and drove away from the water, through olive groves and past fields of artichokes. Finally he came to a village, where he parked the car and walked. He didn't know he was looking for anything until he found the church. He stood in the doorway. While his eyes adjusted to the dim light, he felt awkward and wondered if he should cross himself. Near the door, two old women sat with a box of tapers, speaking in low voices. He put some coins in a plate, and they gave him a candle.

It wasn't a big church, but it was crowded with icons. They had even been painted onto the plaster. Everywhere he looked — the concave ceiling, the arches, the walls — Christ and perhaps a hundred saints returned his gaze. They were serene, comforting. He couldn't remember the last time he'd felt such awe in the face of beauty.

He lit his candle and for a while stood watching it burn. Then he said goodbye to the women by the door and drove out of the village, putting more distance between himself and the resort. Finally he came to the opposite side of the island, a rocky stretch of coast where the buildings were hardly more than shacks.

His son had been right to tell him to take a trip. He felt as if he had been asleep a long, long time.

After driving several kilometers of empty road, he came upon a bright yellow building with a weathered sign that said, "Taverna." He sat at an outside table in the shade. The menu was all in Greek, and the girl who'd brought it couldn't understand his questions. She gestured for him to follow her into the little kitchen. There he met a middle-aged woman who might have been the girl's mother. The two women talked — about him, he guessed. Then the mother called out. A man's voice answered, and a white-haired fellow appeared with a dripping tray of fish on ice. They gestured for him to choose one.

The fish was served with fresh lemons, and he ordered a bottle of Coca-Cola, which was the same in Greek as in English. He ate the fish slowly, both because it had bones and because he wanted to savor it.

A car stopped, and a trio of young female tourists got out, jabbering away in Russian, or maybe Polish. One of the women happened to look his way. He stopped chewing. *Wow!* he thought. She turned back to her companions, but he couldn't take his eyes from her. Such delicate features. He wondered what her hair smelled like. Then the serving girl appeared with menus for them, and she, too, was beautiful. How had he missed it before? Her features were not delicate like the Slavic girl's. She was darker, the lines of her face more dramatic. But she was no less beautiful.

He had forgotten what it was like to really see young women, to drink in their beauty.

All of the Slavic women were dazzling. He looked from one to the next, amazed and full of longing. It seemed they spoke no Greek, and the girl with the menus wasn't having any success in getting them to follow her back into the kitchen. He did his best to politely look away anytime one of the women caught him staring, but he couldn't help himself. He stared.

The middle-aged mother came out. She was beautiful, too! He wanted to kiss the wrinkles around her eyes. Behind her came the white-haired man, bearing the tray of fish, and . . . *Oh, my.* The old fisherman was stunning. What would it be like to touch the sunburned skin of the man's face? A golden light surrounded all of them. They were all so beautiful, he wanted to gather them in his arms, every one.

He blinked. He wiped his eyes with a napkin. He was filled with joy. And fear. He tried to think back to the article he had read describing the first signs of a stroke. And if he was having a stroke, what was that phrase in Greek that means "I need a doctor"? He couldn't remember. Every time he tried to recall it, all he could think was *Hello, gorgeous!* ∎

■ Contributors

The title of each piece in this anthology is listed with its author, along with the issue of The Sun *in which it first appeared. Back issues of* The Sun *can be ordered online at www.thesunmagazine.org.*

— Ed.

STEVE ALMOND (Ecstasy, June 2001) is one of the few Jewish, left-handed twins writing today. He spends much of his time chasing after his daughter, Josephine, and dreaming of a gentler homeland. His new book of essays is *(Not That You Asked): Rants, Exploits and Obsessions* (Random House).

ERIC ANDERSON (Committed Relationships, May 2007) lives in Elyria, Ohio, and has been published in *Prairie Schooner* and *Artful Dodge*. He learned in elementary school that the heart has four chambers, which his teacher, Mrs. Law, said to think of as "rooms." She was a tough old lady who walked sideways and would take off her wooden clogs whenever she wanted to go into stealth mode. Down the aisle she came and then clucked disapprovingly when she caught Eric drawing in red a fifth room of the heart on his mimeographed handout.

POE BALLANTINE (The Empty House of My Brokenhearted Father, February 1996) is the author of two novels (*God Clobbers Us All* and *Decline of the Lawrence Welk Empire*) and two collections of essays (*Things I Like about America* and *501 Minutes to Christ*), all published by Hawthorne Books. His work has appeared in *Best American Short Stories* and *Best American Essays*. For most of his adult life he traveled the country, living in rooming houses and residential motels, working menial jobs, and getting by on four hundred dollars a month. He recently settled down with his wife and son in Chadron, Nebraska.

ROSEMARY BERKELEY (Au Revoir, Pleasant Dreams, October 2002) prefers her pizza plain, her tea highly sugared, and her biographical information kept to a minimum. She lives outside of Boston, Massachusetts, so close to the Atlantic Ocean that she can dangle a cheese curl out her front window and have it snatched from her hand by a sea gull in under ten seconds. She has an MFA from Vermont College, a handsome husband who adores her, and a job writing snide, sardonic pieces for a political-humor website.

NICOLE BLAISDELL (Cover photograph, January 2004) photographs artists, writers, painters, and poets for love; power sanders, screws, and Southwestern kitsch for money. When she was ten and walking with a very cute boy of eleven, a photographer stopped them and asked to take their picture. He said, "Stand closer together and hold hands. Closer." They flushed and held hands awkwardly. Her heart raced. "Great, great," he said. "Write your names and addresses, and I'll send you each a photograph." But the photograph never came. When she became a photographer, she decided always to give her subjects their portrait and never to leave anyone wondering what the photographer saw. She and her husband (poet for love, engineer for money) live in Albuquerque, New Mexico, and are collaborating on a photography-and-poetry chapbook. On a good day her sons play the theme from *Mission Impossible* for her on the trumpet and euphonium. (nicoleblaisdell@yahoo.com)

KRISTA BREMER (My Accidental Jihad, October 2007) loves loitering at her local library, running in the woods behind her house, and peeking at her children while they sleep. Her essays have appeared in *Utne Reader* and *Brain, Child: The Magazine for Thinking Mothers*, and she received a Pushcart Prize in 2008 for her essay "My Accidental Jihad." She lives in Carrboro, North Carolina, and is associate publisher of *The Sun*.

CHRISTOPHER BURSK (How Far Did You Get?, March 1999) is the author of nine books of poetry, the most recent being *The First Inhabit-*

ants of Arcadia (University of Arkansas Press). He inhabits his own arcadia with six grandchildren, who help him ward off the evil spirits.

STEPHEN T. BUTTERFIELD (Bleeding Dharma, May 1996) lived in Shrewsbury, Vermont, and taught English at Castleton State College for twenty-six years. The author of *The Double Mirror: A Skeptical Journey into Buddhist Tantra* (North Atlantic Books), he also sang traditional Celtic tunes and played the guitar and the bouzouki in the band When the Wind Shakes the Barley. He died in 1996.

MICHELLE CACHO-NEGRETE (And Passion Most of All, April 2005) grew up in a Brooklyn ghetto and longed to migrate to Manhattan. She now lives on a former granite quarry in Maine and polishes her written work by reciting it aloud as she walks, which makes her neighbors uncomfortable. Her writing has appeared in *Psychotherapy Networker*, *SNReview*, *Persimmon Tree*, and *Sierra*. She is most proud of her work as an activist and most embarrassed about loving all three *Terminator* films, as well as their TV spin-off, *The Sarah Connor Chronicles*.

MATTHEW DESHE CASHION (An Hour after Breakfast, August 2006) was born in North Carolina, grew up in Georgia, earned an MFA at the University of Oregon, and now teaches creative writing and literature at the University of Wisconsin–La Crosse. He is the author of one novel, *How the Sun Shines on Noise* (Livingston Press), and is currently completing a second, tentatively titled *Our Thirteenth Divorce: A Love Story*. His stories and poems have appeared in *Passages North*, *Northwest Review*, *Fugue*, and *Asheville Poetry Review*. Jazz drumming and blues harmonica were once among his hobbies; now he taps on tabletops and tries to whistle Little Walter tunes. He lives with his wife, Heather, and their three cats, Grendel, Lionel, and Lily.

COLIN CHISHOLM (Green, May 2000) lives in Missoula, Montana, where he works as a hospice social worker. He is the author of numerous magazine articles and the book *Through Yup'ik Eyes: An Adopted Son Explores the Landscape of Family* (Alaska Northwest Books). In the spring of 2010 he plans to climb and ski the 20,320-foot Denali (aka

Mount McKinley) to raise money for children and low-income patients facing the end of life. (www.climbforhospice.org)

ALISON CLEMENT (Suzy Joins the Sex Club, July 1994) is the author of the novels *Twenty Questions*, which won the 2007 Oregon Book Award, and *Pretty Is as Pretty Does* (both Washington Square Press), which was both a Barnes and Noble Discover Great New Writers as well as a BookSense selection. Her short stories and essays have been published in *High Country News*, the *Upper Left Edge,* and the *Alaska Quarterly Review.* She lives with her family in western Oregon, where she practices yoga, rides her bike, and writes a blog in defense of pit bulls. (www.alison clement.org)

LARRY COLKER (The Leap, March 2008) is managing editor of the online magazines *Speechless* (www.speechlessthemagazine.org) and *Poetix* (www.poetix.net) and has cohosted a weekly poetry reading in Los Angeles for ten years. A former university professor and an aspiring blues harpist, he lives in San Pedro, California. You can see and hear him reading his work at www.poetry.la.

DOUG CRANDELL (Foreclosure, July 2008) is the author of two memoirs and two novels, one of which, *The Flawless Skin of Ugly People* (Virgin Books), has been optioned for the big screen. In addition to writing, he finds jobs for people with mental illnesses. He and his family live on a small farm outside of Atlanta, Georgia, where they tend ducks, sheep, goats, and chickens. Crandell recently beat out his childhood hero, former president and noted author Jimmy Carter, for the Georgia Author of the Year Award. Carter has yet to call and concede the race.

PATRY FRANCIS (On Catching My Husband Smoking a Cigarette after Seven Years of Abstinence, December 2000) worked as a waitress for more than twenty years before she was finally able to support herself as a writer. She has published poems in the *American Poetry Review* and the *Ontario Review,* and her novel *The Liar's Diary* was published by Dutton in 2007. She is currently at work on a second novel and also a collection of essays from her blog, *Simply Wait.* An incorrigible night

person, she is trying to train herself to get to bed before 3 A.M. (www
.patryfrancis.com)

TESS GALLAGHER (Sixteenth Anniversary, February 2006) is
spending more time in the West of Ireland, in her cottage on Lough
Arrow, where she raised three varieties of potatoes this year, including a purple one. She is the author of several poetry collections,
including *Moon Crossing Bridge* and *Dear Ghosts* (both Graywolf
Press). She has been working on her *New & Selected Poems* and also her
Selected Stories, as well as hanging out with a group of North Sligo
poets and painters known as the "Wild Bunch."

DENISE GESS (The Kitchen Table: An Honest Orgy, June 2007) is
the author of two novels, *Good Deeds* and *Red Whiskey Blues* (both
Crown). She's recently completed a collection of essays called *Bad
for Boys*. She teaches at Rowan University and lives in Philadelphia,
Pennsylvania.

MICHAEL HETTICH (The Stranger, February 2008) was born in
New York City and now lives in Miami, Florida, with his wife, Colleen.
He has published a dozen books and chapbooks of poetry, including
Swimmer Dreams (Wordtech Communications) and *Flock and Shadow:
New and Selected Poems* (New Rivers Press). His most recent chapbook, *Many Loves*, won the Yellow Jacket Press Chapbook Contest in
2007. A new book of poems, *Like Happiness*, is forthcoming in 2010
from Anhinga Press. Perhaps his proudest moment occurred nearly
thirty years ago in the Colorado Rockies, when he leapt to stop the
fall of a woman who was tumbling down the snowy ridge toward the
rocks below. For once, he didn't think: he just acted. He still remembers how her blue eyes gleamed, this woman he had just met who
would later become his wife. (www.michaelhettich.com)

JOHN HODGEN (This Day, April 1995) is visiting assistant professor
of English at Assumption College in Worcester, Massachusetts. His
book *Grace* (University of Pittsburgh Press) won the AWP Donald
Hall Prize in Poetry. He lives in Shrewsbury, Massachusetts.

KATHRYN HUNT (Greed, June 2002) is a writer and filmmaker living in Port Townsend, Washington. Her writing has appeared in *Open Spaces, Painted Bride Quarterly,* and *Crab Orchard Review.* Her feature-length documentary *Take This Heart* received the Anna Quindlen Award for Excellence in Journalism, and her film *No Place Like Home,* about a ten-year-old girl who lives with her family in Seattle hotels and homeless shelters, was broadcast nationally as part of the public-television series *P.O.V.* She earns her living working for a national antipoverty initiative and is in search of a publisher for a memoir about her mother, titled *The Province of Leaves.* When she's not at her desk, she can be found in her garden, trying to stay ahead of the weeds and the deer.

TOM IRELAND (The Woman in Question, April 2004) has received an NEA grant and a Jeffrey E. Smith Prize and is the author of four books of nonfiction, including *Birds of Sorrow: Notes from a River Junction in Northern New Mexico* (Zephyr Press). He's also known for his ability to balance a broom on his nose while telling the story of how he came by that talent. A native New Yorker, he moved to New Mexico in 1971 and has lived there ever since. He's worked as a builder, a rancher, an animal trainer, and, for the last twenty-three years, an editor with the state's Office of Archaeological Studies. He lives in Santa Fe with "the woman in question" and his cat, Max, who's been with him longer than anybody.

LOIS JUDSON (I Am Not a Sex Goddess, January 2009) is the pseudonym of an author who lives in New England and recently had her nursing license suspended for six months due to alcoholism. The good news is that she is presently enjoying a natural high from four months of sobriety and the election of Barack Obama.

HEATHER KING (Beach Boy, July 1999) is the author of two memoirs, *Parched* (NAL Trade) and *Redeemed: A Spiritual Misfit Stumbles toward God, Marginal Sanity, and the Peace That Passes All Understanding* (Viking Adult). A full-time writer, she lives in LA's Koreatown, where she drinks coffee, ponders the meaning of life, prays, fumes, frets, gives praise, and takes long, purposeless walks, often all at the same time.

JAMES KULLANDER (My Marital Status, December 2007) lives in New York's Hudson Valley and on Nova Scotia's Cape Breton Island — and on the long and winding roads in between the two. He holds a master of divinity degree from Union Theological Seminary in New York City and is editor in chief of marketing at the Omega Institute in Rhinebeck, New York. His interviews with Pema Chödrön, Marion Woodman, and Sister Joan Chittister — all published in *The Sun* — are part of an on-going series of talks with prominent women who have influenced him. He is working on a book based on his essay in this anthology and is also completing a novel. (jameskullander@aol.com)

KATHLEEN LAKE (Prayer for Your Wife, November 1994) is a chronic procrastinator with high testosterone levels whose God-given gifts are hyperbole and free association. She can spell in languages she doesn't speak and has never correctly balanced her checkbook. She lives in Orlando, Florida, where cats come out of the shadows and follow her home.

SUNITI LANDGÉ (Small Things, June 2002) lives with her children in Vancouver, British Columbia. She was born and raised in India but has lived outside the subcontinent for sixteen years, first in England and now in Canada. She writes for *Performing Arts and Entertainment* magazine and has had one other short story published, in the *Alaska Quarterly Review*.

LOU LIPSITZ (Marriage, May 2004) is a psychotherapist living in Chapel Hill, North Carolina, who is trying to deal with his bitterness over not being able to find a publisher for his latest book of poems. He recently changed his study around and can now look out the window at the oak trees and the garden while he writes. Why didn't he think of this before? (www.loulipsitz.com)

ALISON LUTERMAN (Smashing the Plates, September 2004) is adjusting to domestic bliss, milking the chickens and harvesting the cactus with her beloved on their little homestead in Oakland, California. She is the author of a book of poems, *The Largest Possible Life*

(Cleveland State University Poetry Center) and writes a blog at www
.seehowwealmostfly.blogspot.com.

STEPHEN J. LYONS (Blowing It in Idaho, June 1998) is the author
of *A View from the Inland Northwest: Everyday Life in America* (Globe
Pequot) and *Landscape of the Heart: Writings on Daughters and Journeys* (Washington State University Press). His writing has appeared
in sixteen anthologies, and he is a two-time recipient of the Illinois
Arts Commission fellowship for prose. He lives in east central Illinois
(not to be confused with west central Illinois), where he is a full-time
speechwriter at the University of Illinois at Urbana-Champaign. Like
President Barack Obama, Stephen is a White Sox fan and a former
resident of Chicago's Hyde Park. There the comparisons end.

ROBERT McGEE (The Woman with Hair, November 2005) is a native
Texan whose short fiction has been published by the *Raleigh Quarterly*
and *Front Forty Press*. He spends much of his nonwriting time mentor-
ing an autistic teen while carving out a self-sufficient homestead near
Asheville, North Carolina, where he grows (or barters for) most of his
food. His short story in this book comes from *Fragile*, an unpublished
collection of twelve linked stories. He is now at work on a novel called
The Women of Walden Pond.

BRENDA MILLER (The Date, April 1998) is the author of *Season of
the Body* (Sarabande Books) and the coauthor of *Tell It Slant: Writing
and Shaping Creative Nonfiction* (McGraw-Hill). Her newest collection
of essays, *Blessing of the Animals,* is forthcoming from Eastern Washington University Press in 2009. Her work has received five Pushcart
Prizes and been published in *Fourth Genre, Creative Nonfiction, Utne
Reader*, the *Georgia Review*, and *Witness*. She is an associate professor
of English at Western Washington University and serves as editor in
chief of the *Bellingham Review*.

KIRK NESSET (Still Life with Candles and Spanish Guitar, February 2006) has been in love enough times to consider himself a master
of romantic failures. In fact, his book of short stories *Paradise Road*

(University of Pittsburgh Press) is devoted almost exclusively to his shortcomings in relationships. He's also the author of a book of flash fiction, *Mr. Agreeable* (Mammoth Press); a nonfiction study, *The Stories of Raymond Carver* (Ohio University Press); a collection of poems, *St. X* (forthcoming); and a book of translations, *Alphabet of the World* (forthcoming). He was awarded the Drue Heinz Literature Prize in 2007 and teaches creative writing and literature at Allegheny College. To give himself a break from writing, he plays in a Grateful Dead cover group called Unkle John's Band.

TODD JAMES PIERCE (Box Step, March 2004) lives in Santa Barbara County, California, with his wife and their twins. He is the author of the novel *A Woman of Stone* (MacAdam/Cage) and *Newsworld* (University of Pittsburgh Press), a collection of stories that won the 2006 Drue Heinz Literature Prize. His poems and short stories have appeared in the *Gettysburg Review*, the *Georgia Review*, and the *Missouri Review*. For the last four years, he has worked on a nonfiction book about the men who built the first wave of American theme parks in the 1950s. He has a Dalmatian named Indio who often follows him to school, and people in general are far more excited to see Indio than they are to see Todd.

LESLIE PIETRZYK (Ten Things, August 2000) is the author of two novels, *Pears on a Willow Tree* and *A Year and a Day* (both Harper Perennial), and writes a literary blog at www.WorkInProgressInProgress .blogspot.com. She lives in Alexandria, Virginia, and has finally found the perfect recipe for transcendent pound cake, which she will happily e-mail upon request. (Lpietr@aol.com)

LAURA PRITCHETT (Under the Apple Tree, August 2006) is the author of the award-winning novels *Sky Bridge* and *Hell's Bottom, Colorado* (both Milkweed Editions). When she isn't writing about environmental issues and sex, she's dumpster-diving to save what other people throw away or standing naked in the local river to help protect it (www.savedthepoudre.org). She lives in Bellvue, Colorado, with several chickens who follow her around like dogs and try to come inside her house. (www.laurapritchett.com)

BRUCE HOLLAND ROGERS (Hello, Gorgeous!, April 2006) spends most of his time writing, teaching writing, or worrying that he's not writing enough. Learning new languages is the closest thing he has to a hobby, and he has read translations of his work aloud in German, Portuguese, and Finnish — and hopes to do so in Bulgarian and French. He lives in Eugene, Oregon, but has also resided in Canada and England, where he discovered that he loves being an expatriate. He makes much of his writing income selling his short-short stories directly to readers through e-mail subscription (www.shortshort short.com). He's hopeful that, even if traditional publishing abandons them, literary writers may survive by such micropatronage.

EDWIN ROMOND (Alone with Love Songs, June 2007) was a high-school English teacher for thirty-two years, and he always loved that first spring morning when he could teach with the windows open. His favorite singers are Johnny Cash and Johnny Mathis, his favorite meal is macaroni with stewed tomatoes, and his secret wish is to be named poet laureate of the New York Yankees. He lives among the Blue Mountains of Pennsylvania with his wife, Mary, their son, Liam, and their dog, Nabby. Sometimes, when he has the house to himself, he listens to his parents' Kate Smith records. (www.edwinromond.com)

LEE ROSSI (Self-Storage, November 1997) has spent his life in and out of religious institutions: first the Catholic Church, then Buddhism, and then a New Age cult, where he stayed for five years. He recently joined the Unitarians and will probably end his days in that church, since, where there are no bars on the windows, there is no hope of escape. He has two collections of poetry, *Beyond Rescue* (Bombshelter Press) and *Ghost Diary* (Terrapin Press). He lives in the California Bay Area, where he works as a "data shepherd" and writes interviews and reviews for *Pedestal* magazine.

ALISON SEEVAK (Her Shoes, June 1998) lives in Albany, California, with her young daughter and elderly pets. Her poetry and essays have appeared in the *San Francisco Chronicle Book Review*, *Many Mountains Moving*, and *Lilith*.

JASMINE SKYE (Finding a Good Man, January 2000) is a vegetarian cook, house painter, artist, musician, Scottish country dancer, meditator, and diarist who, as a child, won third prize for her portrait of the Easter Bunny. (She dipped the drawing in green egg dye.) A reader of countless self-help and psychology books — with occasional lapses into gothic romance novels — she lives with her seventeen-year-old dog in the middle of a fairy grove near a doughnut shop in Kingston, Ontario, Canada.

SPARROW (Eight Love Poems, June 2007) lives with his wife, Violet Snow, and daughter, Sylvia, in Teaneck, New Jersey, where he is a gossip columnist and small-time reporter. He is attempting to learn gourmet cooking, and his sautéed peppers with polenta (based on a recipe found on the Kraft Cheese website) were a decided success. His work has been published in the *New Yorker*, and he is the author of *America: A Prophecy* (Soft Skull Press).

CHERYL STRAYED (The Boy with Blue Hair, January 2006) lives in Portland, Oregon, with her husband and two children. Her stories and essays have appeared in the *New York Times Magazine* and the *Washington Post Magazine*, as well as in the anthologies *Best New American Voices* and *Best American Essays*. She is the author of the novel *Torch* (Houghton Mifflin) and is currently at work on a memoir called *Wild*, about love, loss, death, sex, divorce, marriage, drugs, and the ninety-four days she spent hiking the Pacific Crest Trail alone.

JOHN TAIT (I Will Soon Be Married, September 2005) has stories published or forthcoming in *Crazyhorse*, *Prairie Schooner*, *TriQuarterly*, and *Michigan Quarterly Review*. He is an associate professor of fiction writing at the University of North Texas and the editor of *American Literary Review*. A Canadian transplant living in Texas, he has come to enjoy barbecue and Shiner Bock as much as he does back bacon and Molson.

RITA TOWNSEND (The Year in Geese, January 2001) is a native Californian with Texas dust in her bones and the Bay Area in her blood. She is the coauthor of *Bitter Fruit: Women's Experiences of Unplanned*

Pregnancy, Abortion, and Adoption (Hunter House) and is currently completing a memoir. She considers herself a friend to all geese, especially the domesticated ones with wild and feverish hearts. (ritatown@comcast.net)

LEAH TRUTH (**My Fat Lover, November 1997**) is the pseudonym of an author of four books of poems and a memoir. She lives in Oakland, California, teaches in the low-residency writing programs of Ashland University and Split Rock, and has a private psychospiritual healing practice. She loves being with her partner, Michelle; rubbing whiskers with her Siamese-tiger feline lover-boy; facilitating transformation; and eating Trader Joe's sea-salt, turbinado-sugar, dark-chocolate-covered almonds. Her essay in this book was originally published under the pen name Judith Joyce. (www.leahtruth.com)

KATHERINE VAZ (**Blue Flamingo Looks at Red Water, May 2002**) lives in New York City with Christopher Cerf. *The Sun* published one of her first short stories in 1988, and since then she has written two novels — *Saudade* (St. Martin's Press) and *Mariana* (Aliform Publishing) — and two collections of short stories, the most recent of which, *Our Lady of the Artichokes and Other Portuguese-American Stories* (Bison Books), won the 2007 Prairie Schooner Prize in fiction. She's currently a Briggs-Copeland Fellow in fiction at Harvard University. Her story in this book is dedicated to her friend Mercedes Gomez, a musician who wrote a solo composition about steering a harp through traffic in Mexico City. The story's title was inspired by a child's drawing exhibited many years ago at an art show in California.

ASHLEY WALKER (**Everything I Thought Would Happen, May 1995**) lives in Dallas, Texas, and is married to Lynn Harris, a writer and video/film producer. Her work has been published in *New Directions*, the *Cimarron Review*, and the *New American Review*, and she has a screenplay in development. Being a freelancer and living by her wits has caused her to experience self-doubt and raw terror, and sometimes she's hated herself for not settling into a comfortable corporate job. Even so, she's kept writing.

JEFF WALT (Evening Voices, June 2001) recently moved back to Honolulu, Hawaii, where he is a massage therapist, barfly, and beach bum. His living space — three hundred square feet at the Waikiki Grand Hotel — is the tiki pad he dreamed about while growing up among coal miners and bricklayers in rural Pennsylvania. (www.jeffwalt.com)

THERESA WILLIAMS (Blue Velvis, August 2004) lives with her husband, two dogs, and six cats. Her life story, to quote Rumi, "gets told in various ways: a romance, a dirty joke, a war, a vacancy." She's the author of *The Secret of Hurricanes* (MacAdam/Cage), a novel, and has a crooked little house on twelve acres in Ohio, not too far from Lake Erie.

ROBLEY WILSON (The Word, February 2003) edited the *North American Review* for more than thirty years. Now retired, he lives with his wife, the novelist Susan Hubbard, and six cats in Orlando, Florida. His most recent story collection is *The Book of Lost Fathers* (The Johns Hopkins University Press), and his latest novel is *The World Still Melting* (Thomas Dunne Books).

GENIE ZEIGER (The Song of Forgiveness, December 1998) lives in Shelburne, Massachusetts, where she leads writing workshops and is writer-in-residence at the Academy of Charlemont. She is the author of three books of poetry and two memoirs. Her sixth book, *What Happened Was . . . : On Writing Personal Essays and Memoir,* will be released by White Pine Press in 2009. To her amazement, she has been married three times. Her third husband, Bill, is one of ten kids from a Catholic home in Ohio. She is one of two kids from a Jewish home in New York City. When her father met Bill, he said, "The other two I could have lived without. You have a good one now, so please don't screw it up." She and Bill have been together for twenty years.

Also Available From *The Sun*

Stubborn Light
The Best of *The Sun*, Volume III   Softcover: $22.95
The most compelling works from *The Sun*'s second decade.

A Bell Ringing In The Empty Sky
The Best of *The Sun*, Vols. I & II   Softcover; each: $15.95
This two-volume set includes the finest interviews, short stories, essays, photos, and poems from the first decade of *The Sun*.

Sunbeams
A Book of Quotations   Softcover: $15.95
A collection of the most memorable Sunbeams from the magazine's back page.

Four In The Morning
Essays by Sy Safransky   Softcover: $13.95
Thirty of editor Sy Safransky's essays.

To order books or subscribe to *The Sun*, please visit www.thesunmagazine.org.